FLIGHT OF THE STAR PHOENIX

Bernard Doove

FLIGHT OF THE STAR PHOENIX

This is a work of fiction. All characters and events portrayed within are fictitious.

Copyright © 2012 Bernard Doove

A production of *The Chakat's Den* – www.chakatsden.com

All rights reserved, including the right to reproduce this book, or any portions thereof, in any form.

Cover art by Kacey Miyagami © 2012

Printed by CreateSpace

ISBN-10: 1480260169
ISBN-13: 978-1480260160

Other books by Bernard Doove:
  Forest Tales
  Transformations
  More Terrible Than Chains
  Other Trails Taken
  Tales From The Chakat Universe
  Life's Dream
  Jazmyn

Contents

Foreword 5
Chapter 1 . . . . Crew Review 7
Chapter 2 . . . . Unexpected Baggage 79
Chapter 3 . . . . Passenger Peril 110
Chapter 4 . . . . Mouse Machinations 135
Chapter 5 . . . . Plague Plot 152
Chapter 6 . . . . Asteroid Adversity 180
Chapter 7 . . . . Changes 243
Chapter 8 . . . . Side Trip 264
Chapter 9 . . . . To Snare A Firebird 278
Chapter 10 . . . Children, Children! 303
Chapter 11 . . . Encounters 326
Chapter 12 . . . Faleshkarti Catch-22 353
Chapter 13 . . . The Final Challenge 368
Character Art Gallery 381

Foreword

While this story is set in my *Chakat Universe*, it follows a different set of characters from my *Forest Tales* series, and stands independent of those stories. However, a certain amount of background knowledge from those other stories would possibly improve your enjoyment of this novel. Nevertheless I have written the story in a way that I believe will stand well on its own.

For those not initiated into this universe, there are three sexes: Male, Female, and Herm (hermaphrodite). Because the herm species have become so common, they created special pronouns for them. They are *shi* (equivalent to he or she) and *hir* (equivalent to his and her).

I hope that you enjoy the story.

Bernard Doove

Chapter 1: Crew Review

*** 18 September 2332 ***

"You look a bit young to be wanting to buy a starship," the salesman on the other end of the videophone remarked.

Martin Yote repressed a sigh. That had been pretty much the response of every starship broker that he had contacted so far. In fairness, not too many twenty-one year olds came shopping for interstellar vessels, let alone something of the size that he was after. Nevertheless, the young coyote morph put on his most professional façade and said, "I assure you that my need is real, and my means are adequate. I would like to send you the specifications of the type of vessel in which I'm interested, and the price range that I am looking at."

"In that case, I would be delighted to help you. We have recently acquired several additions to our inventory, and I am sure that we can find something to interest you."

"Excellent. Let me transmit the specifications and my letter of credit for you to peruse." Martin had the documents ready, and with a touch of the transmit key, they were sent to the broker.

The man opened the files, and his eyebrows arched when he read the letter of credit. Then he checked the specifications and nodded. "You don't aim small, do you?"

"No – I intend that my business gets off to the best start that it can. So... can you help me?"

"As a matter of fact, I have two or three possibilities for you. I see that you are looking at a moderate cargo capacity, and two of the ships that I have might interest you. The third would need some modification, but the added expense would be worth it because of the extra features it has."

"What's so special about that?" Martin asked warily, wondering if the salesman was trying to up-sell him.

"It's an ex Star Corps vessel. It has a longer range than most cargo vessels, better crew facilities, including a holosuite, high-end equipment that government vehicles are required to have, and a few other goodies that the average starship doesn't normally have fitted."

"Sounds a little bit too much for my needs," Martin responded doubtfully.

"I admit that it could be pushing your budget, but I strongly urge you to consider it at least. I will send you the specifications of all three ships that fit your needs, and let you consider their merits. Take your time looking them over, and I think that you'll agree that the Star Corps vessel is a strong contender."

"Very well, I'll do that."

The broker transmitted the documents and Martin shut down the connection. He then settled down to read the specifications of all three starships thoroughly.

Six cups of coffee, one hastily heated bowl of pasta, and many hours later, Martin was feeling torn. He had dismissed one of the two freighters that had been offered because the power core was in need of major overhaul, and much of the other equipment was in need of servicing or upgrade. The other freighter however was close to what he'd had originally in mind for his venture, although it too would need a bit of work. Nothing near as much as the other though, and it would leave him a bit of financial elbow room. The Star Corps vessel was tempting him badly however. It was already designed to carry large amounts of supplies and equipment, and would not take much work to adapt it to more conventional cargo loads. Removing one superfluous crew accommodation deck would give him more cargo space too. It was the other features that made the ship so seductive though, but also that much more expensive. If he chose that ship, he would have to go into significant debt before he lifted one crate from the ground.

He still had not made a decision when his wrist comm chimed with a reminder that he was due to have dinner with his parents that evening. He hastily shut down his work centre and ordered a PTV to pick him up from his apartment. With the efficiency of the artificial intelligence that ran the Public PTV network, one was ready and waiting for him as he exited the apartment. His comm identified him as the person who had ordered the PTV, and it opened to allow him entrance. He entered his destination, and the AI-driven electric vehicle took off and joined the traffic flow seamlessly. Without people controlling them, they were able to make the most efficient decisions, and make the best time, and thus he was able to get to his parents' home with a bit of time to spare.

The PTV turned into the driveway of a fenced estate, the gate already opening to allow him entry as it automatically detected an authorised person aboard. The vehicle drove past manicured lawns and landscaped garden beds and pulled up at the front door of a mansion. Martin disembarked, and as he walked up to the door, it opened for him, but this time with a real person responsible for that.

"Welcome, Martin," the lynx morph butler said with a genuine smile. While he was a professional manservant, he'd been more of a friend and confidante than an employee to Martin while he had been growing up.

"Thanks, Alain. How's Dad's mood today?"

"Quite good, actually. I believe he has been looking forward to this evening's meal with you."

Martin grimaced. "Let's hope that his mood remains good when I tell him what I've done."

"So you've gone ahead with your plans? I doubted that your father dissuaded you from your dreams. Nevertheless I support your decision, for what it's worth. One must take one's own course in life. Anyway, your room is ready as always so that you can freshen up. Dinner will be served in fifteen minutes."

"Thanks again, Alain."

Martin made his way to his old bedroom which was permanently kept in readiness should he wish to visit. It had an en suite bathroom where various toiletries and fresh towels had been left out for him. He freshened up, brushed his fur, and then put on a jacket from the wardrobe. While his father was not a snob, he did expect his son to dress appropriately for a formal dinner. It was, after all, his 21st birthday celebration.

He headed for the dining room, with both a sense of anticipation and dread. Today he officially left the comfort of his father's protection and took off on his own course. However, unlike his siblings before him, Martin was not choosing a career that met with his father's approval, a fact that he had made plain four and a half years ago....

Martin's second brother's birthday was the excuse for this family get-together, having just turned twenty-one and received his father's bequeathal. Like his sister and elder brother, Hank now had to decide how to use that money to set himself up in a business, or buy into an existing one with the goal of making back that money and turning it into a profitable success. It was a generous bequeathal, and an excellent head-start for any young person with the talent and drive to make it a going concern. There was only one catch, but it was a big one – they had to make back that money and show a profit without the slightest extra help from their wealthy industrialist father, and in a maximum of five years. If they failed, they had to give up the business and take a job in their father's company, starting at the bottom. It was excellent incentive.

Brandon, the elder brother, had played it safe and bought one of his father's smaller businesses, Smart thinking and good business practices saw him reach his goal in less than two years. His sister, Clarice, was more ambitious and decided to start her own company, but used her knowledge of her father's conglomerate to ensure that it would succeed. It had not yet, but was on track to do so in a few months, almost exactly as she had planned. Today, Hank would declare his intentions.

Their father was a very busy man, and his spare time was at a premium, but he always reserved these days for his family. He was not a bad father, but he was not at home as much as his children would have liked. His manservant, Alain, had become much like a surrogate father to Martin, but there was no replacing the real thing. Therefore these events were always exciting for him.

The siblings had always gotten along as well as any normal brothers and sisters did. Their father had worked his way up from relative poverty, and never let his hard-earned wealth go to his head, and especially not to his children's. They had never lacked, but they were not spoiled either. The bequeathal arrangement was one way that he made sure that they learned the value of working for their money, but without having to struggle like he had at first. Now that Hank had reached twenty-one, there would be fewer opportunities for the entire family to gather, so they made the most of them when they could.

The dinner culminated in the traditional birthday cake, and it was not until Hank had blown out the candles and the family congratulated him that their father would let anyone talk business.

"So, son, what have you decided to do with your bequeathal? You've discussed several good ideas with us, and I'm curious to know what you've settled upon."

Hank replied, "I'm not going to play it as safe as Brandon, but I'm more cautious than Clarice, so I've decided to go halfway. I've discussed this with Clarice, and I'm going to invest in her business. She has reached a point where she wants to expand, but needs backing. We believe that by pooling our resources, we can both get the maximum benefit. She will reach her goal sooner, and I won't have to start from scratch."

"That sounds like a good compromise. I look forward to seeing the results." Then their father looked in Martin's direction. "And while we're on the subject, have *you* got any idea yet what you're going to aim for? You've only got a year and a half before you complete school and have to decide on tertiary studies."

"I do have a goal, actually," Martin replied. "I want to buy a starship and start my own independent shipping company."

Yote Senior frowned. "This is a joke, right? Shipping is a mug's game. Do you know how many independents fail in their first year of business? Do you know that most struggle with debt for many years, and maybe never make any decent money? Only the big shipping companies make money at that game, and they have the benefit of huge infrastructure and other advantages. You'd be better off buying into one of their subsidiaries."

"No, I intend to be my own boss. I could never be that if I do it your way. Besides, I want to travel, not sit behind a desk."

"If you do well in a safer business, then you will have the money to travel after a few years."

"If all it takes is the money, dad – why have you never left Earth and seen some of the galaxy? Not even one little vacation to Hesperia Asteroid city?"

"An interstellar trip takes weeks – I can't be away from the business for that long just for a vacation. You need a sense of proportion, son."

"And that's why I want to be a starship captain. I want a larger proportion devoted to having a life, not just a business."

"Enough of this foolish talk. Think long and hard, son. You won't have the time or money for interstellar jaunts if you're working in the warehouse of one of my companies after your business fails."

"Believe me, dad, I *will* be thinking about it."

Martin had done little since then but think about how to make his dream work in reality, if for no other reason than to prove his father wrong. His studies had covered every aspect of business connected with commercial shipping, from learning what goods were profitable enough to ship between worlds, to operational procedures for starships, and getting his pilot's licence. Ironically, despite his goal of having more time for a life, those years had left him very little time for socialising, and he did not even have a steady girlfriend yet. He sincerely hoped that would change soon.

His father continued to try to dissuade him from his course, but to his credit, did not actively block Martin's goal in any way. Despite Martin's hard work and thorough preparations though, he doubted that he would ever hear a word of encouragement from his father, and he was resigned to that fact.

"Here's the birthday boy," announced Brandon as he entered the dining room. In fact all his siblings had beaten him here, as well as his parents.

"We were beginning to think that you were going to be a no-show," Clarice commented.

Martin grinned. "This was one event that I was sure that you weren't going to start without me."

"Don't be too sure of that – I'm pretty hungry," Hank retorted.

Martin noted that he had put on a lot of weight lately. He had always been a big eater, and his lifestyle was not doing him any favours.

Martin gave his mother a hug. "Good to see you, Mom."

"You really should visit more often," she gently chided.

His father said, "Sit down next to your mother, Martin, and let's get this celebration under way."

Martin did so, and soon the table was abuzz with conversation as parents and children caught up with each other's lives. While they chatted, appetisers were served, then a fancy main meal, followed by Martin's favourite dessert – passionfruit pavlova. Normally he tried to avoid such foods, not wanting to go Hank's way, but this was his one indulgence. Then of course there was birthday cake.

Martin had been semi-dreading the cake, because it marked the end of the embargo on talking business at the dinner table, and it was also when he would be committed to his course of action. He blew out the candles, there were cheers and congratulations, then the inevitable question.

"So, Martin, what have you decided to do with your bequeathal?" his father asked in a tone that was a faint warning to make a smart choice.

"My mind is unchanged, Dad. I will be buying a used starship to refurbish and start my own shipping company. I have already started shopping around for the ship."

"I suppose you'll be swanning around the space in some leaky rust-bucket that will cost you a lot in maintenance, and I'd be ashamed to be seen in?"

Martin was stung by his father's disdain. "Of course not! In fact I've virtually settled for a former Star Corps ship. It's outdated by Stellar Services standard, but a wonderful start-up for someone like me. Once it's refurbished, I'll not only be able to show it off to prospective clients, but it will also look smart enough for the passengers I intend to take on top of cargo."

"I still think you're being a fool, but on your head be it."

"Gee, thanks for the encouragement, Dad."

"Well, I think you're being bold," Clarice opined. "Perhaps you can show me around when it's ready. I'll even christen it for you if you like?"

Martin smiled gratefully at his sister. "I'll take you up on that, Ceecee."

She and her brothers steered the subject away from Martin's plans for the future in order to restore the pleasant family atmosphere. No more was said on the subject for the rest of the evening, but Martin was uncomfortably aware that he had committed himself to the more expensive starship after shooting off his mouth about it. He prayed that his figures were right, because even if they were, it was going to be a close thing.

Martin dickered with the broker and managed to squeeze out a few extra concessions. He was grateful for the times that his father had let him sit in on negotiations, and so he had a very good idea on how to do it well for himself. He had the ship moved to a shipyard to have the necessary modifications done, and the refurbishment of passenger cabins and facilities. After that, he spent most of his spare time either practicing for his Master Pilot's licence, or tracking down business. He had a firm date set soon, and that left just one important thing left to do – he needed a crew.

Heywood Baxter was a very excited ten year old boy. Of course any boy would be excited on the occasion of their birthday, but the tenth was when he would be getting his Companion. He remembered the tests that they had done with him which they said would determine what kind of Companion he would be getting, but he was never told what the results of those tests were. That was the way they traditionally did things on the Non-Aligned world of Celeste – it was supposed to be a moment of discovery and bonding between a human and his personal morph slave.

He had waited impatiently throughout the birthday party that his parents had arranged for him and his friends. Some of them had their Companions already – Manny had a German Shepherd bitch morph, and Lyle's was a deer buck. Heywood wondered what species his was going to be. They told him that they were psychologically matched to each person – he didn't even really understand what that meant. However he did know that they were supposed to stay with you all your life, so you had to like them a lot.

The moment at last arrived when a van pulled up outside of their house with the logo of a well-known gene-tech factory on its side. Heywood rushed outside to meet the occupants. The driver got out and grinned at the boy.

"Let me guess – you're the birthday boy. Heywood, isn't it?"

"Yeah, that's me. Have you got my Companion?"

"Not so fast, my friend. First I need your parents to sign for the completion of contract, *then* you get to see your Companion."

Heywood raced off yelling, "Dad! Mom! Come out here! Hurry!"

Of course Heywood's parents already knew what had to be done, but they put on a show of reluctance to draw the moment out. Eventually they relented and signed, and the driver opened the sliding door of the van. A small morph got out, spotted Heywood, walked over to him, and waited while he got a good look at his new Companion.

Heywood saw beige fur with very dark brown fur on the forearms and lower legs, a very slim build, and bright eyes surrounded by a mask of dark fur – a black-footed ferret morph. He loved ferrets!

"Hi – I'm Menalippe, and I'm so happy to meet you at last, Heywood," she said.

Heywood grinned hugely. She was perfect! "Come on inside – I want to show you to my friends!"

"I'd love to meet them," she said enthusiastically.

The two ran inside while his parents smiled proudly; their own Companions sharing the moment with them.

As was intended and designed, Menalippe was the perfect companion for the boy. She and Heywood played the same games, read the same books, and shared all their interests. She went to school with him and learned alongside him and his friends and their Companions. At night, she had her own bed in his room. They were inseparable. Years passed and puberty saw him grow into a healthy youth, along with the usual sexual urges – and Menalippe was perfect there too. By this time though, they shared one big bed. It was not until his eighteenth birthday that he got a severe reality check.

"Could we have a word with you, son?" his father asked.

Heywood's mother was there also, instead of out with her Companion, so it had to be a matter of some importance. "Of course, Dad. What's the problem? Mena and I haven't been keeping you awake, have we?"

Heywood's father smiled. "No, nothing like that. Take a seat, son – we have an important matter to discuss."

Heywood settled on a sofa, Menalippe beside him as always, and he waited curiously. His mother sat with her panther morph Companion in a two-seater, but his father remained standing while his rabbit doe morph Companion sat to one side on a chair.

"Next week you turn eighteen, and it's time to announce your betrothal."

"My *what*?" Heywood asked in surprise.

"You will be introduced to the girl you will marry when you turn twenty one."

"But I haven't met anyone that I would even want to go steady with, let alone marry," Heywood protested.

"That has nothing to do with your marriage. Your mother and I arranged your marriage years ago to the daughter of a business associate of ours. This will make stronger financial ties between our families, and of course she will provide you with an heir."

"What if I don't *want* to get married? What if I can't stand the girl?"

His father frowned. "Heywood, you can't be so naïve as not to know how marriages work here on Celeste. Our whole culture has been based on this way of doing things, and it has worked well for us since this world was colonised. You *will* marry this girl. Besides, if you put some effort into this marriage, you will find it has many advantages, and you may even learn to love her. I did not meet your mother until our betrothal, but we respect and care for each other."

"I always thought that I'd have some say in the matter!" Heywood protested.

"Don't be ridiculous. Teenagers aren't qualified to know what's best for them in the future. We're talking security for your finances and your children, and the inter-family bonds that makes our way of life so successful. That's why you have a morph Companion to take care of your base needs so that your marriage may be ruled by your head and not by your emotions."

"I don't find the concept of love to be ridiculous."

"Enough! This isn't a debate. I am telling you what is going to happen next Thursday so that you will be prepared, and won't embarrass us in front of our associate."

Heywood glared at his father, but knew that he was fighting a lost cause. "Consider me advised," he growled, and then got up and marched out of the room with Menalippe at his heels. He stormed into his bedroom, and his Companion barely made it inside before he slammed the door.

"Argh!" he yelled, and kicked an inoffensive sports bag across the room, scattering its contents widely.

Menalippe said, "I hate to say this, but your father was right – you *are* being naïve. You knew what to expect, but you chose to turn a blind eye to it."

"And why should I accept it just because it's the way it has always been done? Heywood demanded. "Why can't there be a compromise? Why should I be forced into a relationship with someone when the person with whom I'm in love is right here in front of me?"

"Shh!" Menalippe said urgently, waving her arms in a manner to suggest that he lower his voice. "You know that's forbidden, and that they would never compromise on that. Talk like that could get you into deep trouble, and might even get us split up. You know that humans and their Companions may love each other, but not be *in* love."

"And yet how can the powers-that-be create for us our perfect companions and expect us not to feel this way? How many others have been forced into loveless marriages while the ones they should be marrying have to stand aside and pretend that it doesn't bother them?" Heywood looked keenly into Menalippe's eyes. "And it does bother you, doesn't it?"

Menalippe's eyes fell, and she nodded. "Yes. I knew to expect this, but it bothers me a lot."

Heywood took the ferret girl into his arms and hugged her. His anger gave way to tenderness, and he said quietly, "I love you, Mena. I love you with all my heart and soul, and whatever happens on Thursday, nothing will change that."

"I know you do, and I love you no less. No human girl could ever care for you more than I do." She tilted her head up and her muzzle met his lips, and they kissed deeply.

Soon their kissing turned to more intimate caresses, and then they were busy removing each other's clothes. Moments later, they were on their bed making love.

A long and satisfying time later, they lay together enjoying the afterglow in silence. Eventually though, Heywood broke their reverie.

"We're going to have to find a way out of this."

Menalippe turned her head to look at him. "Okay, but how?"

He sighed. "I don't know. But I'll have three years to find out before I'm forced into marriage. Maybe I'll get some idea if I sleep on it for a while. Goodnight, Mena."

"Goodnight, my love."

Heywood was still without a plan of action though when his future wife arrived with her parents. One look at her Companion told him volumes about her. He was a horse morph – tall, powerfully muscled, and conspicuously male. There was nothing subtle about her relationship with him, and it was a jarring contrast with the gently intimate relationship that Heywood had with Menalippe. The two humans belonged together as much as fire and water.

Nevertheless, Heywood endeavoured to at least be courteous to Alexandra, if for no other reason than to make life no more unpleasant than it had to be. However, despite her being polite and gentle in return, she nevertheless gave the impression that she was looking at something that had crawled out from under a rock.

While both their parents were having a lively and amiable talk mostly about the future of their children, Heywood and Alexandra endured a chilly and uncomfortable time forced together. It was impossible to tell who was more relieved when she had to leave with her parents.

Heywood tried to escape without having to talk with his parents, but his father caught him at the door.

"So what are your impressions of your betrothed?" he asked.

"Even more than I expected, Dad," Heywood replied, and beat a hasty retreat before his father queried just what exactly he meant by that.

Back in his room, he sank onto his bed with a groan. Menalippe sat beside him and stroked his head.

"I can't live with *that*, Mena," he said with a touch of despair.

"But you will have to. It's not as if you can run away. The betrothal law is upheld worldwide."

Heywood was struck by a thought. "You're right – but only on this world. It doesn't apply on other worlds."

Menalippe frowned in thought. "Are you thinking of leaving Celeste? Your parents would never allow it, and besides it's far too expensive for us to afford."

"If you go as passengers. If I can get a job as starship crew, then cost won't be a factor."

"Again – your parents won't let you take a job like that. In fact your schooling is being aimed at you taking up a part of their business. I don't think that will get you a job on a starship."

"Right again, unfortunately, so I am just going to have to learn a trade without them finding out about it."

"How are you going to do that?" Menalippe asked sceptically.

"Give me time to work it out first, love, but I think I know what to do. I'm going to need an ally though if I'm going to make this work."

That got Menalippe curious. "Who would do that?"

"Why – who else but by beloved bride-to-be!"

Heywood's parents were surprised but pleased a few days later when he requested that he make a trip to visit Alexandra, and could they make arrangements with her parents for a convenient date? They certainly could, happy to see that their son was warming to the idea of being betrothed. Alexandra's parents were equally pleased, and ensured that their daughter was ready and waiting when Heywood arrived to pick her and her Companion up.

The atmosphere was positively glacial in the car, and their Companions were equally uncomfortable, but they did not have to endure it for long. Rather than taking Alexandra to a restaurant as he had implied for some getting-to-know-you talk, he turned off the main road to head for a quiet picnic ground that he had searched out beforehand.

"Where are we going?" demanded Alexandra.

"Somewhere very private," Heywood replied. "Despite what this meeting appears, I have something to discuss with you that you are going to want to hear, unless I'm a terrible judge of character. And we have to do it where I'm sure that we won't be overheard."

"Then why not just say it right here in the car?"

"This may take a while, and seeing as we're supposed to dining, I thought we might as well have something to eat while we're at it."

Despite herself, Alexandra was intrigued. "Okay, but this had better be good."

It was not long before they pulled into the picnic ground. It was one of the more out of the way places, and being the middle of the week, there were no others there, as Heywood had hoped.

"So why here?" Alexandra asked.

"Because we won't look out of place here if someone does come along. We even packed a complete picnic basket to complete the image, not to mention the food." He indicated the basket that Menalippe had fetched from the trunk. She put it on one of the picnic tables and started unpacking it. The others seated themselves around the table.

"Enough mystery – what is it you want?" Alexandra asked impatiently.

"First – a question. I want you to answer me with complete and unvarnished honesty. Do you want to marry me?"

"Not if you were the last human on Celeste," she replied with finality.

"Excellent! he replied, and she looked startled. "The feeling is mutual. So - what if I told you that I have a plan to avoid that fate? How far would you go to help support that plan?"

"That depends on what you have in mind," she replied cautiously.

"First I need you to promise that you will tell absolutely no one about this," Heywood insisted. He did not bother asking the same of Samson, the horse morph – what one would agree to, the other would honour.

"You have my word."

"I intend to leave Celeste on a starship as one of its crew. To do that, I need to take extra classes to learn a trade suitable for a starship, but I can't cover up that much extra time without a good excuse. That's where you come in. We will pretend to have a great deal of interest in each other, and want to go out often. If your parents are anything like mine, they'll only be too glad to encourage us to do so. Of course I'll be at those classes while you can be doing whatever you like in the meantime. We only need to be together when I pick you up and drop you off. Oh, we might have to put in a few appearances together at our folks' places occasionally, just to keep them happy, but I think that we can tolerate that under the circumstances, don't you?"

Alexandra mulled that over, then asked, "How long are we going to have to do this?"

"I'm afraid that it takes a while to earn the necessary qualifications. I think that it will take pretty much three years."

"Ouch! That's a long time to maintain the pretence."

"I know, but I can't afford to buy a ticket – I don't get any serious money until I turn twenty-one."

"What if you used that class time for a job instead so that you can pay the fare?"

"Bureaucracy – Because I'm under twenty-one, I couldn't get a ticket without my parents finding out about it, and they might find out about the job also. I already investigated the possibility and had to give it away. But our society actively encourages tertiary education, so it's easy to sign up for classes. Umm… I might need a bit of financial help to pay for them. I can't attend two sets of classes *and* hold down a part-time job also."

"I might have known there'd be money involved."

"It's going to take every cred that Menalippe and I have as it is, so I'm not asking lightly. Besides, it will pay off well in the end. The long delay has one definite advantage for you."

"Oh? How so?"

"Your birthday is just a few weeks after mine, right?" She nodded. "Request your parents that we get married on your birthday as a special present to you. I'll arrange to leave the night before though, and when I don't turn up, you can be the distraught bride left at the altar. Here's the kicker though – because you'll be a legally totally independent adult as of that day, you will no longer be subject to the betrothal laws any more."

Alexandra looked amazed. "I can't be forced to marry anyone after I turn twenty-one… Yes! Heywood, you've got yourself a deal! Now, how are we going to work this?"

They ended up discussing the details for over an hour, and their Companions served them food and drink while they did so, occasionally offering opinions or suggestions. The journey back to Alexandra's home was far more relaxed now that the two humans were enthusiastic conspirators rather than inevitable spouses. Later they could tell both their parents that the date had gone wonderfully well with complete honesty.

Heywood took some aptitude tests to determine what career would best suit him. He was pleased to discover that he had scored highly in piloting, and enrolled immediately in an appropriate course. He also took an extra course in nav-systems as a back-up. The charade with Alexandra worked even better than they had hoped, although over the ensuing months they had some awkward moments where their plans almost came unstuck. Because he was concentrating so much on his clandestine lessons, his grades in the regular classes began to slip, and his father warned that if they continued to do so, his frequent outings with Alexandra would be severely curtailed. In order to get his grades back up, Heywood had to spend even more time studying. To help him make the most of his time, Alexandra arranged a small apartment where he could concentrate on his studies, while she and their Companions made sure that he ate well, and took care of other distractions. It amused them that in some ways, they were becoming the spouses that they were trying so hard to avoid.

As the months passed, something else changed between them – they became friends. There still was not the slightest bit of romantic interest between them, but respect and liking grew in both. When the holiday breaks came, they took the opportunity to do some things together as friends would do. Sometimes though they deliberately involved their parents to maintain the fiction of an engaged couple growing closer. Their friendship helped make their personal sacrifices much more bearable, and nearly three years later, it was almost a shock to realise that it must soon end.

This evening, the foursome were at a fancy restaurant to celebrate Heywood's graduation and attaining his pilot's licence.

"So, what happens now?" Alexandra asked.

"Now comes the tricky part. I not only have to find employment on a starship, but I also have to get it on a ship that leaves on the morning of the wedding, if possible. If not, I'll have to go into hiding until I do. Despite being twenty-one, the betrothal law remains in effect until the marriage contract is sealed. Neither of us will be free until I leave Celeste's jurisdiction and I can tell everyone that I won't be coming back. That would nullify our betrothal, and you can't be forced into another. So it's up to me to make sure that I get on a ship that day. Any sooner and your parents might slap another hasty betrothal contract on you with someone else, so I can't leave early either. The bottom line is that I need a good dollop of luck for this part of the plan."

"Have you gotten any leads yet?"

"No, but I've registered with a recruitment agency. They tell me that I have a pretty good chance."

"I have a good feeling about this. You've worked hard, and you deserve a lucky break." Alexandra raised her glass of wine. "A toast to you and Menalippe whose love and devotion has brought this day about."

Two weeks later, confidence was no longer so high. The only offers that Heywood had gotten so far were too soon or too late. One was so long after the wedding date that he was almost certainly likely to be discovered. He persisted though, and with just two days to go, he got a bite.

"Alex – I got it!" he excitedly commed her. "There's a ship departing on Tuesday night that needs to replace a retiring pilot, and I've got the position!"

"But that's well after the wedding is supposed to be held – they'll be looking for you all day."

"That's when the ship actually leaves, but I will have to report in long before that, so I'll drive in that morning before the wedding. If everything goes well, I'll be on board before they even start looking."

"Is it a ground-launch ship, or do they shuttle up to it in orbit?"

"Ground launch," Heywood confirmed.

"They might trace your car to the spaceport and locate you before they launch. You need to get there some other way."

"Good point. Don't want to be stymied at the last moment. I can't trust public transport though because the A.I. might be able to trace me, not to mention the difficulty of lugging all our stuff."

"I'll get Samson to take you there. I'll pretend to have him go on an errand for me because I'll be too busy getting ready for the wedding. He can rendezvous with you and Menalippe somewhere discreet, and take you to the spaceport, and then come back here before any questions are asked."

"That should work, and I know a good place to rendezvous."

They set an exact time and place, and then signed off.

On the morning of the wedding, Heywood insisted that he drive himself and Menalippe to the wedding, pointing out that he would be driving his wife to their honeymoon retreat, so he had to have his car there, and he might as well drive it. He also left a little early, saying that he wanted to make sure that absolutely everything would be ready for the big moment. Menalippe and he had carefully packed everything that they thought they would want or need on the starship, and had stowed it in the car the previous night. They did not want anyone querying why they were taking so much.

They rendezvoused with Samson in the car park of a quiet public garden on the south side of town, located well away from the spaceport, but near to a route that suggested that he might be heading for another town further down the coast. They transferred all the baggage to Samson's car and headed off to the spaceport.

The equine morph was normally untalkative – not unfriendly, but not given to chatting much. It was not often that he initiated a conversation, but this time he did.

"I want to thank you, Heywood. My Companion had been

dreading marriage so much that it was hurting both of us. You have given us quite a gift, even if it was started just as a way of getting yourself out of a similar fate. You could have easily abandoned us without taking us into consideration."

"Don't praise me too much, Samson. Alexandra's willing cooperation made my goal more achievable."

"I know, but it's still appreciated. Alex wanted me to pass on a message, knowing that it would be unlikely that she would see you today. She said that if you were the last human on Celeste, she *would* consider marrying you after all."

Heywood chuckled. "High praise indeed. Anything else?"

"Yes. She said that she will not miss her fiancé at all, but she will dearly miss her good friend."

Heywood nodded soberly. "Yeah, I'll miss her also for that reason. We four made a pretty good group, didn't we?"

"Indeed," Samson replied, and then returned to his normal non-chatty state.

Samson helped them unload their baggage onto a trolley at the spaceport. Menalippe gave the big horse a big hug, to his surprise, and then he had to hasten back to Alexandra.

Heywood showed his documents to the security guard at the crew entrance, and was directed to the correct launching cradle where he would find the *Stellar Rose* berthed. There he found one of the crew on duty at the ramp leading to the personnel lock, and once again he showed his documents.

The man looked them over and said, "So you're the new assistant pilot? You've certainly brought quite a load with you."

"It's my first job, and I'm leaving my old life behind. It's possible that we will pare this down over time, but for now I think we're prepared to cover all our needs."

"Fair enough – I remember my first time well. You're a bit early, so take your time unpacking before reporting to the captain at 0300 hours when he's due back. Have your slave report to Hatfield in Ship's Services to be assigned her duties."

Heywood had to remind himself that they were not Celeste citizens, but came from another of the Non-Aligned Worlds where they had different attitudes towards morphs. That had been one of the difficulties in getting a suitable ship, but he had wanted a non-Celeste ship because it was unlikely that they return soon, or cause him trouble with the authorities here. The flip side was that he and Menalippe would have to put up with another world's attitudes towards her.

"She is my Companion, sir, not just a slave," he politely reminded the man.

"That's right – you Celestians have your morphs bonded to you. Don't worry – we're not going to do anything to her. She's just going to have to earn her keep while she's on board with you."

"We expected as much, sir," Heywood replied.

"Good. Get on board and get familiar with the ship. We'll have more than enough time to chat later." He instructed them as to where to find their assigned cabin and sent them on their way.

Heywood and Menalippe took his advice and got settled in. He met the captain at the appointed hour, and found him to be a stern but pleasant man. He was ordered to start his first watch at 0600 hours, so he was free to meet and get to know many of the crew beforehand. It helped keep his mind off the fact that by now there would be a major search for him going on. He fervently hoped that while they might check the spaceport, it would not occur to them to check the crew rosters. He sweated over that right up until the moment that they took off.

"Mr Baxter – you are the pilot in control. Let's see what you've got," the captain ordered.

Of course Heywood was nervous – it was his first professional lift-off, but with the Chief Pilot at the station next to him watching and ready to take over in an emergency, some of the pressure was off him. He set out to impress.

The Chief Pilot never lifted a finger while Heywood launched them from the cradle, boosted the ship through the atmosphere, and set a course away from the gravity well of Celeste.

"Well done, Mr Baxter. I think we'll keep you on," the captain commented.

"Thank you, Captain," Heywood replied, and gave a quiet sigh of relief. He was now officially a spacer, and he and Menalippe were free at last.

A month later, Heywood was surprised to get a note forwarded to him from Alexandra. In it she let him know that it had taken them three days to track him to the spaceport, and they knew that he was on board *Stellar Rose*, so he had better not return because he would be arrested for violation of the betrothal laws. As expected, her parents tried to arrange for her to marry someone else, but she refused, quoting that she was devastated by being abandoned by her fiancé and she could never marry another. Heywood wanted to wish Alexandra good fortune for the future, but thought it inadvisable to make any sort of contact with her. He never heard from her again.

He did receive messages from his parents which ranged from demanding that he return home to fulfil his obligations, to pleading that he think of how this had affected the family. Considering how they had not bothered to think about how it affected *him*, he took little notice of their pleas. He missed them nonetheless, but he could never go home again.

As it turned out, *Stellar Rose* never went back to Celeste. Apparently it had been an unusual port of call for the freighter which plied the routes between the Non-Aligned Worlds. Heywood and Menalippe fitted in reasonably well with the rest of the crew, tempered only by their different attitudes towards the slave species. When Heywood made it totally clear that his Companion was not theirs to command at a whim, the captain ordered the crew to keep their hands off her. She was treated pretty much as a low-level crew member thereafter, except that she did not earn a wage. That did not matter to her and Heywood though because they did not have much opportunity to spend his wages. He did not trust what might happen on most worlds if he brought her along on shore leave, and he did not care to go alone most of the time.

Six years passed, and during that time Heywood achieved his Master Pilot's ticket. Then their Chief Pilot met a girl and decided to settle down planet-side, and Heywood was promoted. He might have been doing that job for the rest of his career except for a twist of fate.

Stellar Rose was adrift light-years from the nearest inhabited world, her warp engines crippled.

"I'm sorry, Captain," the engineer reported, "but it's hopeless. There's no way that I can fix the warp drive outside of a shipyard."

"I see. Then we're left with no option but to call for help."

"You know that the only ones who are likely to respond way out here are the Feddies."

"I know, but it's still better than the alternative."

Twenty eight hours later, a Star Fleet ship came to their aid. Shortly thereafter, all the morphs aboard were 'freed', and Heywood and Menalippe were ripped apart, not to see each other again for many weeks.

Ceres had enjoyed a wonderful childhood in Black Foxtaur village, but always knew that shi was destined for much more. It was not just a feeling, but a hard truth – shi was not the same as hir parents. Or to be more accurate, hir surrogate parents. Although they had mostly black pelts, they also had white fur on their chests, bellies, hands and paws, while shi was solid black from the tip of hir ears to end of hir tail. Even more different was the fact that shi was a hermaphrodite, while hir parents were single sex – both females, but that was hardly unusual for foxtaurs. Vulpamours (lesbian foxtaurs) were a high percentage of the families in any foxtaur community due to their gender imbalance and other factors. But that fact also made them perfect contenders for the Stellar Foxtaur breeding program. Vulpamours already needed to get someone outside of their relationship to get them pregnant if they wanted children. It mattered not that the someone was actually the New Generation Genetics company that was in charge of the breeding program, and who were seeking volunteers to be surrogate mothers for the new breeds of foxtaurs. Because they were similar in looks and build, the Black Foxtaurs were chosen to raise the Starwalker breed of Stellar Foxtaur. Hir parents had wanted children, and the financial and other incentives were enough to convince them to join. Both vulpamours had been implanted with an embryo, and Ceres had a 'sister' named Vesta. Not that they were true sisters because they had none of their parents' DNA, and there was variation built into their own in order to prevent inbreeding when they started having children of their own, but that did not matter to Ceres anyway. Vesta was hir sister in all but fact, and they did virtually everything together as they grew up. Then one day, something happened that would forever push them apart, and as so often happens, it was over a boy.

Ceres and Vesta were only two of a few dozen Starwalkers being raised in that village, but despite being amongst Black Foxtaurs all their lives, they still naturally started gravitating towards others of their kind as they matured and started getting interested in adult matters. Ceres had been no different until shi met Danson one day. The young tod had been raised on a farm at the opposite of the village from Ceres, and while shi might have seen him at one of the community festivals, shi had never really met him. It was at the Harvest Festival not long after shi had turned seventeen that shi had been randomly partnered with him for a dance. Shi found him to be witty, charming and surprisingly knowledgeable for a farm boy, and shi ended up spending the rest of the evening with him. It did not bother him that shi was a herm, and shi liked the way he related to hir. Shi asked to see him again the next day.

When shi told Vesta about him, hir sister had laughed. "You've just got a crush on him. You'll soon wake up and realise that he can never replace a Starwalker like us. Have fun while it lasts though."

That had annoyed Ceres. The things that had attracted hir to him just were not part of the psyche of the average Starwalker. It was the sameness of all the others of hir kind that had held hir back when many of the others were already forming relationships. Shi knew that made hir different from the others, but shi did not think much of it for now. It would be a few years yet before they left the community to really start

Art © Heather Bruton

their lives as pioneers out in the stars, and many things could and would change in that time.

Only as time passed, this did not pass. Instead, the two grew ever closer together until one day Ceres realised that he was waiting for hir to propose. Being a herm, shi never really ascribed to most gender stereotypes, but that did not apply to Danson. In foxtaur society, it was the female who proposed, and in their relationship, that role was hirs, and he waiting patiently for hir to do so. For once in hir life, shi was so flustered that shi did not know what to do, and so consulted with hir counsellor at the Stellar Foxtaur training facility which shi had been attending three days a week since a very early age.

Amongst the facilities there was a zero-G gymnasium, a facility set up specifically for the Starwalkers. None of the other six breeds of Stellars would be working in the environment that shi had been bred for – space – and so the Starwalkers had that to themselves. The first day that they had gone to the training facility, they had been introduced to the gym. They were like birds with clipped wings who suddenly discovered that they could fly again. The joy and freedom of moving around in that weightless environment rammed home to all of them that their future lay away from the grasp of a planet's gravity. The teachers had struggled to get them to leave that first time. Nowadays Ceres used it whenever shi wanted to think deeply about some problem. Hir thoughts seemed freer and clearer when shi was in hir natural environment. This time though, the answer was not clear – shi was bred and destined for outer space, while Danson was anything but. However, shi knew that shi loved him, and now shi knew that he loved hir too. Shi turned to the only other person who ever managed to answer the hard questions for hir – Chakat Cornsilk, who was named after the colour of hir hair. Cornsilk had joined Ceres in the gymnasium at hir request, but while the chakat could never match a Starwalker in that environment, shi certainly was no slouch in there either. Ceres told hir of the problem that confronted hir.

Cornsilk smiled reassuringly at Ceres. "Things aren't quite as bad as they seem, Ceres. It's true that you would never be happy if you stayed on a planet, but don't count out your boyfriend yet. When the Federation started the Stellar Foxtaur program, they did so knowing that the Stellars would have complete freedom of choice when it came to their individual destinies, and thus some of them would not become part of the next stage of the program. In other words, a life in the service of the Star Corps is not your only possible destiny. You could consider another career in space that would allow Danson to accompany you, if he wishes. You said he's farm raised, so have you tried asking him if he might be interested in hydroponics, for example? That's always a valuable position on any starship or space station."

Ceres realised that Cornsilk was right – she *had* been taking a blinkered approach to the problem. It had not occurred to hir that shi did not have to do what shi had assumed shi would be doing. But would Danson be interested?

He was surprised but curious. Although a farm-boy, his association with Ceres had exposed him to broader horizons, and he was willing to look into it... if shi was keen for him to go with hir.

Ceres realised that he was hinting that he was looking for that proposal from hir. Shi made hir decision, took a deep breath, and said, "Danson, would you be my denmate, and follow me to the stars?"

Danson smiled happily. "I would follow you across the galaxy. I accept your proposal."

After appropriately celebrating their bonding, the pair made their plans for the future. Shi concentrated on training for a commercial enterprise, while Danson took Cornsilk's suggestion and studied hydroponics. Vesta thought Ceres was crazy though, and their relationship was strained a bit because of it. That disappointed Ceres, but hir future was more important, and Vesta just had to learn to live with it. Shi was much more concerned about Danson, and whether he would cope with hir crazy plans. He accompanied hir to the Starwalker training facility where he was definitely the odd foxtaur in the group, but still made to feel welcome because he was a symbol of their freedom to choose rather than be destined to work for the Star Corps. The trips to the facility also helped ensure he would not develop the crippling Territorial Attachment Syndrome during the critical years of his development. Although it was far more common in vixens, they did not want to risk it happening to him.

Eventually the time came that the Starwalkers graduated and almost all of them chose to accept the Star Corps offer of employment. Ceres bid a sad farewell to hir many friends, and then shi and Danson went on a search for a starship that would be willing to take on two novice crew members such as them.

R'Murran was enjoying the last day of the *Jahazrah*, a combination family reunion and festival that was only held every two hands (8) of Caitian years, and the previous one happened while he was on a tour of duty, so he was making the most of this one. The leonine alien was not pleased to cut his stay short when he received a call to return immediately to his starship, *R'Verrastrr's Victory*, and report to the First Officer, but it was not entirely unexpected. He entered her office and was told to take a seat. He curled his tail through the slot in the seatback and sat down and waited to hear what Commander M'Tisharr had to say.

"I hear that you are looking to take on a Fourthwife," she said with a warm smile. "Congratulations on finding someone for that role. It's been quite a while since you got your Thirdwife, hasn't it?"

"Yes, it has," R'Murran agreed. "My family has been very happy with the status quo, so finding M'Resk was something special."

M'Tisharr sighed. "I know, and that's what makes what I have to say extra hard. Star Fleet's family policy encourages Fleet personnel to bring their mates and children with them in times of peace, and thankfully the Federation has been basically at peace for a very long time now. Caitians even get extra leeway due to the nature of our gender imbalance compared to the other member races of the Federation. However, there is a limit, and you have just reached it. Because your Secondwife, M'Anissa'tk, is also Fleet personnel, you were able to have three wives on board, two being the limit for non-Fleet crew, but you cannot have another non-Fleet wife and stay aboard this ship."

"M'Rarrtikar warned me that there might be some problems, but I didn't think that it was that bad."

"I'm afraid that the regulations are quite specific on this matter, so let me lay out the options for you. First – You can give up the idea of having M'Resk as Fourthwife, and that would be the end of the problem. Second – You can take M'Resk as Fourthwife, but she cannot join you here on the ship." She held up a hand to forestall a protest. "I know – that's a very poor option, and certainly one that I would not agree to, but it had to be said. Third – You can take M'Resk as Fourthwife, but be forced to take a post planet-side, and never be part of a ship's crew again, unless you lose one of your non-Fleet wives, goddess forbid. Fourth – You leave Star Fleet and do what you see fit with your life without any interference from us. This is a big decision to make, so I suggest that you discuss it with your family and get back to me. I'm afraid that I will need your answer by 0200 tomorrow ship time in order for me to arrange a replacement for you if necessary."

"Yes sir. I will do that as soon as possible." R'Murran got up to leave.

M'Tisharr had one last thing to say though. "I must admit that I am a little bit envious of you, R'Murran. If I hadn't been so focused on my career, I might not be unmated today. You would have made a fine choice for me if I was just a bit younger. I would happily trade some of my rank for your status. Don't let your career get in the way of doing what makes you happy, okay?"

"I won't, sir. Thank you."

As he made his way back down planet-side, he reflected on his relationships and what had brought him to this turning point.

R'Murran was an unremarkable looking Caitian. His mane was nice enough, and at 155cm (5' 1"), he was taller than the average male although not the tallest. However, what distinguished him was his exceptional engineering talent, which had caught the eye of a Star Fleet recruiter. He had accepted a scholarship to the Star Fleet Academy straight after graduating from Katten'rrtsk University, and there he studied starship design and operation. It had left him little time for socialising, and thus it wasn't until he had been at the academy for several months that he had met his future Firstwife. It was the midyear break, and he had been enjoying doing a whole lot of nothing for a change. He was lazing at the side of the pool when he was whacked by an errant ball. An apologetic female had collected the ball, and on a whim he had asked her name and invited her to dinner with him. Her name was M'Rarrtikar, and she said yes.

They had hit it off well, and thereafter he tried to make as much spare time as possible to see her. Upon graduating from the academy, they exchanged vows in front of a Mentarkan priestess and became husband and wife. When he was assigned to the Federation starship *R'Verrastrr's Victory*, M'Rarrtikar accompanied him and took one of the civilian positions suitable for her skills as a qualified accountant. It was Star Fleet's policy to free up Fleet personnel for more important work by utilising their non-Fleet mates to do such jobs during peacetimes, and in doing so, helped maintain better morale by keeping families together.

Inevitably on a Caitian-operated ship, he had attracted the attention of several other unmated females, but the one who interested him in return was a maintenance technician named M'Anissa'tk. M'Rarrtikar recognised the attraction and compatibility with them and, as was her right and duty, proposed to M'Anissa'tk, who accepted the position of Secondwife, with the Aspect of Strength.

Soon after, M'Rarrtikar gave birth to their first child, a daughter whom they named Keera. They took leave for a few weeks for the event, during which time they met M'Lertiña, a teacher and volunteer paramedic. They liked her immediately, and spent much of their leave with their new acquaintance. When it was time for them to return to *R'Verrastrr's Victory*, M'Rarrtikar formally asked her to be R'Murran's Thirdwife, and she accepted, taking the Aspect of Fertility due to her high libido, which was unusual for a Caitian. By tradition, the wife who takes that Aspect must get pregnant within a year of the ceremony of bonding, and M'Lertiña happily did so, bearing them another daughter whom they named Ner'ritn. Because of her paramedic training, she worked as a nursing assistant on board the starship.

About a year after Ner'ritn was born, M'Anissa'tk decided that it was time for her to contribute to the growth of the family, and asked him to get her pregnant. She eventually gave birth to a son, a very welcome addition for a species where about 83% of children are female. They named him Kannekin.

His family settled into a comfortable routine for thirteen years during which he was promoted several times. A male with three wives had a significant amount of respectable status, they all had jobs they enjoyed, and family life was wonderful. It may have stayed like that for many more years if it had not been for the big clan celebration that coincided with their shore leave one year.

R'Murran, his three wives and their three children were all looking forward to the big event. It was on the sixth day of the Jahazrah that he ran into M'Resk, a young woman who had been only five years old when they had last met. She had stuck in the memory of the then fifteen year old R'Murran because she had been such a joy-filled child who always made him smile. She had said to him with all the seriousness of a five year old that one day she would be his wife, and he had smiled and said he'd wait for her to grow up. Grown up she had, and into a beautiful and joy-filled adult. He asked her to enjoy the festival with their family, and by the time they were almost due to go back to the starship, R'Murran was thoroughly taken with her. He asked M'Rarrtikar to consider her as Fourthwife.

This had troubled M'Rarrtikar. She liked M'Resk, but she was significantly younger than R'Murran, although that did not seem to be a problem to either. The biggest obstacle was not something that she could do much about, and that was Star Fleet's policy on families. She had told him that she would think seriously about it, but needed some time, and he had to accept that. She had spent that time considering the pros and cons, and then went back to the starship early to talk with the officer in charge of personnel. The result of that meeting had brought him to this moment, and the big decision that would have to be made.

R'Murran returned to the others and called a family meeting, and then related what M'Tisharr had to say.

"So those are the choices," he said in conclusion. "'Nissa – this is going to affect you a lot also. You're the only other one of us with an actual career in Star Fleet. What are your thoughts?"

M'Anissa'tk gathered her thoughts for a moment, then replied, "I only ever wanted to work in space, and Star Fleet was a means to that end. If we can get another job on a starship, I would be satisfied."

"Good. 'Tiña – any comments?"

"No, husband. I will be happy anywhere that I can be with you and my co-wives," M'Lertiña replied.

"That just leaves the Firstwife's opinion. So what is it to be, 'Tika?"

31

Art © Xian Jaguar

"Husband, you make this difficult. The question that must first be answered is whether *you* can be happy away from Star Fleet. It has been your life since the Academy. Are you going to turn your back on it for love?"

"I had it easy, Firstwife. I got the choice of career handed to me with a scholarship, and I've learned so much since then. Perhaps it's time to spread our wings and fly somewhere else to put what I've learned to the test. I think maybe it's time for me to abandon the safe route and see what else life has to offer."

"Then if no one else has anything to add, I will consider our options and give you my decision tomorrow. As the Terrans say, I'm going to sleep on it."

Risha de Mar was quite an attractive cougar morph fem – long hair, glossy fur, curvaceous body, and a nice bust. Nevertheless, she did not find it easy to get boyfriends. It was the extra pair of arms that usually put them off. Set one above the other, they were perfectly integrated into an otherwise totally normal physique, and Risha quite like having the extra limbs. Unlike most other people, she had never had a job where she wished she had an extra pair of hands. She was a not a freak – her kind had been deliberately gene-engineered this way well before the Gene Wars, and because it was a dominant trait, it bred true even when they mated with normal two-armed cougars.

However, liking her extra limbs did not mean that they did not cause her trouble. She had suffered the taunts of her peers while growing up, and even had to physically defend her two younger siblings from harassment when she was older. Now though, the biggest problem was finding men who did not find her four arms a turn-off. That was why when she had met Carson and he had found her intriguing and exotic rather than freakish, she had fallen hard for him.

Carson was a male cougar about a year older than her. He had a great zest for life, and loved to share it with Risha. She was drawn into his world, and soon they were spending as much time together as they could. Inevitably they became lovers, and spent many passionate nights together. Risha soon could hardly remember sleeping alone, and certainly had no intention of ever doing so again on a regular basis. He asked her to be his wife rather than settling for the usual mating contract, and she had enthusiastically agreed, setting a date for the wedding.

A few weeks before that came to pass, they set off one weekend for some off-road bike riding. Risha was inexperienced on the trail bikes, but was enjoying learning from Carson. A whole morning went by in no

Art © Jameless

time, and they quickly worked up an appetite. They found a small town with a café that catered to the passing trade, and had a light meal before continuing on. Some time later, Risha began to feel nauseous. As it grew worse, Carson suggested that they head for the cabin that was their base camp. The cabin had been in Carson's family for generations, and was used intermittently for various reasons, and was perfect for their weekend jaunt. As they reached the cabin, Carson took a look around the darkening sky.

"Looks like there might be a storm approaching. I should have checked the weather forecast before we came up here."

"Right now, I don't really care," Risha replied. "I just want to lie down for a while. It can pour rain if it wants to."

"Is it getting any better?"

"No – worse." Risha swayed on her feet, and Carson hastened to support her into the cabin. She immediately sprawled on the bed with a groan.

"Sounds like you might have food poisoning. Last time I'm going to *that* café. Anything I can get you?" Carson asked solicitously.

"No – just leave me to my misery."

"Sorry, Love. I'll just put the bikes under shelter."

Carson barely beat the downpour. The storm hit them with a wall of wind and rain that hammered on the roof, but the cabin was well maintained, so they remained dry and warm. However, after about an hour of the torrential downpour, the power failed. Carson found and lit a couple of kerosene lanterns that were amongst the variety of recreational equipment with which the cabin was stocked.

By this time, Risha's condition had worsened. She had to rush to the toilet several times, and lay sweating on the bed in between. Carson was getting very worried.

"Hon – you need some medicine or something."

"How… are you going to get it… here in the middle… of nowhere?" Risha managed to ask.

"I'll ride into town and find help."

"In this weather? No… Stay with me… I'll survive."

"A little rain won't hurt me. I'll be back before you know it," he replied confidently.

Risha wanted to protest some more, but another spasm stopped her.

Carson donned his riding gear and opened the door. The howling gale momentarily pushed him off balance and sent loose items blowing around the room, and then he was through and gone. Risha did not even hear the sound of his bike over the noise of the storm.

For Risha, her illness seemed worse without Carson there to comfort her. She fretted constantly, then when she realised that more time had passed than could be accounted for by a round trip, even in this bad weather, she really started to worry. She weakly searched for her comm to try to call him, but discovered that she had forgotten to charge it, and the battery had died. She was alone and out of contact, and too sick to ride out on her own in this weather. Only exhaustion finally caused her to fall into a restless sleep.

She awoke some time in the morning – exactly when she could not tell without a clock or her comm. The power was still off, and she was still alone. She felt weak and ill, but far better than last night. She managed to hold down a little food and drink.

And she waited.

By now she was in a panic. She could not imagine why Carson had not returned. Eventually she decided that she had regained enough strength to ride out herself. She left a note on the table for him, although it was unlikely that she would miss him riding in. There was only one dirt track to the cabin after all.

The storm was gone as if had never been, leaving a cloudless blue sky. Risha noticed that everything was saturated though. She would have to take extra care while riding. She took it very easy along the track, and slowed down a lot on the curves. She had nearly reached the paved road when she was forced to a stop. Only her slow speed prevented her from running into a landslip that covered the road. The saturated soil had slid off the hillside, completely blocking the road. On the other side of the landslide was a police vehicle. Risha carefully picked her way over the rubble and approached the officer.

"What's going on here, sir?" She asked. "Can I get through?"

"Yes, ma'am, but would you happen to know a cougar morph bike rider?"

Risha grew alarmed. "Yes – my fiancé, Carson. He went out last night and didn't come back."

The officer looked sorrowful. "A local farmer found a rider this morning. Apparently he hit the landslide and crashed heavily. It's with much regret that I must inform you that he is deceased."

Risha crumpled to the ground, wailing her anguish.

For a long time after the tragedy, Risha refused to be left alone. It took her a long time before her life resumed a semblance of normalcy, and even longer before she started dating again. Nothing ever lasted though because the men found her too clingy, or suffering in comparison to her dead lover. Risha realised that she had to make a break from her previous life in order to start afresh. She could think of no bigger break than to leave Earth altogether.

Two chakats entered the family restaurant and looked around for their daughter and hir lifemates. It did not take Lavenderbreeze and Twitchtail long to spot a couple of hermaphrodite felitaurs like themselves, and made their way over to join them. The chakat with light reddish-brown fur with bold red 'socks' noticed them coming, and bounded over to greet them.

"Mum! Dad! I'm so glad that you could make it!" Hotfoot exclaimed as shi hugged hir parents enthusiastically.

"How often do we get to see you, what with you always travelling? Of course we had to come," Twitchtail responded. "But isn't it odd that you, a master chef, should be celebrating at a restaurant?"

Hotfoot grinned. "I'm not *that* obsessed with cooking, Dad, and even I like to have a day off from cooking for a change. Besides, you never know what ideas you can pick up in places like these," shi added with a wink.

Lavenderbreeze replied, "At least this way you aren't in the kitchen half the time. And how is my daughter-in-law?" shi asked as Hotfoot's tiger-patterned mate came over for a hug of hir own.

"I'm doing very well, Mama Lavender," Burningbright replied. "It's good to see you again."

"Where's Zelkie?" Lavenderbreeze asked, looking around for Hotfoot's other lifemate.

"They've got a fancy ice cream soda bar here, and Zelkie took the cubs to get a drink of their choice. Actually, here they come now," Burningbright pointed out.

A reddish-tan chakat with white spots and stripes was approaching with three 13-year-old cubs in tow, each of them holding a huge glass with an elaborate ice cream soda concoction. Only the fear of spilling their marvellous drinks restrained the cubs in their enthusiastic greeting of their grandparents. Only after each had gotten their hugs was Zelkie able to get one of hir own.

"I'm glad that you were able to come at such short notice," Zelkie said. "We had not expected to be so tight for time when we originally planned this get-together."

"So why the rush? And are your parents coming also?" Twitchtail enquired.

"Both my and Burningbright's parents intend to be here to help us celebrate our 14th anniversary as lifemates. You two just happen to be the first to arrive. As for the rush – we'll explain that when the others get here."

"I suppose that's fair," Twitchtail conceded.

Art © Mendhi

Shi and Lavenderbreeze seated themselves at the table, signalled a waiter, and ordered drinks. They engaged in small talk until three more chakats arrived – Burningbright's parents – Dandelion, Pawtapper, and Tailkicker. Another round of hugs ensued and they were barely done when another chakat arrived, this time though with a Bluepaw skunktaur partner in typical male phase. Zelkie was in the arms of hir parents – Truenote and Zuko – in a trice. The cubs weren't far behind, and a laughing Zuko fended them off with hys telekinetic ability. Two cubs hung in mid air giggling, while the other one had the chance to give the skunktaur and chakat a huge hug before being hauled into the air to be replaced by one of the others.

While they were occupied, Zelkie turned to an 18-year-old skunktaur who had accompanied the others. "And how is my young brother? Still giving Dad and Mum a hard time?"

Darkwave grinned. "You know me – the perfect son."

"Yeah, *sure*," Zelkie said with a grimace. "I'm glad you came along anyway."

With everyone finally gathered, they placed their orders for the main meal, and munched on the appetisers that had been ordered in advance.

"Okay, so now that everyone's here, what's the big news?" Tailkicker asked. "And why the big hurry?"

Zelkie answered for them all. "Of course we wanted to celebrate our 14th anniversary on the actual date. It's the first time that we've been able to do so in many years because our interstellar travels haven't coincided until now. Not since we first declared ourselves lifemates after graduation, in fact. We had originally planned to spend a week on Earth celebrating with our families, but we have also decided on a career move. We resigned from the cruise ship as of this trip back to Earth."

"I thought that you loved your jobs there?" Twitchtail remarked.

"We did, but the fact is that it had become routine. We did the same runs every trip, and did the same things every time. We wanted a career in space because we wanted to see new things and places, and get a bit of a challenge to our abilities. Of course finding another ship that fitted that need and would take all three of us and the cubs was not going to be easy. However, we did find one, but it leaves tomorrow afternoon. It's a freighter with a hard departure time, so we have to squeeze in as much as we can before then."

"Well, I'm glad that you were able to find a new ship so quickly, but I'm sorry that it's at the expense of family time. We'll just have to make the most of these moments together. So what's the name of this ship?"

"It's called *Scott's Venture*, and to tell you the truth, we're all wondering what it's going to be like. It's going to be a big change from the cruise ship."

"No doubt. I hope that you fit in well though. I'm sure that you'll let us know soon enough. In the meantime, let's hear all the news from your latest trip."

Burningbright spoke up. "Lemondrop has decided that shi would like to follow in my footsteps and be an environmental engineer."

Pawtapper beamed at hir grandchild. "That's great news. How are your studies coming along, hon?"

"My tutor says that I'm doing really well, Gramma," Lemondrop said excitedly, and proceeded to tell all the details while hir parents proudly listened. Then the other cubs had to tell all about what they had been doing too. The evening was getting off to a great start, which boded well for their future course.

Several weeks later, they disembarked at Big Sur spaceport in disgust.

"The first thing that I am going to do is take a long bath, and then another. I want to get the stink of that ship out of my nose permanently!" Hotfoot declared.

"Better be a big tub, because we'll be joining you," Zelkie agreed fervently.

"At least you two didn't have to work with the biggest pervert," Hotfoot snarled.

Burningbright grimaced. "No, but I could not help sense his slimy feelings every time I was near him."

"I still can't believe we were hired because the captain thought that all chakats were sex maniacs and would put out for his crew," Hotfoot added.

Zelkie snorted. "My handpaw crushing his balls soon disillusioned him as to that matter."

"Didn't stop the rest of the crew trying to cop a feel at every opportunity, did it? If we wouldn't have been left stranded at that outpost, I would have jumped ship long ago."

"Yeah, so you keep saying, Burningbright," Zelkie said tiredly, having heard it a thousand times. "I know that your strong empathic Talent made it hard on you, but the rest of us had to deal with verbal and physical abuse that was just as bad."

"Thank God they left the cubs alone," Hotfoot added.

"Let's just all forget about it and find a hotel with taur facilities and get that bath," Zelkie suggested.

"You're right. We all deserve a vacation," Burningbright

concurred.

They herded themselves and their cubs through the spaceport's bureaucracy and took a Public PTV to a hotel that advertised taur amenities. There they did their best to unwind and think about anything but the ship of horrors that they had just escaped from. It wasn't easy though because they were hurting financially from the early termination of their work contract. Eventually Zelkie sighed and hauled hirself out of the spa and stepped into the fur-dryer.

"I'm going to start making enquiries for work. With the three of us needing to find positions on one ship, we need as much of a head start on that as soon as possible."

"Maybe our old cruise line will take us back?" Hotfoot suggested.

"They warned us that it might be hard for all three of us to get our jobs back when we served notice," Burningbright reminded hir.

"Yeah, you're right," Hotfoot said glumly, "But a small chance is better than nothing."

As it turned out, it was no chance, and it was a fortnight before anything likely came along. The adults made sure that their cubs made the most of the time after the poor experience on *Scott's Venture*. In fact they treated it as a holiday, and everyone's spirits were quite bolstered after several days. Nevertheless, Zelkie was quite excited when shi brought in some good news one morning.

"There's a ship now hiring crew. It's a new commercial trader, so there won't be an entrenched mob like the last one, and it notes that because they won't have any set route, and it could take a while before they returned to Earth. That means we could get to see lots of new places, and because they need an entire crew, that means that it's likely that they'll need all three of us."

"That sounds really promising," Burningbright said. "When are the interviews being held?"

"Tomorrow. I've already put our names down. Just waiting for a reply."

Hotfoot said, "In that case, I'm going shopping. I need a few ingredients to cook up my résumé!"

"Buy some bananas! I haven't had a banana in ages," Zelkie ordered.

"Weren't you playing with my banana just last night?" Burningbright asked with a leer.

Zelkie rolled hir eyes and then hit hir mate with a pillow.

Not far from the White Sea in the north-western part of the Russian

Territories lay Arkhangelsk, a small city noteworthy for its timber and paper industries, microbiology laboratory, and a large gene-engineering facility. The latter was responsible for turning out many a morph species up to and throughout the Gene Wars. The city managed to survive the worst ravages of the wars, and grew into one of the country's major commercial cities afterwards. One of the last species that the gene-tech facility had produced before controls were put on creating new morph breeds had been intended as a war beast, but instead they missed out on most of the fighting. Russia had been left with a large number of Amur Tiger morphs that it no longer needed, and pretty much abandoned to their fate. The gene engineers had done a masterful job with them though, and the clever and hard-working tigers soon established a firm foothold in the population of Arkhangelsk, contributing much to its prosperity and growth. It now boasted about half of its population as Amur Tiger morphs, their numbers quickly rising due to the fact they had been intended to rapidly breed replacements naturally while technological resources were under strain from the wars. To maximise this, they made it so that *all* the tigers could get pregnant – in other words, they were hermaphrodites.

However, just because they were all of one gender and bred specifically for one reason, it did not mean that they were all alike otherwise. Their builds varied as much as their personalities. Some were powerhouses, while others were lean and fast; some were more feminine and some more masculine. And that was what drew Valentina's attention to Anastasiya as they both enjoyed one of Arkhangelsk's many nightclubs. Valentina had a definite feminine bent, which made Anastasiya's leather-jacketed form and masculine attitude very attractive to hir. Their eyes met and Anastasiya gave hir a roguish smile. Shi came over and wordlessly invited Valentina to dance with hir, which shi willingly accepted. They spent the rest of the evening enjoying each other's company, and later exchanged comm numbers.

Eight months later, they were still together and contemplating getting engaged. Valentina could already picture married life with Anastasiya. Only one thing spoiled that vision – Anastasiya refused to give up running with the gang whose leathers shi wore. More than once shi had arrived at Valentina's place in a bad way – fur ripped out, bloodied nose, and multiple aches and pains. But at least shi came every night.

But tonight shi had not.

Anastasiya groaned and tried to stand up, but the stab of pain from the gouge in hir side, and the dizziness from loss of blood, foiled hir effort. Shi sank back into a snow bank already deeply stained with hir life fluid. Shi fumbled for the comm in hir coat pocket. After a ridiculous amount of effort, shi managed to extract it, only to let it drop to the ground in despair, shattered by the same assault that had so seriously wounded hir.

Shi gave a humourless laugh. "So here I die in badly lit back street, and I've never even left Arkhangelsk. Big tiger of world I turned out to be." Shi realised that shi didn't feel cold any more, and knew that hypothermia was setting in. "Stupid fool! Why did I listen to Nadia? Should have told hir to go fight Rostovs by hirself, but no, I had to go along. Must be in rut – too much testosterone. 'Tina told me not to.... Sorry 'Tina... so... sorry...."

Consciousness slipped away. An unknown time later, shi became aware of a voice calling hir name. Shi tried to focus on the person leaning over hir, shaking hir shoulder, but shi blacked out again.

To hir great surprise, Anastasiya woke again. The first thing that shi noticed was that shi was cosily warm. The second thing shi noticed was the sharp jab of pain in hir side when shi tried to move. Shi moaned in pain.

"Don't try to move, my love. You're safe now."

Anastasiya opened hir eyes to see a vision – Valentina was leaning over hir with a concerned look on hir face. "Urr... not sure if I have not died – I see an angel."

Valentina smiled. "I'm as close to heaven as you will get for now. Med techs have patched you up and you are going to be fine."

"I am glad; it gives me chance to ask your forgiveness."

"Forgive you for what? For nearly getting yourself killed?"

"Yes. And for being idiot. And for not listening to you."

"No, I cannot do that."

Anastasiya was shocked, then saddened. "I am sorry, 'Tina. I knew that I would go too far one day, and I would lose you."

"You are still being that idiot, Ana. I cannot forgive you because you always say that you will stop this madness, but then you go right back to doing it when your so-called friends ask. Only way that I will forgive you is for you to break with gang, get real job, and marry me."

"You would marry a fool like me?"

"If no longer fool. I love you, Ana, but I want real future, and it's not with gang member. Grow up and be responsible. Come home to me and make family with me."

"I will, Tina, I swear..." Anastasiya began, only to be stopped by Valentina putting a hand over hir muzzle.

"No, Ana; no swearing this time. You do as I tell you. Just one moment." Valentina took out hir comm and tapped in a code. When shi got a response, shi said, "Anastasiya is awake", then disconnected again.

Anastasiya was about to ask what that was all about when a strange hum filled the room. To hir surprise, a glittering form took shape and coalesced into a familiar figure.

"Aunt Svetlana! What are you doing here?"

The Amur Tiger was dressed in Star Fleet uniform, with a rank badge of Port Admiral. Shi glared at hir niece and said, "Trying to get you out of trouble again, hopefully for last time. I have been talking with Valentina, and we have decided that you are going to school when you have recovered sufficiently."

"School? I am too old for that, and how would that help anyway?"

"You are not too old for this school, although considering grades from before you dropped out, that might be good also. But no, this is school for security trainees. Put that wild energy into something that you should be good at. Learn how to fight properly, defend even better and, God only knows, perhaps learn to think before you act."

Anastasiya had to admit that it sounded intriguing, but before shi could ask any questions, a nurse bustled in and glared at Svetlana.

"Where did you come from? No, don't bother answering. Out! The patient needs more rest. You too," she said, looking at Valentina. "You've seen that shi's alright, so you can leave now. Shoo! Go home!"

Valentina held up hir hands in surrender. "I'm going! I'm going! But first..." Shi leant over Anastasiya and planted a kiss on hir muzzle. "Get strong soon."

Valentina and Svetlana were hustled out of the ward, leaving Anastasiya to ponder what shi had just been told. Considering that shi had not expected to survive, things were looking up. Perhaps shi should have been near-fatally stabbed sooner!

The second day after shi was released from hospital, shi was enrolled in the training college. The first day was mostly devoted to Valentina, but also to rearrange some things in hir life. The first couple of weeks at the college were spent hitting the books mostly because shi was not yet fit enough to participate in the more physical side of things. When shi did finally get into martial arts training, shi discovered how little shi really knew about fighting, to the point of being embarrassed at hir ineptitude compared to the other trainees. Shi made sure to quickly change that situation. Hir instructors were also pleased at how well shi took to the more cerebral problems such as planning security arrangements, identifying weaknesses in defences, and usage of sophisticated technologies.

During the months spent on the training, shi came home to Valentina every night. Valentina supported them both with hir work at a logistics company. Shi was in a modestly paid job in warehousing, but it paid the bills and kept food on the table. When Anastasiya graduated from hir course, shi was immediately offered a position in a prestigious security firm. Shi came back from the interview with a broad grin and a huge bunch of flowers.

Valentina accepted the flowers with a smile. "I take it that they were happy with your interview?"

"Better than that – they gave me job starting tomorrow!"

Valentina hugged Anastasiya and they kissed deeply. Then Anastasiya gently pushed hir beloved back to arms-length. "Time for me to keep another promise. Valentina, will you be my wife?" shi proposed.

"Of course, my love. Is next Sunday soon enough?"

"What? Don't you need to make preparations? Is big event!"

"I have been preparing since you left the hospital. I had faith in you and booked the church long ago. Told parents and relatives and friends to keep day free but not tell you."

"What if I had not passed course? Or got job?"

"Would have married idiot anyway. I love you, Ana."

Anastasiya shook hir head in amazement. "What did I ever do to deserve such good fortune? I love you so much, Val, and next Sunday will be just fine."

The wedding went off without a hitch. Hir new employers had told hir to take the Monday off for a brief honeymoon when they found out, and the couple took advantage of it to spend a day and a night at a nice hotel beside the White Sea. Three weeks later, Valentina announced that shi was pregnant, and in due time they had beautiful cub whom they named Katarina. When Valentina had to go on maternity leave, Anastasiya had supported them, and encouraged hir wife to take as much time raising their child as shi saw fit. Valentina only went back to full-time work when their child was two years old. Katarina was seven and a half before they made another life-changing decision.

They were seated around the table eating their dinner when Valentina said, "Ana, how satisfied are you with our life here?"

Anastasiya looked at hir wife quizzically. "I do not understand? It's a good life – we eat well, we have good home and not half-bad cub." Shi winked at their daughter who stuck hir tongue out hir sire.

"No, not that. I mean – we never leave Arkhangelsk. The furthest that we have ever been is to that hotel on the White Sea. I'd like to see more."

"What brought this on so suddenly?"

"We have a new customer. He is an alien – a Caitian. I was given his account to take care of. I've never seen an alien except on vid screen. We talked about many things not business related, and I soon realised just how tiny our part of the universe really is. I don't want to spend my life in just this cosy little speck of the galaxy."

Anastasiya thought about that for a little while, then said, "Did you have any ideas about bringing this about?"

Valentina was relieved. Shi had been unsure what to do if Anastasiya had been resistant to the idea. "Talking to the Caitian also suggested course of action – we find jobs on starships and get paid to see galaxy!"

"That is a very big step, Val. And what of Katarina? We cannot simply take hir out of school and away from hir friends."

"Hey! I'd *love* to go on a starship!" Katarina said excitedly.

Anastasiya shook hir head. "It isn't that simple, young one."

Valentina replied, "There are ships that take families and have tutors aboard and other children for hir to play with. Shi is still young enough that a break from hir social group here won't be too hard on hir. If we leave it too long, it will only get harder."

"I see that you are very determined about this idea. Very well, I'm sure that you must have brought home much material to help try convincing me. We will discuss it after meal."

Valentina had far less difficulty persuading Anastasiya than shi had expected. In truth though, Anastasiya had been getting a bit bored with hir job. Shi was very good at it – so good that it had become too easy, and thus dull. It was time for hir to move on to something else, and the something else that Valentina offered was very tempting.

They made some enquiries, looked into some shipping companies, and then eventually made a decision to apply for work on a cruise ship. Because neither had any experience on starships before, both had to take relatively junior positions, but they did achieve their goal to start seeing more of the galaxy. They spent over a year on that ship before deciding to move on again. It was not because it was a bad place to work; in fact it was so good that the ship had a high employee retention, and neither was likely to see promotion any time soon because of that. The ship also had a limited route, and another ship could offer them more to sate their curiosity. When they finished their latest voyage and disembarked at Earth, the first thing that they did was start looking for possibilities that would take both of them. Only one stood out as filling their requirements nearly perfectly.

Art © Mayra Boyle

Commander Second Class Bethany Oakwood was very much a career-oriented Star Fleet officer. She had little time for socialising when that time could be put to better use. Nevertheless she did not want to end up alone for the rest of her life either, so she went out on shore leave occasionally with her shipmates, and kept her eyes open for a good prospect. An attractive grey fox vixen like herself had no trouble getting attention from males of many species, but she was a lot more choosy. Then after she was transferred to a new ship, she eventually set her sights on its First Officer – a handsome red fox morph named Edward Russ. He was not only a capable officer, but also a compatible species – an ideal match for someone in the Service – a fact she did not hesitate to point out to her friends.

It did not take long to attract his attention in return, and when they took shore leave on Earth, he asked her out with him. The day passed very pleasantly, and Bethany decided that she had made a good choice. They had dinner at an upmarket restaurant, at the end of which he suggested that they finish the night with coffee at his apartment.

Bethany was a little surprised – few career officers bothered to maintain a permanent residence planet-side. Nevertheless she was curious to see his place.

"Well – okay, but just coffee," she insisted.

"No problem. I just want this day to last a little longer," he assured her.

The apartment was small but cosy rather than cramped, decorated with items garnered from various worlds. It did not look very much lived in, which was hardly surprising.

"I just use this as a home base when I'm on leave, and my family know where to find me when I'm in town," he explained as he started to prepare the coffee.

"I suppose it might be handy," Bethany conceded. "I don't think I'd have any use for one, but it's nice to have some place that isn't on the ship."

"Yes – some things are better away from the workplace," he agreed.

He brought over the mugs of coffee and handed one to her as he sat down beside her on the sofa.

"Mmmm... good coffee," Bethany said appreciatively. "This is a nice cap to this day out together."

"It could be even nicer," Russ replied, putting his hand on Bethany's thigh.

Bethany frowned at the offending appendage. "That's not appropriate for a first date, Edward."

"Come on, Bethany – you know what you want. *I* know what you want. A fair portion of the crew know that you have the hots for me. Just go with the flow."

"Commander Russ," Bethany began formally, putting down her coffee, "I insist that you take your hand off me right now."

"Your words say no, but your body says yes. I can scent your desire."

"My hormones don't dictate my mind, Commander. This ends now!" she said, rising from the sofa.

Russ yanked her back down again. "No, it's just begun," he told her forcefully. His hand groped her breast as he pulled her in to kiss her.

Bethany buried her fist in his solar plexus, and the tod reflexively released his grip. She slipped out of his grasp and headed for the door, grabbing her shoulder bag along the way. "I'm seeing that you go on report for this, you prick!"

"This isn't over yet!" he gasped out as she closed the door behind her.

Bethany took the next shuttle back up to the ship, and the first thing that she did was stop by the Security chief's office to swear out a complaint. Only then did she head off to her room, fuming all the way.

"Smeg! Why did he have to ruin things? Who does he think I am? I'm no cheap slut! It's obvious why he has that apartment now. Damn it! We could have had something good if he wasn't such a bastard."

Still angry when she went to bed, it took her a while to get to sleep.

The next morning as she prepared for her duty shift, she received a message to report to the Security Chief's office.

'Some action already on my complaint, I suspect,' she thought as she headed there. She was a little surprised to see Russ there already. It bothered her to see that he had a smirk on his face. The Security Chief asked her to be seated.

"Commander Oakwood, I am officially warning you that we may be charging you with attempting to bribe a superior officer with sexual favours, assault on a superior officer, and attempted blackmail."

"WHAT?" yelled Bethany, jumping to her feet. "He was going RAPE me, and you're charging ME?"

"Sit down, Commander! That is your story. His version is that you pursued him with the intention of gaining extra favours and privileges through offers of sexual acts. He claims that you took advantage of what was supposed to be a quiet coffee at his place to half strip and flaunt your body, and when he rejected your advances, you assaulted him and threatened to blackmail him with false allegations."

"And you *believe* that crock of shit?" she asked incredulously.

"Where is your evidence otherwise, Commander? It's your word against his, and he has a clean record, while it's common knowledge that you have been eyeing Commander Russ."

"That only means that he has always gotten away with it before this in that private apartment of his. I want to contest the charges, and I'll be insisting on a court telepath to verify my allegations."

"That's your privilege, Commander. I don't think we can allow it to get that far though."

"*We can allow*? What do you mean by that?" Bethany asked suspiciously.

Russ spoke up then. "It means, my dear, that if you go ahead with that, I'll probably get off with little more than a reprimand due to my good record and the little that actually happened, but your career will be destroyed. You will never be promoted, you will get all the worst assignments, and your reputation will be trashed."

Bethany looked from Russ to the Security Chief, and she suddenly realised that they were in collusion. "And what if I drop the charges?"

"Then we can resume where we left off last night," Russ replied with that smirk back on his face.

Bethany realised that she was trapped. No matter what path she took, her future was ruined. She knew a man like Russ would continue to wave his threats over her, and if she acquiesced to his demands, she would only give credence to his lies. There was only one thing left to do under the circumstances, and it cut like a knife to do it.

"I won't be your slut, Russ, but I acknowledge that you could and would ruin my career if I tried to fight you. So I am going to do the one thing that I can to get away from you. I'm going to resign my commission. The captain will have my letter of resignation on his desk within the hour. Now, unless you plan to arrest me, I will bid you two miserable excuses for civilised sentients goodbye, and I hope to never have the misfortune to meet either of you again.

Bethany left the room unopposed, perhaps because she had surprised them with her decision.

The captain was very surprised to receive Bethany's resignation, and she quoted personal reasons when he queried why. He reluctantly accepted it, and she was on a shuttle back dirt-side as soon as she could pack her belongings. She had gotten the shuttle to Big Sur Spaceport, which was the width of the continent away from Russ' apartment, wanting to be as far from that memory as possible. She could not help thinking how ironic it was that she now needed a place to stay. It was the middle of the night here, and not a good time to call family. Fortunately she had plenty of money saved, and could well afford a hotel room for a night or two.

After that first night, Bethany ended up staying with her younger

Art © Shawntae Howard

sister who, aside from badgering her constantly about her reason for leaving Star Fleet which she did not want to talk about, made her feel welcome as a guest for an indefinite period. With that settled, Bethany's thoughts focused on the future. She had never made alternative plans – as far as she had been concerned, she had intended to stay in Star Fleet until she retired. Starships were her life, and she did not want, nor was she really trained for, any other career. After spending a week taking a holiday at her sister's insistence, she got down to the task of finding a job in a commercial starship company. Ex-Fleet personnel were always in demand.

Except for some reason, she was not.

It took a long time before she found out why, and for the first time in her life, genuinely wanted to murder somebody. Her reputation had been systematically trashed, and she was on every company's blacklist. Not one would even let her get a foot in the door or give her a chance to defend herself. Russ had done a thorough job of getting back at the vixen who had dared defy him.

It was with increasing desperation that she started looking through the advertisements for little independent ships. She found one that was a brand new start-up business which sounded more promising than most. She made an appointment and, to her relief, got an interview for the next morning. In fact she was asked to be the first for the day. Bright and early, she got dressed in her Fleet uniform (minus the insignia), and left to meet her fate.

*** 13 November 2332 ***

Martin had been worried that he would not be able to get the crew that he needed by the deadline. It was one thing that he could not plan meticulously, although he his research suggested that the time allotted should be sufficient. He had visited the shipyard to inspect the work being done on his starship, and found it to be on time and on budget, and so he had been able to lock in a departure date. Some of his potential clients required that firm date before they would commit to a shipping contract, so he was glad to have passed that hurdle. It had only left him a limited time to put together a crew, and for that he contracted the services of a recruitment agency. The word was put out to fill the vacancies in all departments of a medium-size freighter, and then he waited.

In less time than he thought, the agency informed him that they had

Art © Jameless

several applications. He looked through them and was quite pleased with the results, but he was particularly surprised by the application by a former Star Fleet officer, which seemed too good to be true. Her file came marked with a warning however, but he was desperate enough for an experienced professional that he was more than willing to give the person an interview. In fact he scheduled her for the first of the interviews that would start the next day.

Martin was assigned a temporary office at the recruitment agency from which he could conduct the interviews. He made sure that he was early, and that the receptionist had an up-to-date list of the interviewees.

Promptly at the scheduled time, a grey fox vixen immaculately dressed in uniform turned up. It made Martin wish that he had worn the fancy formal uniform that he'd had made to impress clients, but his standard duty uniform would have to do.

"Please be seated, Ms Oakwood." Martin picked up the PADD with her résumé on it. "This is an extremely impressive record – three years at Star Fleet Academy, qualifications in nav systems, computers, and field command, seventeen years of exemplary service, with a rapid rise up the ranks, and with quite a potential for a lot more." He put down the PADD, folded his arms and looked at her keenly. "So what on Earth brings you to an infant starship service like mine?"

Bethany looked uncomfortable when she replied, "I was forced to resign from Star Fleet, but I'm a career spacer, and I want to be back among the stars."

"That still doesn't answer my question though. Someone with your qualifications could have the pick of employment opportunities. I could never afford someone like you, and you know it."

The vixen was silent for a long moment, and then she sighed. "Will you please keep what I have to say strictly confidential?"

"You have my word."

"I left Star Fleet with some prejudice. My name is mud with all the big commercial operations."

"And why would that be? What sort of problems would I be inheriting if I take you on?"

"None – the allegations were trumped up. I chose to resign rather than to fight them."

"And what were those allegations?" Martin pressed.

"Conduct unbecoming an officer. Bribery. Indecent assault. A few others." The vixen's voice was bitter.

Martin's eyebrows rose. "That certainly sounds like grounds for a court martial. What was their story?"

"That I tried to seduce a superior officer in order to gain promotion, and then got violent when he rejected my advances."

"And what's the real story?"

There was a flash of gratefulness from the vixen when realised that she was not going to be dismissed immediately. "It's true that I had made advances to that officer. He was a handsome tod, and I had made no secret to the other crewmembers that I found him very attractive. I managed to get a date with him when we were on shore leave, and I thought things were going quite well when he had asked me back to his apartment for coffee. I had told him that it had better be just coffee for the first date, and he had assured me that that's all it was. To make a long story short, it wasn't. He made sexual advances and I told him to stop. He didn't, and things went downhill from there. I pressed charges against him the next day, but he countered with false charges of his own, and because I had made such a big deal about chasing him, his word would be believed over mine."

"Surely an investigation would have exonerated you though?"

"He has powerful friends. He made it clear that if I pursued the charges, my career would be ruined. I'd get all the worst assignments and have zero chance of promotion. I'd always have to look out for subtle harassment. If I dropped the charges though, then he would drop his, but then he would get to have his way with me. I'm no fool – I took the only way out and resigned. I didn't count on them dragging my reputation through the dirt anyway to ensure that I could not cause trouble later. Because of it though, no big commercial operation will even touch me. No offence, Mr Yote, but your ship is something of a last resort for me."

"No offence taken, Ms Oakwood, and for the record, I accept your story. While Star Fleet might have a great reputation, it is hardly perfect, but their loss is definitely my gain. I would like to offer you the position of First Officer. How soon can you start?"

"Immediately, Captain."

Martin noted her immediate switch to formality as he held out his hand to say, "Welcome aboard, Bethany."

She shook his hand and replied, "Thank you, Captain, but please call me Commander Oakwood. This is strictly a professional relationship."

"Very well. It's quite obvious that despite being owner-captain, I lack experience. In fact I'll be counting on you to keep me from making bone-headed mistakes. My main function is the business side of shipping, determining where we go and when. I have a Master Pilot licence, but virtually no practical experience. We will have to pull together a working crew, and you're the one whom I'll be counting on."

"I appreciate you being candid with me. I'll be happy to help you out in any way, sir."

"Very good. I have several other interviews to conduct today, and I want you to sit in on them and offer opinions where necessary."

"Certainly, sir."

"And Commander, please remember that this is a civilian ship, not a military one. While respect for command should be maintained, I don't want stiff formality. Try to get used to that."

"Yes sir," she said with a hint of an apologetic smile.

Martin grinned. "Okay, while we're waiting for the next applicant, let me show you an overview of the ship...."

They spent the next forty minutes going over aspects of the ship, and Martin's goals for it, by which time Bethany was feeling much encouraged by her choice of last resort. Despite his youth, Martin seemed to have a good grasp of the basics, and a viable plan for the future. Shi in turn had responsibility for an entire ship and its crew. It might not be a Star Fleet ship, but it was not a clunker either, and any hope of being an XO on a Fleet ship had been years away still. Under the circumstances, she reckoned that she had come through the situation fairly well, and she was determined that she would make the most of it.

The receptionist announced that the next group of applicants had arrived for their appointment, and Martin asked her to send them through.

"Group?" Bethany queried.

"Three chakats put in applications together. I'm assuming that they're mated."

A moment later, the three chakats in question entered the office. The first was a classic tiger pattern with auburn hair. Shi was followed by one that had an ochre coat with random brown spots, and 'boots' of dark red fur. Hir tail tip and hair were the same colour as hir paws. Last to enter was a light tan chakat with cream stripes reminiscent of a spotted skunk. Hir hair was a rather spectacular shade of red. When all three taurs had entered, the small office was rather cramped for room.

"Thank you for coming. My name is Martin Yote, and I will be the captain of the ship for which you are applying for positions. This is Commander Bethany Oakwood, our First Officer. I assume you are a mated triad?"

"Lifemated, yes," answered the one with red paws.

"I'll go out on a limb and guess that you're the one listed as Hotfoot?"

Shi grinned. "Yes, that's my name. Care to guess the others?"

Martin shook his head. "No, although Zelkie and Burningbright are very distinctive names."

"May I guess?" Bethany asked before Hotfoot could say more.

"Sure!"

Bethany pointed at the tiger-striped one and recited, "*Tiger, tiger, burning bright, in the forests of the night...*"

The chakat smiled. "You caught the reference. Not everyone knows that old poem by William Blake."

"That means that you must be Zelkie," Martin said to the last one. "A rather unusual one for a chakat, isn't it?"

"My full name is Zelkie Sandblossom, and I was named like that because my sire was a skunktaur." Shi pulled down hir blouse a little bit to reveal a paw-shaped blue-coloured patch of fur over hir right breast. "That's how I got this too."

"Did you inherit the skunktaur Talent also?" Martin asked curiously.

The PADD on the desk in front of Martin suddenly lifted into the air, pirouetted in front of his muzzle, then settled down gently again.

"That would be a yes," Martin answered his own question. Anyway, let's get down to your applications. I see you all spent twelve years on the *Star Odyssey* before resigning. Why did you leave?"

"We chose a career on starships to see different worlds," Hotfoot replied. "The work was good, but our choices were too limited, so we eventually decided to try another type of ship."

"Fair enough. If everything goes as planned, there won't be many places in the Federation that we won't go. However, you have a gap here in your résumé between then and now. What happened to your plans?"

"That's a time that we'd rather erase from our lives, and we're ashamed to have on our records. We signed up on a freighter, but found out too late that they had rather perverted ideas about what chakats are like. We got off that ship at our earliest opportunity."

"My sympathies. Racial stereotyping just never seems to go away, no matter how advanced that we think we are. That accounts for the gap; now let's have a look at your qualifications. Let's see... Burningbright – I see that you have applied for the position of environmental engineer. I've gotten your records from *Star Odyssey*, and they are glowing in their praise of your work. My ship is a lot different from a cruise ship though, so will you be comfortable with the new system?"

"Provided that I get a chance to review it beforehand, yes. The basics are still the same; just the equipment and application is different. Give me a couple of days with the equipment and I should have a good grasp of it."

"Good. And what about other systems? Could you help the Chief Engineer if they need an assistant? Our ship will have just a small crew, and most of us will need to have a secondary duty."

"That's no problem. Environmental is my speciality, but hardly my only field of competence."

"Excellent." Martin turned to the next chakat. "Now, Zelkie, you're after the post of Loadmaster – what are your piloting qualifications?"

"I'm fully rated for both passenger and heavy-lift cargo shuttles," shi replied.

"What about starship piloting?" Martin asked hopefully.

Zelkie shook hir head. "I started studying that, but never pursued it seriously."

"That's a pity – I could do with a good starship pilot. Nevertheless your current qualifications will be very useful for when we load and unload cargo. We usually need a fast turnaround."

"It's no different on cruise ships. Time is money, and you need to be very organised. I was quite good at the job, even if I do say so myself," Zelkie added with a hint of pride.

"Yes, your record indicates that they were sorry to see you go. I think you'll do well on my ship." Martin then turned to the last chakat. "Hotfoot – your résumé is rather odd. You have indicated that you were Assistant Chief Chef on *Star Odyssey* when you left?"

"Yes – I would have been Head Chef if Pierre had retired, but he liked his position there, so there was no chance of further promotion."

"Yes, I suppose it would be hard to get ahead if you had stayed on. Anyway, the bit that I find odd is that you only have a small amount of detail, plus a note to say that you will be bringing along the rest of your résumé with you. Why? What did you mean by that?"

Hotfoot held up a box that shi had brought with hir. "Words can only say so much about a cook. The proof is in the pudding, as the saying goes. Or in the pastries in this case. Here are samples of my work that I whipped up just for this interview. Please try them."

Martin looked at the contents of the box. There were both savoury and sweet pastries inside, and he tried some of both, indicating to Bethany to try some too.

Hotfoot continued, "I was tempted to bring along a hot dish also, but I didn't know if I could keep it in ideal condition by the time we were interviewed."

Martin licked his lips and grinned. "I might think you were trying to bribe me with these delicious goodies."

Hotfoot just smiled a little smugly. "A bribe can only work if it's really tempting, and if my little sample is really that tempting, then I think my ability is proven, don't you?"

Martin laughed. "Impeccable logic! You're as good as hired. Commander, do you have any questions for these three?"

Bethany nodded. "Just one. I'm assuming that you have children. How many?"

"Just three cubs," Hotfoot replied. "We each had one soon after we mated. We didn't want to have to deal with a large family while travelling."

"That's sensible, but we don't have a teacher or child-minder as yet," Martin said.

"That's okay. We have plans in place if you don't get one."

"I did expect to get some families though, so it's on my agenda. I'll let you know if I find someone suitable."

"Does that mean we've got the jobs?"

"Not so fast. First you should know what we're going to be doing. *Then* you can decide if you want the jobs."

"We're pretty easy, as long as we can be together."

"Still, you should realise that we'll be away from Earth for months at a time. The nature of my business means that I won't have a set schedule, and I'll only be coming back to home port only when I am returning with freight. That means that you won't be able to see your families for an extended period, and I know how important that is to you chakats."

"That's okay, Captain. We came to terms with that possibility a long time ago."

"Good. I'm also hiring with a long view. I want to have a crew that I can hopefully rely on keeping for at least four and a half years."

"Why that long in particular?"

"Because if I haven't turned a decent profit by then, I'll be selling up and quitting the starship business, so I want stability."

"I see." Hotfoot looked at hir mates, who gave hir a silent nod. "We're agreed – we'll stick with you for that long at least."

"Excellent! Welcome to the crew. I will have your employment contracts sent to your comms. In the meantime though, I have a favour to ask. Would one of you stay and give your empathic impressions of our applicants?"

Zelkie said, "Burningbright has the strongest empathic Talent of us all. Shi would be the best choice."

"Gee, thanks for volunteering me, Zelkie," Burningbright said in mock outrage.

Zelkie just grinned back.

"Okay, I'll do it."

"Great! I'll give you a bonus 'consulting fee' for that," Martin told hir.

Burningbright laughed and stuck hir tongue out a Zelkie.

Martin continued, "I will be letting you all know when and where to meet to begin work in a few days. In the meantime, I recommend making the most of your time left here on Earth."

Zelkie and Hotfoot insisted on a parting hug.

When they had left, Martin said to Burningbright, "While we're waiting for the next applicants, perhaps you would like to have a look at our environmental systems?"

Burningbright nodded. "Could I get a copy of the specs so that I can look them over in detail later?"

"Not a problem."

They spent the next twenty five minutes looking over the specifications until the next applicant arrived – a male wolf morph who was applying for the job of Chief Pilot. Neither Martin nor Bethany were particularly impressed with him, but put him down as a maybe.

The next two applicants were two tiger morphs. There résumés said that they were both herms, but Martin's first impression when they walked into the interview room was that one was definitely masculine biased, and the other more feminine. The masculine one introduced hirself in heavily Russian-accented Terranglo as Anastasiya Tartikova, and the other as Valentina Tartikova.

Martin began, "I see that you have quite extensive experience in the security field on Earth, Shir Anastasiya, including a small local spaceport, but only about 16 months on a star cruiser. Why leave that to take on a job with a commercial trader?"

"Valentina and I felt stifled back in Russia – we spent all our lives in one small area, but we wanted to get out and see universe. Also, there was too much emphasis on staying and keeping everything in community. Cruise ship jobs were our way of making clean break, and that was very good then. But there was no chance to advance our careers on cruise ship, and we felt that your ship could offer better future, and see more worlds."

"Fair enough. I can certainly empathise with the desire to see other worlds, although my constraints were more personal rather than cultural. Do you think that you will be comfortable working in a totally new environment though?"

"I studied requirements and see no problems."

Bethany asked, "Do you have the appropriate licences for weapons?"

Anastasiya produced copies for them.

"Hmm… you have quite a broad licence allowance. That allows us a few more options. We'll have to talk about your recommendations for equipping our ship."

"I would want to do thorough evaluation of whole ship first."

Martin nodded. "Yes, that would be a good idea. Anything else?"

"Not security-wise as yet, but I can also offer services as physical trainer when not needed on security job."

"I never thought about that, but it would be good to keep the crew fit between ports of call." He looked to Bethany. "So what do you think, Commander? Does shi fit the bill?"

"I would have preferred someone with actual experience on a commercial trader as that is a lot different from passenger cruisers, but hir credentials are otherwise excellent. I would find hir acceptable."

"Good. Now, Valentina, I see that you gave up a job as a logistics manager at a large manufacturing company. Do you think your skills translate across to interstellar shipping?"

"More than that, Captain – I have already dealt with several interstellar customers and suppliers."

"Very good. You would be working directly with me to coordinate our routes and goods."

"Not a problem, sir."

"Then let me fill you both in with what sort of business we'll be doing, and where we'll be going." Martin did so, and then asked them if they would be prepared to commit to a job under those circumstances.

Anastasiya answered, "That is very close to what we imagined job would entail, so we would commit."

Martin looked at Burningbright who had been quietly listening to one side. "What are your impressions?"

"Very positive," shi replied. "I'm already looking forward to chatting to them."

"Then it's settled." Martin turned back to Anastasiya and said, "I will send you and your mate your contracts, and I will talk to you again soon about when to start your jobs."

"Thank you, Captain, but must correct you. Valentina is my wife, not mate. We were married properly in church!"

"I stand corrected," Martin said with a smile.

After the tigers had left, Martin said, "We seem to be doing quite well so far."

Bethany replied, "I agree, but from my limited knowledge of commercial shipping, don't think that it's all going to be that easy.

Her words turned out to be prophetic. The next interview was with a badger morph who was applying for the post of Chief Engineer. His qualifications seemed okay, but his record showed him moving from ship to ship on a regular basis. When queried, he replied that he had itchy feet, and did not like to be tied down for long, although on one occasion it was a case of not fitting in well with the crew. Martin was going to query him more when Burningbright caught his eye and firmly shook hir head. Martin decided to cut the interview short and told the badger that he would let him know if he had the job.

With the badger gone, Martin looked to Burningbright who said, "He was deceiving you, Captain. Bending the truth in places; outright lies in others. I would class him as being big trouble."

"Thanks – that confirms my feeling that there was something wrong. I just hope that I can find someone else who's qualified for the job. I'm curious though – why didn't you pick up on the bad vibes of that last job that you had?"

Burningbright grimaced. "Several reasons. First – we were rushed into it, and didn't take the time to look further into the prospective jobs. Second – the one who interviewed us wasn't one of those who was... *interested* in us, so he was focused on the actual jobs that we were applying for. Third – we were interviewed away from the ship, just like here, so I couldn't pick up on the negative emotions until too late."

"I see. A hard lesson learned."

There was some time before the next interviewees were due, so Martin suggested that they go out for lunch. Enquiring with the receptionist, they were told of a nice sit-down restaurant about a block away. There they had a nice meal while chatting, although it was really mostly the chakat enthusiastically talking about hir family and travels.

When they got back to the interview room, Martin reviewed the next appointment.

"Another couple – foxtaurs this time. A Black Foxtaur applying for the hydroponics job. That sounds promising. The other is a Starwalker. What the heck is a Starwalker?"

"Hire hir," Bethany said definitely.

Martin blinked in surprise. "I haven't even said what this person is applying for yet."

"It doesn't matter – although I could narrow it down. Shi will be perfect for whatever shi's applying for."

"Going by the pronouns, this person must be a herm, but what else is special about these Starwalkers?"

"They are one of seven special breeds called Stellar Foxtaurs. Hir kind was specially bred to be perfectly at home in space, and they are all very well trained in their chosen fields. I don't know why shi did not join the Star Corps program like the others, although I'm guessing that it might have something to do with that Black Foxtaur, but shi would be an invaluable asset."

"I bow to your superior knowledge," Martin conceded.

When the duo arrived, it was quite obvious that they were mates by their body language. The Starwalker introduced hirself as Ceres, and hir mate as Danson. Shi was applying for the post of astrogator, with a side speciality of E.V.A. expert. Danson had a brand new degree in hydroponics, and knowing how much the average foxtaur liked their natural ways, it was an interesting contrast to the high-tech farming on board a starship. Ceres made a point of the fact that they would have to take both of the foxtaurs, or neither – they would not split up. Martin could not see sufficient reason to reject Danson just because he was inexperienced, and Bethany was still keen to hire the Starwalker. He supposed that he would find out for himself just how good the Stellar Foxtaur was. He hired them both on the spot.

Their next appointment nearly did not get an interview. They were reviewing the résumé of the next couple – a human and a ferret morph. Martin was interested until he came to a certain point, then he exclaimed, "*What?* They're from the Non-Aligned Worlds! You know what that means?"

"The ferret jill was probably a slave," Bethany commented.

"More to the point – he was a slave-owner!" Martin said angrily.

"That does not necessarily follow, but it's likely."

"No way I'm going to hire him! I'll tell the receptionist that their appointment is cancelled." He reached for the intercom.

"No, we'll interview them," Bethany firmly contradicted.

Martin was startled. "I thought that a former Star Fleet person like you would agree with me?"

"It's precisely that which is why I want to give him a chance. Star Fleet usually sends LNAW people back to their world and confiscates their slaves. But here we have that human not only here, but with a morph that should not be within a hundred kilometres of him. I want to know the reason."

"I think you're reading too much into it, but okay."

When the couple in question arrived, the first thing that Martin noticed was that they were holding hands, and Burningbright's ears pricked up with interest, a small smile on hir muzzle. Something had made hir like them already. The ferret girl certainly did not look submissive at first glance. In fact she was very normal for her kind, and dressed in a nice off-the-shoulder top and skirt – dressy without being too formal, and perfect for the interview. She could have been the girl next door, and she looked quietly confident.

The human by contrast was definitely nervous.

"Please be seated," Martin instructed. When they had done so, Martin looked at the PADD in his hand. "I see that you're applying for a job as a starship pilot, with a Master's licence and six years experience on the *Stellar Rose*... a Non-Aligned World ship." Martin put the PADD down and folded his arms. "Tell me, Mr Baxter, why should I hire someone whose people practice slavery of my kind?"

Heywood Baxter had been going through this kind of thing for many weeks now, and this was the furthest that he had gotten so far and he was desperate to make a good impression. "Firstly, sir, even though I have... *had* what you would call a slave, I am not a slaver. She was

Art © Michele Light

given to me when I was ten, and I certainly didn't have a say in the matter. Nevertheless I was glad that they gave Menalippe to me. She has been my closest companion for years, and she means more to me than you would ever think for a slave. The Non-Aligned Worlds differ in their approach to slavery. On mine, every human gets a companion for life, usually on their tenth birthday. The morphs are not intended to be there simply to wait upon us – they share our lives, help us when it's needed, and even be our lovers when we mature."

Martin interrupted, "You're not doing much to dissuade me yet. It seems to me that Menalippe didn't have much say in the matter."

"That's not true, sir. Mena was bred to match my personality, so she wanted the same sort of things that I wanted without coercion. The slave bond that you are so worried about is as much for her protection, because it means that she is only responsive to my needs and can't be commanded by another human."

"I'd heard differently – that they must obey any human's orders unless they contradicted their master's."

"That may be true on other worlds, but not on Celeste, my home world. We do not see eye to eye with many of the others. Also, our situation was a little different."

"How so?" Martin asked, his curiosity aroused.

Heywood was relieved when it seemed that the coyote was going to hear him out. "The companions are supposed to satisfy all our base needs and desires, including dealing with hormone-stoked teenagers. However, the only social and legal relationships we could have were with other humans. We would marry for money, politics or power. Some of us had our marriages arranged long before we even got our companions. Sex with our spouses is purely for producing an heir while our companions continued to serve our more visceral desires. At the age of twenty one, I was to be wedded to a girl whom I'd only met for the first time at my eighteenth birthday whereupon I was told she was my betrothed. I knew that I did not want this, not only because I knew nothing of this girl, but also because I was in love with Menalippe. Captain – you can do almost anything with your companion morph, but falling in love with them is a big no-no. I spent the last three years before my forced marriage learning my skills, and then on the day I was supposed to be wed, I left home to take a job aboard a starship. I broke the law and tradition, left my home and family, and bound my life to a morph, all because I love Menalippe more than anything else in my life."

Burningbright spoke up for the first time. "And how do you feel about this, Menalippe?"

Martin realised that the chakat was not merely looking for information, but trying to get an empathic response.

Menalippe said, "It's all true. We companions are expected to love our humans, but not allowed to be *in* love, if you appreciate the distinction. Heywood risked everything for me though, and I could do no less. I am a ferret morph companion, and I am proud to say that I am in love with my human. He *deserves* a fair chance from you."

Burningbright looked at Martin, then smiled and nodded.

Martin was satisfied that they were telling the truth, but his curiosity was aroused. "So how did you come to be here in Federation space?"

"Pirates," Heywood replied. "They don't just attack Federation ships, y'know? The starship that I was serving on was attacked and disabled. A Star Fleet cruiser rescued us, but that put us under their jurisdiction, and once in the Federation, slaves are never returned to the Non-Aligned Worlds. Once they finished their well-intentioned meddling, they returned Mena to me, knowing full well that I could never go back without her. So now I'm a probationary Federation citizen looking for a job to support both myself and my beloved. Will you give us that opportunity, Captain?"

Martin glanced in Bethany's direction and she gave him a curt nod. He decided that if an ex-Star Fleet stiff like her could give Baxter a chance, then he could put aside his prejudices too.

"Mr Heywood Baxter, I offer you the position of helmsman and chief pilot." He held out a PADD with the contract on display. "Here are your salary and benefits. Do you accept?"

Heywood barely glanced at the contract before replying, "Yes, as long as Menalippe stays with me."

Martin hmmed, then said, "We don't have room for non-paying passengers."

Heywood began to look distressed.

Martin continued, "However, we could use someone to perform Ship's Services – in other words, all those odd jobs that don't fit into anyone else's responsibilities." He took back the PADD and changed screens and tapped in a few new figures, then held it out to Menalippe. "Here's my offer."

Menalippe's eyes widened in surprise. "That is most generous, sir. So does that mean that we get to stay together?"

"Of course. Can't be breaking up lovers, can I?"

Menalippe smiled gratefully, then said, "I see that you have put my name down as Menalippe Baxter. I am just Menalippe, sir."

Martin frowned a little. "You love Heywood?"

"Yes, sir – with all my heart."

"But have you formally mated?"

"No, sir."

"Then I expect you to produce a mating contract by this time tomorrow or else I will not take either of you on."

Heywood said, "I'll see to it today, sir."

Martin nodded. "Good. That will be all for now."

The pair got up and thanked him before departing. When they were out of earshot, Bethany said, "What was that mating contract business all about?"

Martin leaned back in his chair. "I don't intend to let it be known that she is a former slave, or even a 'companion' as they call it, because it could cause problems. If however it does get out, they will have a legal document to show that they are mates – husband and wife, not master and slave. It's time that they started thinking that way too, and making them get the mating contract will help reinforce it. Besides, do you know what a pain in the butt it is dealing with bureaucrats who won't accept that a person hasn't got a surname?"

Bethany gave him a hint of a smile. "Devious coyote," she murmured.

Martin flicked an ear and asked, "What was that?"

Bethany said, "Nothing. Let's interview the next applicant."

That applicant was solo for a change, but startled everyone as none had ever seen a four-armed morph before. The 23 year old cougar woman seemed otherwise quite normal though.

After introductions, Martin said, "Before we start, Ms de Mar, I have to ask…"

"Yes, they're natural and normal for my kind," Risha interjected. "I come from a long line of four-armed cougars, both male and female."

"Must be an interesting family. Anyway, back to business. You haven't applied for any specific post, although you list your skills as storeperson, handyman, and office manager. That's an interesting mix. Would you care to tell us more?"

"My father owns a repair business. He taught me all of his skills as I was growing up, and I'm pretty much a jack-of-all-trades. I worked my way through college at his workshop by helping him fix things, procuring parts, and running the office part-time. I can put my mind to most things related to that kind of business."

"Flexibility is very useful when you only have a small crew," Martin admitted. "We could use you in various roles such as quartermaster, handyman, and perhaps you can handle comms?"

"It would not take me long to learn the systems if necessary."

"And that brings us to the next point – you have never been into space before, according to your résumé, so why the interest now?"

"I need to get away from here, away from a part of my life that is now finished. The reason is very personal though, and I would rather not talk about it. I assure you that it would not affect my performance."

"That is your privilege, so I won't press you, but going by your résumé, you would seem reliable. We will consider your application and let you know. Thank you for coming, Ms de Mar."

After Risha had left, Martin said to Burningbright, "I'm not quite sure what to make of her. What's your opinion?"

The chakat sighed. "She's trying to cope with a very deep sorrow. She's lost someone very close to her, and she hasn't really coped with that as yet. She feels very lonely and struggling to reach out again. However, I sensed no deception with regards to her application for a job. My opinion is that she's running away from the hurt, but that shouldn't affect her work, as she said."

Martin considered what Burningbright said, then asked Bethany, "Have you anything to add?"

"Most people have emotional baggage of some sort, myself included. As long as it doesn't interfere with her work, she is worth considering."

Martin nodded in agreement. "And as I said, it's good to have someone with versatility. If we get no other applicants for her job who might be better, I think I will hire her."

There was a lull for a little while. One applicant cancelled their appointment, and no more had been scheduled. Martin had the office booked all day though, so he waited to see if any more applicants would call in. He put the time to good use though with further discussions about the starship systems with both Bethany and Burningbright.

With just a bit over an hour to go, the receptionist called to say that a number of Caitians had arrived and wished to be interviewed as a group. Martin told her to send them in.

Although he knew what Caitians were, Martin had never personally met one, and now he had a whole group of them coming in. He wondered what the alien felinoids were doing here on Earth applying for a job.

The first entered – a male, closely followed by four more adults – female this time. Then three teenagers – two females and one male – also squeezed into the interview room.

"Good grief! How many more of you are there?" Martin exclaimed.

"This is all," the male adult answered. "My apologies – I did not realise that the room would be this small."

"Okay, but why bring the whole family?"

"Because we want you to be aware that if you employ us, this is what you would be taking on."

"I see. Point made though, so could I have the children please wait out in reception while the interviews are done?"

The male turned to the eldest child and said, "Keera, take your sibs and wait for us outside."

"Yes, father," Keera replied, and herded the others out.

Martin then introduced himself, Bethany, and Burningbright before saying, "Because you have just turned up without an appointment, I haven't had a chance to review your résumés, so please introduce yourselves and the jobs for which you are applying."

The male said, "My name is R'Murran, and I am applying for Chief of Engineering."

A female then spoke up. "I am M'Rarrtikar, his Firstwife. I look after our family's finances, and I'm a qualified accountant. I offer my services as your ship's Purser."

"I am M'Anissa'tk," said the next. "I am Secondwife, and a maintenance technician fully qualified for starship systems."

"And I am Thirdwife, M'Lertiña by name. I am a teacher by trade, and a licensed paramedic."

The last female was noticeably younger, and she said, "My name is M'Resk, and I am Fourthwife. I do not know if your ship can use my services, but my skills are in hospitality."

Martin was a little overwhelmed. "Pardon my ignorance, but you're *all* his wives?"

M'Rarrtikar spoke up. "Yes, we are. This is not unusual for our species as females greatly outnumber males. Our culture revolves around the *Rrurwanz* – a Pride or Harem in Terranglo, with one male and up to six wives."

"I see that I'm going to have to learn a bit more about your species if you are going to join the crew," Martin admitted, "but for now we had better stick to business. Your résumés have now been loaded onto my PADD... and R'Murran, I see that you have recently retired from Star Fleet. Why is that?"

"Too many wives. It was either them or Star Fleet. My wives are my life; Star Fleet just a job. The choice was easy."

"I can empathise with that, but why would you want to work for my fledgling shipping business. It's quite a come-down for someone of your training." Martin had a strong sense of déjà vu.

"Again, too many wives. It is not easy to find a ship that will take all of us. That is why I brought the entire family in at first so that you could see what you would be in for up front. We tried to get employment on Kà'iît, but there were no multiple positions available. Star Fleet allowed me to remain on board my ship until we reached Earth so that we could try our luck here. So far yours has been our best chance."

Art © Sara "Caribou" Palmer

"I can see where you would have problems, but I'm glad that I have so many vacant positions. I'd even stretch things a bit to get hold of a Fleet engineer such as yourself." Martin scrolled through R'Murran's list of qualifications. "Heck, I think you should be interviewing *me* as a suitable captain for your needs!"

R'Murran grinned a toothy smile at that.

Martin continued, "Let's assume that you've got the job, so next we skip to... M'Anissa'tk... did I say that right?"

"Close enough," she replied.

"You're ex-Fleet also. I assume you resigned to follow your mate? Or should that be husband?"

"Either will do, and yes."

"I see that you are very well qualified also. I intend to have a strong maintenance program in mind for my ship, so I know that I can keep *you* busy, and you could be R'Murran's back-up."

"I'm not an engineer, sir."

"No, but your mate would be the only engineer aboard, and we need some people to take over or help out in some situations. I would not expect you to do everything he does, but you would be more competent than most to handle those duties."

"I see. Yes, I can do that much," M'Anissa'tk agreed.

"Now – M'Rarrtikar – your record shows that you were a civilian employee on the Star Fleet ship. What did you do there?"

"I did a range of jobs, from keeping track of expenditures, to payroll."

"In other words, the same things that you reckon that I will need doing?"

"Exactly," she replied with a small smile. "You always know exactly how your finances stand with me in charge of them."

"Considering my tight budget, that would be useful, and I can't spend as much time on it as an employee dedicated to the job. Okay, I admit that I could use you. Now, as for M'Lertiña..." Martin looked to the Thirdwife. "I cannot afford to have a full medical doctor on staff, but a paramedic in conjunction with the ship's autodoc is almost as good. And you're a teacher as well? I have at least three teenage chakat cubs and a tiger morph who will need tutoring, not to mention keeping out of trouble. Think you'd be up to the task of handling them as well as your own children?"

"I already did far more than that on the Fleet ship," she replied confidently.

"Excellent That just leaves us with..." He consulted his PADD to refresh his memory. "...M'Resk. Believe it or not, your skills will be quite useful. Independent commercial ships like mine frequently take on passengers. We offer a cheap alternative to the cruise lines for those who want to do interstellar travel on a small budget. It's very much a no-frills operation. They get a small cabin with a bed and basic facilities, somewhat like a backpackers hostel. They eat in the crew mess hall, use the same recreational facilities as the crew when they're not in use by them, and there are almost no extras whatsoever, but we do want to keep them occupied during the long trip. I really could use someone for Passenger Services who could look after them from the time they step aboard, until the time they leave. Help them settle on board, keep them amused, and make sure they stay out of the crew's way during the trip. Would you like that job?"

"Yes, I'd love it!" she replied enthusiastically. "It's certainly better than being a deadweight, which I feared might happen."

"Then I think that we can come to an arrangement, unless the Commander has any problems with this?" Martin looked at Bethany who had been perusing the résumés a bit more thoroughly while he'd been talking.

She shook her head. "I see no objections nor concerns."

Martin looked to Burningbright and asked, "Would you be satisfied with M'Lertiña tutoring your cubs?" Of course he was also discreetly asking hir opinion of them based on hir empathic assessment.

"I believe that she will do fine, Captain," Burningbright reassured him.

Martin then turned back to R'Murran. "I would like to formally offer you the post of Chief Engineer, and your wives their appropriate posts. Your wage was advertised, but we'll have to negotiate the others. Do you find this acceptable?"

"I would," R'Murran agreed.

Martin ended up doing the negotiations with M'Rarrtikar. As she had said, she handled the family's finances, and he was quite impressed by her aptitude when they had all finished and signed up.

Both parties were quite satisfied as the Caitians left. Bethany had to comment though that Martin had stretched things a bit far for some of the wives.

"I said that I would if I had to," Martin replied. "But I've managed to get myself an ex-Fleet engineer rather cheaply in exchange, so I'm not complaining. Besides, in one sense I didn't stretch things at all. One of my aims is to make my shipmates more family-oriented rather than just people thrown together as a crew. I believe that between them and Burningbright's family, it's going to work out much as I wanted.

Bethany looked thoughtful. "I suppose so. I'm afraid that after years in the Service, I'm too used to thinking of things from a military perspective."

"You're not in the Service any more, Commander, so I suggest that you practice loosening up a bit."

"Yes, sir," she replied.

'*Too soon for her,*' Martin thought, and let the subject lie.

With the Caitians gone, Martin checked with reception to see if there were any other latecomers, but was told that there were none.

Bethany asked, "Do you feel that we have enough crew to properly man the ship?"

"Barely," Martin replied. "Although you would probably be able to gauge that better than I. We got lucky in a few places, but we're still lacking a specialist comp-tech. I know that you are competent in that field, but still…. Anyway, I should count my blessings. I could have done a lot worse. Getting R'Murran was a huge load off my mind."

"So your planned departure is locked in now?"

"Yes. I suggest that you start considering how best to set watches with these personnel, and anything else that you're more experienced at planning than I." Martin turned to Burningbright. "Thank you for your input – it was quite useful. I'll be sending everyone the details of where and when to meet later on. I suggest that you make the most of the next couple of days."

"We'll do that, thanks. I'll see you then." Burningbright then offered a parting hug which Martin accepted.

After shi departed, Bethany said, "You really should reserve a more respectful relationship between the crew and yourself, Captain."

"For chakats, that *is* respectful," Martin replied with a grin. "Now if shi tried to grope me while we hugged…."

Bethany resisted the temptation to roll her eyes. She suspected that he was trying to get a rise out of her, and remembered his suggestion to loosen up. "If you won't be needing me any more today, I'll be heading home now. I'm sure that my sister will be happy to hear that I will be out of her fur soon."

"Have a good evening, Commander."

Martin hung around the office until time almost ran out, and started to pack up. Heywood and Menalippe arrived just as he was about to leave the office, and they proudly showed Martin the mating contract. He congratulated them, signed them up officially, and then told them to go home, pack, and wait for the call in a few days.

*** 16 November 2332 ***

In one of the warehouses bordering the Big Sur Spaceport, the brand new crew gathered bright and early three days after the interview. Martin was there to meet and greet them as they arrived, and had them gather in the office where he had drinks and snacks. The youngest of R'Murran's wives – M'Resk – was not as experienced with meeting other species, and was somewhat intimidated by the large tiger morphs, but seemed to be putting a brave face on. In fact, all the Caitians were much smaller than the tigers, being naturally a small species, but the rest were used to dealing with much larger species. The tigers' nine year old child, Katarina, was already as tall as they were. Shi was a little bit shy of the others, but seemed to be more comfortable around others hir size, despite the fact that they were adults.

The various other children were already getting to know each other. Martin had been startled to meet the chakat's three children. While he knew that wildly varied fur patterns were the norm for chakats, these three were exceptional even for their species. The first was Lemondrop who was the least remarkable with hir base of white fur with splashes of orange and yellow on hir shoulders, back, feet and tail. The second was Candycane, and shi was tiger-striped… in pink! An otherwise normal stripe pattern was startling in pink on white, with pink hair to top it off. Martin could figure that red fur could have been lightened enough to produce the eye-catching colour, but that could not explain the final cub. When Pixiepaws stepped into view, his jaw hit the floor.

"Bright green?" he gasped. "How is that even possible? Is it a dye job?" he asked Zelkie while trying to take in the sight of a cub with green fur with white chest, belly fur, and other markings, and yellow-green hair.

Zelkie grinned. "Nope, it's completely natural. Gotta admit that it startled us just as much when shi was born. Best we can guess is that it has to do with my skunktaur genes." Shi pointed to the blue paw-shaped mark on hir fur where it showed above hir halter. "We reckon that shi was going to be a normal yellow-furred cub, but it mixed with the blue skunktaur colour genes, and this is the result."

"Shi certainly wouldn't be hard to pick out in a crowd. Does it bother hir to be green?"

"Well, chakats are varied enough that even an odd colour like hirs didn't result in too much teasing, and shi seems to like being so distinctive. I'd say so far it hasn't affected hir adversely."

"Let's hope it continues that way. So, how old are they?"

"They're all thirteen. When we three den-mated, we decided to all get pregnant at once, so they were born within a few days of each other. Candycane is the eldest of the three." Zelkie smiled affectionately. "Shi sometimes feels that as being the firstborn, that makes hir responsible for hir sisters. Don't be surprised if shi occasionally tries to act too adult. Watch out for Lemondrop though – shi seems to have just two speeds: stop and go. Shi tends to do everything at breakneck speed."

Art © Megan Giles

"Shi gets underfoot sometimes?"

"Yes, but on the other hand, shi's always the first to finish hir chores."

"Anything distinctive about Pixiepaws; besides hir colour, I mean?"

"Shi's an artistic type. Shi loves to dance, and shi's getting pretty good on the piano keyboard."

"I'll look forward to hearing hir play."

Last to arrive were Danson and Ceres in a rental truck with a large sturdy crate amongst more traditional luggage in the flatbed.

"What do you have there?" Martin asked curiously.

"Would you believe a couple of tonnes of soil?" Ceres replied with an apologetic grin.

"What on Earth is that for?"

Danson answered, "It's some of the soil from my home. I wish to have a traditional garden growing in that soil as a connection to my family and clan."

"I see. That's… unusual, but I suppose it can't hurt. Anyway, get unloaded and join the rest of us as soon as you can. I'll send out Risha to operate the lifter for that crate."

When that was accomplished and everyone was gathered back in the office, Martin called them to attention. With him was a female coyote morph dressed in business attire, and a petite lynx girl.

"Ladies, gentlemen, and shirs, welcome to the first day of what I hope will be a long and prosperous venture. Let me introduce you to a couple of people first. This lovely lady is my sister, Clarice, whose warehouse facility this is. Clarice has agreed to be my agent here on Earth, and all goods bound for this spaceport will go into or come out of this warehouse. Of course Clarice doesn't handle these things directly, which brings me to this other lovely lady – and extremely competent warehouse manager I might add – Beliz Carlotta. In addition to storing or expediting our freight, this office is our default point of contact on Earth, so I'll suggest you all get to know Beliz so that she can help you out as needed."

There was a pause as the chakats insisted on giving Beliz a hug, then Martin continued.

"Now I suppose a few of you are wondering which ship you have signed onto. Well, the reason that I haven't mentioned her name yet is because she hasn't been properly dedicated as yet since her refit. Clarice asked me long ago for the privilege of doing so, and I ask her now to step forward."

Clarice stepped up and Martin handed her a PADD. A monitor on the wall lit up with a view of a starship with all of its ports unlit, and

Art © Mendhi

only minimum navigation lights on. It was mostly visible only by the stars it eclipsed.

Martin gestured at the image. "This is our ship, and the view is from a remote drone that is fitted with a special piece of equipment. Clarice, please do the honours."

Clarice said, "I hereby name this ship the *Phoenix*. May good fortune smile upon all who sail her." She touched a button on the PADD which sent a signal to the drone. There was a slight shudder in the scene on the monitor as the drone spat out millions of tiny pellets in a very precise pattern. The pellets impacted on the hull of the ship and burst, releasing their load of special gilt paint. Like magic, the name "*Phoenix*" appeared on the hull, glittering in the floodlight of the drone. On cue, the ship then lit up everywhere, and the crew cheered.

"Thanks, Marty," Clarice quietly told her brother. "That's something that I thought I'd never do."

"You're welcome, Ceecee," Martin replied. Then he addressed the others. "As this is a professional outfit, I have provided with uniforms in various styles which you will find in the next office. They've been tailored to your specifications, so they should fit perfectly. So, please grab yours to take with the rest of your luggage, and make your way out to the warehouse where our two shuttles are waiting. My fellow crewmates, we are now in business!"

Chapter 2: Unexpected Baggage

As the crew filtered out into the warehouse, they were directed to the shuttles by Martin.

"Zelkie, as our primary Loadmaster, our bigger shuttle is your baby. The main pilot's station has been preconfigured for taurforms. There are a limited number of stowable passenger couches, enough to take your family plus Ceres and Danson. Beliz has already arranged to have some of our cargo loaded, but there's still plenty of room for everyone's luggage. I'll leave the rest for you to check and prepare for lift-off."

"Everyone else, stow your luggage on the other shuttle which I'll be piloting. You should all have an information packet that was with your uniforms. You'll find your assigned quarters marked on a map. Please drop off your belongings as soon as you can, but leave settling in until later. Change into your uniforms and head for your duty stations. Until we leave Earth orbit, everyone is on duty; Commander Oakwood will assign watches after that. While Zelkie and I return for more loads, I expect all crew to familiarise themselves with their posts and equipment in preparation for departure."

Martin then looked at the group of cubs. "I know that most of you are familiar with space travel, so I hope that you know to keep out from under our feet. Either stay in your cabins, or with M'Lertiña until we depart. In the future we will probably be able to give you more leeway, but for our first time, we need to keep things as uncomplicated as possible, please."

He turned his attention back to the adults. "Okay, we're on the clock now, so let's get going!"

There was organised chaos while everybody sorted themselves out. Zelkie insisted on checking the manifests for both shuttles before allowing them to seal up. Ceres took the co-pilot's seat next to Zelkie, while Heywood was Martin's co-pilot. Martin got clearance from the spaceport's control tower and was soon accelerating up into Earth orbit, with Zelkie only a few minutes behind him. He felt exhilarated! Although he had made many such lift-offs while achieving his pilot's

Art © Windpaw

licence, this was the first time as captain of his own ship and head of his own business. His dream was really coming true!

Martin parked his shuttle in its assigned bay, well aware of Heywood's scrutiny. The man had many years of experience over him, and he did not want to be found wanting. They were met by the skeleton crew from the shipyard who had been manning the ship until the real crew turned up. The foreman ceremoniously handed over a small PADD emblazoned with a phoenix symbol which contained all the ship's access codes, and congratulated Martin. He passed on a copy to Anastasiya who would be responsible for changing them away from the shipyard defaults.

After the crew had dropped off their luggage and changed into their uniform of choice, they headed to their posts, Risha returning to the shuttle bay to help unload the cargo, while Zelkie and Valentina were doing the same in the second bay. Martin's smaller shuttle was unloaded first, and he took the yard crew back to their orbital base before heading back to Big Sur. Zelkie had beaten him down though, and was already loading up. The coyote and chakat were kept busy shuttling for a few hours before their entire load was stowed.

Martin was pleased to see that Bethany seemed to have everything running smoothly when he stepped onto the bridge. "All stations report," he ordered as he took his place in the captain's chair.

Bethany said, "Flight plan filed with Earth Orbit Control and approved, Scheduled departure is in nine minutes."

M'Anissa'tk said, "Engineering reports power cores up to full readiness. Engines on stand-by and ready whenever you give the word."

"Course laid in," Ceres reported from the navigator's station.

"Pre-flight checks completed," Heywood added.

Burningbright said, "Environmental systems all in the green."

Anastasiya spoke next. "All ports secured. Cargo scans completed and clear. Non-crew are all in their assigned cabins."

Martin's final lift had included half a dozen passengers. They had been met in the shuttle bay by M'Rarrtikar who had checked their tickets and passports before handing them over to M'Resk who had cheerfully and efficiently got them squared away in their cabins as if she had been doing the job for years.

"Excellent work, everyone. Any questions?" Martin asked.

There was a slight pause before Burningbright asked with a smile, "Hotfoot wants to know when you want to have the celebratory dinner?"

Martin grinned. "I almost forgot that. Let's schedule that for after second shift. Ask hir to have normal meals ready for those of us coming off first shift. I don't know about you, but I've worked up quite an appetite!"

The rest of the remaining time was spent in light banter until the chronometer told Martin that the time had come. He touched the comm controls and said, "Earth Orbit Control – this is the *Phoenix*. Awaiting clearance for scheduled departure."

A few moments passed before a voice replied, "Earth Orbit Control to *Phoenix* – you are cleared for departure on vector Delta Niner Charlie. Bon voyage, Captain."

"Delta Niner Charlie – thank you Earth Orbit Control. *Phoenix* out." Martin switched off the comm and said, "You have a go, Mr Baxter."

"Aye Captain," Heywood replied.

The human expertly manoeuvred the ship out of parking orbit and into the departure lane. They accelerated away from Earth's gravitational influence, and at a predetermined point, engaged the warp drive. Their voyage was well and truly under way.

Martin had Bethany stand down the crew members who would be taking the second shift, then left the bridge in her control. With the pressures of loading and getting under way, he'd had no time to think about food or drink, but now that those pressures were relieved, he realised how hungry and thirsty he was. He made his way to the mess hall where he intended to use the replicator to make a snack to keep him going until meal time, only to be confronted by Hotfoot who firmly steered him to a seat.

"You're hardly the first hungry captain that I've had to feed after departure," shi commented. "I have a light meal prepared for you and the others. Just tell me what kind of drink you prefer, and I'll have it here in no time."

"You're a gem, Hotfoot," Martin replied gratefully. Coffee with cream, please."

Hotfoot returned quickly with a tray of food and a mug of coffee, Martin thanked hir before shi went to attend the other crew members who'd had the same idea as Martin.

After his meal, he did a tour of his ship, checking on how the rest of the crew were doing. He was pleased to see that even the inexperienced members were settling well into their roles. However, he had to be reminded of certain other people not on duty. His wrist comm beeped, and he answered it. "Captain Yote here."

"Pardon me please, Captain," the voice of Keera, the eldest Caitian child came. "The children would like to know if they can leave their cabins yet?"

Martin castigated himself for forgetting them. "Yes, it's okay. Get yourselves something to eat if you're hungry. The holosuite is programmed with a large assortment of scenarios if you'd like to check them out."

"Thanks, Captain," Keera replied before disconnecting.

"Better get used to taking them into account," Martin murmured to himself.

It had been several hours since he had risen from bed for a very early start to the day, but he was still too keyed up to go back to his cabin and relax. Now that they were under warp, there was no great need for him to be on the bridge, so he decided to head to the holosuite to see if the kids would check it out. He found that half of them had already gotten there before him, and a seaside program had been chosen. They were in the middle of choosing sides for a game of beach volleyball when he arrived.

"Captain! Can you be our umpire?" Ner'ritn asked. None of the children wanted to be left out of the game.

Martin smiled indulgently. "Sure," he replied. He pulled up a deck chair, took off his jacket and hung it off the back, and then propped up an umbrella to shade himself from the warm holo-sun while he watched the game.

Six minutes later, he was sound asleep.

An insistent beeping from his wrist comm finally woke Martin. He was startled to realise that the volleyball had been finished without him, and there were only a couple of chakat cubs sporting in the water. He answered the comm. "Yote here."

"Captain," came Bethany's voice, "could you come to the bridge to relieve Mr Baxter and myself so that we can have a meal?"

"I'll be right there, Commander," he replied, wondering just exactly how long he had been asleep. He regretfully levered himself out of the comfortable chair, realising that there were going to be many such minor interruptions with this small crew running this big ship. But that made the job more interesting. Martin never wanted his dream career to turn into mind-numbing monotony.

Of course there were a few teething problems as they all settled into their roles on the ship. M'Resk slowly got used to the presence of the big tigers. Heywood, despite a willingness to treat the morphs as equals, still had to get comfortable with the social dynamics. Anastasiya got a little too gung-ho about hir physical training sessions, and had to be asked to lighten up on the crew. Bethany continued to be stiffly formal, which grated on many people's nerves. The latter particularly bothered Martin as he needed her experience badly, both to operate the ship smoothly, and also to learn from her in order to be a better captain. A week into the voyage, he had to call her into his office and have a heart to heart talk about the matter. The result was a promise to try harder to be social and friendly, but Martin knew there was not going to be an overnight change.

The biggest surprise that Martin had though, happened shortly after his talk with Bethany. He was about to head off to bed when the door to his quarters chimed. Clad only in his shorts, he opened the door to find Risha standing there, dressed only in a casual one-piece ship-suit.

"Is there anything that I can do for you, Risha?"

The cougar fem looked uncertain and hesitated before replying, "Would it be possible for me to sleep with you tonight?"

Martin looked at her quizzically. "Are you looking for sex?"

She shook her head. "No! Not that. I mean... I just can't stand being left alone. I thought that I could cope, but.... Please, Captain, I just need the company."

Martin was half tempted to demand to know why, but refused to pry into something that could be deeply personal, although he still suspected her motives. "Okay. It's not as if I wouldn't mind a bit of company myself. But that's all."

He stood aside to let her into his quarters and indicated the door to his bedroom. As the captain and owner, he had a fairly luxurious cabin with a spacious living area separate from the sleeping area. She stepped into the bedroom and Martin followed.

She stopped next to the king-size bed and waited for Martin to say something.

"I sleep on the right side normally," he said, moving in that direction.

"Okay. Umm... I prefer to sleep nude. Will that bother you?"

"So do I, so if that doesn't bother you, you won't bother me."

"Thank you." She started stripping off the ship-suit, and Martin did the same with his shorts. The lithe and curvaceous form of the naked cougar started stirring his interest, and he quickly climbed under the sheet, turning his eyes away from the stimulating sight. Risha climbed in next to him, settling down on her side, facing away from him. As she had said, she just needed the company, and she quickly fell asleep.

Martin wished that he was able to do so also. It had been a long time since he had been able to spend some intimate time with a fem.

Risha was gone in the morning when he woke, although the residual warmth in the bed next to him indicated that she had been there until very recently. He could hardly expect anything else though – if she wasn't going to explain last night, she was unlikely to do so now.

Martin did not bring the subject up when he encountered Risha in the mess hall, although he did feel that she looked cheerier than she normally did in the morning. He could not decide though if he was imagining it in light of what had happened the previous night.

In retrospect, he should not have been surprised to see her again the next evening at the same time, but he was.

"May I?" she asked simply.

Martin stood aside and waved her in wordlessly. Like the previous night, she disrobed and climbed into her side of the bed, and he climbed into his. He awoke the next day as she was getting out of bed. She noticed and stopped to give him a smile.

"Thank you," she said sincerely, before dressing and leaving.

The next ten days, Risha joined Martin for all but two of the nights. She never said why, but by now he was certain that her demeanour had improved. It was obvious that she had security issues, but he still refused to pry just to sate his curiosity. It was her business, and she would tell in her own good time if she wanted to. Meanwhile, one of his crew was happier, and he had to admit to liking the company also.

On her next visit though, things changed. He noticed her scent immediately when he opened the door for her – she was in heat. The pheromones were the wrong kind to stimulate him directly, but knowing that she would be horny and in his bed was enough to provoke a reaction.

"Risha, are you sure that you want to sleep with me tonight?" He did not bother mentioning her conditioning – she knew to what he was referring.

"I especially don't want to be alone tonight," she replied.

Martin shrugged. "Okay, if you think you know what you're doing."

Risha climbed into bed with him as usual, but instead of lying down on her side with her back to him as she normally did, instead she faced him and started stroking the fur on his chest.

"Risha…" he began.

"Captain," she interrupted, "please shut up." Her hand wandered lower and found his sheath.

That was more than Martin could resist, and his manhood rapidly unsheathed. Despite what she had said, Martin tried protesting. "Risha, I know that you're horny as hell, but don't do anything that you will regret in the morning."

Risha stilled his voice by covering his muzzle with one of her hands. One other continued to play with his manhood, while a third resumed stroking his chest. "Captain, I've always enjoyed an active sex life until recently. I want to resume that, and I want to do it with someone whom I can trust. Will you be that person for me?"

Martin gave in to the inevitable, but not without a sense of anticipation. "As you wish, but with one proviso. My name is Martin; I'm not your captain tonight."

Risha's smile was filled with pleasure and the promise of delights to come. "Very well, Martin, let me show you what a four-armed lover can do for you."

And she proceeded to do exactly that. While Martin was not a virgin, his ambitions had left him little time for a social life for several years, and he was far from experienced in the ways of making love. Risha was quite the opposite, and quite aggressive in her techniques. She nearly blew his mind with pleasure, even as he tried to give his utmost in return.

It was quite some time later that the two lay panting in each other's arms, exhausted but satisfied. Then Martin noticed the tears leaking from Risha's eyes.

"What's wrong, Risha. Please tell me that this wasn't all a mistake."

Risha shook her head, a smile coming to her muzzle. "No, Martin, it wasn't a mistake. It was catharsis. I needed this more than you think. I needed to start laying to rest the ghost of my past."

"You don't have to tell me any more. I'm just happy to be able to be here for you, although I'm not sure if you haven't done a lot for me too."

"But I want to tell you. I need to get this off my chest while the moment is right." She proceeded to tell Martin about meeting Carson, and their plans for a life together. Then she related the events that led to his death, and her loss and despair. Her sense of abandonment at a moment of vulnerability had left her with a constant feeling of insecurity, and being alone at home was no longer tolerable. Basically she had to leave home to escape the memories and the loneliness. As the only unmated male on board the ship, Martin had been the only lifeline for her insecurity, but being the captain, she had been hesitant to approach him at first. When she could bear it no longer though, she had sought him out, and that had been enough then. Her heat had reawakened other needs and desires, and in the comfort of the security of being with him, she had reached out to him for both physical and emotional fulfilment.

"And now I feel better than I have in many months," she concluded. "The loss and loneliness have started to fade, and I have you to thank for that. You never pushed; you never questioned; you were just there when I needed it. I couldn't have asked for more."

"You're welcome, Risha. I'm very happy that I was able to help." Then Martin grinned. "Although I must say that I thoroughly enjoyed the way that I got to help."

Risha laughed. "Then you'll be happy to know that I'll be wanting more… *therapy?*"

"As long as it's tomorrow. You've worn me out completely."

"And you've done a pretty good job of tiring me out too," she replied. "Tomorrow it is."

They then snuggled up together to sleep facing each other for the first time, and were soon fast asleep.

Martin woke to the sound of the shower running. Unlike the previous nights, it seemed Risha was freshening up before leaving. Considering how they both smelled after last night, he realised that he would soon be following suit. The shower stopped, quickly replaced by the sound of the fur-drying cycle. Martin entered the bathroom to see her turning around with all four arms raised to allow the jets of warm air to thoroughly dry her. She smiled when she saw him, unconcerned that they were both naked. After last night, that would never be an issue between them.

After Risha stepped out, Martin showered thoroughly, noticing through the glass door that Risha had started brushing her fur. She was working on her hair when he stepped out, and started to brush his own fur. She asked him to brush the fur on her back, and then she returned the favour. Both enjoyed the grooming process thoroughly. Then she got dressed, kissed him on the cheek, and left without saying a word.

Neither person even hinted at the previous night all that day, but that evening she was back at his door, and they made love again.

The next day, Risha's heat had abated, and she did not show up at his room. He went to bed, keenly feeling her absence.

From then on, Risha would turn up four or five days every week, and half the time she was in the mood for sex. Martin never pushed her for more. He realised that he was not her boyfriend; he was a source of security and satisfaction for someone who was rebuilding her life. It did not matter – he was enjoying the status quo for now, and for however long it lasted.

There was one related incident however. One evening as Risha was joining Martin, Bethany happened to be walking down the corridor. She frowned a little, but did not stop or say anything. The next day though, she stopped by Martin's office while he was there by himself.

"Captain, may I speak frankly?"

Martin was a little surprised at that opening question. "Certainly, Commander. What's bothering you?"

"Are you certain that it's a good idea to be fraternising with the crew? You are the captain and should not be showing favour to anyone." She left her own experience unspoken, but clearly indicated.

Martin sighed. "Commander – need I remind you that this is not a military ship? While I do need to retain a certain amount of respect for my position of authority, when I'm not being the captain, I am still a person who has normal interactions with other people. If I choose to have any sort of a liaison with a woman, that is *my* business, not the ship's, and certainly not yours."

Bethany was still stiffly disapproving. "It *is* ship's business if she is trying to gain advantage and privileges through sexual favours, and causing resentment amongst the other crew members."

"Enough! For the record, she has neither asked for, nor would I give her, anything for sexual favours. For reasons that are very personal to her, Risha is very insecure and needs the company – she hates being alone. So unless you find a *valid* reason for being concerned, Risha will continue joining me whenever she wishes, and you will keep your nose out of it. Am I making myself quite clear, Commander?"

"Perfectly, sir." She then turned and left, but Martin could tell that she was very angry indeed. Not that he could completely blame her, considering her recent past, but he was not going to let her misfortune affect his own relationships.

Despite the best efforts of M'Lertiña, it was not possible to keep all of the children occupied all of the time. Although their school studies kept them busy for some of the time, that still left them plenty of time to get into mischief. Fortunately most of the time they were able to amuse themselves in the holosuite with its extensive library of locales to try out, with multiple safeguards built into the programs. Nevertheless there was still the urge to explore the ship that was their home for the foreseeable future, and occasionally they had to be ejected from places where they did not belong.

This day found two chakat cubs checking out places that they had not been in yet on deck seven. They noticed Ceres in the corridor ahead of them and, wanting to avoid questions about being on this deck, ducked down a side corridor. Peeking out, they realised that Ceres had apparently not noticed them, and shi was opening a door that was marked: '*CAUTION: Z-G SHAFT*'.

"Hey, that door was locked before," Lemondrop said.

"Must be one of those places the grown-ups want us to stay away from," Pixiepaws replied.

"They're always too cautious and won't let us into the fun places. Let's follow Ceres."

"We can't go in there!" Pixiepaws protested.

"Why not? Shi's left the door unlocked."

"The door says 'Caution'. It has to be locked for a reason."

"If it was dangerous, it would say '*Danger*', not '*Caution*'. I'm going in for a look. You can stay out here if you like."

"What if someone sees you?"

"Better keep a look-out for me then," Lemondrop said with a confident grin that did not quite match what Pixiepaws could sense shi was feeling.

"No, I'll follow you and watch your back."

They approached the door and looked about to see if there were any witnesses, then Lemondrop hit the door switch and rushed inside while Pixiepaws followed, looking over hir shoulder to make sure that nobody saw them going in. Because Lemondrop was so hasty, shi did not notice that the floor simply stopped about a metre inside the door until almost too late. Shi teetered on the edge of an enormous drop with a *meep* of fear. That turned into a squall of terror as Pixiepaws, hir attention distracted, bumped into hir, toppling hir over the edge, all hir limbs flailing futilely…

… and hung there in mid air.

What neither cub knew was that Z-G stood for Zero Gravity, and the Z-G Shaft was a broad corridor without artificial gravity that went down most of the decks of the ship. It's original purpose when it was a Star Corps vessel was to provide a ready means of moving equipment about a ship that needed to be flexible in layout and purpose out on the frontiers where there were no ship docks and other facilities. It was not as essential for its new life as a trader, but the crew found it handy to move cargo pods between the decks – a tractor beam mounted at the end of the shaft quickly and safely moving anything that could fit inside. Most of the time though, it was not needed, so it was kept locked, and when it was needed during loading procedures, the children were required to be out of the crew's way, so they never learned about its existence before now.

Having heard Lemondrop's cries of fear as shi exercised, Ceres rose rapidly from below, skilfully bouncing off the walls to propel hirself quickly and exactly where shi wanted to go. Shi brought hirself to a halt next to Lemondrop who was still desperately trying to grab something to stop falling, not realising that shi was in fact merely drifting slowly *across* the shaft.

"What are you cubs doing here?" Ceres asked. "You should realise that this place is out of bounds."

Pixiepaws hung hir head guiltily. "We just wanted to see what you were doing. Ummm… can you get Lemondrop, please?"

The Starwalker looked at the panicky cub. "I suppose shi's learned hir lesson by now." Shi looked back at Pixiepaws. But don't you have your sire's Talent for telekinesis too? You could pull hir back yourself."

"I can't lift that much yet!" Pixiepaws protested.

"Shi's in freefall – you don't have to lift hir at all. Just pull hir back to the edge."

"Oh, yeah." Pixiepaws was embarrassed not to realise that. Shi reached out with hir mind and tugged at hir half-sister, who drifted over to the edge.

The moment that Lemondrop's paws got traction, shi hauled hirself over the ledge and shot out into the corridor. Shi stopped there, panting wildly.

Ceres exited the shaft and put an arm around the quivering cub. "Relax – you're safe now. In fact you were never in danger," shi said reassuringly. "Haven't you ever been in freefall before?"

"No," Lemondrop replied in a very small voice.

"I thought you spent years aboard cruise ships with your parents, and I know that they have zero grav recreational facilities for the passengers – so didn't you ever want to try them?"

"Yeah," Pixiepaws answered as shi cuddled hir sister, "but the crew weren't allowed to use them – only passengers."

"What? Not even at night shift?"

"Starships don't have a real night, and cruise ships are active 24 hours a day. There isn't a night shift."

"Well that must have sucked," Ceres said sympathetically. "Tell you what – I'll have a word with the captain and see if he will allow you to play in the Z-G Shaft under my supervision. You can learn how to handle yourselves in freefall." Ceres lifted Lemondrop's head to look into hir eyes. "And not be afraid if you ever need to use it." Shi gave the cub a grin and wink.

Lemondrop smiled weakly back. "Yeah… okay, I guess."

"And don't rush in where you don't belong in future," Ceres added.

The cubs nodded guiltily.

Ceres got Martin's approval and let the chakat cubs know. They not only told their sister, Candycane, but all the other cubs as well. Consequently the shaft was quickly filled with a cloud of inept children. It took a while before the Starwalker was able to get them organised so that shi could start properly teaching them how to handle themselves. While some of them were uncomfortable at first, at least none of them threw up due to the precaution of having them all take anti-nausea medication beforehand. Once shi was satisfied that they had the basics down pat, Ceres introduced them to a variant of a game that shi and the other Starwalkers had played at the training academy, with some adaptations due to the unusual locale. It had elements of basketball and soccer, with makeshift goals mounted at either end of the shaft. Plenty of bumps and scrapes were accrued, but nobody minded because they were having so much fun, except perhaps for Kannekin who remained clumsy and very uncertain. The game somehow acquired the name of Shaftball, and became one of the more popular means of entertainment, and not a few of the adults also. Ceres was more than pleased because shi got to exercise in hir natural environment without it becoming a boring chore. M'Resk took advantage of it also to give the passengers another option for keeping entertained.

Martin remarked to Bethany while watching one of the games, "And to think that I once thought that the Z-G Shaft was mostly a waste of space. If it hadn't been handy for moving cargo between decks, I would have had it taken out during the ship's renovation, but it wasn't cost effective at the time."

Bethany nodded. "It wouldn't be the first time that something turned out to be unexpectedly useful. As long as I was in Fleet, I still regularly came across unusual but ingenious adaptations of old things. Some things are worth sitting on for a while to see if something pops up to make them useful again. It's certainly helping to keep people fit."

"Yes, Anastasiya was quick to point that out too. Shi wants to incorporate regular scheduled matches into the fitness regime. Want to pick teams and have a little competition?" Martin asked.

Bethany eyed him with a small smile on her muzzle. "You're on, Captain, but don't forget which one of us has many years of experience in space."

"It's a team sport, Commander, so let's see who can put together the better team. And I'm choosing Ceres to be on *my* team," Martin declared with a grin.

By the time that they reached their next port of call, the Commander's Commandoes were beating the Captain's Conquerors by five games to three.

Although he had hoped otherwise, Martin had not expected his refurbished ship to perform absolutely flawlessly. So it came as no big surprise to him when Burningbright stopped by his office a day before they were due to arrive at the planet, Bounty.

"Have you got a moment, Captain?" Burningbright asked from the doorway to his office.

"Sure, come in," Martin replied. "What's up?"

"It's the number 2 air scrubber – it's performing well below specification."

"Is that the new or reconditioned unit?"

"The reconditioned one."

"Hmm… I'm going to have to have words with the shipyard about that when we get back to Earth. Anyway, what do you recommend that we do about it?"

"I'd like to take it offline and determine why it's malfunctioning. That way I can give you a full report on the problem. The other units should be able to cope with the load well enough meanwhile."

"Sounds good to me. How long should it take? We're going to need all hands when we get to Bounty."

"That depends. I could do it by myself, but if you want to get it done before we reach Bounty, then it's a two-person job. I'd like to enlist M'Anissa'tk's help to do that.

"I regard this as a priority job, so go ahead and get her to help you."

"She's on second shift, Captain."

"Ah, okay. Hmm… go have a talk with her and arrange a mutually agreeable time for you to work on this together, then go see Commander Oakwood and confirm the change."

"Will do, sir. Umm… while I'm here, there's something else that's concerning me. It's a bit more personal though."

"I'm always ready to listen, 'Bright."

"It's M'Resk. She's putting on a good façade, but I can sense that she's tired and stressed. Forgive me for asking, but might you be working her a bit too hard?"

Martin was genuinely surprised. "I don't understand why that would be. M'Resk's responsibilities shouldn't be that onerous."

"Perhaps you should talk to her about them," Burningbright hinted.

Martin nodded. "I will. Thanks for the heads-up. In fact, if you sense any other possible problems, let me know so that I can deal with them before they get out of hand."

"Aye, Captain," Burningbright agreed, then departed.

Martin then tapped his comm. "Captain Yote to M'Resk – please report to my office at your soonest convenience."

After a brief pause, M'Resk replied, "*Acknowledged, Captain. I'll be there in about ten minutes.*"

Nine and a half minutes later, M'Resk tapped at his door.

"Come in and sit down, please, M'Resk."

The Caitian did so, and because Martin was looking for the signs, he realised that Burningbright was right – she did look tired.

"M'Resk, how many hours have you been putting into your work lately?"

M'Resk looked uncomfortable. "I don't have a set shift because of the nature of my job," she replied evasively.

"I know, but that isn't what I asked," Martin said gently.

"Captain, I know you only took me on because you wanted my husband as your engineer. I know that what I do isn't very important, so I try to do as much as I can to make up for it," she replied earnestly.

Martin sighed. "So you've been working basically from the time that you get up until you go to bed again, right?"

M'Resk hesitated, then nodded silently.

"My dear lady, whatever gave you the idea that what you do is unimportant? You can't measure yourself up against your husband. I can't do what he does, but that doesn't make *me* less. We all need to do whatever we're best at doing, and your job of looking after passengers is just as important because of that. Bored passengers can cause problems, or simply get under our feet. We need their money, but we don't need them interfering with ship's business, and you're helping to keep that from happening. On top of that, a happy customer tells others about their experience, and word-of-mouth brings in more passengers. This all helps our profit margin. However, as important as these things are, it's still just a job, and one that I don't expect to put more hours into than the rest of the crew does. In the end, this is a trader ship, not a pleasure cruiser, and we are not expected to keep our passengers entertained constantly, nor attend to their every whim. Do you understand?"

"Yes sir."

"Good. There's no such things as make-work on this ship, and I want you to know that I am very happy with what you've been doing. But now I want you to take more care of yourself, and in future try to stick to no more hours than a standard shift."

"Yes sir," M'Resk said again with more assurance.

"Now go wrap up whatever you're doing, and take the rest of the day off. Do whatever *you* want. Go take a nap might be a good idea. But if I see you doing some work again today, I'm going to knot your tail, get me?"

M'Resk grinned. "Believe me, I don't want a kinked tail."

"Excellent. Now get out of here," Martin said with a smile.

"Thanks, Captain!"

Martin noted that aforementioned tail was waving a lot more jauntily as she departed. "I hope future problems will be as simple to solve as that," he murmured to himself before he called Bethany to let her know about M'Resk, and then getting back to his work.

A young voice came from the doorway of Martin's office. "Pardon me, Captain. Could I talk to you?"

Martin looked up from his work to see the eldest of the Caitian children waiting for an answer. "Sure, Keera. Come on in."

The girl walked up to his desk and fidgeted for a moment before saying, "I'd like to learn how to operate a starship; maybe even become bridge crew."

Martin was curious. "How long have you felt that this would be your choice of career?"

"I thought about it back when we were still with Star Fleet, but I didn't much like the military aspect. Since we've been on your ship though, I've liked the way it's run, and I think that this is what I really want to do."

"Fair enough. You do realise though that it takes good grades in a variety of subjects to qualify for training in careers suitable for bridge crew?"

"Of course, Captain. I already have good grades at my current level, but rather than wait until I graduate to start training, I thought that maybe I could come onto the bridge and get a head start on learning stuff – only when you're not busy, of course."

Martin nodded. "Work experience – not a bad idea. I wish that I could have done the same. Tell you what – I'll run this by Commander Oakwood, and if she's agreeable, we'll set up some kind of regular training class. Find out what suits you best, and then you can focus your studies towards that goal."

Keera smiled happily. "That would be perfect, Captain. Thank you!"

"Whoa! I have to square it with the commander first. She's responsible for running the ship, and I won't override her if she feels it's inappropriate for you to be doing that."

Keera tried to quell her excitement, but she still felt optimistic. "Okay, Captain."

Martin ran the idea past Bethany the next time they met on the bridge. She nodded thoughtfully and after a moment said, "I think that's an excellent idea. I'll speak to her and set up a schedule."

Soon after that, Keera was a regular visitor to the bridge, and she took turns with whoever was on duty to go through some exercises at various stations. She even got to wear a ship's uniform, although it did have 'Cadet' on her ship's badge.

M'Rarrtikar came to Martin's office soon after Keera started her training.

"I'd like to thank you for allowing Keera to learn from the bridge crew. It not only means a lot to her, but it relieves a worry for us also."

"For you? How is that?" Martin asked in puzzlement. "Didn't you think she was going to get a good enough education?"

M'Rarrtikar smiled. "No, nothing like that. You're not a parent, so

Art © Michele Light

you probably haven't thought about it, but Keera is a teenager, and while our cultures might vary in some things, there are some things that are universal. In this case, it's Keera reaching that time of life when she gets rebellious and dissatisfied with the way things are. By giving her this training, she's focusing on what *she* wants, rather than *our* expectations. I'm sure that it will help make the next few years smoother for all of us."

"You're right – I hadn't thought of it in those terms. However, by the same token, what happens when she starts getting interested in finding a mate?"

M'Rarrtikar sighed. "I wish I had a good answer for that. Back when we were still in a Star Fleet ship, there were other Caitian families with young males. We fully expected Keera to find someone amongst them, or at least keep her happy until something better came along. On this ship though, the only male is her brother. The only way that she's going to find a potential mate is to meet one when we're in port somewhere. If she doesn't, it's possible that we would have to leave her with family back on Cait."

Martin frowned. "But if she has her heart set on a career in space, I don't think that will go down very well."

"Yes, you see our problem. As her parents, we must look after her best interests. However, what *are* they? Her career? A family? It isn't an easy choice."

"I would think that establishing a career would be the best thing to do first."

M'Rarrtikar shook her head. "You aren't taking Caitian culture into account. How well you do in your career depends not only on what you know, but on your status. You can gain status in various ways, but the simplest is to get mated. Our family has a fairly high status due not only to R'Murran's career achievements, but also because he has four wives. It doesn't matter how well Keera does academically – if she competes with another Caitian female with similar qualifications but is also mated, that person's status will always win over Keera's unmated status. She *needs* to find a suitable mate to do well in a career."

Martin grimaced. "I see. That makes things complicated. So what do you intend to do?"

"For now – nothing. While she is happy with the way things stand, we can afford to wait and look for answers. With luck, something will come along before it becomes a crisis."

There were a few more teething problems amongst the crew on that first leg of their voyage. The Caitians especially were concerned about their disparate schedules, but a bit of fine tuning with their shifts alleviated that situation. Nothing was perfect of course – they had too small a crew to give everyone what they liked.

Heywood, while proving able to fit in with a crew of anthros quite readily, nevertheless occasionally grated on people's nerves because of his strong opinions on various subjects which were often at odds with the majority of others. They quickly learned to avoid debating certain subjects with him, and that mitigated that problem.

The chakats, outside of their duty shifts, tended to be a bit lazy, and weren't thrilled about being required to attend Anastasiya's physical fitness sessions. Ironically, they were some of the most enthusiastic players of beach volleyball, and other very physical games available in the holosuite, and later the Shaftball matches. Martin put the moaning about the exercises down to being rather boring, and asked Anastasiya to make the sessions more interesting. In the end it was Valentina who came to the rescue with some well chosen music to help make the sessions more lively.

Danson proved to be somewhat reclusive. Martin wanted him to socialise with the crew a lot more, but was not going to force him to do so. However, a word with Ceres led Martin to realise that it was not shyness, but a discomfort with the sterile environment of the ship that kept him in his gardens most of the time. Martin solved this with a twofold approach. Firstly, he asked Danson to make planters that could be placed in the corridors and various public rooms about the ship to alleviate that sterile feel. Secondly, he dug up a holosuite program that had his native forests in it, and with Bethany's help, added sub-programs from other sources. Basically he made an imitation of a foxtaur festival. Its resemblance to the real thing was somewhat crude, but good enough for Danson to willingly join the others in the festivities. Thereafter, similar social events were regularly scheduled for his benefit, but also because the rest of the crew enjoyed them.

It was therefore a fairly well integrated and happy crew that reached Bounty.

The *Phoenix's* first port of call was an agricultural colony. While the world had been a disappointment in terms of resources, it had been a godsend to the early space explorers. Much of planet Earth was still recovering from decades of war that had ruined so much prime agricultural land. It had been let regrow naturally, and today much of it was either grasslands or forest inhabited by the various species of wildlife that had survived the devastation. Despite the regrowth though, the soil remained dangerously unsafe for growing food crops, and would remain so for decades, or even centuries. Earth desperately needed new food growing areas. Bounty proved to have a geography and climate that was near perfect for large scale cropping, the only type that was truly economical for interstellar shipping. Even so, only the urgent requirement for lots of food made it a viable proposition at first. Nowadays, vast improvements in technology and starships made it a thriving worldwide business. There had been objections at first to the wholesale changes to much of the planet's ecology, but the needs of the people of Earth were greater, and Bounty became the new food basket for the regrowing population.

Still, to maximise profitability, foods were shipped in bulk wherever possible. Stasis units kept perishables as fresh as newly harvested for their long trip to Earth or other destinations in massive freighters. The world's import needs were also generally served by those freighters which would otherwise have returned empty. This helped keep costs way down. However, occasionally someone on Bounty needed something that could not wait for that long, and that's where the independent traders came in. Martin had been able to offer a far cheaper rate than any of the big multi-planetary shipping companies, and he had scored an impressively large consignment. All he had to do was to deliver it on time.

As this was their first test making a delivery as a new crew, Martin ordered a rehearsal of the procedures, which pointed out some minor bugs that they were able to iron out ahead of the real thing. When they pulled into orbit, M'Rarrtikar had all the I's dotted and the T's crossed on the paperwork, and Zelkie and Martin quickly and efficiently shuttled loads down to the spaceport where Risha coordinated the unloading with the ground crews. On Martin's first trip down, he took one of *Phoenix's* passengers, a young rabbit morph who had been sent to Earth to further his studies at a university, and was now returning home to take up a career.

The deliveries went without a hitch, and Martin was delighted to pick up a couple of priority deliveries for his next port of call. On his last trip down, he took several of the crew and cubs to get a few hours of fresh air and sunshine before they had to depart. Bounty had no tourist facilities whatsoever though, so there was no point in stopping longer.

Once under way again, Martin asked Hotfoot to prepare a special celebratory dinner. He scheduled it to overlap the change of shifts so that everyone could enjoy it about the same time. Right at the end of the first shift, everyone was in the mess hall except for Bethany, who was listening in from the bridge, and Martin called for everybody's attention.

"Before the second shift has to go take their posts, I want to express my thanks to everyone for their fine efforts at Bounty. Everything went very smoothly, with everybody giving their best. Even the cubs helped out here and there, even if it was just to fetch refreshments for the rest of us. The bottom line is that we worked together as a crew should, and I'm proud of the lot of you. If the rest of the voyage goes as smoothly as this, I'll be absolutely delighted. Thank you for vindicating my choice of you as the *Phoenix's* crew, and my shipmates." He raised a glass of sparkling wine that had been served to all who drank such, with other appropriate drinks to those who did not. "A toast to the continuing success of the *Phoenix*, and the people who make it so!"

There were cheers, glasses clinked, and the various crew congratulated each other. It was a very happy ship that proceeded to their next destination.

After Bounty, their next port of call was Erdatta, a Voxxan colony world, then Voxxa itself. Then they started looping back via another Voxxan colony, a Federation relay station, a Terran mining colony, then finally back to Earth. Aside from the air scrubber which Burningbright and M'Anissa'tk successfully repaired, systems on the *Phoenix* performed flawlessly, and the crew were now operating just as well. M'Rarrtikar reported a very profitable trip which Martin was able to apply to repaying part of his debt. He gave the crew two days R&R before they had to leave for their next voyage. Nobody realised that they had one unaccounted for passenger though.

*** 2 February 2333 ***

Anastasiya had discovered the mouse morph when a routine security scan of a crate had revealed the presence of anomalous contents. The tiger had hauled the short, slightly zaftig girl dressed in a comfortable pair of leisure overalls, up to the captain's cabin where a bemused Martin had interrogated her.

"Just what do you think you were doing? You surely didn't think you could get away with stowing away? You'd have had to leave that crate long before we got to our next destination."

"I didn't have to stay hidden for the entire trip," the mouse explained. "Only for as long as it took for it to be too late to turn back."

Martin had to admit that she had a point – there was no way that they would have turned back once they were under warp for their

Art © Jenner

destination. "Okay, you're right, but how the hell did you avoid detection until now? Security at the spaceport isn't *that* lax."

"I had help."

"And..." Martin prompted.

"And I'm not saying any more. My helper doesn't deserve any repercussions for my actions."

"That's a matter of opinion, but it's not my place to do the job of law enforcement at the port. However, it is my job to look after the welfare of this ship. So why were you trying to stow away? And don't just say – 'to get to Chakona'."

"But that is half my reason anyway," she replied as if it was perfectly reasonable. "The other half is that I want to get away from some people."

Martin frowned. "Are you in trouble?"

"Not yet," the mouse replied with an impudent grin.

"What do you mean by that?"

"It means that my parents would hit the roof if they find out."

"What do you mean 'if'? We'll be taking you back down on the next shuttle and handing you over to Port Security. I doubt that they'll be slow to let your parents know."

"I'm hoping that you won't do that. In fact, I'm hoping that you'll let me stay on."

That surprised Martin. "Now why would I do that?"

"Because I'm eighteen and old enough to make my own decisions, and I'm prepared to work my passage. Also because you'd screw up my life if you send me back."

She gave Martin her best wide-eyed helpless waif look, which might have worked a lot better if she wasn't so well fed and sexy.

Martin sighed. "Alright, let's assume that you may have some skills that I might want. I'd still like to know why I would be doing you such a disfavour by putting you off my ship."

The mouse grimaced. "Because if you do, my parents will force me to marry Edward."

That sounded like a terribly familiar story to Martin. "So you don't like the guy, and you reckon that leaving the planet is your best alternative? Surely you could just leave town?"

"Oh no, I really like Edward – he's a genuinely nice guy. I've known him for years."

Martin was confused. "Then why are you avoiding marriage so drastically?"

"Captain, if I'm going to marry anyone, it's going to be to the *fem* of *my* choice."

"Oh, you're gay. Sorry, I should have thought about that

possibility. Still, there's no need to leave the planet just for that."

"It is if your name is Penelope Windsor."

Martin's eyebrows raised in surprise. "Windsor? As in Windsor Imports? You're the daughter of the owners of one of the biggest import companies on Earth?"

"Yep, that's me," Penelope said with a grin. "And Dad has quite a long reach when he tries."

"I know – my father deals with him big time, and now he's one of *my* clients also. Now I'm beginning to see where that inside help came from. It also makes me a bit nervous about doing anything that might harm our business relationship."

"Even if the girl you found was named Penny Lane?" Penelope asked ingenuously.

"Huh? What do you mean?"

Penelope reached inside her coveralls, pulled out an ID card, and handed it to Martin. He looked at it and saw the name 'Penny Lane' printed next to Penelope's picture.

Martin looked at the mouse. "If I put this into a reader, I'm betting that I'll get a really good fake ID, won't I?"

Penelope's grin never faded. "Yep."

Martin rolled his eyes. "OK, so why Chakona?"

"Why not? I've always wanted to go there, and I should be able to make a new start for myself, and not as Daddy's little girl."

Martin had to admire her spirit, and it reminded him of his own desires to break free of the mould and do his own thing. Still, there were financial considerations. "So what can you do to earn your passage? And how are you planning to pay for the food that you'll consume, plus all the other expenses?"

"Oh, that's not a problem." She took another object out of her pocket and showed it to the coyote. "I may not be able to take a regular commercial passenger service because Daddy would track me down in an instant, but I certainly could afford it. This e-cash card has a large stash of Fedcreds on it – quite untraceable. I'm sure that we can come to some arrangement."

"No doubt we can," Martin said drily. "But what can you do for us? I can't take you on as a paying passenger – I won't fake the paperwork for that. An unknown stowaway has to work for her keep though."

"I'm an entertainer. I play the keyboard and sing. I tell jokes and really good stories. I'm a great game partner. Try me and see!" Penelope said enthusiastically.

Martin grinned. "I can see why your father's plans didn't fit you. Are you *sure* you're his daughter? You sure don't sound like the child of a big businessman."

Penny nodded rapidly, her smile never fading.

Martin could not help but be amused by her unwavering cheerfulness, and he figured that she might just work out after all. "Okay, you've managed to appeal to both my curiosity and my own dreams of independence. You can stay. I'll hold onto this e-cash card for now, and we'll work out expenses later."

"Thank you, Captain!" The mouse gave the coyote an unexpected hug.

"Um... yeah... don't do that, please," Martin said, acutely conscious of her plush breasts pressing up against him. He turned to Anastasiya who had been awaiting the verdict. "Anastasiya, let the record show that Ms Lane was discovered an hour or so after we went into warp. Now find her a spare cabin while we finish loading up. We don't want her spotted by anyone before we depart."

"Aye, Captain," Anastasiya replied with a grin.

And so that was how Penny started as the ship's Entertainment and Morale Officer. Her fake ID had been sufficient to gain her a visitor's visa at Chakona, but Martin had advised her that if she wanted to try for residency, it would never hold up under the closer scrutiny. The point had become moot however when the girl had formally requested to stay on as regular crew. By then she had so enamoured herself with the rest of the crew that Martin would have been very hard pressed to say no. In fact, most of them had come with her when she had made the request. The only one who had been less than thrilled when Martin had agreed was Bethany, although not for the reason that the mouse constantly flouted formal procedures, or was less than satisfactory as regular crew. No, it was a lot more personal. Penny had developed a crush on the flustered vixen despite being informed that she was firmly heterosexual only. Martin was constantly amused by the fact that the normally unflappable commander was nearly helpless before the cuteness onslaught of the little mouse. As much as he valued his First Officer, sometimes he reckoned that she needed to have her cool exterior rocked a bit, and that was best done by someone who didn't directly affect the running of the ship.

*** 8 May 2333 ***

Phoenix completed another voyage without incident, along with another nice profit margin. M'Rarrtikar was able to report that Martin was well within the parameters of paying off his debt within the stipulated time, and that pleased the coyote greatly. The one sour note was that the workload on the crew was beginning to show on a few of them. *Phoenix* needed a couple more personnel to relieve that pressure, but Martin's budget did not really have sufficient margin to allow him to hire more people yet. He wanted to, but until his debt was repaid, he could not take the risk. There was too much to lose if he came up short. Unexpectedly, a solution presented itself from a surprising source, although it did leave him feeling bemused at first.

Martin had been in his cabin working on his contacts in order to secure more cargo contracts when Bethany let him know that if he could spare a moment, he had important visitors. He told her to send them up, and he went to meet them as they emerged from the translift. One of them was in Star Fleet uniform – a jaguar fem – no, a herm, he noticed. Shi was accompanied by two incredibly cute fennec fox morph children – about twelve years old, he estimated. The only thing wrong was that Martin happened to know that there weren't any fennec fox morphs on Earth.

"Captain Yote, I presume?" the jaguar asked.

"That would be me," he confirmed as he held out his hand to shake hirs.

"My name is Commander Aileen Ramirez, and we come to you with a request from the Federation Council."

Martin's eyes rose in surprise. "What on Earth, or anywhere else for that matter, could I do for the Council?"

"First let me introduce these people," Aileen said as shi gestured to hir companions. "These are Loander and Presaith, representatives from the planet Nameth. They are Faleshkarti, an alien herm species, not Terran morphs."

Martin smiled at the Faleshkarti and said, "No offence intended, but I have never heard of that world or your species, and aren't you a bit young to be representatives?"

The one identified as Loander replied in softly accented but precise Terranglo, "It is hardly surprising that you have not heard of us as we have only recently opened up relationships with the Federation. As for our apparent age, while you are correct when you say that we are young, in fact we are both at the beginning of our professional careers, and at a very normal age for our kind."

"You will find them to be quite remarkable," Aileen added.

"Why would I find them anything at all? What did you come to see me for?" Martin asked.

Aileen replied, "The Faleshkarti people have requested to send a number of their kind out into the Federation to observe and assess how they might fit in. We would be grateful if you could take Loander and

Art © Kacey Miyagami

Presaith with you so that they can experience shipboard culture and how you interact with other worlds."

Martin was a little puzzled. "Isn't a small commercial vessel an odd choice? Wouldn't they be better off going in a Star Fleet ship or visiting communities on Earth?"

"Believe me, Captain," Presaith answered, "there are plenty more of our kind doing precisely that and many other tasks. Loander and I specifically requested a ship of your nature because it fits in best with our skills and desires."

"Not that I'm agreeing to take you on, but what kind of skills are we talking about?"

"I am a starship systems engineer, and Loander is a comptech."

Martin's ears pricked up at the latter. "We don't have a specialty comptech amongst the crew, and we have a software glitch that has been giving us problems. Let's see if you can do anything about that, and then maybe I'll consider taking you on. You are familiar with Terran computer systems, I hope?"

"Of course," Loander replied, "or else there would not be much point in applying for the post, would there?"

Martin noted that while they looked like children, they sure didn't talk like them. "Hmm... right. Come with me."

Martin led them all up to the bridge and showed Loander one of the workstations. He logged into the station and pulled up one of the system programs. "This program has been regularly crashing despite being reinstalled. Our engineer has determined that the equipment that it monitors is in perfect working order, so that doesn't seem to be triggering it. Although we have competent comp operators, we have no programming experts, so we haven't tracked down the problem as yet. Do you think that you can do anything with it?"

Loander nodded. "If the situation is exactly as you described it, I can find it," shi replied confidently.

"Good luck," Martin said, then turned his attention to Presaith. "Now you said that you are a starship systems engineer; what kind of experience have you had with Federation systems?"

"Not a lot," Presaith admitted, "but I am fully rated on Faleshkarti systems, and I can't see a problem learning the differences."

Martin was sceptical that a twelve year old could be a fully rated engineer, but he was not about to say that in front of the Star Fleet rep. He said to Ceres who had been standing watch on the bridge, "Keep an eye on our Faleshkarti guest, Ceres, while I take the others to meet R'Murran."

"Aye, sir," the Starwalker replied.

Martin led Presaith and Ramirez down to Main Engineering where he introduced them to his Caitian engineer.

R'Murran was as surprised as Martin had been, but a tad less sceptical. "Let's see your qualifications," he said.

Presaith handed him hir PADD which listed hir qualifications with the Federation equivalents next to them. After scrolling through them, he said, "These look fine, but let's see what you're like in practice. Computer! Set controls to training mode alpha."

"*Training mode alpha engaged*," came the neutral voice of the ship's A.I.

"Alright, Shir Presaith," R'Murran said as he tapped a few buttons, his claws tik-tik-tikking over the surface of the controls, "I'm setting up an emergency cold start scenario. Show us what you can do to get us going with the least amount of harm to the ship."

Presaith nodded and looked over the controls to familiarise hirself with the layout. Although they were set a bit high for someone of hir stature, shi acted confidently and with little difficulty. After several minutes shi said, "Done – optimal output reached."

R'Murran smiled. "That was very well done considering that you are new to this ship's systems. I'll set up another scenario. Once again his short fingers played expertly over the keys to set up the problem, and once again the Faleshkarti handled it with little difficulty.

R'Murran turned to Martin and said, "For someone who has never laid eyes on this ship's particular design, Presaith did extremely well. I'm confident that with training, shi could almost be at my level in a short time. Captain – I know that we've been a bit shorthanded due to economic considerations, but I would really like to take hir on as Engineer 2nd."

Martin nodded. "I'll take your request into consideration, Chief." He turned to the others and said, "Let's go back to the bridge and see how Loander is doing."

Martin was surprised to see that Loander was not at the computer station, but chatting with Ceres instead who seemed to be showing hir some of the other bridge equipment. "Was there some sort of problem holding you up, Shir Loander?"

"No, Captain. I have found and fixed your software bug already."

The corner of Martin's muzzle twitched. "You… fixed it already? You went through that complex program and found in under 45 minutes what my crew had failed to find in days?"

"Yes, sir. I found the problem in about thirteen minutes and wrote and applied the fix by about twenty. I've been conversing with your astrogator about your voyages since then. I hope that you will seriously consider taking us on so that we can share your travels."

Martin blinked in mute astonishment for a long moment, then

107

asked, "Are you sure that you're only twelve years old?"

Loander nodded. "In Terran years, yes."

Martin absorbed that, then shook off the shock. "Shir Loander, Shir Presaith, Commander Ramirez – please accompany me to my office."

Once back in his office, he sat behind his desk and waited for the others to make themselves comfortable. Then he said, "Okay, what's the deal, Commander? If you've checked us out thoroughly, you should know that we're a very new outfit, and while we're making very nice progress, we still aren't in the black and won't be for at least a couple more voyages. R'Murran's request notwithstanding, I really can't afford to put on two new crewmembers as yet, especially ones as highly competent as these two obviously are. We're stretched a fair bit, but almost everyone is cross-trained and can cover for other people now. So even if I wanted to, putting these two on the payroll would not be a good idea until I can afford a larger crew."

Ramirez replied, "Yes, we did check you out and know exactly how you stand, but we have an offer for you. The Federation Council will pay Loander and Presaith a wage commensurate with their positions on your ship. You will provide meals, accommodation, equipment and uniforms. This agreement will be effective for one complete round trip after which the situation will be re-evaluated."

Martin leaned back in his chair, clasping his hands behind his head. With a sly smile, he said, "Commander, let's talk details."

The Faleshkarti had proven to be excellent additions to the crew, although even now Martin still had a sense of unreality of having two children fulfilling their jobs in the manner of adults twice their age. That voyage had done much to enlighten Martin, however, and he empathised with their race's plight – a race that lost much of its intelligence when they reached sexual maturity and entered their breeding phase. He also had to admit to being a little relieved to find out that they weren't really a super-intelligent species – they just got up to that level much faster, but then plateaued at that level that much sooner, with just a few years of productive life before they lost it again. Martin fervently hoped that the Federation scientists would quickly find a solution to their dilemma. They both still had several years leeway though, and Martin was more than happy to sign them up for another tour of duty after the *Phoenix* completed its third voyage. Commander Ramirez had made it plain though that if he wanted to continue using their services after that, the Federation would no longer be paying their wages.

Martin had been bemused to see them acquire a liking for hot chocolate and start spending their free time with Katarina. Despite their intelligence, sense of responsibility, and professionalism, in the end the Faleshkarti were still children, and they identified best with the tiger child who, despite being a couple of years younger, already was much taller than the fennec-like aliens. Anastasiya and Valentina were happy for the Faleshkarti to be hir friends as they seemed to inspire their child to higher achievements. Valentina even seemed a bit maternal towards them. This somewhat puzzled Loander and Presaith as they had absolutely no experience with the phenomenon. No Faleshkarti knew hir parents, nor was brought up in anything that Terrans would recognise as a family. However, they found it pleasant and tolerated the tiger's attentions. Like everyone else, they had found their place in the crew, and they in turn accepted them.

Chapter 3: Passenger Peril

*** 3 August 2333 ***

It was time to depart for their fourth voyage, and Martin finished off the remainder of his coffee. With the last of the crew now present in the mess hall, barring M'Resk, he could start the pre-flight ritual that had evolved over the past voyages. He nodded at Bethany who had been awaiting his signal. At a touch on her PADD, the bosun's pipe blew in the room, bringing conversations to a halt.

Martin said, "M'Rarrtikar – have all our passengers arrived and been checked in?"

The Caitian replied, "Yes, Captain. M'Resk reports that they are all settled into their cabins for take-off. We have one extra – one of the passengers brought along his son at the last moment. I charged him full fare plus a late booking fee."

Martin nodded. "A bit more income won't go astray. Risha, have we got adequate reserves to feed an extra mouth for the duration of his stay aboard?"

Risha replied, "The passenger was booked just early enough for me to get some extra supplies loaded onto the last shuttle at the last moment, so we still have the normal optimum reserves."

"Excellent. Valentina – what is the cargo situation like?"

"All freight is stored and secured," the tiger replied. "We are expecting priority parcel still though. Is due by courier drone within ten minutes – five minutes before lock-down."

"That's cutting it a bit fine, but it's a high priority item and they've paid in advance, so we'll wait until the last moment. We cannot afford a fine for missing our departure slot though, so keep a close eye on the situation." Martin was aware of what the item was, but part of the contract stipulated total confidentiality as well as urgency. Only he, Bethany, and the two tigers knew exactly what they were carrying, and why it was being delivered so close to deadline.

Valentina nodded and turned hir attention to hir PADD to do precisely that.

"Department heads – sit-rep please," Martin continued.

"Everything's in the green, sir. We're good to go," reported R'Murran.

Baxter said, "Scheduled diagnostics and maintenance completed on navigation and helm systems. All nominal, Captain."

Burningbright spoke next. "Environmental systems flushed and replenished; all is green across the board."

Anastasiya was the last to report. "All cargo scanned. No suspicious goods or devices detected. No stowaways found," shi added with a wink to Penny. "All ports secured except for main cargo hatch which is awaiting priority parcel."

"Which is just arriving," Valentina interjected. "Pardon me, Captain, while I take delivery."

Martin nodded and said, "Go." As the tiger left, he continued, "My friends, this voyage will mark a milestone for our young business. With the successful completion of it, Phoenix Incorporated will be halfway to the goal of being in the black, well within the time I allocated, and that means well deserved bonuses for all."

There was a chorus of cheers at that news.

Martin continued, "We have been fortunate to acquire some lucrative contracts, but it has been your hard work and dedication that has been a large factor in our success, and I thank you all. Now let's make this the best voyage yet. Hotfoot has agreed to cook up something special for the main meal tonight, but until then, may your gods smile upon us as we get under way. Everybody to stations – we depart in eighteen minutes."

Exactly on schedule, the control tower gave *Phoenix* clearance to depart from its slot at Earth's gateway station, and make its way along the carefully plotted route through the crowded spaceways around that world. Once clear of Earth's gravity well, the starship's warp drive engaged to begin its historic fourth voyage.

The first hint that anything was abnormal did not come from Anastasiya. In fact it came from the least likely source on the ship. Yote was in his office and had just completed the day's paperwork. He turned the chair around and leaned back to relax while watching the stars streak past in the viewport. It was all an illusion of course – even at top warp speed, stars simply did not go by that fast. In fact it was an artefact of hyperspace that was not really fully understood. There was some speculation that they were stellar objects in that plane of reality, although they didn't seem to show on scans other than as purely visible light. No one had actually encountered those objects – at least none that survived to tell about it. Nevertheless, they gave people the sense of moving fast, and they were pretty and relaxing to watch.

There was a knock behind him, followed by a voice that said, "Pardon me, Captain, but could I have a word with you?"

Martin swivelled around to see Penny standing in the doorway. "Come in, Penny. What's bothering you?"

The mouse entered, and Martin could already see that the normally irrepressible girl was upset about something.

"It's the passengers, sir – there's something odd about them."

"Odd? In what way?"

"Well... normally they spend the first couple of days chatting, getting to know each other. There's not a whole lot to do besides watching vids or watching one of my little performances."

"And they're not this time?"

"That's just it – it's as if they're carefully avoiding unnecessary public contact. The passenger bookings suggest that they have nothing to do with each other, but I still have this odd feeling... I can't really put my finger on it."

Martin considered her words. "It's only your third voyage – heck, it's only the fourth for many of us. There are plenty of circumstances that we haven't encountered yet. We'll probably run across many unusual situations in the years to come. I think we'll just have to wait a while and see how things work out."

"Oh... okay." Despite accepting his words, Penny didn't move to leave.

"That isn't what's really bothering you, is it? You can tell me, Penny."

"It... it's something a lot more personal," she said hesitantly.

"I'm prepared to listen if you really wish to tell me about it."

"It's that teen canimorph – the one that came along with his father at the last moment. He recognised me."

Martin frowned. "How is that possible?"

"His father works as a security guard at the spaceport. The boy was visiting his father there on one of the days that my father dragged me along in the vain hope of getting me interested in his business. I was wearing a cheesy dress at the time, so I tried to persuade him that he'd gotten the wrong person, but he was adamant that he was certain that it was me. And Captain – he says that there's a reward posted for information leading to finding me."

"Damn. So the guy wants to claim the reward. That will make things awkward when we get back to Earth."

"It's worse than that, Captain. He wants to blackmail me."

"**What?**" Martin was outraged. "I'll kick the bastard off the ship at the next port! Wait – what could he be blackmailing you for if not the reward money?"

The mouse remained unhappily silent.

Martin put two and two together and got even more pissed off. "Did you try telling him that you're a lesbian?"

Penny nodded. "He said, 'Doesn't matter to me. You're going to be my bitch for the rest of the trip, or else daddy gets a message for where to find his stray lamb.' He then left me to think about it. I think that he's confident that I'll give in."

"I think that he's wrong. Why didn't you tell him flat out to go to hell?"

"I didn't want to cause you trouble with the passengers, or with my father if I did that," Penny said earnestly.

Martin got out from behind his desk and gathered Penny into an embrace. "Oh, Penny dear, I'd rather take on a hundred such people than let any of *my* people come to harm. You're more than just crew to me, y'know?"

Penny sniffled and nodded. She hugged Martin back and said, "Thanks, Captain."

"Now go back and give that guy your answer – preferably one that involves kicking him in the balls. Don't tell anyone that I told you to do that though. I suggest that you take Anastasiya along with you in case he doesn't like your answer and tries to cause more trouble."

Penny's smile was returning. "I'll do that, Captain." The mouse girl left with the bounce back in her step.

Martin sat back down at his desk and considered what Penny had told him. Despite his reassurances, he was a little perturbed by the news. In the few times that he had met them, the passengers had given him a vibe that he didn't like, but just as with Penny, he couldn't put his finger on it. Penny's observations only added weight to that feeling. He would have to have a word with Anastasiya after shi dealt with dog boy.

Penny contacted Anastasiya and arranged to meet hir at hir office. There she explained the situation and the captain's recommendation.

Anastasiya nodded. "I will wait out of sight. If boy is smart and let's things lie, I will let the matter stay just between you two. If not smart, I will be there if you need me."

"Thanks. He's usually in the passenger lounge. Let's get this over with," Penny said determinedly.

The German Shepherd morph was alone in the passenger lounge, playing a video game. He glanced up as Penny entered, and he grinned. "Finally realised that you'd better play things my way?" he asked as he paused the game and got up out of his chair.

"Oh yes, I've come to let you know my answer," Penny said as she reached up as if to embrace the boy. Instead of hugging him though, she pulled him in closer and kneed him in the groin as hard as she could.

With an anguished cry, the dog collapsed n the floor in agony.

"I hope that I made my position crystal clear," Penny said sweetly. "Don't harass me any more, understand?" Without bothering to wait for an answer, she turned and exited the lounge.

Unfortunately she did not see the boy struggle to his feet while grimacing in pain. He stumbled after the mouse and caught up to her while she was waiting for the trans-lift. He took her by surprise, grabbing her by her jumpsuit and spinning her around to face him. "Nobody does that to me, you bitch! Now learn your place!" he yelled hoarsely. He hauled back his fist to bash the terrified mouse, only to have it stopped in mid-swing. His arm was yanked painfully behind his back, and he was hoisted up until his toes lifted from the floor.

"So you like it rough, boy?" came Anastasiya's growl. "I like it rough too, and I think I'd like to play with you for a while. Do you like that idea, boy? Are you man enough for me?"

The dog knew who and what Anastasiya was, and he went cold with fear. "No!" he gasped.

"Pity – you could have been such fun. If you don't like it so much, why are you bothering my friend, Penny? I don't like it when my friends get hurt. I like to hurt people who hurt my friends."

"Pl... please, don't," he begged as Anastasiya's grip tightened and hir claws dug in to emphasise hir words.

"Foolish child," Anastasiya said contemptuously, releasing the painful grip that shi had on him.

He collapsed on the floor, only to be hauled back up to his feet by his shirt. The tiger then shoved him into the waiting trans-lift, saying, "I have good room waiting for you. Ship's brig is nice and clean and never been used."

The tiger came by Martin's office to report the incident, leaving nothing out.

Martin thanked Anastasiya for hir good work, and then added, "I'm going to throw the bastard off the ship at Elantra. I don't care that it's a small colony that hardly gets any passing traffic – it'll be his problem to find his way to his destination, or back home. I just want him off our ship as soon as possible. Better inform his father, of course."

"I will make arrangements," Anastasiya assured him.

Martin wasn't surprised to see the adult German Shepherd barging into his office shortly thereafter.

"What the hell do you think you're doing to my son?" the dog yelled without preamble.

Martin noted that he was a rough-looking character with a torn ear. Although none of the passengers who chose to travel on a tramp vessel like the Phoenix had much money, this person's dress was a distinct notch below the norm, and he was coming across as a homeless bum rather than a thrifty traveller.

"Your son sexually assaulted one of my crew, Mr Shepherd," Martin said coldly. "He has been put under arrest and will remain in the brig until I deliver him to the authorities at Elantra."

"You can't do that! He has to come with me to the Landrau colony."

"I am the ultimate authority on this ship, Mr Shepherd. I can and have the right to eject any undesirables. Your son will *not* be going to the Landrau colony with you."

"You can't do that! He's got a ticket through to the Landrau colony. You're obligated to take him there. I'll sue you if you don't!"

"You should have read your copy of the rules and conditions, Mr Shepherd. You haven't a legal leg to stand on. However, if you don't wish to be parted with your son, I will quite gladly put you off at Elantra also." Martin already had just about enough of this obnoxious morph.

"What? This is outrageous! I'm warning you, Captain – don't cross with me!" The dog leaned over the desk with his teeth bared in a snarl.

"And I'm warning you, Mr Shepherd, that I won't tolerate any misbehaviour on my ship. You are on the brink of joining your son at this rate."

"Don't lecture me, you smug coyote! I've had to deal with your kind before – you and your arrogance. Think you're better than me?" He started poking Martin in the chest quite forcefully. "I'm onto you. You're just another stuck-up son of a bitch to me, and if you don't let my son out of the brig right now, I'm gonna make you regret the day you were whelped!"

Martin had taken all that he was going to. "Anastasiya, would you take Mr Shepherd to see his son and acquaint him with the facilities there?"

"With pleasure, Captain." The tiger grabbed Shepherd's shoulder in a vicelike grip.

Shepherd winced in pain, but as he was dragged off, he defiantly yelled, "You're going to regret this, you bastard! And sooner than you think!" He was hauled out of sight, but his ranting continued. "And I won't be forgetting you either, you cock-bitch freak. Arrgh!"

Martin smirked. Somehow he felt that Anastasiya hadn't appreciated Shepherd's comment. He hoped that shi didn't get *too* rough with the fool. He didn't want to be explaining too much to the Elantra authorities.

*** 15 August 2333 ***

With eight days to go before they reached the Elantra colony, Martin was glad that everything seemed to settle down to normalcy. The passengers still seemed unusually stand-offish, but nobody gave them trouble like the Shepherds did. He reviewed the passenger list – five morphs, two Voxxans and a human – all bound for the Landrau colony on business of some kind. Only the human had booked onwards to their next port of call, another colony world, and then to Voxxa. The others would have to wait until another ship came along eventually to either go back home or to another destination. The Landrau colony did not have regular shipping as yet, and starships like *Phoenix* which were contracted by the Star Corps to supply them, were almost the only means of getting to and from the world. If the passengers had done their homework though, their stay might be a minimal one if another starship from another planet arrived soon after *Phoenix*. That was their problem though.

Eleven days passed without incident. When they were still twelve hours out from Landrau, Martin took himself off the bridge, leaving Ceres on watch with Baxter at the helm. He headed off to the mess hall to see what Hotfoot had available for supper before he retired for the 'night'. As he exited the bridge into the passageway to the trans-lift, he came across an odd sight. Ner'ritn was patiently feeding a cable from a reel into an open service conduit. The cable appeared to be being pulled by something unseen.

"What are you up to at this time?" Martin enquired curiously of the Caitian girl.

"Oh, hi Captain. I'm helping Momma M'Anissa'tk replace a faulty sensor cable," Ner'ritn replied without halting the careful feeding.

"Well, it's a sure bet that your mother isn't in that tiny passage, so how's it being pulled through?"

"Menalippe is in the conduit. Mom was cursing the narrow service ducts when Menalippe walked by and volunteered to help."

Martin nodded. "Makes sense – she's the smallest of any of us, and very flexible. You should get the job done in half the time."

"That's the idea."

"OK, carry on, but don't make it too late. It's your bedtime, I know. As for me, my stomach is reminding me that it's time for me to eat.

Good night, Ner'ritn."

"G'night, Captain."

Martin continued onto the mess hall where he found that Hotfoot had been forewarned that he was on his way, and shi had a meal served up and ready for him. The two Voxxan passengers were there also. One looked up at Martin, nodded in curt greeting, and then turned his attention back to his food. Martin was about halfway through his meal when that Voxxan got up from his table and walked over to Martin's.

"I believe that you have two passengers in the brig?" he asked without preamble.

Martin glanced up. "Mr Kavenak, isn't it? Yes, I do. Is that a problem?"

"Yes it is, Captain. I would like it if you would release them immediately, please."

"Sorry, but that isn't going to happen until we reach Elantra."

"I'm afraid that I am going to have to insist."

Martin suddenly found himself staring at the business end of a weapon. It was a curiously makeshift-looking device, but Martin was instantly sure that it was nonetheless effective. He noticed that the other Voxxan had gotten up and pulled out a similar weapon, and moved to cover the entrance to the galley. There would be no heroics coming from Hotfoot. He glared up at Kavenak. "How did you get those aboard my ship?" All people passing through the spaceport were automatically scanned for weapons, but most starships did their own additional scans for full security. Martin had no reason to believe that Anastasiya had lapsed in hir thoroughness.

"That's not important. What is important is releasing your two prisoners and forgetting about leaving them on Elantra."

"Why are they so important to you?"

"Stop asking questions and get up. We're going to the brig now, and you're going to behave yourself or else. Hand over your comm and don't try any tricks. Revendi, bring along the chakat."

Hotfoot was very upset at being rousted from hir kitchen at gunpoint. The fact that shi was obviously being used to ensure Martin's good behaviour disturbed both of them. They left the mess hall and headed for the trans-lift. They called a car, and moments later they were herded inside and headed up a few decks into parts of the ship that were out of bounds to the passengers. Biometric controls normally kept them out but allowed the crew to have easy access. Unfortunately it also let in anyone who was with the crew.

Anastasiya's office was next to the brig, of course. Martin hoped that the tiger had retired for the night, but it was not to be. Shi was sitting at hir desk, working on something, but as soon as Martin entered, shi turned hir attention to him. Shi immediately sensed something was wrong and threw hirself out of hir chair in an effort to take Kavenak by surprise... and amazingly succeeded. One powerful hand pushed his weapon aside as the other went to deal him an incapacitating blow. Unfortunately shi had not yet seen his companion. Revendi's weapon hummed and Anastasiya screamed and dropped like a sack of potatoes.

"Anastasiya!" Martin cried out, bending over the tiger to check hir out.

"Leave hir!" commanded Kavenak. "Shi's just stunned. Now release Shepherd or I will shoot hir again. That will be enough to stop hir heart."

Martin glared at the Voxxan, but did as he was told. He led them into an adjacent room which had three cells. Father and son Shepherd had been given the luxury of a cell each. Martin went to the control panel and released the electronic locks on both.

The adult dog rushed out of his cell and gave Martin a roundhouse punch to the face. Martin was knocked to the floor, dizzy and in pain from the huge blow. "That's for locking me up, you son of bitch!" Then he turned to Kavenak. "What the hell took you so long to free me?"

"Shut up!" Kavenak snarled. "You got yourself into this mess. You and your idiot son have nearly ruined our plans. If we didn't need to keep this out of the authorities' view, I would have cheerfully left you to your fate. Now try to be of some use and lock this chakat up. The tiger is unconscious in the next room. Drag hir into a cell also before shi comes to. Captain – you're coming with me."

Martin had no choice – the nerve-shock from the heavy-duty stunner at his back was just as capable of killing also, as Kavenak had threatened to do to Anastasiya. As they headed out, he noticed Revendi at the controls of the security systems, and he suspected that the Voxxan was disabling many of the measures that prevented their free movement, such as the trans-lift and compartment locks. As they continued out towards the trans-lift, he asked, "What do you intend to do with us?" He didn't really expect a reply, but he got one anyway.

"For now, you will all get to enjoy the comforts of your cells. When we get to Elantra, we will need you to reassure the authorities that everything is okay. Then you will proceed to Landrau as planned."

"We've got cargo to unload there, What about that? If we don't, it will look very suspicious."

"You'll unload that too, and you'll even have some help."

"Help? How so?"

Just then the trans-lift arrived and the doors opened. One of the other passengers, a European lynx morph, was inside and also brandishing a stunner, which was pointed at Penny and M'Resk.

Kavenak stood aside to let the others out. "The brig is ready for those two, Anders," he told the lynx. "Hurry back – we need to round up the entire crew before someone can raise the alarm."

"Right," the lynx replied, and they headed off while Kavenak and Martin entered the trans-lift.

Penny and M'Resk arrived at the brig just as the two Shepherds had finished dragging Anastasiya into a cell. The younger grinned nastily when he saw Penny and grabbed her arm.

"I told you that you'll be my bitch, Now I'm going to make up for lost time. OW!" His father had backhanded him on the muzzle, and his eyes watered from the pain.

"Can't you keep your cock in your pants for even five minutes? I'm sorry I let you talk me into bringing you along. If it wasn't for you, we wouldn't be in this clusterfuck right now. Put her in the cells with the others! There'll be time for that later."

The younger Shepherd glared hatefully at his father, but did as he was told.

"Stay here and help put the prisoners in the cells when they're brought in," the elder Shepherd ordered. "I'm going back to join the others."

Meanwhile Martin and the two Voxxans had reached the bridge. The extra security there could not be overridden from Anastasiya's desk, so Martin was needed to access it. The coyote had been trying to think of a way out of their predicament without success, and he was distressed that he was being forced to put the rest of his crew in danger also.

Ceres was surprised to see Martin return. "Is there a problem, Captain? Why are these passengers on the bridge?"

"Yes, there's a problem, Ceres, and they are it. Martin indicated the weapons that now covered the foxtaur and human too.

Kavenak said, "Don't try anything stupid, and no one will get hurt. Captain, I want you to disable all the security systems and release the controls to us. I'm familiar with the procedures, so don't try any tricks. Try to send out a warning to your crew and I will kill you, and then get Blackie to do it instead."

Martin had no choice but to take that statement at face value, and he reluctantly did as he was told, knowing that it would leave the entire crew vulnerable and helpless. "It's done."

Kavenak activated his wrist-comm. "Kavenak here – all the security has been disabled. Take over Engineering and round up the remainder of the crew." He turned his attention back to the others. "Put everything onto full automatic. You won't be needed here until just before we get to Elantra. Everyone off the bridge now!"

They were herded back to the brig where they found R'Murran and Presaith already incarcerated. They looked questioningly at Martin who could only shrug helplessly. He presumed that the hijackers must have been waiting outside of Engineering for the word to be given in order for them to have been rounded up so quickly. He was immensely relieved though to see that Anastasiya had recovered consciousness, although shi seemed to be nursing a huge headache.

Gradually the rest of the crew and all the children were being rounded up and crammed in the cells with the rest. The hijackers swept the ship deck by deck, rousting some of the ship's complement from their beds. Zelkie, Burningbright and all the chakat cubs came in all at once with three people covering them with their weapons. Zelkie had a grim look on hir face and was carrying an unconscious Candycane on hir back. When the villains had left Martin was able to ask what had happened.

"They caught us totally by surprise, Captain," Zelkie explained. "We were all asleep in our common room when suddenly those three were in our room and trying to wake us up."

Martin knew how deeply chakats slept once they settled down, so it was unsurprising that they had had a hard time rousing them.

Zelkie continued, "The wolf decided to 'encourage' me by pistol-whipping me," shi said as shi touched hir fingers to a bright red stain on the fur on hir forehead. "Between being too dizzy from the blow, and with too many guns pointed at the cubs, I wasn't able to fight back."

"What happened to Candycane?"

"Shi attacked the wolf after he hit me. Shi was knocked unconscious for hir effort. I couldn't protect hir," Zelkie said bitterly.

"It's okay, Zelkie. No one is blaming you. If you want to blame anyone, blame me. I disabled all the security, including the locks on your cabins."

"Why did you... no... you had a gun pointed at you too. I can't blame you for that, Captain."

"But I will take responsibility for it. All is not lost though. We just need to bide our time for now."

"Not much else we *can* do."

Next to arrive were Risha along with the Caitian children – Keera and Kannekin. Risha looked dishevelled and seriously pissed-off – the angriest Martin had ever seen the usually placid cougar. Keera wasn't happy, but she was relatively calm. Young Kannekin though was really upset, and he was sniffling and generally not listening too well to what their captors were telling them to do. The wolf bellowed in anger and shoved Kannekin towards the cells. He stumbled, fell hard, and started bawling, tears flooding his eyes.

There was a scream of rage from the cougar, and she leapt upon the wolf, heedless of the weapons trained upon her. Caught unawares, the lynx didn't bring his weapon to bear upon her until too late, and she had the wolf between them as a shield. She grabbed both of the wolf's wrists in two of her hands, restraining them while the other two rained blows on his face and abdomen. Her claws opened long gashes in his fur before the lynx was able to get around and shoot her. Risha yowled in agony for a brief moment and then collapsed. The wolf swayed on his feet, almost joining Risha on the floor. One eye was already swollen shut, and blood matted his fur in a couple of places.

The lynx cursed, unlocked the least crowded cell, and then stepped back a safe distance. "Get her and those kids into your cell – **now!**" he demanded as he waved his weapon menacingly.

M'Anissa'tk, who was already in that cell, came out to gather up Kannekin, while Ceres and Baxter gathered up the unconscious cougar.

The lynx reactivated the lock and then took the time to examine the wolf. "Shit, Marko – you're a mess!"

The wolf growled and seemed to be recovering. He pushed the lynx away. "I'll be okay, Anders. Just let me at that cunt!"

Anders restrained Marko. "Don't! Kavenak's running this show, and he says that they stay unharmed."

The wolf snarled, but relented. However, as he turned to leave, he said, "I *will* get payback later though."

Eventually the cells were filled with the remainder of the crew, plus their one human passenger who was complaining bitterly about his mistreatment. Martin murmured to Burningbright who was in the cell with him, "'Bright, can you do a scan of that man? I need to know if he's genuinely a prisoner like us, or if he's a plant here to keep an eye on us."

Burningbright nodded and Martin addressed the man. "Mr Davies, are you alright?"

"Yeah, sure I am. Being dragged out of bed at gunpoint is the highlight of my trip."

Ignoring his sarcastic comment, Martin looked at Burningbright questioningly. The chakat gave him the thumbs-up sign. Satisfied with hir verdict, Martin said, "We're not too thrilled about it either, but hang in there, and we'll try to get you through this unscathed."

"Big promises from a guy behind bars," scoffed Shepherd Senior who had brought in the man and had paused to gloat.

"That reminds me," Martin said, turning his attention to the dog. "Kavenak never did explain how you got those weapons on board my

Art © Lis Boriss

ship." He was not sure if the dog would answer either, but it did not hurt to try fishing for information.

Shepherd looked smugly proud. "They're my invention. I used my knowledge of security scanners to create them. They came aboard in pieces which, when scanned, resembled other harmless items. The focusing crystals were encased in a scan-absorbent substance that masqueraded as packing material. The batteries were uncharged so that your scanners could not sense the high energy potential. All we had to do was bring the parts together, assemble them, and then charge them up. Piece of cake, really," he boasted.

Martin knew that fooling the sensors was not quite that easy, and yet this person had achieved it. He had to admire that skill even as he made a mental note to upgrade the scanners... if they lived through this. The dog's willingness to talk did not bode well for the crew's future – they knew too much.

"Enjoy your stay in the brig," Shepherd smirked. "If I remember, I might even bring you something to eat later." The dog then walked out, presumably to rejoin his fellow conspirators.

Martin was glad that the canine morph did not hang about. "It's about time we got left alone. Now we can start fighting back."

Davies stared in disbelief at Martin. "Fight back? We're all locked up – what the hell do you think we can do from in here?"

"More than you think, but first – does anyone know where Menalippe is?"

M'Anissa'tk replied, "If she's smart, she's still hiding in that service duct. I'm afraid I quite rudely slammed the cover down in her face when I realised what was happening. Hopefully she's figured out what's going on and stays safe."

Martin nodded. "Good. Now I know where everyone is, I can act more confidently. Once we get our comms back, we might be able to use her, seeing as our captors don't seem to be aware that she's on the crew."

"Menalippe has been working second shift with me, so I don't think she's met any of the passengers yet," explained Baxter. "I'm glad she's safe, and I hope that what you have in mind won't change that, Captain."

"Don't worry, Heywood, I plan to bring us *all* through unharmed. First priority – getting out of here. Zelkie – can you deactivate the cell locks?"

"Yes, Captain, if someone tells me what switch to hit."

Anastasiya said, "Look at panel that I am pointing at – see row of blue-lit buttons? Depress and hold any of those for two seconds."

As Martin and the others watched, all three buttons were depressed telekinetically, and after two seconds, they turned red and the cell doors opened.

"Told you we need biometric switches," Anastasiya commented as they eagerly exited the cells.

"But aren't you glad that they weren't in the budget?" Martin asked with a grin.

"Am glad that they didn't know Zelkie is a K5 Talent, or else they would have used disabler."

"True, but let's count our blessings. Everyone grab your comms." Martin picked up his from the pile on Anastasiya's desk where they had all been dumped. "Right now we have the advantage of surprise. We know exactly how many there are – seven including Shepherd's idiot son. I'm presuming that they have at least two or three competent spacers amongst them, as they couldn't count on us to cooperate with absolute certainty, so there are probably two on the bridge, and at least one down in Engineering.

"That still leaves two or three unaccounted for," Ceres pointed out.

"Not for long." Anastasiya keyed in a command into hir security system. The screens lit up with data and images. "Voxxan named Revendi and horse morph on bridge. Lynx in Engineering. Kavenak and wolf in Cargo Bay One. Two curs in recreation room."

"Shepherd has probably done his bit," Martin speculated. "Now he's just extra muscle when needed."

"Why are those two in the cargo bay?" M'Anissa'tk asked. "They've hijacked the whole ship, so why bother?"

"Probably because they know about our special consignment which is located there," Valentina guessed.

"'Tina..." Anastasiya began warningly.

Martin held up his hand. "It's okay. They've gone to far too much trouble to hijack a ship that would only give them a modest return for their efforts, which implies that they know that we have something of rare value aboard, and if *they* know, you might as well know also."

"You're talking about that secret consignment that Valentina wouldn't talk about, aren't you?" Zelkie guessed.

"Yes, and judging by how our pirate friends are homing in on the secure store, I'd say that the guess is confirmed. They're after the mind-matrix generator."

"The what?" Danson asked in confusion.

"It's what makes a Transporter more than an oversized replicator. Without it, you cannot send any person through it because they'd come out mindless at the other end. It's the Federation's most closely guarded secret. Places like the League of Non-Aligned Worlds reverse-engineered replicators long ago, but the creation of the mind-matrix generator was a major leap in science – literally a stroke of genius that has never been duplicated. The strategic value of the Transporter is enormous, and the knowledge of how to create one of those generators is fanatically guarded. The units themselves are sealed in such a way that any attempt to scan or tamper whatsoever will cause them to self-destruct into an unrecognisable mess. A working unit is worth a king's ransom to certain people."

"But I thought that pirates already have transporters?" M'Anissa'tk asked.

"Some do – ripped from their victims' ships. However, the matrix generators have a limited lifespan. After a set period, they become inactive. Legitimate operators can get theirs replaced; pirates end up with a big paperweight. The Landrau colony, which is where our unit is destined for, has to get in a special tech just to activate this one. He travels separately from the unit for security purposes though."

"If it needs to be activated, then what good is this unit to them?" Risha asked.

"Is simple," Anastasiya answered. "If they found out about shipment despite security, is most likely they know how to activate one, or arranging capture of tech also."

Martin nodded in agreement. "Indeed – there's no such thing as a perfect secret, although Federation safeguards are incredibly complex. Anyway, enough talk – it looks like Kavenak has discovered that they can't get into the secure store. That means that they will be coming back to get me to open it up for them. Anastasiya – let's prepare a little surprise for them."

"Already on it, Captain," Anastasiya replied as shi keyed the biometric sensor on the weapons locker. Shi passed out phasers to Martin, Oakwood, Valentina, Ceres, R'Murran and M'Anissa'tk.

"What about us?" Hotfoot asked when it became apparent that no more phasers were forthcoming.

"You have licence or Star Fleet training?" the tiger enquired. When it became apparent that none of the rest did, shi continued, "I think that is something we must rectify in future. Meanwhile, you can have stunners, but only as a last resort to use." Shi handed over the defensive weapons to those who wanted them.

"Okay – listen up!" Martin commanded. "I want everyone back in their cells except Anastasiya. Close the doors to make them look like they are locked. When those two get here, they'll be looking for me, so they shouldn't notice Anastasiya's absence until too late. Shi will conceal hirself and come up behind them when they enter the brig, and then take them out. Those of you with weapons, keep them concealed and don't use them unless something goes wrong. Now hustle! They'll be here shortly."

Everyone hastened back to their cells and closed the doors. Martin placed himself at the front in full view so that the hijackers wouldn't start looking around. In the end their trap was almost undone due to the indicator lamps on the door lock buttons still glowing red, but the wolf who noticed that, hesitated for just long enough for Anastasiya to silently come out of hiding from behind hir desk, and shoot them without warning.

"Are they dead?" Loander asked as they emerged from their cells once again.

"No – heavy stun setting only. Killing is too good for these." Anastasiya kicked the Voxxan contemptuously. "Hope they enjoy headache it gives them as much as I am enjoying mine."

"Search them and remove everything on them, then lock them in a cell," Martin ordered. "We've got four more to capture, and the rest aren't likely to be so obliging as to walk into the same trap. Any ideas?"

"I know how to get the dogs," Penny spoke up. "All we need is a little distraction."

"Go on," Martin encouraged.

The sound of the door opening immediately drew both sets of Shepherds' eyes. Abruptly, Penny was shoved through it and the girl stumbled and nearly fell. She turned and yelled at the unseen shovers, "There's no need to be so rough, you bastards!" Then she turned, spotted the dogs, and froze. "Oh, shit."

Shepherd Junior grinned. "Looks like I've finally been given my toy, hey Dad?"

Shepherd Senior gave a bark of laughter. "Yeah, and now's the time to play while you have the chance."

As the youth approached the mouse, Penny stepped back and shrunk up against the wall, and then tried to move away from him, but was soon backed into a corner.

"I told you that you were going to be my bitch, girl. I'm gonna make you regret the trouble you've given me."

The father watched in amusement. He knew his son's tastes – they weren't so different from his own. With his eyes on the two though, he did not notice his weapon lift from the table next to him and silently fly across the room into the hand of a chakat. He did notice when his son's fist suddenly froze in mid-swing.

"Dad! Something's grabbed me. I can't move!"

Penny stopped cringing and suddenly smiled. "Don't worry, you'll have other things to worry about. Here – let me remind you." She then kneed him in the balls, and then did it a second time for good measure before Zelkie allowed him to drop to the floor, weeping tears of agony.

Shepherd Senior had not been idle. He had grabbed for his weapon, only to find it missing. He whirled around and found himself staring at the emitter of the phaser held by Anastasiya.

"Hello, doggie. Want to play? No? Please do something stupid. You are pathetically easy to catch."

The tiger's taunts goaded the dog morph into action, and he leapt at Anastasiya, who pistol-whipped him as shi effortlessly dodged his attack. Shepherd crashed to the floor, but started struggling to his feet again. The tiger shot him using the heavy stun setting, and he collapsed unconscious.

"Very obliging doggie," Anastasiya said happily. Shi went over to Shepherd Junior and nudged him roughly with hir foot. "Want to play too, pup?"

"N-no," he grated out between clenched teeth.

"Pity," shi lamented, and then knocked him unconscious also.

After stripping the Shepherds of everything, they locked them in the next empty cell.

Martin smiled. "Well done, everyone. Penny – you were incredibly brave to play bait like that."

"My pleasure, Captain. Really!" She had genuinely enjoyed getting the better of the young dog and his father.

Zelkie added, "And I'm pleased to not have weapons pointed at my crewmates so that I could use my Talent safely.

"It was probably a good thing that you didn't dare use telekinesis when you were captured," Martin opined. "If you had, they might have been chasing you around the ship while the rest of us remained locked up, or you might still have been captured and rendered helpless. Either way, we would not now be in a position to fight back."

"Good point," Zelkie admitted.

"Okay, people, listen up. This is going to be the tricky bit. The bridge is going to be a lot more difficult to retake safely, and time is against us. Sooner or later, these four are going to be missed, so what I want you to do...."

"*Revendi to Kavenak – what's taking you so long?*" came from Kavenak's confiscated comm.

Martin groaned. There went that plan.

"*Kavenak! Answer me!*" ... ... "*Marko, are you there? Where are you and Kavenak?*" ... ... "*Shepherd, report! Have you seen Kavenak or Marko?*"

Martin shut down all the comms and sighed. "One unanswered

comm they might put down to equipment failure, but several will ring alarm bells. Any bets that they haven't sealed off the bridge yet?"

"Is sucker bet," Anastasiya said from behind hir desk console. "Bridge has gone into security lockdown."

"Any suggestions anyone?" Martin asked.

"I have an idea of how to get the drop on them once I'm on the bridge," Ceres offered. "Of course, first we need to get that door open."

"Which is designed specifically *not* to be opened during lockdown," Bethany added.

The crew were quiet for several moments while they tried to think of alternatives. Then the silence was broken by a very soft voice whispering from Martin's comm.

"*Menalippe to Captain Yote. Can you hear me, Captain?*"

"Mena's okay!" Baxter shouted with relief, and the others made happy responses also.

"Sshhh! Quiet! If Menalippe needs to whisper, you might be heard when I reply." Everybody immediately quietened, and Martin hit the reply button to quietly reply, "I'm here, Menalippe. Are you safe?"

"*Thank heavens, Captain! I'm safe for now. When I overheard the Voxxan tell the horse that he thought something had happened to his partners, and you might have escaped, I took the chance of trying to contact you.*"

"We did escape, and we've captured four of them. That just leaves the two on the bridge and one in Engineering. Wait! You said that you overheard them. Where are you?"

"*I'm still in the service ducts. I crawled up to the bridge to see if I could do anything, and I saw Heywood and Ceres being captured. I've been waiting here ever since.*"

"Stand by, Menalippe. I might have something important for you to do."

"*Okay, Captain. Standing by.*"

Martin looked over to Ceres. "You said that you had an idea how to get those two on the bridge?"

Ceres nodded. "There's one thing that isn't locked down, and that's the artificial gravity. If that could be shut down, there's no way that either of them could keep up with me long enough to shoot me, let alone catch me. All you need to do is get the bridge doors open the moment that the gravity plates are turned off, and I can bounce around inside and pick them off."

Martin shook his head. "Too dangerous. I've seen you practice your zero gee manoeuvres, and you're pretty amazing, but the bridge isn't that big, and you still have to get through the door first. There's such a thing as a lucky shot too."

"That's possible," Ceres conceded, "but I'll come in high, and those two will be aiming for normal level, and besides, while I'm doing that and distracting them, Zelkie can hold one of them and Anastasiya can come in low. Remember that we'll have the advantage of surprise because they won't be expecting an attack... if we can get that door open, of course."

Martin asked, "Zelkie, can you telekinetically hold both of them?"

Zelkie gave an apologetic shrug. "Sorry, Captain, my Talent is very strong but not very selective. I might be able to try holding both, but I also might end up losing control of both. I'd rather concentrate on one."

Martin considered the suggestions and knew that there were still risks, but he didn't exactly have a lot of alternatives. "Okay, we'll do that. I just hope that those nerve stunners are the only weapons that they have. It'll take at least two hits from them to be fatal." He tapped his comm. "Menalippe – the duct that you're in – it comes out under the console near the door, doesn't it?"

"*Yes, Captain.*"

"Is it possible for you to remove the access panel quietly enough to slip onto the bridge and hit the door override button without being seen?"

"*I.. I think so, sir.*"

"Captain! That's too big a risk for her to take!" Baxter objected.

"I'm sorry, Heywood, but if we don't regain control of this ship, *all* our lives may be at risk. Menalippe is our best, and perhaps only hope of getting onto the bridge in time."

Baxter wanted to argue further, but without a reasonable alternative to suggest, he shut up.

"Menalippe, we're going to take positions outside the door. When you're ready, give me the word. Then I'll give you three seconds to get out and hit the switch. We'll be shutting off the gravity then, so make sure that you dive clear of the doorway."

"*I understand. I'm going to need a few minutes to get the access panel off without being heard.*"

"Right. Signal us when you're ready." Martin switched off the comm. "R'Murran... where is he?"

Loander said, "He and Presaith have gone to Engineering already. They'll be able to switch off the gravity plates from there after they take care of the lynx."

"Of course. Ceres, Zelkie and Anastasiya – let's go."

"I'm coming too," Baxter said firmly.

Martin could not deny the man, so they all headed for the trans-lift. When they got to the bridge level, they emerged into a corridor illuminated by red flashing lights indicating emergency lockdown. They walked past the captain's ready room and the conference room, up to the sealed bridge door. The word 'LOCKED' glowed next to the door controls. Anastasiya and Zelkie took up positions on either side of the door.

Ceres said, "Captain – I'm going to need something to push off against when the gravity goes. There's no wall or anything to brace against facing the door. I'm going to need your help and Heywood's."

"What do you want us to do?"

"Squat on the floor with your back to the door. Heywood – you squat behind the captain and brace yourself against him. I'll put my hind paws against your back and shove off hard. Your combined inertia will give me enough to work with, and by squatting, you will be far less of a target if things go wrong."

They got into position and Martin turned on his comm. "R'Murran – are you ready to turn off gravity on the bridge level?"

"*Just give the word, Captain.*"

"Stand by." He tapped the comm again. "Menalippe – we're ready. What's your status?"

The little ferret morph was scared stiff. She was feeling cramped in the narrow tunnel. It had never been intended for anyone to move through it – not even lithe mustelids. Trying to remove the panel in those confined conditions was not only difficult, but every little noise she made, sounded very loud within the duct, and she was terrified of being caught at any moment. With a final creak, the access panel popped off. She barely managed to stop it from clattering to the floor. After a moment to confirm that the two hijackers had not noticed, she replied to Martin.

"*I'm ready, Captain,*" she whispered.

"Right. Three seconds – go!"

Menalippe slid out of the shaft as quickly as possible and stood up… and stared right into the eyes of the horse morph who gave a startled oath. Menalippe gave out a frightened squeak, but remembered to lunge for the door controls. She slapped the door lock and then attempted to dive for cover. Because she had caught them by surprise though, they were a fraction slow to react, and she was safely out of harm's way when the doors opened. A moment later, the gravity shut down, throwing off the horse's aim. The Voxxan had recovered quickly, but was still unprepared for the Starwalker foxtaur shooting through the doorway and over their heads. Between Ceres and Menalippe, the distraction was enough to cause them to overlook the others for a critical moment. The horse's weapon was suddenly ripped from his grasp and he froze. Then he collapsed as a phaser shot followed. Meanwhile the Voxxan tried to track Ceres but, lacking an anchor, futilely swivelled in the air. The foxtaur bounced off a couple of bulkheads, completely at home with the weightlessness, and calmly shot him a moment after his colleague.

"Clear!" Anastasiya called from the doorway.

Baxter shot onto the bridge, desperately looking for Menalippe. He spotted her helplessly squirming in the air near the ceiling. "Mena! Are you alright?" He manoeuvred to reach her.

"I don't feel so good, Heywood."

"Oh no! Where did they get you?" he asked solicitously as he reached her and drew her into his arms.

"They didn't hurt me, but could you please turn the gravity back on. I think I'm about to puke." Unlike most of the crew, Menalippe had never been tempted to try out freefall in the Z-G Shaft, and she was seriously distressed with this novel experience.

Heywood laughed in relief, and shoved off the ceiling to get them back to the floor. He grabbed a handhold and called out, "Captain – could you re-establish artificial gravity before Mena succumbs to space-sickness!"

A few seconds later, the gravity plates switched back on. All the crew were braced for the return of their weight, but they allowed the hijackers to crash to the floor unimpeded.

Martin walked over to the couple and gave the ferret a quick hug. "You're a hero, Menalippe. I don't know if we could have done this without you."

Ceres, Zelkie and Anastasiya also came over to add to their congratulations. Menalippe was still feeling queasy, but she smiled and felt a little embarrassed for all the attention.

Martin said, "Anastasiya, could you please clear the trash from my bridge."

"Delighted to be obliging, Captain. Ceres – would you please to be assisting me?"

Martin sunk into his captain's chair with a sigh of relief. He keyed the ship's P.A. system. "This is the captain speaking. The ship is now completely back under our control. My thanks to everyone, especially Zelkie and Menalippe, without whom we'd still be in deep trouble. Second watch – please report to your stations. All others – I suggest that you get some rest. We reach Elantra tomorrow."

Martin shut off the P.A. and then keyed a private link. "Yote to M'Resk."

"*M'Resk here, Captain.*"

"Could you please make sure that our one legitimate passenger is placated. Offer him something special from our private stores. Davies happens to be a representative from the company that manufactures the

Art © Diana Harlan Stein

matrix generators, here to oversee the transfer to the customer, and I want him to leave *Phoenix* with a good impression of what our crew will do in the face of adversity."

"*Will do, Captain.*"

Martin leaned back and closed his eyes, trying to force himself to relax. A minute later he heard Bethany say, "I relieve you, Captain. Please go to bed."

"It's not your watch, Commander," Martin replied. He looked about. "Where's Heywood?"

"Mr Baxter is currently comforting his mate. Considering the risk that Menalippe took, I think that we can excuse him for a while. I will take his watch until he's free."

"Fair enough. Ceres should be back shortly. The bridge is yours, Commander."

Martin was only halfway back to his room when the weight of fatigue hit; the stress of the incident finally catching up to him. Back in his cabin, he started undressing, only to be interrupted by the door chime. Not unexpectedly, he found Risha waiting outside the door. He waved her in and closed the door. The four-armed cougaress immediately embraced Martin, leaning her head against his shoulder. He could feel her shaking – coming down from the tense situation was affecting her too.

"I saw how you defended Kannekin. I think that you're going to be a great mother someday."

"Thank you, Martin," she responded. After a moment's silence, she continued, "Would you like to be the father of that child?"

Martin was surprised – she had never hinted at anything more to their relationship than the casual sex and comforting company in bed. "Er... I don't even know if we're genetically compatible."

"Sorry – that's not what I meant. I would be pleased if the father of my future children was like you."

"I see. In that case, I would be honoured to be chosen to be the father of your children."

"Thank you." She let go of him and started undressing.

Martin continued disrobing also, and they climbed into his bed.

"Just hold me tonight, please," Risha requested. "I feel safe in your arms."

Martin was not in the mood for sex either, but he was happy to hold the sexy cougar while they both drifted off to sleep.

The worst part of dealing with the hijackers turned out to be dealing with the Elantra bureaucracy. Martin spent many hours writing reports, answering questions, and dealing with the endless hassle of the unending stream of petty details that the situation demanded. And when one department finished with him, another came along and started asking for all the same things again. For the third time, he gave them his thoughts on the matter.

"I'm fairly certain that they had originally intended to take control of the ship between here and the Landrau colony. My intention to turn the Shepherds over to the authorities here would have stirred up too much unwanted attention to them, with the risk of their plans being leaked, or even balked, so they moved up their timetable. They probably only kept me and others alive so that we could help them get through your bureaucracy without suspicion, keeping the rest alive as hostages to ensure our good behaviour. If their original plans had gone ahead, I'm betting that we would have been unlikely to survive the takeover, unless they decided to take us as slaves, of course."

"And your cargo was really that valuable that it was worth going to so much effort just to hijack your small ship?" the man asked sceptically.

"You have no idea," Martin said fervently. Ships the size of mine specialise in high-value consignments rather than bulk goods."

"And you still won't reveal the nature of the particular item that they were after?"

"Not until after it has been delivered – that's the terms of the contract. The information will be provided to you immediately after that – well before those hijackers come up for trial."

"Very well, Mr Yote. I will follow that up in due course. That will be all for now." The interviewer turned off his PADD.

"Thank the stars!" Martin murmured, getting up from his chair. He left the office and found both Bethany and Risha waiting for him. "You're still here?" he asked with a grin. "I thought that you would have given up on me ages ago."

"They kept us long enough with giving statements that we thought that we might as well wait," Bethany explained.

"Well, I'm grateful that you waited anyway. I declare that we are now officially on shore leave for R&R. How would you ladies like to go to Elantra Port's swankiest restaurant – my treat?"

Risha smiled broadly. "I'd love it!"

Martin arched an eyebrow at Bethany. "And you?"

"Oh, alright. I think I'd like that."

"Great!" He took Risha's arm in his and offered the other to the normally taciturn vixen.

She eyed it reluctantly, sighed, and then took it.

Martin gave hir a big grin and said, "Commander – there's hope for you yet!"

Chapter 4: Mouse Machinations

Anastasiya groaned and tried to stand up, but the stab of pain from the gouge in hir side, and the dizziness from loss of blood, foiled hir effort. Shi sank back into a snow bank, barely noticing that it was deeply stained with hir life fluid. Shi fumbled for the comm in hir coat pocket, but let it drop to the ground, shattered by the same assault that had so seriously wounded hir.

Shi gave a humourless laugh, certain that shi was going to die, and berating hirself for hir stupidity. Most of all shi regretted that shi would not see Valentina again.

Consciousness slipped away. An unknown time later, shi became aware of a voice calling hir name. Shi tried to focus on the person leaning over hir, shaking hir shoulder, but shi blacked out again.

Anastasiya sat up in bed with a yell, and then panted heavily as shi tried to regain hir bearings. Shi became aware of Valentina's arm about hir, and started to calm down.

"It was that dream again?" Valentina enquired. "The one where you almost died?"

Anastasiya nodded mutely. Shi was aware of the throb of pain from the imperfectly healed wound that had almost claimed hir life.

"Father – what's wrong?" came the voice from the doorway of a worried Katarina, woken by the yell of hir sire.

"Go back to bed, Kat, dear. Your father had a bad dream – that's all."

"Okay," Katarina said, only partially mollified. Shi had seen the look on hir father's face and knew that shi was in pain.

"Lie back down, Ana'. Let me massage you. You know that eases pain."

"It is you who eases pain, 'Tina, not massage," shi replied even as shi complied. "You who make my life complete. You who saved my life that night. Without you, I would have been just another dead rebellious youth."

"You get so maudlin when you have that dream," Valentina said as shi massaged the stiff muscles of Anastasiya's back.

"Not all bad memory though. Led to me getting act together and us getting married."

"Only after you promised your Aunt Svetlana to train and get discipline, and to stay away from gang," Valentina pointed out.

"Only did for you, 'Tina."

"No, you did it for *us*." Valentina leaned in close and kissed hir. "And I loved you for that."

"I would do anything for you, my love."

"Oh? When will you have child that you promised?"

Anastasiya groaned. "Not this again. It's not good time – job is too new. We need more savings. I don't want to risk child while I'm working."

Valentina dug hir claws in a little, and Anastasiya winced. "Excuses! After four voyages, our jobs look more secure than ever. We have good work, good friends, and we even will have bonus from share of reward for capturing pirates. Life is risk – if you worry about every little thing, you will die childless. Katarina needs a sister. I think that I will accidentally forget prophylactic when you are next in heat."

"You would do that?" Anastasiya asked plaintively.

"Only making you keep promise," Valentina declared firmly.

Anastasiya sighed in resignation. "You win, 'Tina. Next heat we try for sister for Katarina. Right now though…" Shi rolled over, pulling Valentina under hir. "I'm still in male phase, and I want you."

"No less than I want you," Valentina replied as shi opened hirself to hir lover.

Martin contemplated his next move. His opponent had him cornered, and his options were severely limited. A bold move could see him break free, but also leave him vulnerable elsewhere. However, being constantly on the defence would not gain him his objective. He made up his mind.

"Rraikarr to Karnass 4," he said, moving his piece.

"Rasst'kn to Siskinrek 6. Killing strike!" M'Rarrtikar declared.

Martin slapped his forehead. How *had* he missed that? He sighed. "I concede. Well done. That puts you two up on me, doesn't it?"

"Three," M'Rarrtikar reminded him as she packed up the pieces of the Caitian equivalent of chess that they called Lirkar-Kr'rin – the Stalking Game. It had great similarities to the Terran game of chess, with its variety of pieces with their set moves, and even a board of eight by eight squares. Where it differed were the five extra two-by-two areas located *above* the main board at each corner and the centre. These were said to represent trees that gave either refuge or vantage point for pouncing.

Martin had found it easy to pick up, but tricky to master. "Enough of the games – how is our budget faring?" he asked as he keyed in an order to the replicator for coffee.

As usual, the Caitian did not have to consult her PADD for answers. "As projected, we have come out of this voyage with a modest profit. If we throw in the reward money, we can add to the budget for making improvements and upgrades," she added hopefully.

"No, I promised to share that with the crew. Upgrades can wait a little longer."

M'Rarrtikar had expected as much, but she'd had to try. "Judging by the goods that we are scheduled to pick up from Earth, we might be able to afford a number of them the next time around. However, the ship will be due for a major service then, so we will need to put aside some funds for that."

"I was hoping to give all the crew a raise by the end of the next round trip."

M'Rarrtikar shook her head. "Unless you have lined up some extra profitable consignments that I don't know about, that will have to wait until at least one more time around."

"Nuts! I've been half-promising that I'd boost their wages soon. I must admit that having Penny on the payroll might be good for morale, but it didn't do wonders for my original wage projections."

"Are you suggesting that we lay her off?"

"Good grief, no! Besides liking Penny and what she does for us, I think the crew might lynch me if I tried."

M'Rarrtikar smiled. "I'd say that was more than likely."

"We'll get by. We're doing okay and we have a pretty happy ship, and that make me sleep well at night." He sipped his coffee, and then continued. "My agent has a list of prospective customers to check out when we get to Earth. Maybe we'll get lucky and they will have something extra profitable for us. If nothing else, the way we handled those hijackers gave us extra credibility in the reliability department."

"I expect that as the news spreads, we may see more benefits come from that ugly situation," M'Rarrtikar agreed.

"And that's half a dozen rogues who won't give anyone problems for a very long time," Martin added.

*** 23 October 2333 ***

Martin piloted the shuttle to Terra Gateway himself, leaving Baxter and Valentina to start organising the freight to be taken down to the spaceport while he attended to the inevitable paperwork. As usual, he offered a ride to those of the crew who weren't directly involved with the unloading, as well as their two paying customers who had to go through Customs. That included M'Resk, who accompanied their passengers, Anastasiya, Hotfoot, M'Rarrtikar, both Faleshkarti, and Penny.

"I'm sure not missing a chance to do some shopping at Gateway Plaza!" declared Penny. "I still don't dare go dirt-side, and I have Fedcreds burning a hole in my pocket."

"Wouldn't dream of leaving you behind, Penny," Martin replied with a grin.

On the way over, the voice of Gateway Control came over the comm. *"Phoenix shuttle Baker – change of port. You are now assigned Port 116."*

"Acknowledged, Gateway Control – Port 116." Martin switched off the comm. "That's odd. Level one hundred is usually reserved for important passenger transfers, not starship crews."

"Maybe they're extra busy today and the other ports are tied up on the normal levels?" suggested M'Rarrtikar.

"Perhaps, but I hadn't noticed any exceptional traffic." Martin shrugged. "Doesn't bother me – it's closer to the office where I need to go anyway."

They docked without fuss and allowed their passengers to alight first. The rest followed but stopped just outside of the airlock when several Star Fleet Security people held them up. A jackal morph holding a PADD saw Martin and checked whatever was displayed on the device. "That's him."

One of the Security personnel stepped up to the coyote and said, "Captain Martin Yote – you are under arrest."

Martin was flabbergasted. "What?! What the hell are you talking about?" he began angrily before realising that the FedSec had his phaser firmly pointed at him, and he decided to calm down quickly.

"You are hereby charged with kidnapping, illegal imprisonment, and psychological coercion."

"Being explaining this nonsense!" Anastasiya spat out.

"Careful," said the jackal. "The scanner says shi's armed.

Two more of the Security people levelled their weapons at Anastasiya and one said, "You will very carefully remove your weapon using just two fingers. Move slowly, or I will shoot."

"Am registered security officer licensed to carry weapon," objected the tiger.

"You are all also under arrest as accomplices to Captain Yote. Now remove that weapon as I instructed and put it on the floor and then step back."

Anastasiya did as shi was told, glaring balefully at the guards all the time.

"Who are we supposed to have kidnapped?" Martin asked.

"You are accused of taking Ms Penelope Windsor from Big Sur Spaceport on August 3, 2333. What have you done with her?"

"Me?" Penny squeaked from behind the pack where she had been lurking unnoticed.

The jackal quickly scanned her. "Positive ID. That's her alright. Please step forward, Ms Windsor. You're in safe hands now."

"What? I wasn't kidnapped! I'm here of my own free will with my friends."

The jackal grimaced. "Stockholm Syndrome – just as we were warned." He tapped his wrist comm. "Bates – the Windsor girl is here at Port 116. Come collect her."

A tense half minute later, two female Fleet Security personnel – a vixen and a tabby cat this time – turned up. The vixen immediately spotted Penny and said, "Please come with me, Ms Windsor. We have some anxious people waiting for you."

"The only person I know who would be anxious to get me back would be my father, and I have no intention of going."

"I'm afraid that I am going to have to insist, Ms Windsor. Please don't make me resort to harsher measures."

Penny just folded her arms defiantly. "There's nothing that you can do that's worse than making me go back to my father."

The vixen sighed. "Very well." She nodded to her cat cohort, and they each grabbed an arm and started half-carrying, half-marching her off.

Penny didn't go quietly. She was abusing and arguing with her captors for at least as long as the others were in earshot.

The jackal said, "You will accompany us to the Security Block. If you attempt to escape, you will be shot and charges of resisting arrest will be added to your list of crimes. There you will be interviewed and formally charged. You will be entitled to one comm call. Better make it a good one, considering the deep shit that you're in. Now move!"

Martin had never felt so furious or frustrated in his life, and that included the incident with the hijackers. It was plain that the Security personnel had already made up their minds about their guilt, and were only trying to extract details from them and find more evidence of their crimes. That there was not any to be gotten had irritated their Security interrogators considerably, making them even less charitable towards their suspects. The coyote noted how they seemed to be referring constantly to a list of details regarding the ship, its crew, and its itinerary. It was all very accurate up until the point that Penny was involved, but from there the facts got horribly skewed. The crimes that they were accused of started from an opportunistic kidnapping at the spaceport, claims of ransom demands, enforced servitude, and breaking Penny psychologically. It read like a drama script, which it basically had to be because none of it was true. It was only when an interrogator let a detail slip that the light dawned on him.

"The Shepherds!" Martin exclaimed. "Junior said he'd make her pay. He must have somehow gotten in contact with Penny's father. Now it's starting to make sense."

"That isn't what I asked you about," the interrogator growled. "Answer the question!"

"Not much point in doing so as long as you're referring to that fairy story that Windsor has fed you," Martin replied.

"Your failure to cooperate will only count against you when you go to trial."

"Your failure to be able to distinguish truth from fiction is only going to make you look stupider if you persist with this idiocy."

"Are you trying to make me believe that all this..." he waved his hand at the PADD, "...is not true, and you're just innocent dupes? How gullible do you think I am?"

"Very, apparently," Martin replied with one of his best annoying grins.

It worked. The interrogator snarled and said to the guard in the room with them, "Take him back to his cell."

Martin was relieved. Even a jail cell was better than listening to all that rubbish any longer.

Captain Abel Karnak was a jackal morph of 64 years, 45 of which he'd spent in Star Fleet in Security Division. He had been appointed Head of Security of Terra Gateway Station seven years ago, and had dealt with a large number of incidents in that time. This latest one involving the recovery of a kidnapped heiress was going to look good on his record, and he hoped for another promotion before his retirement. The tip-off and the information that had brought about the recovery of Ms Windsor had come belatedly, but swift action on his part had caught the rogues unawares. He was feeling pretty good about his world in general.

His desk comm beeped, and his executive assistant's voice came through. *"Sir – there's an Admiral Tartikova from Star Fleet Command here to see you."*

Karnak blinked in confusion – he had not been expecting anyone from Command, and that name was dreadfully familiar. "Send the Admiral in, please."

A moment later, he began to get a sinking feeling in his stomach when a herm tiger entered his office. He stood up and saluted. "This is most unexpected, Admiral."

Admiral Svetlana Tartikova returned the salute and said, "I will cut to chase, Captain. Why have you arrested my niece?"

"I gather that Anastasiya Tartikova is your niece? Shi was arrested as an accomplice to the kidnapping of Penelope Windsor, amongst several other serious charges."

"Bullshit, Captain. Shi did not do any such thing."

"With respect, sir, even high-ranking Star Fleet officers can have criminal relatives."

"Aware of that I am. Only stating fact, not opinion. Anastasiya was a wild youth, but matured into responsible and respectable adult. On what are you basing your charges?"

"I was given a comprehensive report on Ms Windsor's abduction, subsequent ransom demands, and a list of subsequent sightings at various interstellar locations where private investigators had tracked her down. She was found in the company of Captain Yote and his crew, wearing one of their ship's uniforms, displaying evidence of Stockholm Syndrome – behaviour identifying with her kidnappers and very atypical of an heiress of a business empire. We acted on a tip-off that Yote was intending to smuggle her through Terra Gateway using the alias of Penny Lane, and everything we found matched the details in the report."

"And when did you receive tip-off and report?"

"About a quarter hour before Yote came aboard the station."

"And in this quarter hour, you comprehensively checked all facts, of course?" the admiral asked drolly.

"Er... no. We had to organise the arrest hastily."

"Odd then that alleged kidnapping was never reported at time it was supposed to have happened. Parents of kidnap victims invariably either call authorities, or pay ransom and then call authorities, which in this case would be Star Fleet. There was no call. Would you care to explain anomaly?"

"The parents could have responded to threats to kill their daughter if they reported the kidnapping?" offered Karnak.

Admiral Tartikova nodded. "Not impossible. Extremely unlikely considering great efforts that Windsor has supposedly put into finding their child, but not impossible. So, having located their daughter, what made you think that she was displaying evidence of Stockholm Syndrome?"

"I was supplied photographs for identification purposes. She was pictured in a smart business dress at one of her father's business meetings, apparently learning more of the business. Very serious demeanour. We were warned that the investigators had found significant changes in behaviour in the time since her abduction, and that's what she exhibited when we arrested Yote and the others."

"I see. And you got services of registered Telepath to verify this, of course?" the tiger asked deceptively sweetly.

"Um... no. As I said, we were rushed to take advantage of the opportunity to catch the kidnappers."

"So you took everything that was given to you at face value?"

"It all fitted!" Karnak protested.

"Best lies consist mostly of truths, as you should know. Penny was never kidnapped. At least, not until *you* abducted her from her crewmates and handed her over to her father."

"What... what do you mean? How could you know this?"

"Told you – my niece is a good child. Writes often. Calls me on comm whenever shi can. Anastasiya informed me of how Penelope Windsor was caught trying to stow away on *Phoenix*. Told me how she became friends with the crew. Introduced me to her on one occasion. I get email from Penny now also." Shi pulled out a pad from hir jacket's pocket, opened a file, and then showed it to Karnak. A video began with Penny's cheerful face filling the screen.

"*Hi Svetlana! We've just got back from Voxxa, and I've been saving up some new jokes for you. Have you heard the one about the chakat, the Voxxan, and the Rabbi?*" Penny proceeded to tell a string of jokes and funny stories until Tartikova switched it off.

"Does that look like missing person?" shi asked.

Karnak shook his head mutely.

"Does that look like someone under duress?"

Again the jackal had to indicate the negative.

"Do you think Stockholm Syndrome can turn serious business woman into cheerful comedian?"

"No, Admiral."

"You have been manipulated, Captain Karnak. You were given carefully constructed pile of partial truths with very little time before Windsor girl arrived. As Head of Security, responsibility is yours to check and verify *all* data, *and* have registered Telepath on hand to verify allegations before attempting arrest. Instead you acted in haste and falsely arrested innocent people, took Ms Windsor away, and placed her in the hands of controlling and overprotective father. Your actions and position on this facility will be up for review in light of this. Now – why are my niece and hir friends still in jail?"

Karnak slumped in his chair and hit the comm. "Lieutenant Katz, Captain Yote and his entire crew are to be released immediately."

"*What? Have they all been bailed already, Captain?*"

"No – we've been had. They're all innocent and all charges are now dropped."

"*Oh. I'll attend to that immediately, sir.*"

"Did anyone track the shuttle that took away Ms Windsor?"

"*No, sir. We had no reason to do so.*"

"See what you can do about locating it, then report back to me."

"*Aye, sir.*"

"If you would accompany me, Admiral, I'll take you to see your niece."

Martin was surprised to be released so abruptly and politely. Although he had made a comm call to his lawyer, he hadn't expected to be bailed so soon, or at all, considering the charges against him. The sudden release was soon explained though.

"Our apologies, Captain Yote. It appears that we have been misinformed and all charges have been dropped. You and all your crew are free to go," Lieutenant Katz told Martin.

"That's what I have been telling you idiots for the past few hours," Martin replied hotly. "Don't think that this is finished. Your actions have cost us dearly in time lost, and personally too. What has happened to Penny?"

"Ms Windsor was released into the custody of her father," Katz admitted reluctantly.

"You morons! You've put a helpless girl back into a situation that she was trying to escape. I had a pretty high opinion of Star Fleet until this incident. I'll certainly think twice about approaching you lot in future."

"Please, Captain, we were acting on information that said otherwise."

"You wouldn't let us get away with a feeble excuse like that," Martin pointed out. "Why should I let you?"

Katz had no reply for that, and merely led Martin out to join the steadily growing crowd of his released crew members, including the ones that had been originally left on *Phoenix*.

Moments later, a herm tiger in Star Fleet Command uniform

entered with Captain Karnak. Anastasiya's face lit up with pleasure.

"Auntie! I knew had to be you that got us out of custody." Shi went over to hir aunt and the two exchanged an embrace and cheek kisses.

"Always you getting in trouble and I am getting you out," the Admiral said gruffly.

"At least not *my* fault this time," Anastasiya replied unrepentantly.

Martin approached the pair. "Hello, Admiral. Anastasiya has told me a lot about you, and how you turned hir life around. I gather that we have you to thank for our release?"

Admiral Tartikova nodded. "Yes. My niece used hir comm call to contact me and explain situation. I researched charges and information on my way here. Was not too hard to see what really happened – something Head of Security should have found out for himself, if not had head up backside."

Martin noted with satisfaction as Karnak winced at that statement. "I'm glad that you sorted this out so quickly. I'm very concerned about what has happened to Penny though."

"I also, Captain. Attempting to trace her whereabouts already."

"If she has her comm with her still, we can trace her with that," Martin suggested.

"Unlikely that she has comm still, but is worth a try. Karnak – assist Captain Yote with his efforts."

"Yes, sir. Please follow me, Captain."

Martin said, "Everybody except Anastasiya – go back to the ship. We have cargo to unload and we're way behind schedule. Leave is cancelled until this situation is fully resolved. Anastasiya – come with us."

Karnak led them to Security's operations room. They gave the tech in charge the comm frequency and encoding, and they set out to trace Penny's comm. A few minutes later, the tech shook his head and said, "No response."

"Perhaps she's out of range of Gateway Station?" Martin suggested.

"Star Fleet relays cover the entire globe, sir. The comm is either shielded or destroyed. If they are trying to hide Ms Windsor's whereabouts, I would suspect the latter. However, we're not defeated yet. Does she have an implanted transponder?"

"Yes, but they're so short-range that they're useless for tracking people planet-side."

"Not with our resources, sir. We do need to narrow down the search area though."

Karnak turned to Lieutenant Katz. "Has Ms Windsor been tracked as yet?"

"Partially, sir. We know that they landed at Big Sur Spaceport as per their flight plan. However, they transferred to a private aircar that was flown to a large private ranch in Oregon Territory. That is a huge property though, with several residences scattered about it, and we are unsure as to which she may have been taken, or if she's still there at all."

"Send in locator drones to all possible sites. A transponder key will be provided shortly."

"Aye, sir."

Karnak look at Anastasiya. "I believe that you're in charge of security aboard *Phoenix*. Can you provide the key?"

"Need my personal PADD, which was confiscated when we were arrested."

"Those items are being returned to your ship. I'll see if I can locate it." A few minutes later, the device was handed over to Anastasiya. Shi unlocked it and found the information, transferring it wirelessly to the tech's station.

"Beaming in locator drones now," the tech said. A moment later, he added, "It would seem that there is a sophisticated security system in place on three of the properties. The drones have tripped alarms on all three."

"Continue the search," Karnak instructed. "We have reasonable cause."

"Scramblers have been activated, but we are still maintaining contact with the drones."

"Military grade circuitry not easily overcome," Admiral Tartikova commented to Martin. "Good sign though – they have something to hide."

Everybody's attention was on the screens displaying the progress of the drones. Each flew low over the residences in a search pattern until suddenly one double-beeped.

"Transponder key detected!" the tech announced.

Karnak tapped his comm. "Squad Two – prepare for beam down. I will join you shortly."

"I want to go too," Martin said.

"No, Captain. This situation has been screwed up too much already without adding your presence. Trust me to bring Ms Windsor back safely, please."

"That's Ms Lane to you, and I *don't* trust you after this experience."

"I'm truly sorry for that, sir, but you're still not coming with us." Karnak then turned and left.

Admiral Tartikova restrained Martin from following. "Karnak is correct. Be patient."

Martin was at least able to watch though. The drones were

repositioned to cover the front door, as well as various other exits. The lens captured the arrival of the security team which spread out around the house. Karnak and one other approached the door. After a delay, the door was opened by what appeared to be a butler who reluctantly let them in. Then the watchers were forced to wait while nothing happened for several minutes. Abruptly, the security people left outside regathered and were beamed out.

"What's going on?" Martin queried.

The tech replied, "It would seem Captain Karnak has beamed back without exiting the house, so the team has withdrawn."

The truth of his words soon became apparent when a familiar voice was heard approaching, and the colourful language that was being used to describe Karnak and the rest of the Security people quite impressed Martin who had no idea she was so well versed in it.

Penny spotted Martin the moment that she entered the Operations Room, and she squealed in joy and rushed over to hug him. "Captain! Am I ever glad to see you! So you finally managed to make these idiots see the light?"

Martin was a bit shocked at her appearance. The mouse was most uncharacteristically garbed in a very feminine dress and dainty shoes, but she still did not act anywhere near ladylike. "Glad to get you back, Penny, but I'd still be languishing in jail if it wasn't for a friend of yours." He indicated Admiral Tartikova who was standing to one side.

Penny's eyes widened in delight. "Svetlana!" She gave the tiger a hug also. "What a way to meet in person for the first time, hey? I bet Anastasiya called you to kick some butt."

Svetlana grinned. "Yes, many butts to be kicked to get back my favourite mouse. You have more jokes for me, I hope?"

"Don't I always? But first – one more favour, please?"

"And that would be…?"

"Get me home so that I can get these ridiculous clothes off!"

"Svetlana grinned even more. "True – they not suit you. By 'home', I assume you mean *Phoenix*?"

"I do mean *Phoenix*, and my friends who are more family to me than certain blood relatives."

"I will take you and your Captain there myself in my shuttle." Shi turned to Karnak. "I trust that you will sort this all out and submit report by tomorrow morning?"

"Yes, sir."

"Good. Penny – Ana – Captain Yote – please to be accompanying me."

"One moment," Penny said. She unbuckled the fancy shoes and tossed them aside. "God, that's better!" she said fervently as she

Art © Jenner

wriggled her freed toes. "Let's go!"

The admiral took them over to the *Phoenix* where those not involved in moving cargo down planet-side welcomed Penny back enthusiastically. When Svetlana's role in their release and Penny's recovery was fully explained, there was much thanks, handshakes, and of course hugs from the chakats.

"You'll stay for dinner, won't you?" Hotfoot asked. "I'll make anything that you like – just name it!"

"Would be shame not to take advantage of being here to visit niece and sample your cooking. I accept."

Martin said, "Glad to hear it. Now pardon me – I need to join the others and try to make up for lost time."

The evening had been convivial and very enjoyable. Martin had not let an early hint of trouble spoil it for himself or anyone else. This morning though, things were looking grimmer. Bethany found him staring glumly at whatever was being displayed on the screen on his desk.

"Are you aware of the delays in our cargo pick-ups?" she asked.

Martin nodded and sighed. "Sadly, yes, and I think I know why."

Bethany sat down opposite him. "This sounds bad. What's happening?"

"Many of our scheduled cargoes have been cancelled, and I keep receiving more notices of delays and cancellations. It's playing havoc with the shuttle loads, not to mention that we have too little to break even on this trip."

"Dare I guess why?"

"What's to guess? We've trod on the toes of a powerful enemy, and now we're seeing the results." Martin shut off the screen and leaned back in his chair with a sigh. "You know that Windsor didn't have to go through that elaborate charade to put the snatch on Penny. He did it to make a point – you don't mess with him and his baby girl. If things had gone as he had planned, we would have been tied up with the judicial process for so long that it would have ruined us financially. If it wasn't for the fact that Anastasiya had a relative in high places, he would have succeeded."

"And what about the false accusations against us?"

"What about them? He could claim that his investigators got it wrong, or come up with some legal excuse with his team of high-priced lawyers. He might get away with little more than a slap on the wrist. Although there is a chance that something else will backfire on him."

"What's that?"

"Loander and Presaith. Those two are not just crew, but observer representatives of the Faleshkarti, and the diplomatic repercussions of the false arrest might overcome his legal machinations."

"We can only hope."

"At least Star Fleet has extended their sponsorship of Loander and Presaith in partial compensation for their screw-up, so I won't have to find more money to pay their wages this voyage."

Bethany and Martin were quiet for a long moment, thinking. Bethany eventually shook her head. "This kind of thing is beyond my expertise. Have you any idea what to do about this?"

"Yeah, but it's not something that I want to do."

"Why not?"

"Because it involves going to my father."

"Is that such a problem?"

"Yeah. The terms of my bequeathal expressly forbids me from getting help from him during the five year probationary period, and besides I had no intention of calling on my father's resources ever. He had his doubts that I could succeed in this business, and I wanted to present him with a strong and healthy interstellar shipping company. Instead we may be teetering on the precipice of ruin."

"We're not dead yet, Captain, and I think you're going to have to swallow some pride and try."

Martin gave Bethany a twisted grin. "You're right, of course, but it's still not going to be fun. Oh well, it looks as if it has come time to fight fire with fire." He typed a code into his comm, and his screen lit up with the image of a female lynx. "Hi, Yvette. Would my father be available, please?"

"*Hello, Martin. It's been a while. Let me see if he's free.*"

A moment later, the image shifted to that of an older coyote morph, slightly scowling back at him. "Well, well, if it isn't the son with the stars in his eyes. Still gallivanting around the galaxy?"

"Yes, Dad, and I was doing very well at it also."

"*You were? So something's gone wrong and you're crawling back to me for help? You know the terms of the bequeathal – you have to start a business, pay back the full amount of the bequeathal and make it profitable within five years, or come back and work your way back up through the company.*"

"I know that, and I can report that I was actually well on course to get into the black on schedule."

"*You have the figures to back that claim up?*"

"Of course."

"*Hmmph! Yet I sense a big 'but' in there, and you're now calling me. Why?"*

"I need to deal with an extraordinary problem that is beyond my means."

"I've got only a bit of time to spare, so tell me, and make it quick."

Martin told his father the entire story, with his father only interrupting occasionally to ask some pointed questions. At the end, the old coyote grimaced. *"Well that explains at last why his goons have been sniffing around and interfering with my business. Nevertheless, the terms of the bequeathal require you to deal with this problem yourself."*

Martin felt shattered. If ever there was a good reason to make an exception, he thought that this would be it. Before he could say anything though, his father continued:

*"But Windsor made a **big** mistake messing with **my** business too, so in order to teach him a lesson not to screw with me, I'm going to help you out this one time. Send me a copy of your list of cancelled shipments. Fortunately I think I can divert enough of my shipping needs to fill some of the gaps in your load, but only up to the value of the freight that you lost, and not a cred more. By the time you get back from your voyage, I expect that I will manage to get things mostly back to a level playing field again. Expect no more help after that."*

"What do you plan to do?

"Son, there are some things you are better off not asking, but I'll give you a hint. When you butt heads with someone willing to play dirty, you gotta know when to fling a bit of dirt yourself."

"Gotcha, Dad."

"Good. Now when can I tell your mother to expect you for dinner?"

"Would seven be okay?"

"That would be fine. Now I've got to get back to work. This company doesn't run itself, you know?"

"One last thing, Dad – would you mind if I bring a couple of friends with me?"

"Hell! Bring them all. Give us a chance to see what kind of company you're keeping. Now be off with you! Time's money!"

"Sure, Dad. Bye." Martin cut the connection.

"Your father seems rather gruff," Bethany commented.

"That's damn near soppy by his standards. I think he's actually missed me. I suppose I've missed him too, although I wouldn't have thought I would when we last talked and parted company. He still manages to surprise me occasionally though."

"But wasn't it rather hypocritical of him to deny you help until it was *his* business that was being harmed."

Martin grinned. "You're not looking at it in the right light. Dad is scrupulously fair with us kids – he can't be showing me any favouritism. *But* if he's only responding to a rival's attack on his business, and I *happen* to benefit from it, then he can say he wasn't directly helping me. Yeah, it's smoke and mirrors, but it's all for the best."

"I don't suppose it's easy to run a huge corporation and be a good father at the same time."

"No, it isn't, which is why I don't intend to ever grow that big. When I have a mate and children, I want to be able to spend more time with them than my father did with me and my mother. Still, even though he scarcely shows it, he cares what happens to his children, and that means a lot." Martin got up from his chair, and Bethany followed suit. "I've got a few things to finish before I head down to make that dinner appointment. Speaking of which – would you care to come along?"

"I think that I'd like that, thank you."

"You're not going to make me call you Commander Oakwood all the time that we're there, are you?"

"I suppose, under the circumstances, it will be okay for you to call me by my first name then. This is not a date though," she warned.

"Considering that I intend to ask the others if they want to come also, I think that you can trust me on that point."

"Good," the vixen replied, and then headed out the door

Oddly enough, Martin thought he detected a slight note of disappointment in that single word. He shrugged it off though – there was no way that Bethany was ever going to let herself get close to a colleague again. But she was family now, and Martin cared about her, and all the others, in ways he would not have dreamed of when he had started his venture. "We all get by with a bit of help from family," he murmured as he followed the vixen out.

Chapter 5: Plague Plot

*** 23 October 2333 ***

Captain Yote called the crew together for his customary pre-flight meeting a little earlier than usual. He took their reports, happy with their normal efficiency. There was an air of expectancy when the last of them had reported.

Martin finished off his coffee first before calling for their attention. "Most of you already know most of what I'm about to say, but I'll sum it up so that everybody knows where we stand. The recent unpleasantness with regards to Penny's father is still having repercussions as he uses his influence to inflict his displeasure upon us."

Penny snorted a humourless laugh. "If by displeasure you mean that he's as pissed off as a rattlesnake that's been trod on, you might be close."

"We get the idea, Penny. Anyway, many of the freight consignments that we were due to pick up were either cancelled or delayed beyond our departure date. Fortunately my father was able to pull strings of his own, and we have some replacement cargo. The bad news is that there are still far fewer consignments. The good news is that they are generally of higher value. Nevertheless they didn't quite bring us to the break-even point, so I had to take on a couple of extra jobs that I would rather have preferred not to."

Martin paused and looked regretfully at his empty coffee mug.

"Let me refill that for you, Captain," Hotfoot volunteered.

"Thanks, Hotfoot. Anyhow, the bad news is that I've accepted a re-supply job to Winchester Way-station."

There were a few groans from those familiar with the destination.

"Yes, I'm afraid that's about the right reaction. For those who don't know about Winchester, it's a private enterprise that has gone sour. It's an unpleasant place – run-down and full of shady characters. However, even they need occasional legitimate supply runs, and we're it. I'm recommending that no one takes shore leave there, and anyone who does go, does so in groups of no less than three. More on that when we get there. Before that though, we have one other destination that people avoid like the plague – literally."

Hotfoot handed Martin a fresh brew, and he paused to take a swig from his refilled mug. "How many of you have heard of the colony planet Asahikawa?"

Bethany put up her hand, as did R'Murran. Martin knew that Bethany was already aware of their destination, but had not known if any of the other crew had heard of it.

R'Murran said, "Isn't that the world that they call the Planet of the Herms? I thought that was totally quarantined?"

There were a few murmurs amongst the crew when the Caitian mentioned that it was quarantined.

"Even I hadn't heard of it until I was approached to take some passengers from there to Earth. I must admit that I wasn't thrilled about the idea, but it pays very well, and I have been assured that it's perfectly safe."

"Safe?" Heywood frowned. "You're talking about a quarantined world and bringing people from it. That doesn't sound safe to me. And why is it called the planet of the herms? Was it colonised by herms only?"

Martin shook his head. "No, they only had a handful of herms amongst the colonists who settled there. However, every one of those colonists is now a herm."

"What!" Burningbright exclaimed. "How did that happen? Is there something in the environment that changes them?"

"Yes and no. It wasn't there when they colonised the planet. The truth is a long story."

Heywood said, "I'm sure that we would all like to hear about it so that we know exactly what we're getting into."

"Hence why I called this meeting early." Martin took another drink of his coffee before continuing. "Asahikawa was colonised by a Japanese contingent who basically wanted to start a new Japan with its traditional culture. It consisted of about half humans and half morphs of various kinds, and aside from their cultural goals, was much like most new colony groups. Amongst their number, they considered themselves extremely fortunate to have the services of an expert genetic engineer by the name of Dr Osamu Hiro. Normally colonies just have gene techs to help deal with problems, adapting animals and plants, and coping with potential new diseases. To get someone of his skills was a real coup for the colony."

"I can sense a big 'however' coming," commented M'Rarrtikar.

"And you would be right," Martin conceded. "Hiro had taken the position because he had been fired from several reputable genetic engineering firms for misuse of company resources and unauthorised research. You see, he was pursuing a personal agenda, and the colony position put him in charge of the division with little oversight, and freedom to pursue his personal goal – he wanted to be a fully functional hermaphrodite."

"Wait – haven't the gene techs been able to change people's sex for decades?" objected Burningbright.

"Yes and no. They've been able to remodel bodies to be indistinguishable for a long time, but *not* fully functional. Being able to reproduce as the opposite sex is a relatively recent accomplishment, and this incident took place 34 years ago. Besides, it's a hideously expensive process, something that only the very rich could afford, and Hiro wasn't that rich. Anyway, he managed to achieve this years before they did back on Earth. Unfortunately, although he was undeniably brilliant, he was also sloppy and careless. He modified a symbiont that he discovered on Asahikawa as his means of reprogramming his body's entire genetic code, and it worked excellently. It took several weeks to make the complete change, but he – now shi – was now a perfect fully-functional hermaphrodite human. Disastrously though, that symbiont was also very contagious, just like a virus, and Hiro had done little to isolate himself during the change, and not at all afterwards as shi showed off hir accomplishment. Everyone who came in contact with Hiro also contracted the symbiont, and everyone who came in contact with them also got it. Because it took a little while for the effects to become noticeable, and because the colony was still so small, soon every man, woman, and child, human and morph, and even some farm animals and pets, had contracted the symbiont, and all of them were turning into herms also."

"It's really *that* contagious?" Penny asked.

"Unfortunately, yes. The only thing that saved the rest of the Federation was that Asahikawa being such a young colony world, it rarely got visits from starships, and by the time one did come along, they had slapped a class one quarantine on the world."

"So tell us why in Heaven's name are we picking up passengers from there?" Heywood asked belligerently. "No offence meant to the herms in this crew, but I have no desire to be one."

"Nor do I," Martin agreed. "Star Fleet maintains the quarantine very diligently for that very reason. However, they also inform me that they found a way to deactivate the symbiont, and the people we are scheduled to pick up I am assured will be totally safe."

"Then why aren't Fleet transporting them to Earth?"

"Because while maintaining the quarantine is extremely vital, providing a taxi service for a handful of relatively unimportant people isn't, so they foist that kind of thing onto civilian sub-contractors. And due to the unpopularity of the place, there aren't many who will take the job except those who are rather desperate for work – like us."

"If they can deactivate the symbiont, why don't they do that for everyone on Asahikawa?" Penny asked.

Martin shrugged. "I don't know every detail. I suppose you can ask our passengers when they come aboard. I was only told enough to explain the situation we would be going into. I'm passing it on so that none of you will be going into this blindly, but the decision has been made, and we *will* be taking this job however you feel about it. If you reckon that you cannot deal with the situation, then you are welcome to leave the crew without prejudice. We won't be picking them up until the return leg of our voyage, so you'll have plenty of time to think about it."

"Well I don't need more time to think about it," declared Penny. "I know that you wouldn't deliberately put us in any danger, so I'm not worried at all. In fact, I'm looking forward to meeting these people. I've got a thousand questions that I'd like to ask them."

The rest of the crew joined in an affirmation of their faith in their captain, some perhaps a little less enthusiastically like Heywood, but none objected.

"Thank you everyone," Martin said with a relieved grin. "We lift in twelve minutes – final preparations and report readiness!"

The crew scattered to their posts, leaving Martin and Bethany to make their way to the bridge together.

"That went better than I had feared," Martin commented.

"I wish that I had as much faith in Star Fleet as I used to," Bethany said. "However, I don't think that they'd let something that dangerous get out, so I'd say that we have nothing to worry about."

"Considering how many that I'm told didn't survive the transformation, I fervently hope so."

The outbound leg of their voyage was basically uneventful. They had their quota of goods to deliver or pick up from various space stations and worlds. Martin was relieved to be able to pick up some extra consignments along the way that would help their books nudge further into the black. Their halfway point was T'Karr Paradisio, a world jointly colonised by Caitians and Terrans in a cooperative effort soon after formalising relations between their worlds. It was also the crew's last opportunity to have a relaxing shore leave before having to face the less pleasant aspects of this voyage.

After all the shipments had been dealt with, R'Murran and his wives took one shuttle down to Arrartenen, a city located on the hot, dry plains that were so similar to the savannahs of Cait. The Faleshkarti elected to join them. Martin chose to go down to the other major city, Hartsburg, which was located in a more temperate and wetter climate. The rest of the crew came with him – all except Ceres who had drawn the short straw and was left to keep watch on *Phoenix*. Shi consoled hirself by switching off the artificial gravity and having some freefall fun.

Despite the naming of the cities, each had both species living, working, and socialising together, although climate preference did mean that more Caitians lived in Arrartenen, while more Terrans made Hartsburg their home. The planet had been colonised by idealists who saw a great future on a new world, working alongside an alien race. It had been a remarkable success, and it showed in the melding of cultures. Each world had contributed the best it had to offer, and from that grew new and unique arts and crafts. It was not unusual for Caitians and Humans to be mated, and that had led to the creation of new customs and laws. Very often, a cross species couple would seek out another, only with sexes reversed, in order to have children. Sometimes those families would remain together in a loose bond, and the children would have three parents – their mother, their father, and their sire. It all worked so well that their world was often held up as a shining example of interspecies cooperation, and T'Karr Paradisio remained an extremely popular place to immigrate.

It was also a great place for tourists, and had the crew of the Phoenix not been trying to keep a tight budget, they would have quickly spent their wages on its many attractions. It was a tired but very happy bunch of people who returned to the ship two days later. Martin was fresh as a daisy though because he had swapped out with Ceres after the first day to give the Starwalker a day's shore leave also. He used the time to catch up on both paperwork and sleep. He made a point of talking loudly and jovially around those of his crew who came back with hangovers just to make a point, then sent them off to their cabins to sleep it off until second watch. As none of the crew had had second thoughts about going to Winchester and Asahikawa, the Phoenix left with a full complement, although the crew was quieter than normal as they approached the planet of the herms.

They were halfway into the star system when they were hailed. "*This is Star Fleet patrol ship* Esperance – *you are entering a restricted zone. Bring your ship to a halt for identification procedures. I repeat – you will bring your ship to an immediate halt for identification.*"

Warned that this would happen, Martin ordered an immediate full stop to all drives, and they coasted at relatively trivial sub-light speeds. He keyed the comm and replied, "This is the commercial trader, *Phoenix* for a scheduled pick-up of four passengers from Asahikawa. Authorisation code Gamma Zeta 710239."

"Confirmed," came the reply. *"We are sending you a flight plan. Follow it precisely and without deviation."*

Martin could hear the unspoken 'or else' in the person's voice. "Acknowledged, Esperance." After Heywood nodded to him to indicate that the flight plan had been received, he continued, "Will comply."

Phoenix dutifully followed the flight plan, shadowed by the wary Fleet patrol ship. They docked at a rather small space station that was orbiting Asahikawa.

"I wonder why they have such a small station?" Heywood commented.

Ceres replied, "Probably because they aborted plans to expand upon the original module due to the quarantine, and now they just use it as a base for the Star Fleet patrol ships."

"Makes sense," Heywood conceded.

The comm came to life again. *"Commander Hasluck to Phoenix."*

"Captain Yote here, Commander."

"Captain – you and your First Officer may now proceed to my office. All other crew members are to remain aboard your ship. Do not attempt to use any Transporter devices."

"On our way, Commander. No worries about using a Transporter because we aren't rich enough to afford one."

They were met at the airlock by a morph with whose species Martin was unfamiliar, but was later informed was a quoll. She smiled a friendly but toothy carnivore's smile and introduced herself.

"My name is Lieutenant Stone, and I am the Commander's executive assistant. Follow me and I will take you to see him." The trio moved off, and she continued, "Sorry if people have been a bit terse, but we take our duty very seriously here. This isn't the kind of job where near enough is good enough."

"I quite understand, Lieutenant, and I've been quite happy to stick to the letter of the instructions."

Lieutenant Stone showed them into the Commander's office without the need to announce themselves first. Behind the desk was seated a male human, while seated on one side of the room were two more humans, and on the other side two fox morphs. The Commander got up and came around his desk to meet Martin and Bethany.

"Welcome to Asahikawa Patrol Base, Captain Yote, Commander Oakwood," he began with a serious but not unfriendly demeanour. "Thank you for accepting this assignment. I know that you must be uncomfortable with this – heaven knows we live with it for months at a stretch. However, once again I reassure you that there is no danger involved. Let me introduce you to your passengers."

He turned to the humans, and Martin was able to look them over more carefully. They were both of Asian descent – unsurprising considering that it was basically a Japanese colony. One was about Martin's height and looked like an effeminate male, although D-cup breasts ensured that shi would never be mistaken as such. The other was several centimetres shorter and looked like a butch female, but with exceptionally large breasts that looked far too big on hir. Asian people weren't generally known to be very busty, and Martin wondered about that. They were both dressed in clothing that Martin could only describe as modern traditional Japanese style.

Commander Hasluck said, "These are Akira and Hikaru Yamato, a married couple who were two of the original colonists, and are the appointed representatives of the Asahikawan council. Gentles shirs, this is Captain Martin Yote and Commander Bethany Oakwood of the *Phoenix*, who will be taking you to Earth on your mission."

Original colonists? Martin was puzzled – the herm plague started over thirty years ago, yet neither of this couple looked that old. It was a mystery to be solved later though.

The couple bowed to him, and Akira said, "It is an honour to meet you, Captain san. We look forward to an interesting journey with you."

Martin tried to return the bow, and while it was a little clumsy, the couple seemed satisfied with the result. "We too anticipate a good voyage, but be prepared to answer a lot of questions. My crew are very curious about you."

Akira smiled. "Most understandable, and we welcome your curiosity. Our mission is to raise awareness of our world and society so as to improve our colony despite the unfortunate barrier between us."

Hasluck then directed their attention to the fox morphs. Now that they were standing up, Martin noticed something that had not been obvious when he had entered the office – they both had two tails. A memory tickled the back of Martin's mind – kitsune. That made sense; the Japanese gene engineers would have been likely to make morphs based on their own folklore.

The kitsune were of similar size and build, both with D-cup breasts, but of significantly different fur patterns. The first was a typical red fox, and shi was dressed in what Martin guessed was a modern samurai outfit, complete with katana, but with a holster on the other hip for some kind of energy weapon. The other kitsune was a silver fox, and shi wore a traditional kimono dress.

"This is Shintaro, the Yamatos' bodyguard, and Kiku, their personal assistant. They will be coordinating with the Federation officials when you get to Earth, and seeing to the Yamatos' particular

Art © Mayra Boyle

needs throughout their mission."

The kitsunes both bowed, much lower than the Yamatos had. Martin returned the bow again, although not as low as he had with the humans, suspecting that it was best due to their relative ranks.

Neither kitsune said anything at that particular point, and Hasluck continued, "I'm officially passing responsibility for these four onto you now, Captain. All their documentation is on this data chip, and the rest of your instructions remain unchanged from when you accepted the job. Now I would like to invite you to a meal, but this is a military base, and we don't do social events here, so I will hasten you on your way. I wish you all a safe journey and a successful mission."

"Thank you, Commander," Martin replied.

"We thank you also for your efforts over these past weeks," Hikaru said, and all four herms bowed to Hasluck.

"Lieutenant Stone – please see our guests to the airlock."

"Yes sir. Follow me please, gentle beings."

They were soon all aboard *Phoenix*, and Martin handed off the care of their guests to M'Resk who informed him that their personal belongings had been transferred while he had been with Hasluck. Before the Yamatos left though, he said, "We have planned a formal meal for your benefit to be held once we leave the star system. I'd like to introduce you to the rest of the crew then, if that is to your satisfaction?"

"That would be most enjoyable," Hikaru replied.

"Excellent! I will see you there then. M'Resk will fill in the details for you."

Martin left for the bridge, and *Phoenix* departed the space station, following the same type of rigid flight plans to leave that star system behind.

The meal was preceded with refreshments and appetisers, giving the crew a chance to mingle with their guests, with Martin giving formal introductions. Some had to stay on duty, of course, but Martin kept a comm line open so that they could listen in on the conversations. Once the formalities were out of the way, the Yamatos relaxed into quite genial guests. Shintaro was polite and not unfriendly, but clearly regarded hirself as being on duty still, and so did not totally relax. Kiku was quiet – almost shy – and remained attentive to the humans. The Yamatos however were quite forthcoming, especially Akira.

"Knowing Star Fleet, you are probably short on details of our world. In the interests of better understanding each other, I invite you to ask whatever you like of us, and we will endeavour to answer your questions as completely as possible."

Heywood had been waiting for the opportunity to talk. The herm humans made him feel uncomfortable, and while he had no problem with other species being hermaphrodites, for humans to be dual sexed seemed too unnatural. He practically jumped at the chance to ask some questions.

"If Fleet knows how to neutralise the symbiont that makes people into herms, why don't they do that for everyone on the planet?"

"That is a more complex question than you seem to realise, young man. The simple answer though is that it's an impossible task. The symbiont doesn't just affect people – it has spread to every Terran mammalian species that is on Asahikawa, right down to lowly vermin. Neutralising of the symbiont does not make you immune to it, and re-exposure brings you right back to where you were before the neutralising. If only one insignificant mouse was to be missed, it would re-infect everyone again, whether by direct contact, or indirectly, such as a cat catching the mouse, then that cat coming into contact with someone. In all of humanity's existence, no one has ever totally eliminated vermin from any major settlement, not even space ships like this."

"Then remove the people a few at a time, cure them like you, and then re-settle them elsewhere."

Akira smiled benignly. "That assumes that we *want* to be cured."

That confounded Heywood. "But... surely...."

"I said that this was more complex than you realised. Bear with me while I elaborate. When the plague hit the colony, it caused enormous disruption. Many died during the transformation because it is so stressful on the body, and because virtually everybody went through it at the same time, there was no one in condition to look after the worst affected while it happened. Of those that recovered, some could not cope with the change, and they suicided. Some tried surgical removal of the unwanted genitalia, only to find that it all grew back again. The symbiont has a template that it imposes on the body, so if something tries to change it, the symbiont restores it. However, that is true of the entire body, not just the new genitalia. If I was to lose a hand, it would grow back again, and faster than it does for chakats. In fact, to do its job, the symbiont actually took over the immune system. None of us has been sick since we recovered from the transformation. How old would you say that I am, Mr Baxter?"

"You look to be in your early thirties, although the way you talk implies that you were an adult when the plague hit."

"You are correct. I am 65, and my wife is 63. We have not visibly aged since the plague. The symbiont preserves us, keeps us totally healthy, and repairs major injuries. The majority of the survivors mentally adapted to being hermaphrodites, and those born since have always been herm. To take this so-called 'cure' would be considered a major disaster to most of us now."

"And yet you took it to make this trip," Martin pointed out.

"Our cause is more important than the sacrifice. It is imperative that Asahikawa gets access to the rest of the Federation again, especially for trade. It is our goal to facilitate this somehow. And of course, once we have finished our mission, we intend to rejoin our Asahikawan brethren and regain our abilities. With the aid of the herm symbiont, we expect to live double, maybe triple the normal human lifespan, and perhaps even longer. It is too soon yet to know the full ramifications of our nature."

"Wow, I would never have imagined that," Penny said. "You really do seem a step up from the rest of us. Mind if I ask a more personal question though?"

"I said to ask what you will, and I meant it," Akira assured her.

"Okay. You have quite a full bust, but Hikaru has breasts that are excessive for hir body type. Is that an effect of the symbiont too?"

Hikaru answered, "You have noticed one of the few failings of the transformation. Doctor Hiro wanted D-cup breasts, so the symbiont was programmed to give him them. All males like my husband ended up with D-cup breasts, but unfortunately for the females, this was imposed on top of what they already had. Before the change, I already had fairly large breasts, but the symbiont made them so much larger. And like those who tried surgical removal of genitalia, breast reduction surgery did not work – they grew back to their new size. More former females have cursed these oversized breasts than the additional genitalia. They are very heavy, and cause us frequent back aches. Fortunately for the new generation, all grow to a D-cup and no bigger."

M'Rarrtikar spoke up. "I notice that you still call each other 'husband' and 'wife'. If you have adapted to being herms, why not call yourselves 'mates'?"

Akira answered. "We *have* adapted. I have even borne two children sired by my wife. However, aside from such things, our relationship has stayed basically the same, and we have seen no reason to redefine it. Some have chosen to use the term 'mate', while others have used neutral terms such as 'partner' and 'spouse'. A few even resort to calling each other 'wife' because they see our universal ability to bear children as a feminine aspect. Our society is still feeling its way in some matters such as this."

Valentina got in the next question. "Did you already have any herms amongst morph colonists, and if so, how were they affected?"

"Yes, we did have a few herm species. You are probably familiar with the problems of a lot of the early herm creations; not all were as successful as yours. Some had male physiques that were unsuited to childbirth, for example. Others had hormonal troubles. Some didn't even always breed herm children because the trait was a very weak recessive. The symbiont fixed all that, and they are happier and healthier for it... with the obvious exception of breast size. I feel sympathy for those who were already very well endowed before the change."

"What about chakats?" Burningbright asked. "Were they affected? If you had any, of course."

"We do have two extended family groups, and you have hit on the only time that the symbiont has failed. Because your species was engineered specifically to be explorers resistant to injury and alien disease, they were the only ones who were immune to the herm symbiont. We also had some foxtaurs who were starting a new clan. None of them survived the changes that were being forced upon them. Unfortunately for the chakats though, like Typhoid Mary, while immune to the symbiont, they are nevertheless carriers, and can no more leave the planet than we can without the neutralising treatment. Nor can they have more of their kind join them while the quarantine is in place. Those two families were going to establish a community which was going to be the starting point of an influx of their clan members. Those hopes and dreams have been put on hold for over three decades."

M'Resk took her turn asking a question. "What about non-Terran species? Does the symbiont affect Caitians, or Voxxans, or Rakshani?"

"I must admit that I do not know the answer to that. We have no non-Terran species in our colony, and I have not heard if the Federation scientists have tested to see if the symbiont would affect them. I'm fairly sure though that because we can share environments and even most foods, you could at least be carriers of the herm plague."

"What happened to Doctor Hiro?" enquired Risha.

"Shi is currently serving a life sentence for hir crimes. Shi was convicted on hundreds of counts of criminal negligence resulting in death, and breaking various colonial laws. Rather than execution or imprisonment, shi is required to work for the colony for no personal gain. Shi worked with Star Fleet to find a way to neutralise the symbiont so that we could travel. Shi is also barred from any personal relationships, so that shi's denied much of what shi hoped to have as a herm. Shi is guarded every moment of the day by several people who lost close relatives, and so have no sympathy towards hir. The people of Asahikawa will make sure that the doctor will know their displeasure for the rest of hir very long life."

M'Lertiña asked, "Going back to what you said about herms whose physiques weren't suitable for child-bearing, the same could be said of all males. I notice that your hips are quite wide – I assume your pelvis got restructured? What was it like?"

"Yes, our pelvises were restructured, and it was the most painful part of the transformation. I could not walk for days, and I had to learn to walk a little differently after the change was complete. Doctor Hiro got that part right though – no one on Asahikawa has problems birthing a child due to narrow hips."

"I hear a lot about physical changes," Bethany observed, "but what about social ones? You set out to create a more traditional Japanese culture on Asahikawa – how has that changed?"

Akira grimaced. "A lot. Some things in traditional Japanese culture simply do not translate into a herm society. Gender roles have virtually been eliminated since the new generation started exerting its influence on those of us who clung to our former values. We now concentrate mostly on those things that are not tied to gender – arts in particular. However, we have not made as great strides as we had originally planned due to the plague and our isolation. We have been undermanned and under-resourced for three decades. That is what our mission seeks to correct. We are hoping to persuade the Federation Council to find ways not only to safely trade with us, but also allow more immigrants."

"What!" exclaimed Heywood. "But they'd also get the herm symbiont!"

"Of course," Akira replied with equanimity. "However, I think you underestimate the number of people who would be prepared to undergo that transformation in exchange for perfect health and very long life."

The crew were all a little stunned as they pondered that. Hotfoot spoke up into the silence. "The main course is ready. I suggest that we all be seated for the meal and continue discussion then."

There was a murmur of agreement, and everyone took their places at the table. As they did so, Kannekin asked, "What about you, Shir Shintaro? How did the plague affect you?"

Shintaro smiled at the young Caitian boy. "I was born after the plague, young one. I have never known what it is to be like other than a herm. My mother, however, was a former male who was quick to embrace hir new sex, but still raised me in the tradition of the samurai warrior. It is my honour and duty to serve the Yamato family."

"I would like to see those skills demonstrated," Anastasiya commented. "Would you do me pleasure of sparring match?"

Shintaro inclined hir head. "It would be my honour, Anastasiya-san. With weapons or unarmed?"

"Both. My Aunt Svetlana had me study several disciplines. I

expect that you will be far superior with sword, but should be interesting anyway."

Hotfoot served up the meal with the assistance of Menalippe. As shi did so, shi passed next to Hikaru. "Your husband said shi had two children since the change – what about you? How many have you had?" shi asked curiously.

"I bore my husband three children before the change. I have not felt the need to do so again since."

The chakat sensed an odd negative reaction to hir question, so shi decided not to pursue the subject.

Aside from that incident, the meal went well, with pleasant conversation as the crew learnt more of the little details of an all-herm society.

So what's your opinion of our Asahikawan guests?" Martin asked Bethany later in his office.

"Not what I originally thought. The kitsunes are okay – much as I expected them to be like, if just a touch servile, but the humans come across as a bit intense. They have a certain fervour about the change that I find unsettling."

"They do have a point though – there are a lot of advantages to what they have become."

"I don't mind that, and I suppose that if Asahikawa is going to send representatives, they would be particularly enthusiastic ones. I just can't help the feeling that there's something not quite right though."

"Oh? What makes you feel that?"

"It's what happened when Hotfoot asked Hikaru about how many children shi's borne since the change. Did you notice Akira's reaction?"

"No – I was paying attention to Hikaru."

Bethany hesitated. "I'm not really sure, but shi looked dismayed for a moment."

"So? It might be a touchy subject that's none of our business."

"Why? They unhesitatingly talked about everything from breast size to suicide. Why would a question about babies be such a touchy subject?"

Martin had no answer for that.

Bethany continued. "I don't believe that their relationship has remained the same as Akira said. From what I recall of traditional Japanese society, like many old societies, the females were very subordinate to the males. Now suddenly Hikaru is just as male as Akira and shi feels empowered, while Akira is now just as female as Hikaru and feels equally disempowered. Akira readily had two babies despite being male all hir previous life while Hikaru chose not to. It's easy to see who is now the dominant one in that relationship."

"Okay – so what's your point?"

"If they're lying about that, what else are they lying about?"

Martin considered the question, then shrugged. "Maybe they're just politicians – willing to say anything to sell their view."

The vixen nodded. "Could be. I hope so. A politician's empty words I can live with, but not a deliberate attempt to deceive." She got up from her chair. "I'm going to sleep on it. Goodnight, Captain."

"Goodnight, Bethany."

The fact that she did not correct him to say 'Commander' instead told him how preoccupied she was with the humans' motives.

The next day, Martin approached Burningbright.

"Good morning, 'Bright."

"Good morning, Captain. Is there anything that I can do for you?"

"Maybe. Last night at dinner, did you get any sense that the Yamatos were lying to us at all?"

"Captain – people tell little white lies all the time. They are the lubrication of a properly functioning polite society. I don't 'listen' out for deliberate attempts to deceive unless I have cause to do so."

Martin sighed. "Nuts! Could you do so in the future when you're in the presence of the Yamatos. Bethany has gotten some misgivings about them, and I'd like to clear this up one way or the other."

"Okay, Captain."

"Thanks, 'Bright."

Despite the Commander's suspicions, the rest of the day proceeded without any unusual incident. Anastasiya arranged a time with Shintaro to have their match-up, and several of the off-duty crew members came to watch.

The pair started with unarmed combat. Both were highly trained, and despite hir greater strength and reach, the tiger had a difficult time defeating hir opponent three falls out of five. You would not have known that the kitsune had lost by the pleasure that shi took in the skilful bouts. After a break to recuperate, they then matched their abilities with swords – wooden practice ones replacing the real thing. Despite their disparate styles, it was clear who was the superior swordsperson, with Shintaro disarming Anastasiya rapidly and frequently.

Eventually Anastasiya laughed and said, "Enough! Is clear that I'm overmatched. I bow to your skills, my friend." The tiger matched word with deed.

Shintaro bowed in return, a soft smile on hir face. "It was a pleasure to fight you. I think that you have the potential to do much better."

"Thank you, but I know amount of time and effort needed to truly master sword, and I don't have that much to spare."

"A few lessons, perhaps? I would be willing to teach you."

"You want to be my sensei?" Anastasiya grinned. "I might take you up on that."

The tiger did take lessons over the several days that it took to get to Winchester Way-station. During that time, a camaraderie grew between the two, both skilled in what they did and proud of their work. For all the uneasiness that the humans engendered, the kitsune by comparison were open, honest, and quite likeable. When they arrived at the station though, Shintaro immediately became business-like again, and Martin could hardly blame hir. As a precaution, he forbade any of the Asahikawans to disembark there, much to the relief of Shintaro.

Martin wondered why the Yamatos would want to visit Winchester in spite of being informed of the rough nature of the place. He could only assume that after being confined to their world for 34 years, any new place seemed attractive. Business dealings forced him to visit in person, but he went armed, and with Anastasiya along as a bodyguard. The Amur Tiger would make anyone but a Rakshani think twice. His loadmaster, Zelkie, was instructed to stay with the shuttle at all times and keep hir comm open. Bethany rode with hir, armed and watching the chakat's back while shi was distracted with the unloading. None of the rest of the crew felt any inclination to visit the rundown station, much to Martin's relief. He concluded his business there as fast as possible, then headed back to the *Phoenix* with a small consignment to take back to Earth.

Martin docked his shuttle without incident and said, "I want you to do extra thorough security scans on that load before letting Valentina stow it."

Anastasiya nodded. "Was already going to do that."

It seemed anticlimactic when they departed and nothing untoward happened, but Martin put that down to good preparedness as much as luck. All that remained to do was a very ordinary supplies delivery to a mining outpost, and a milk-run to a Star Corps research station, then back to Earth.

The Yamatos continued to be persons of interest during the journey. Akira surprised them with a demonstration of sleight of hand, flawlessly performing various magic tricks with the panache of a professional. Shi demonstrated various card tricks, and made objects disappear and reappear elsewhere, all without the Phoenix's crew being able to see how shi did it.

Penny was enchanted. "Could you teach me how to do those tricks also?" shi asked Akira after one demonstration.

"It is not something that you can learn in a few days, Penny-san. This has been my hobby for over forty years, and I practice frequently. It takes much dedication."

"I'll settle for being taught how to do a few of them, and practice those every day."

Akira smiled at the mouse's enthusiasm. "Very well. If we can arrange to practice in privacy, I will show you some of my tricks."

Every day until they reached Pellucidar III mining outpost, Penny diligently practiced with Akira coaching her. However, the lessons were postponed upon arrival in orbit around the world. From there, the planet looked similar to Mars, although a little bigger than Venus in size. Despite having an atmosphere and being in the sweet zone where it got just the right amount of sunlight, the world had never developed life. Although people could walk around on the surface with just ordinary clothing, the air was poisonous, and anyone outside of the protective domes and huts had to wear breathing apparatus. Despite being so inhospitable, the population there was quite large because the mining corporations had discovered vast deposits of rare minerals, and they had established several highly profitable mine sites. The main settlement was inside a pressurised dome that contained housing, offices, shops, and an entertainment precinct. It even catered to the passing trade due to the large number of ships that constantly visited the world. And because it was a large, successful operation, it attracted the higher class of professionals, so Martin had no hesitation in authorising shore leave.

Zelkie and Martin took down most of the crew and all of their guests in the first trips down in the shuttles. While the two continued to shuttle freight back and forth, the rest went sightseeing. Not really being a tourist town, the Pellucidar settlement didn't have much to offer besides a change from the boredom of ship life, but it did have one claim to fame – the Crystal Mountains. A restaurant had been built abutting the part of the dome that faced north-east, which gave a perfect view of the mountain range in whose foothills the settlement had been built. Natural crystal formations dominated the geology, and as the local star set, they glittered and glowed spectacularly.

Kiku was excited. Shi had spent some hours in the company of the two Faleshkarti, Ceres, and Penny, while hir mate was preoccupied with accompanying the Yamatos. Shi had come across a store that was selling souvenirs, amongst which shi had found some of the native crystal mounted in a representation of the Crystal Mountains. A concealed battery powered a UV light source that caused the crystal to glow a beautiful soft pink – the Lady Hikaru's favourite colour. As shi knew that the Lady's birthday was very soon, shi bought it with some of the money on the credit chit shi had been given by Star Fleet. When shi enquired, shi found out that the Yamatos had already returned to the Phoenix, so shi took the next shuttle back with Zelkie.

In hir haste and excitement to present the gift to Lady Hikaru, the kitsune forgot to announce hirself first, and shi entered their cabin unexpectedly. Shi bowed to the startled humans and said, "Forgive my intrusion, please, but I have brought you a gift, Honoured Lady."

She lifted her eyes, and only then noticed a small plastic box on the desk next to them. Hir eyes widened in surprise. "I do not understand – why do you have those here?"

Hikaru sighed regretfully. "Oh, Kiku – why did you have to come in without permission? Akira – you know what must be done."

Akira nodded and got up, a troubled look in hir eyes. Kiku backed away. "No – please… I am your faithful servant." Shi bowed deeply.

A moment later shi collapsed n the floor, and the crystal lamp slipped out of hir grasp and bounced on the floor, jolting the light to life.

Hikaru picked it up with a touch of sorrow. "Such a beautiful and thoughtful gift. I will always treasure it."

As people gathered for the evening meal, Shintaro asked, "Has anyone seen Kiku?"

Hikaru replied, "I have not seen Kiku-san since shi returned from sightseeing, and left me with a gift that shi had bought for me."

Nobody admitted to seeing hir since then, so Martin said, "Anastasiya, could you please trace hir."

"Aye, Captain." Anastasiya pulled out hir PADD and tapped it a few times. Shi frowned at what it displayed. "Excuse me, please. I must check this."

A few minutes later, Martin's wrist comm vibrated to indicate a discreet call. He tapped it and held it to his ear. "Yote here," he murmured.

"Please to be coming to deck five, Captain." Anastasiya's voice carried a sense of urgency.

"On my way." He tapped the comm off and stood up. "Excuse me, folks – I have to attend to something important."

Stepping out of the trans-lift at deck five, he found the tiger waiting for him. "What's wrong, Ana?"

Without replying, Anastasiya pushed open the door to the adjacent stairwell. Near the bottom of the steps coming from the deck above lay Kiku, hir head bent at an impossible angle to hir body, hir eyes staring sightlessly.

"Oh hell! How did this happen? Why was shi using the stairs instead of the trans-lift?"

"Looks like shi was in hurry and had not patience to wait for trans-lift. Took stairs hastily, tripped on pretty dress, and broke neck."

Martin sighed. "I'm going to have to break the news to Shintaro and the Yamatos. Have you taken videos for the official report?" Anastasiya nodded. "Okay, then take hir up to sick bay for M'Lertiña to pronounce the official cause of death. I don't want anyone to see hir like this – it's a pretty upsetting sight, so try to make hir presentable."

Martin returned to the others and called for their attention. "I have some terrible news – there's been an accident. Shintaro – could you please come with me."

Hikaru spoke up. "Captain – has something happened to Kiku?"

"Shi has had a bad fall, Lady Hikaru." Martin didn't want to say more before giving Shintaro a chance to see hir.

"No!" exclaimed Shintaro. "Please, Captain-san, take me to Kiku quickly."

Martin did as he was asked, and he tried to forewarn the kitsune, but shi seemed utterly focused on getting to hir mate and did not appear to hear him. When shi saw Kiku's body laying on the sick bay bed as if asleep, shi rushed over to hir. Shi picked up Kiku's hand and called hir name, but of course there was no response.

Martin put his hand on Shintaro's shoulder and said gently, "I regret to say that Kiku died as a consequence of hir fall. My condolences for your loss."

Tears were brimming in the kitsune's eyes. "May I be alone with my beloved for a while, Captain-san?"

"Of course. Please let me know if there's anything more that I can do for you."

Shintaro nodded, and Martin left the room to let hir mourn. He found Anastasiya standing outside the door. "Ana – could you stay here for now and keep an eye on Shintaro. If shi needs anything, try to help."

"Shintaro is my comrade – I will do whatever is needed."

"Thank you. And now I have to go back and tell the others that we lost Kiku today."

*** 19 January 2334 ***

They made one more unexceptional stop – a routine re-supply job for a Star Corps research post – and they headed back to Earth. The mood was sombre for a few days. Shintaro maintained a stoic façade, but each evening shi stopped by the stasis capsule in which Kiku's body was preserved until it could be properly dealt with. There shi placed flowers that shi had begged from Danson's hydroponic garden and grieved for a while before going back to hir cabin for the evening.

Normal routine prevailed. While Kiku's death was tragic, it did not affect the ship's normal activities. Burningbright was doing a scheduled maintenance task on the environmental systems on the passenger cabin deck when a stray scent caught hir attention. Shi stopped what shi was doing and took a deep sniff. There it was again – extremely faint – so much so that only a chakat or a bloodhound might smell it.

"Damn it," shi murmured. Shi tapped hir comm. "Captain? I think we may have picked up some unwanted guests back at one of our ports of call."

"How so, 'Bright?"

"I am fairly certain that I can smell mice."

"Smeg! Where?"

"I'm on the passenger deck at the moment."

"Oh great, of all the places.... Okay, see if you can confirm it, and then deal with it any way you can. The only mice that I want on my ship stand on just two legs."

"Understood, Captain." Shi tapped hir comm again. "Hotfoot – can you bring your talented nose down to the passenger deck, please."

"*As long as I can bring the rest of me,*" came the amused reply.

Minutes later, the ship's cook was using hir discerning nose to test the air. Used to dealing with subtleties of aromas in the kitchen, shi was able to easily pick out the offending smell. "Yep, that's mouse scent. I don't want those vermin finding my kitchen."

"Let's see if we can narrow it down. We'll check out the unoccupied cabins first, Don't want to annoy our guests if it isn't necessary."

Burningbright handed Hotfoot a scanner set to detect small life signs like mice, and they each took a room and started checking them out with both nose and device. When they both came up negative, they moved onto the next. Eventually they eliminated all the cabins except those of Shintaro and the Yamatos.

"I suppose that was inevitable," Burningbright sighed. "Oh well, let's try Shintaro's cabin first.

Shi touched the tone pad, and a moment later the kitsune answered the door. After explanations, shi willingly let the chakat scan the cabin.

"Clear," came the verdict. "And that just leaves just one place the bastards can be hiding. Looks like we're going to have to bother the Yamatos."

"I will accompany you," Shintaro offered. "I will explain the necessity to them."

"Thanks, Shintaro."

The kitsune and the chakats stopped outside the Yamatos' cabin, and Shintaro used the door announcer. Moments later, Akira answered the door, and Shintaro bowed respectfully.

"Akira-sama, Burningbright-san requests permission to inspect your cabin. Shi has detected the presence of vermin, and it is hir task to find and remove them."

Akira looked at the chakats with a frown. "No, you may not come in and disturb my wife and I."

Shintaro was just as surprised as the chakats by the swift refusal. Burningbright stepped forward.

"Shir Akira, the health of the crew and the hygiene of this ship requires me to deal with these small problems before they become big ones. I must insist that we be allowed to scan your cabin."

"And I insist that our privacy be respected. I will say no more on this." Akira closed the door in hir face.

Shintaro shrugged apologetically. "Akira-sama has spoken. I am afraid that I must ask you to respect my lord's wishes."

"With respect, Shintaro, they do not have that right. I'm going to call the captain about this."

Several minutes later, an irritated Martin met up with the chakats. "Right – let's sort this out right now." He touched the tone pad. When there was no response, he tried again, but once more nobody answered. He then called out loudly. "Akira-san, Hikaru-san – this is Captain Yote. Please answer the door."

No one responded.

Martin was genuinely annoyed now. He tapped his comm. "Anastasiya, please report to the passenger deck immediately."

The tiger was there within a minute. "Yes, Captain – what do you need?"

"Override the lock on the Yamatos' cabin, please."

Anastasiya tapped hir PADD, then nodded. "It is now unlocked, Captain."

Martin touched the door control, and the door slid open, to the startlement of Akira who was standing close by.

"What is the meaning of this, Captain? I specifically said that we do not wish to have your crew disturbing us."

"I'm afraid that I must demand that they be allowed access. Health and hygiene regulations demand that I deal with vermin as a priority." Actually it was not *that* urgent, but the Yamatos were really rubbing him the wrong way, and he was not in the mood to compromise.

Akira looked grossly offended. "We are the duly appointed representatives of Asahikawa, and as ambassadors, we demand privacy. Have you not got anything better to do with your time than to chase mice? You would be better off doing more worthwhile projects – repairing dangerous stairs comes to mind. Now leave us! Shintaro – guard the door and do not let these fools pass."

Shintaro pushed past Martin and Anastasiya, and took Akira's place in the doorway. Shi laid one hand on hir katana, and the other on hir phaser pistol. Martin immediately regretted allowing the kitsune to retain hir weapon as part of hir bodyguard duties.

"My apologies, Captain-san, Anastasiya-san, but I cannot let you pass. My first duty is to my lord and lady, and their will is mine."

"No offence taken, Shintaro, but as captain of this ship, I am the absolute top authority aboard this ship, and my commands override theirs."

"Nevertheless I must obey my lord's command, Captain-san."

Martin was flabbergasted. "This is crazy! Why so much reluctance to a trivial scan for vermin? Am I going to have to use force just to…." Martin's voice trailed off as something suddenly clicked in his mind. "Akira – why do you think the inter-deck stairs need repairs?"

"What a foolish question! They are obviously unsafe, otherwise dear Kiku would be still with us."

"I told everyone that shi died in a fall. I had hir moved to sick bay so that the sight would not distress people. How did you know that shi died on the stairs?"

Akira look flustered for a moment, then said, "Shintaro must have mentioned it."

The kitsune was looking confused. "While I mourned the loss of my mate, I had no wish to talk about how shi died. I said nothing to you, my lord."

Martin said, "Only Anastasiya, M'Lertiña, and I knew exactly where shi was found dead. Again – how did *you* know?"

"**Fool!**" Hikaru shouted, coming into view for the first time to berate hir husband. "You never know when to shut up, and now you have jeopardised our mission."

Shintaro was looking stunned as the implications struck hir. Martin moved to push past the distracted kitsune, only to be brought to a halt

173

once again as he saw Hikaru take a clear container out of the box that shi was holding. It contained two mice – the probable source of the scent that Burningbright had detected.

Hikaru held up the box and said, "If I drop this box, it will shatter, and then nothing can save you all from being infected by the herm symbiont that they carry. Now, withdraw from this room immediately. Shintaro – make everybody stay away from the door."

Shintaro made no move to obey. "You... killed Kiku? Why would you do such a thing?"

Hikaru frowned. "Your mate intruded upon us without permission and saw us tending to the mice. We could not trust that shi would not speak of it, so shi had to be silenced. Shi had failed in hir duty – do not fail in yours."

"No! You have betrayed my loyalty and destroyed my dreams. I cannot in all honour serve you any more, and my Kiku must be avenged." Shintaro drew hir katana and started advancing on the humans.

Akira produced a weapon from nowhere and shot the kitsune, who instantly collapsed on the deck.

"Martin was shocked. "Fuck! Where the hell did that come from. That wasn't on the authorised list. Have you murdered another person, you bastards?" He felt ready to lunge at the humans right then despite the weapon now pointed his way.

Anastasiya restrained him, "Is stunner, Captain. Shintaro still lives."

Martin looked carefully and saw that shi was indeed still breathing. He glared at Akira anyway, then backed off as he calmed down.

Akira said, "My weapon can kill also. Please carefully disarm yourself, Anastasiya, so that I do not have to prove it."

Anastasiya did as shi was instructed, while Martin made a show of retreating. "Don't let this door close, Ana," he instructed, then more quietly he discreetly told Burningbright, "Get Zelkie down here *now*."

He turned his attention back to the Yamatos. "Why are you doing this? Why do you want to bring disaster to Earth, and perhaps to the whole Federation?"

"Disaster, Captain? No, we bring a gift – the greatest gift bestowed upon humanity and its children in millennia. Look at us! We are healthier, stronger, and longer lived than the best of humanity, and even the morph species have gained nearly as much. We are your superiors in every way, but we are willing to share, to elevate you to our greatness also. But is our gift appreciated? No – we are treated with fear, and we are cut off from all other civilisation. Like the lepers of old, we are treated as unclean. So if you will not accept our gift with open arms, we will bestow it upon you anyway so that we may once again be part of the Federation, and mankind as a whole will take its next big evolutionary step!"

'*Oh great, they're raving fanatics.*' Martin mentally groaned. "And what about all the people who die during the transformation? If you infect everyone virtually at once, there won't be enough people to care for the one's who have a worse time than the others, just as they did on Asahikawa."

"Those who die are obviously inferior, and are thus unworthy of being elevated to our greatness."

"And foxtaurs? Their genetics would seem to be incompatible with the herm symbiont template. You would kill an entire species?"

"You seek to sway me, Captain, but our destiny is clear even if some must die to see it realised. You will continue on to Earth and deliver us there If you still reject our gift, then you may leave without its blessing."

"I will not do that, Akira. I will not have the death of thousands, perhaps millions, on my head, all for a destiny that none will have chosen for themselves. You are possibly right in saying that many will choose to accept your gift – it is very tempting. You should give up on this mad plan and continue the mission as it was first explained to us."

"Our world would still be cut off from vital trade, and it would not fulfil our destiny. That is our foremost duty!"

Martin saw Zelkie arrive out of the corner of his eye, but he kept up the talk. "Then why didn't you just let the mice loose on our ship before anyone caught wise instead of resorting to murder to keep your secret?"

Hikaru sneered as shi answered, "Do not pretend to be stupid, Captain. You know as well as we do that you would show symptoms of the symbiont long before we got to Earth, and no one would ever be allowed to leave the ship." Shi looked at Anastasiya. "You are already a herm, so the gift would be easy for you to accept. Help us to achieve our destiny and you will be so much greater than these others who would deny us our quest."

Anastasiya rolled hir eyes. "Who wants huge breasts?"

"Give it up," Martin insisted. "No one on this crew will willingly help you do this, and I cannot be coerced.

Hikaru looked at Akira who said, "Then we will kill members of your crew until you comply."

"I think not," Martin demurred. "Zelkie!"

The box of mice that Hikaru was still holding up to dash on the floor at a moment's notice, suddenly wrenched out of hir hands and into Martin's. At the same time, Akira's weapon was wrested from hir grasp and into Anastasiya's.

The humans were stunned for an instant, then Hikaru lunged for the box, only to be met by a tiger's fist to hir nose. Shi fell to the floor, blood pouring profusely from the broken appendage.

"Superior humans bleed very well too," Anastasiya observed.

Martin examined the box – it was barely big enough for the mice. Space was taken up by an inbuilt water supply and a food cache that could be triggered to dispense pellets without having to open the box. A filter allowed air to be exchanged while stopping things like the symbiont – or at least Martin fervently hoped so. The filter also allowed a trace of the scent of the mice to escape – completely unnoticeable by the humans, but after accumulating for weeks, detectable by the sensitive noses of the chakats.

He turned around and handed the box carefully to Burningbright. "Here are your vermin. Take them to M'Lertiña and have her thoroughly scan and document them for evidence *without* removing them from the box, then have them ejected from the ship as soon as possible."

"Yes sir." Burningbright gingerly carried them away.

Martin then looked at Anastasiya. " 'Who wants huge breasts?' " he repeated ironically.

Anastasiya shrugged. "You already said all best words."

Martin grinned and turned to Zelkie. "Please help Anastasiya take the Yamatos to their new accommodations in the brig."

"Delighted to do so, Captain."

"And thank you – you saved our hides once again. I don't think I could have caught that box if Hikaru had tried to break it."

"You're welcome, Captain. Just remember that when it comes to handing out bonuses."

Martin could feel hir empathically broadcasting hir pleasure. Since the episode with the hijackers, Martin had instructed the chakat to never use hir Talent around anyone who was not a crew member. Hir telekinetic ability would be their secret ace in the hole, and Zelkie had agreed. Getting hir young offspring to not carelessly show it had been a greater challenge, but they had made a game of it. They designated one of the crew to be the token 'stranger', and if they concealed their TK ability from that person all day, then they were rewarded with a special treat. Each day a different crew person wore the armband that indicated that they were the stranger, which forced the cubs to be diligent and observant in order to win the reward. The game had worked, and the Asahikawans never knew about the Talented chakats.

Hotfoot was the only one left, and Martin indicated Shintaro's prone form on the floor. "Help me take Shintaro up to sick bay. Shi's going to feel terrible when the stun wears off, and shi might even need more help as shi comes to terms with these events."

Hotfoot nodded, and they lifted the kitsune between them. As they carried hir away, shi said, "You know shi's the real victim in all of this. Hir mate was murdered and hir loyalty betrayed. I wonder how shi's going to cope?"

Martin wished he knew the answer to that.

A group of the off-duty crew were in the mess hall, drinking their favourite brews, and reviewing the recent events and speculating on how they came about. The Yamatos certainly weren't going to enlighten them.

"I still don't know how the Yamatos got that box of mice past Star Fleet," Martin admitted. "Although it's small, it's not something that is easily overlooked, and the staff at the station didn't strike me as anything but diligent."

"It's not so puzzling as you might think, Captain," Penny said.

Martin's eyebrows raised. "Oh? How?"

Penny held out the toy that she used to practice the sleight of hand that she had been taught. Then with a flick of her hand, it was gone. "A little bit of magic. The art of the magician is misdirection, and Akira is an expert at that. Star Fleet was obviously not expecting a deliberate attempt to smuggle the symbiont, so they were able to be misled by Akira who probably put a lot of time and effort into the deception. Shi brought the box in right under their noses."

"Makes sense, I suppose," Martin admitted. "A procedural failure rather than carelessness. Commander Hasluck isn't going to be happy when he finds out. Anyway, that's as close as I ever want to get to a sex change."

"What do you suppose they'll do with the Yamatos?" Hotfoot asked.

Bethany replied, "Most likely try them for terrorism, murder, and attempted hijacking."

"If I were sentencing them," Heywood said, ""I'd ban them permanently from returning to Asahikawa. Think about it – without the symbiont active in their bodies, they are just ordinary humans, except for being herms. No rapid healing, and no extended life span. Just imagine how those bastards will feel to be deprived of their precious 'gift' for the rest of their lives."

There was a murmur of agreement amongst the rest of the group.

Bethany said, "It seems to me that if they genuinely represented the people of Asahikawa, they may have seriously harmed their cause. I can see Star Fleet recommending to reject their appeal on the basis of the

Yamatos' actions. After all – where there are two fanatics, there are surely more."

"But there's also likely to be far more who genuinely want what we were told they wanted to do," Penny replied. "After all, it is a *very* attractive incentive that they have to offer." At the looks that people gave her, she laughed. "I said it was attractive, not tempting. The price is way too high for me. However, I'm willing to bet that others will find it irresistible."

Just then, the discussion was interrupted by Shintaro entering the mess hall. Shi walked up to Martin and bowed deeply. "I most humbly beg forgiveness for drawing arms against you, Captain-san." Shi drew and held out hir katana to Martin. "I surrender my weapons and submit to your justice."

Martin waved it off. "Put back your sword, Shintaro. I cannot fault you for your loyalty, however misplaced it turned out to be."

Shintaro re-sheathed the katana gratefully.

"How are you coping, Shintaro? Your life must be turned upside down."

"I am adrift. My lifemate is dead, and I have turned against those I swore to serve. I have been dishonoured and lost face. I can never return to Asahikawa with that shame over my head."

"I don't find it shameful to do the right thing in the end, but I don't pretend to understand exactly how your society works. I'm more concerned about you though – what will you do without a mate or any others of your kind?"

"I will cope with the knowledge that part of Kiku lives on in me."

"Will that be enough to deal with the loneliness though?"

"You misunderstand, Captain. I am with child. I will never be alone."

"Oh! I hadn't realised. Forgive me for the preconception, but I thought that Kiku would have been the far more likely mother of any child that you two might have."

"I begged Kiku's indulgence. I was my mother's firstborn, and I was the one that shi trained in the way of the samurai. I wished to do the same with my firstborn. Kiku impregnated me shortly before we left on our mission."

"That's wonderful news in all this sadness, but what are you thinking of doing for the immediate future?"

Shintaro hesitated. "I cannot go back to Asahikawa, and I would feel out of place on Earth. I think that I would like to wander and find my place in the universe. To that end, I request that I may join your crew."

That startled Martin, and most of the others in the room. Martin frowned in concern. "Shintaro – I like you, but I really can't afford to put you on the payroll at the moment."

"I have no need to be paid, Captain-san – I just desire meals and a place to sleep. Star Fleet gave us all credit chips to cover expenses while on our mission, and you are welcome to take that to cover my upkeep. I also have other skills to offer besides the obvious."

Martin was still undecided – Phoenix's budget was terribly tight, and their future was still uncertain due to Windsor's commercial sabotage. Then again, Penny had set a very positive precedent. His musings were interrupted by Anastasiya.

"Captain – I wish to support my comrade's request."

A moment later, Loander added, "I think that our friend, Kiku, would be happy for Shintaro to join us," Presaith seconded Loander's opinion.

"Shintaro belongs with us," Penny stated firmly.

Martin held his hands up in surrender. "Okay! Okay! I give up!" He turned back to the kitsune. "Shintaro – these people aren't just crew, but more like family, and the family has spoken. Do you feel that you can fit in with us, not just do your job, but to take an active part in our lives?"

"I will do my humble best, Captain-san."

"M'Rarrtikar is going to kill me for this, but… welcome to the crew of the Phoenix!"

Chapter 6: Asteroid Adversity

*** 8 February 2333 ***

"It just isn't right!" Martin complained.

"You've said that a dozen times already, Martin," Risha replied patiently as she groomed the fur on the coyote's back. "Now stop tensing up so much."

Martin tried to take her advice. Their mutual grooming sessions were usually very pleasantly relaxing, but he was too keyed-up by recent events. He grabbed one of the four arms that were brushing him, and looked her in the eyes. "Doesn't it bother you that we're losing a stack of money every hour that we're stuck here idle?"

Risha shrugged. "I have a job that I like and a place to call home. Everything else can be dealt with in its own good time."

Martin sighed in exasperation. "If that idiot, Karnak, keeps us in quarantine too much longer, we won't even have that. Cargo has to be delivered by a deadline. Other cargo has to be picked up. Deals have to be made. Bills have to be paid. The *crew* has to be paid."

"You can't blame Karnak for the quarantine. After he screwed up so badly with Penny, it's hardly surprising that he's doing everything strictly by the book. We're stuck here on the ship until he can be 100% sure that we aren't infected with the herm symbiont."

"Ha! I went to great lengths to document exactly what happened just so that we wouldn't have to go through all of this. I bet it's Karnak's way of getting back at us for making him look like a fool."

Risha bopped Martin on the head with one of the brushes.

"Ow! What was that for?"

"Stop being so paranoid. Besides, the fact that Star Fleet is taking this so seriously can only play to our advantage."

"What do you mean?"

"We foiled a plot that could have devastated the entire Federation. Don't you think that you could use that as leverage to make some lucrative deals?"

Martin stared at her for a moment, his jaw hanging open. He snapped it shut and rolled his eyes. "Of course. I've been so pissed off with Karnak that I haven't been thinking straight. Damned if I'm going to let them off easy after what we've done for them."

"That's more like it. Here – take these." Risha handed the brushes to Martin, then leant back to sprawl on the bed. "Your turn to groom me."

"You don't need *me* to groom the fur on your front," Martin remarked, even as he admired her sexy nude body.

"No, but I'd like you to anyway," she replied sultrily.

Martin grinned. "Your wish is my command, and I know just where to start."

"I knew you would."

Martin was glad that at least he did not have to put up with the Yamatos. They had been beamed over into a secure quarantine facility on the station soon after they had arrived. It was also better for Shintaro that the people who had murdered hir mate were gone from the ship.

Without those distractions, and in a better frame of mind since Risha de-stressed him, he put his mind to figuring out how to make the best of the present situation. First, he put in a call to Captain Karnak.

The connection was made gratifyingly quickly, and Martin had to admit to himself that if Karnak really had it in for him, there would no way that he would be able to get to talk to the Fleet officer so easily.

The expression on Karnak's face was polite but firm. "If you've called yet again to ask for the quarantine to be lifted, I regret that you have wasted your time, Captain Yote. You will not be given clearance until tomorrow at the soonest."

"No, I haven't called about that this time. I'm calling in a favour or two."

Karnak's right eyebrow raised. "Really? And why would I owe you a favour?"

"Aside from screwing us around with Penny? Your good record may have enabled you to get away with little more than a reprimand from Admiral Tartikova. If I was a bastard, I could sue Star Fleet and cause a nasty stink, and after that I'm pretty sure that the top brass would have a thing or two to say about you and your career. However, that's not my style. I'd rather have you on my side and doing me a favour instead."

"Sounds a little like blackmail to me," Karnak commented.

"On an open comm line? What do you think I am – an idiot? I'm laying down the facts for you – I'm only interested in keeping my shipping company afloat, and my crew paid. To do that, I need income from somewhere. If it has to be through the courts, I won't pull any punches, and I'll have my father's legal resources behind me. On the other hand, if I can secure some reliable cargoes, I won't need to pursue that course. All I'm asking for is your help."

"And if I were to agree, what kind of help would you require?"

"We've proven ourselves with the delivery of the mind matrix generator, the capture of the hijackers, and the foiling of a plot that would have seriously harmed the entire Federation. We've got the score on the board, and now it's time we reaped the rewards, I want to get my hands on one of those lucrative Fleet contracts. I would like you to make contacts for me and add your recommendations. That's it. Nothing illegal – I'm just after the inside track."

Karnak seemed to mull it over for a while, then he seemed to come to a decision. "I will look into it. It's not exactly my speciality, but I have someone on staff who knows how the system works, and I'll put him onto you. He'll be able to help you, while keeping things within the rules."

"Thank you, Captain, and are you sure I can't start shifting my cargo this afternoon?"

"Nice try, Yote," Karnak replied with a half-smile. "Tomorrow morning after the med techs give their clearance, and not a moment sooner. However, I will have your documents processed and ready to go the moment that you do get that clearance. So if that is all, I have other pressing matters to attend to."

"That's all for now, Captain. Thanks again."

The comm disconnected, and Martin leaned back in his chair with a feeling of satisfaction. "Step one completed – let's hope that step two goes as well."

Karnak was true to his word, and Martin was contacted by a Fleet officer – a male human named Lieutenant Smails.

"Captain Karnak has explained your desires to me, Captain Yote, and I will endeavour to procure you some work from Star Fleet. However, before you get your hopes up too high, I will point out that most regular contracts are awarded months in advance. The only jobs available immediately are the type that you have been doing – the odd, irregular ones."

"I figured that might be the case," Martin admitted, "but I'll take what I can to help keep my business going."

"Excellent! If you could give me an idea of your itinerary, I will find which ones would best suit your needs."

Martin transferred his planned itinerary to Smails. "There's a bit of room for deviation in that itinerary," he informed the lieutenant.

"Thank you, Captain. I will call you back later this afternoon. Good day, sir."

Martin signed off, satisfied with the progress so far. Not as good as he had hoped, but not as bad as he had feared.

Precisely at 9:00 UTC the next day, the med techs gave the *Phoenix* their official 'all clear', the quarantine was lifted, and all their paperwork was approved. Martin had everyone who could do anything at all to help speed up the shifting of the cargo, put to work. Martin and Zelkie had everything planned to the minute to ensure that the work was done as swiftly as possible, and for once they encountered no hold-ups. Seeing as delays were an inevitable part of every job, Martin suspected that they had gotten a bit of discreet assistance there, for which he was grateful.

Much to Martin's relief, they had acquired a large number of passengers, including one Star Fleet courier for whom they were paying a premium. The only condition to that well-paying fare was that nobody was allowed to ask his business, as confidentiality was an absolute requirement. Martin had no problem with that, and far from being a mysterious agent, the courier was quite a genial and pleasant ermine morph.

Martin was finalising the paperwork in preparation for departure, when a call came in on his comm from his father. "Hi, Dad. Nice of you to call, but as you keep reminding me, time is money, and we have a very tight schedule to keep."

Yote Senior smiled at that. "I'm glad you have your priorities straight, but I haven't called to chat. You need to go over to the station right now and meet up with an associate of mine. He has a proposal for you that I think that you should consider."

Martin hesitated for barely a moment – he knew that his father wasn't the kind of person to waste his time. "Okay, I'll go right now. You can tell me the details while I'm on the way."

His father nodded and ended the call. Martin called up Bethany on his wrist comm as he headed out of his office to go to the shuttle bay. "Commander – I need you to work on the departure documents because I have to go over to the station right now. Not sure how long this will take, but I hope to be back very quickly."

"*Aye, Captain,*" came her reply.

As Martin piloted the shuttle over to the station, he contacted his father.

"*You'll be met by a rabbit morph by the name of Haydn Cottonfield. He and I have been doing business for many years, and we've occasionally socialised. When he learned of your business, he approached me to ask me to arrange a meeting with you. When he explained why, I agreed. I'll let him explain exactly what, but I think it should work well with your unusual set-up.*"

"I trust your judgement, Dad, but how is that going to be of benefit to me?"

"*An unusual fare – one that should pay well, with the potential for long-term income.*"

"Cryptic, but intriguing. We've got a pretty full passenger complement though. I'm not sure if we can fit another in."

"*Believe me, that's not going to be a problem.*"

"Oh, I'm going to have to get even with you for all this mystery," Martin warned his father.

"*Like I said, Cottonfield will explain, and you're going to have to see the client for yourself.*"

"Well, I suppose I'll find out soon enough. So why are you sending this my way? Didn't you say that you wouldn't be helping me anymore?"

"*Cottonfield asked a favour of me – I'm merely passing it along as he requested. That it helps you is just lucky for you, not a contradiction on my part.*"

"Sure, Dad. Gotta go now – I have to concentrate on docking."

"*Farewell, son.*"

Martin docked without incident and, as promised, found a well-dressed rabbit morph waiting for him outside the airlock. Accompanying him was a human female.

"Captain Martin Yote, I presume?" the rabbit said as he extended his hand.

Martin shook it and replied, "That would be me."

"A pleasure to meet Arthur's son. I would like you to meet my wife, Adele," he said, indicating the woman.

Martin was a little surprised by that, but not exceptionally so. Mixed human-morph matings weren't that rare, but few actually went as far as making it a formal marriage. "A pleasure to meet you, ma'am. Now, while I would normally be happy to chat at length, I am currently on an extremely tight schedule, and we need to get down to business."

"I appreciate that, Captain. Please accompany us to a nearby holosuite where we will explain everything, and you will meet our daughter."

They started moving off, and Martin asked, "Why couldn't your daughter meet us here?" He wondered if they were talking about a rabbit or a human daughter, but figured he'd find that out soon enough.

"Because she cannot, Captain. Some years back, she and her mother were involved in a serious accident. My first wife died, and Madeline, my daughter, almost did also. Such were the extent of her injuries that she lost both legs and her spine was crushed beyond repair. She is a quadriplegic on permanent life-support. Technology gives her a chance of a life, nevertheless, and that's where you come in."

They stepped into a translift, and it whisked them down a few floors to the entertainment levels. They made their way to the holosuite section, and the rabbit keyed the door to one of them. Stepping inside, Martin found himself in what looked like an arboretum. Sunshine filtered through a canopy of trees, dappling the path that led through the trees which opened up to reveal a small swimming pool. Martin started thinking that the pool would be forever being choked by leaves before realising that in a holosuite, that would never be a problem. Lazing by the side of the pool in a patch of sunlight was an attractive female rabbit morph, maybe 18 or 19 years of age, with soft warm-grey fur, dark blond hair, gold eyes, and dressed in a bikini bathing suit, reading a book while sipping on an iced drink. When she noticed them approaching, she got up to meet them, bringing along her drink.

"Is this the starship captain, Daddy?" she asked.

"Yes, dear. Let me introduce you to Captain Martin Yote. Captain, this is my daughter, Madeline."

"A surprising pleasure to meet you, Ms Cottonfield, especially since I was expecting a quadriplegic."

She grinned mischievously. "And one with two fewer legs, I suppose? Can you guess why the contradiction?"

"You're a hologram."

"Bingo! Although I really am here too." She pointed to one side where the holographic environment faded to reveal an object resembling a motorised sarcophagus. "I'm really in there. A sophisticated holo-program gives me a pseudo body though, one that enables me extremely realistic interaction with the real world." She held up her drink. "For example, I was really enjoying this fruit juice while lazing in the warm sun. It has some advantages too." Her clothing abruptly changed to a smart casual outfit of slacks and shirt. "The only catch is that I'm confined to holosuites, but it's better than the alternative."

"I can certainly concur with that. However, what has that got to do with me?"

"I want a job on your ship."

That stunned Martin. "What?" was all he could ask.

"Let me explain," Haydn spoke up. "My fortune could give my daughter the means to have a semblance of a normal life, but within

Art © Megan Giles

severe limitations. The only places that she can do so are within holo-fields, and one of the few places outside of entertainment precincts to have such are starships. I am proposing that I pay you to take Madeline on as an apprentice."

"And how is that going to work if she's confined to the holosuite?" Martin asked.

Madeline interrupted. "I'm not quite that limited, Captain."

"Please elucidate then."

"I have learned to interface directly with computer systems. That's one reason why this holographic simulacrum of mine is so close to perfect. I've studied starship computer systems, and I've been looking into starship design with an eye to becoming a systems controller. My life-support containment would be plugged directly into the ship's computer systems, and from there I can do my job directly, and I would also be able to connect with your holosuite facilities. You do have a good holosuite, I presume?"

"Yes, as a matter of fact. The equipment was so tightly integrated into the holosuite that it wasn't worth the effort to remove it when the Star Corps decommissioned it, and me and my crew find it invaluable for the boring parts of the voyages."

Haydn said, "I already made sure of that before I went ahead with this proposal. Anyway, that's what we propose in a nutshell. I want my daughter to have a fulfilling life, and she wants to be a starship systems controller. I am willing to cover all costs, plus a generous amount as a fee towards taking her on with you. This agreement would last for a full round-trip, with the option of renewing it each time you returned to home port. I have a contract prepared which outlines the fine details, and the money involved."

He held out a PADD. Martin pulled out his and the contract was transferred. He glanced at the screen. The figure quoted was quite impressive, and he nodded. "Mr Cottonfield, you are aware that I must leave extremely soon, and as such I do not have the time to read that contract properly before signing it. However, on the face of it, I will give my verbal agreement. I will take on your daughter, subject to review of the contract."

"I would have been very surprised if you had signed without checking the contract, and I am prepared to accept your verbal agreement." He turned to Adele. "My dear, would you see to disconnecting Madeline's support unit."

"Of course. Madeline, hon, time to withdraw from the holosuite systems."

"Okay, Adele. Just one sec though." Madeline went over to hug her father, the holosuite's sophisticated force-field generators exactly reproducing the feel of the real thing. "Thanks, Daddy. I love you." She then hugged Adele too. "And thanks for all that you've done for me also."

"You're welcome, hon. Now better hurry – we don't want to keep the captain waiting."

"Bye!" the rabbit girl said before abruptly disappearing.

Adele tapped on the life-support unit's control panel, and the holographic arboretum faded out. "We're ready, Haydn."

"Good. Let's get it to the captain's shuttle and get them on their way."

They exited the holosuite, with Adele controlling the motorised unit. As they hastened along, Adele said, "Everything that your engineer needs to know about installing Madeline's life-support unit into your ship's systems, can be found in the manual copied onto the unit's computer system. All it will need immediately will be access to power, and that will be sufficient for a few days, giving you plenty of time to get the rest hooked up. The other supplies are in the crates by the airlock. There's more than enough for two trips in there."

"Won't Madeline get bored while she's disconnected for a few days?"

"For starters, she shouldn't be disconnected that long. That's just how long her onboard systems can cope by themselves. All she requires immediately besides power is a high-speed data link, and she can be interacting with the rest of you immediately. Secondly, even if she was cut off for some reason for an extended period, she does have an entertainment system built in also."

Haydn added, "I made sure that she got the best and most foolproof equipment. I also made sure she got the best care by marrying her therapist." He grinned at Adele, who blushed a little.

Martin said, "Judging by the hug she gave her stepmother, I'd say that Madeline approved."

Haydn nodded. "It's funny – I'm always trying my best to make sure my little girl is happy, but she has never stopped trying to make me happy too. She never felt that I was forgetting her mother when I started going out with Adele. I am a very fortunate father, Captain. Do you see why I would do anything for my child?"

"I do, Mr Cottonfield, and I'm a little bit envious."

"Find the right female, Captain. I was luckier than most, because I found two."

Martin thought about both Risha and Bethany back on the ship, and how they both had their merits. "I wish it was as simple as that, sir."

"Call me Haydn, Captain. I'm trusting you my most precious possession – I expect that we'll become a lot more familiar soon enough."

Possession? Martin marvelled at the difference between Madeline's father and Penny's. One would not let go, while the other would not hesitate to do so if it made his daughter happy. "Then call me Martin. I promise not to let you down, Haydn."

"Thank you, Martin."

They reached the airlock, and loaded Madeline's unit aboard. While he secured it, Haydn and Adele brought in the crates of supplies on anti-grav sleds. With those stowed, Martin was ready to leave.

"I hate to make this such a hasty departure, but I will be in contact with you again soon."

"Bon voyage, Martin," Adele said, and Haydn followed up with a firm handshake.

Martin got clearance to depart immediately and made his best legal speed over to the *Phoenix*. On the way, he commed Bethany. "Is everything ready to go?"

"Everything but you," she replied. "We've been given a departure window in seven minutes – are you going to be able to make it, or will I have to call in a delay?"

"I'll be there and docked in time. Be ready to leave precisely on schedule."

"Aye, Captain."

Martin parked the shuttle on board and sealed up the shuttle bay with a couple of minutes to spare. He dashed to the trans-lift and got to the bridge with seconds to go. Bethany was seated in the command chair, and she gave him a stern look.

"Cutting it a bit fine, aren't you?" she asked as she rose out of the chair.

Martin waved her back. "You have the con, Commander. I'll explain as soon as we get under way."

Bethany nodded, and right at the appointed moment, they left their parking orbit and manoeuvred through the local traffic until they were sufficiently far out of the Earth's gravitic influence, and then they went to warp.

"All systems nominal, Captain," Bethany reported.

"Good. Ceres, you take the con. Commander, come with me." As they left the bridge, Martin tapped his wrist comm. "M'Rarrtikar and R'Murran – report to my office, please."

Bethany and Martin made their way to his office where they waited for the Caitians to arrive. In the meantime, Martin used the office's replicator to prepare everyone's favourite drinks. M'Rarrtikar arrived first, and R'Murran a minute later. Martin let everyone settle down with their refreshments first before saying anything.

189

"First of all, I'd like to thank you all for your excellent work today. We achieved a great deal in a very short time, and it's a credit to everyone on this ship that it all went so smoothly. I'm very proud of this crew, and I'll be telling that to everybody later. Right now though, there's a couple of things that need to be done. R'Murran – you, Presaith and Loander have to install something that I brought with me."

"What needs both engineers and a comptech?" R'Murran asked.

"A life-support unit belonging to our newest crewmember."

M'Rarrtikar looked startled. "Captain! We *can't* afford another person on crew. Adding Shintaro was bad enough."

"Whoa! Take it easy! This crewmember won't cost us anything. In fact, we're being paid to take her on as an apprentice."

M'Rarrtikar calmed down, then asked, "What kind of crew person needs a life-support unit?"

"Good question," Martin replied, and then proceeded to tell them all about his meeting with the Cottonfields. "So your priority is getting Madeline integrated with our ship," Martin concluded.

"Aye. I'll get onto that right away," R'Murran acknowledged as he rose from his chair.

"M'Rarrtikar – let's have the financial report."

The Caitian called up figures on her PADD which she set to display on the main screen. "The good news is that in spite of the late penalties, we have scraped past the break-even point. As long as nothing goes wrong on this voyage, our figures will stay in the black. The bad news though is that the ship will be due for essential servicing, which will not be covered by the profits made on this voyage as they currently stand."

Martin nodded in agreement. His ballpark figures had nearly matched the actual ones. He tapped his own PADD and changed the main display. "Thankfully, that may yet be fully covered. Smails got back to me just before I went over to see the Cottonfields, and he has a couple of shipments for us to pick up along the route. Add to that the money that Haydn Cottonfield is paying us for taking Madeline, and I think we'll be doing nicely."

M'Rarrtikar swept her expert eyes over the figures, and then she smiled. "Now that's much better. I forecast a modest profit in light of this news. Before you ask though – it's still not enough to give the crew a raise. Perhaps a little bonus though."

"Do the figures and let me know what we can afford," Martin instructed.

"If we've got the financial worries out of the way," Bethany said, "we should look at another impending problem."

Martin's brow furrowed. "And what's that?"

"The crew needs a break. Because of the quarantine, nobody got shore leave. By the time that we get to our next destination, a number of them may be getting cabin fever, and going by the current itinerary, they aren't going to get much of a chance for R&R there either."

"Hmm... good point. Okay, I authorise pushing up our speed above standard cruising. Figure out what speed we need to make in order to give the entire crew at least half a day of uninterrupted shore leave. We can spare a bit of anti-matter," Martin said, looking pointedly at M'Rarrtikar.

"Aye, Captain," Bethany replied. "In the meantime, I suggest that we step up the cross-training exercises. We've also got an apprentice to train. That will have the added benefit of keeping their minds occupied."

Martin leaned back in his chair with a sigh of satisfaction. "Looks like we may finally be back on track. Between my father, Star Fleet, and myself, we've lined up some significant work for the next voyage, so the *Phoenix* may soon be rising from the ashes once more."

***

Three days into the voyage, Ilya Minsk was already a bit bored. Although his Star Fleet assignment was important, it was far from exciting, and the ermine had nothing to do until he reached his destination. The *Phoenix* was hardly a cruise ship with a plethora of forms of entertainment, and he didn't really want to sit around watching vids all day. He was told though that they had a holosuite that he could use, as long as the crew was not using it already.

He was disappointed to find that it was in use, but at least it was not closed to him. It seemed that a number of the crew were engaged in various forms of exercise and training, and the holosuite was currently configured as a gymnasium. One of the tiger morphs was engaged in unarmed combat with a two-tailed fox, with a grey fox vixen apparently refereeing. A couple of Caitians were doing gymnastic exercises, while two Faleshkarti, a mouse, and a rabbit were playing handball. The latter aroused his curiosity as he had briefed on all the crew as a matter of basic security, but there had been no mention of a rabbit doe on the list. She had the crew badge on her sports halter, so she was not a fellow passenger, all of whom he'd been appraised of anyway. He stepped up to watch the game and get a closer look at her. Aside from the halter, she wore gym shorts like the others, and nothing else, so he was able to admire her lithe athletic figure. Only a few years younger than himself... not bad! A nicer match for him than the more full-figured mouse fem, or the two herm aliens who were still children anyway.

Ilya kept watching until the game played out, which took quite a while because they seemed to be fairly evenly matched in skill. The result seemed of little concern to them as they appeared to be just doing a fun form of exercise rather than any serious competition. He did notice one odd thing though – while the Faleshkarti and the mouse were all breathing hard from their exertions, the rabbit seemed fresh and rested. He had to find out more.

Approaching the rabbit, Ilya said, "Good game. You must be really fit because you don't look the least bit tired."

The rabbit grinned back at him. "I have an unfair advantage there – I don't *get* tired."

Ilya raised his eyebrows sceptically. "Pardon me for saying so, but I find that hard to believe. I'm Ilya, by the way."

"I know – the Star Fleet courier – and I suppose you're partly right. I mentally tire. My name is Madeline, and I'm the new apprentice Systems Controller."

"You mentally tire, but not physically tire? Now you've really got me puzzled. Mind if I test that statement and challenge you to a game?"

Madeline's grin grew wider. "Want to see who gets tired first?"

The two Faleshkarti giggled. The girl was hiding something, but he could not figure it out yet. Still, it had given him a good opening line, and Madeline seemed willing to play along. An hour later though, after continuous hard-fought matches, he was almost worn out, while she still was not flagging in the slightest. That grin of hers was starting to get infuriating.

"Enough!" he exclaimed. "I see that you will eventually win even if through sheer indefatigability. How do you *do* that?"

"I think I'll see if you can figure it out. No cheating by asking any of the other crew though."

"Okay. I'm going to go back to my room now and take a shower. Can I meet up with you later?"

"Sure – I'll be in the rec room."

"Great! I'll meet you there then." With a wave, he headed off to his room. If he had looked back though, he may have wondered where the rabbit had disappeared to.

After refreshing himself, Ilya made his way to the rec room where various crew and passengers were playing vid games, Lirkar-Kr'rin, or just chatting with coffee and snacks. As promised, he found Madeline there, having a conversation. She spotted him entering, and waved him over.

"Have you figured out my secret yet?"

He shook his head. "The only morphs that I know of that have enhanced endurance are all former war beasts, and I'm sure rabbits were never included amongst those."

"I wouldn't know that, but you're right – that's not the answer."

"Want to give me a clue?"

"OK." She stood up and moved her chair in front of her. "Take this chair."

Puzzled, Ilya attempted to do so, only to have his hands pass right through it. "Wha...? It's a hologram! But if you were sitting on it...." He reached out to try to take Madeline's arm, but again he could not touch anything solid.

"Unlike down in the holosuite, I'm insubstantial here." Madeline pointed to the holo-emitters on the ceiling of the rec room. "Those units can only project an image, and a focused sound projector make my voice seem to come from my mouth. However, there aren't any force-field projectors and other systems to give me a physical presence."

"So I was playing against a solid hologram? No wonder you never got tired. But what are you? An A.I.?"

Madeline gave him a look of genuine disappointment. "Oh, come on! Do I *sound* like an A.I.?"

"No, no you don't. But I know that *Phoenix* is not a brain ship. Those are very rare and well known."

"You're right – *Phoenix* isn't a brain ship, but you would have been a lot closer than your A.I. guess."

"Put me out of my misery and tell me, please."

Madeline relented and told him her story. He was surprised and concerned for her, but he had to admit that she was dealing well with her situation. "So you work in conjunction with the ship's computer, rather than replacing it?"

"That's right. By being directly plugged into it, I can multitask way beyond the abilities of any normal person, and control various ship's systems directly. It also enables me to flawlessly replicate my body as a hard hologram in the holosuite, except of course it doesn't physically tire."

"Quite an advantage," Ilya conceded. "So, can you go anywhere on the ship as a hologram?"

"Sadly, no. While I can be aware of most places through the ship's systems, only this room and the bridge have the auxiliary holo-emitters so far. Between them, they give me a real presence in the most important places – my primary work and relaxing environments."

"So you still need to relax despite everything else?"

"Sure! There's a real body tied into this ship's systems, and I still need to unwind, and even sleep occasionally."

"And you're restricted to the ship too, aren't you?"

Madeline's face fell. "Yes, I'm afraid so."

Ilya was annoyed with himself. Madeline did not need reminding that in spite of all the technology, she was nevertheless still severely handicapped. "I'm sorry – I should not have brought that up."

Madeline shook her head. "No, don't let it bother you. I'm still luckier than most in my condition, and I've made peace with that fact. I'm determined to make my life a worthwhile and fulfilling one within those restrictions." Her grin returned. "And how many quadriplegics get to control a starship?"

Ilya smiled back. "None that I know of. But next time, I'm going to play some game against you that doesn't involve physical exertion!"

Madeline laughed. "Deal!"

They chatted conversationally for a while until Ilya excused himself to head off to the mess hall for a meal. As the ermine departed, Risha smirked and commented, "I reckon he's got the hots for you."

Madeline nodded. "Yeah, and he's cute. Fun to tease too."

"So, are we going to see a little shipboard romance?"

Madeline stuck her tongue out at the cougar. "Don't be silly. Besides, you don't know me very well yet. You're not going to be able to figure out what I find attractive until you do," she added cryptically.

*** 14 February 2334 ***

Phoenix's first stop was an asteroid. However, it was far from being just a barren rock. The star system in which it was located had been a big disappointment because despite having an ideal star, its planets were unsuitable for any form of colonisation. One had potential for mining, but there were more economical sources. The system might have been written off if it hadn't been for its extensive asteroid belt with rare metals in relative abundance. The star's location at a point roughly central to four colony worlds made it ideally placed to not only supply materials to all of them, but also act as a central transfer point between those worlds.

The six kilometre long asteroid was named Hesperia, and it had been mined extensively, leaving it riddled with a maze of passageways and enormous caverns. The Hesperia Mining Company had decided to seal off the tunnels and fill it with air to make it into a habitat, and then they began filling it with offices, shops, and residences. In a surprisingly short time, Hesperia had grown into a vibrant and exciting city. The HMC prided itself on not only providing living facilities, but recreational ones also. Just about every form of entertainment could be found there, and with them came the gambling venues. Many shipping lines used Hesperia as regular R&R port, and the city was often referred to as the New Las Vegas of space, named after the famous city in the middle of a desert that died when the Gene Wars began. Like that old city, the asteroid was lit up like a Christmas tree; all the more to impress the tourists who flocked there as they gazed from the observation lounges of the starliners. Less impressive were the docks that serviced the freighters that kept the city in space supplied with everything from fresh packs of cards, to tankers of water and air.

It was to one of these that the *Phoenix* was directed. Heywood deftly piloted the ship into position where the automated docking tractor beams took over. The sound of the magnetic mooring cables anchoring themselves signalled their arrival. There was not much to be unloaded there as the city was serviced regularly by the much larger freighters that docked daily. Their consignments were of a more urgent and critical nature that couldn't wait on the slower ships, and thus paid a handsome premium. As Martin had instructed, *Phoenix* had arrived early, which would not only make their customers happy, but would give the crew a much-needed break.

"*Welcome to Hesperia City,*" a voice over the comm announced. "*You have been assigned cargo bay 72. Please report to the Portmaster's office before commencing unloading.*"

"That's my cue," Martin said. He touched the P.A. button. "All hands – commence unloading procedures. We will be using cargo bay 72 upon receiving clearance from the Portmaster." He turned off the P.A. and turned to Bethany. "Mr Oakwood – you have the bridge."

Martin departed for the personnel airlock where a docking tube had already been extended to the ship, sealed, and filled with air. "very efficient," Martin murmured in satisfaction. He picked up a couple of VIP parcels that were boldly marked, '**PERSON TO PERSON – SIGNED DELIVERY ONLY**', and headed for the Portmaster's office. Zelkie, as Loadmaster, had transmitted their manifest immediately, and it was waiting for his biometric imprint after the Portmaster gave clearance to start unloading the goods. The duty officer at the interplanetary courier desk accepted Martin's urgent parcels, and then the coyote headed back to the ship to help with the unloading.

Because they were docked directly to Hesperia, they were able to save a lot of time due to not having to shuttle it down. The freight was therefore unloaded very quickly, and Martin was soon able to make the long-awaited announcement.

"All shore leave parties are now free to enjoy themselves as they see fit. You have ten and a half standard hours before you have to be back for a prompt departure at 2200 hours ship time. Any latecomers will have their pay docked, but other than that, I don't want to see you back here, okay?"

There was cheer amongst the crew, and then a mass exodus. Soon there was no one left aboard the ship except for Martin, and of course

Madeline. Her holographic image blinked into existence on the bridge, and she gave him a curious stare.

"Aren't you going on shore leave, Captain?"

"Someone has to stay on watch on the ship, and it's best that the rest of the crew get the opportunity for R&R first."

"You need some R&R too – I could stay on watch. It's not as if I can go anyway."

Martin noticed that there was a touch of wistfulness to that statement, rather than envy. He hoped that it would remain that way because there was nothing that he could do to change that situation. "Maddy, you're doing a great job so far, but you're still only an apprentice. The watch officer needs to be one of the command staff anyway."

"Oh, I see. I understand," Madeline conceded with disappointment, but then she rallied. "But *you* still need a break."

"And I'll get one. R'Murran drew the short straw, and he'll be back in five hours to relieve me. Then I will take a few hours R&R."

"What did you intend to do?" she asked curiously.

Martin shrugged. "Probably take in a live show. Maybe go visit a bar and shoot the breeze with a few other spacers. Whatever takes my fancy."

"What will you do until then?"

"Kill time somehow. Want to play a game?"

"Always! I play a mean game of Scrabble if you think you're up to the challenge?"

Martin grinned. "You're on!"

They were midway through their third game, score tied at one game each, when Madeline's ears pricked up. "I've just '*heard*' an all-ships announcement."

"What is it?" Martin asked curiously.

"There's a bulk freighter, *The Olympian*, limping into the system. They were attacked and badly damaged by pirates. They apparently have very limited control, and all ships are advised to avoid their flight path until they are picked up by a tug ship and docked at the repair facilities at Vulcan Shipyards."

The shipyards were used for all maintenance and repair facilities for the asteroid miners, and were located on another of the floating mountains located conveniently close to Hesperia. "Is that going to affect our departure at all?" Martin queried.

Madeline cocked her head as she examined the flight computer's data. She shook her head. "No – it's due to arrive an hour, more or less, before we depart."

"Good. One less thing to worry about. At least it's not *us* in trouble for once."

Later, after a meal break and change of games, R'Murran turned up on the bridge. "I'm here to relieve you, Captain."

Martin looked at the chronometer. "That time already? I hardly noticed. You might want to take up this game with Madeline – it will help pass the rest of the watch."

"I might just do that. Have fun, Captain."

"I intend to. Sorry that you had to cut yours short."

Having never been to Hesperia before, the first thing that Martin did was wander around Hesperia, gawking like any other tourist. He resisted the temptations of the various Renzar merchants hawking their wares along one of the many shopping districts. Then he passed into the central main cavern and gaped in awe. It had to be at least half a kilometre to the roof! Transit tubes criss-crossed the empty space, but it was the spectacular light display that riveted his sight for several minutes.

Eventually though, he tore his eyes away and accessed Hesperia's entertainment guide, checking for live theatre performances. Deciding that he'd had enough of real-life drama, he chose a comedy instead. That killed about half of the time that he had available, but he felt that it was worth it, giving the show at least four stars out of five.

Feeling a bit of thirst, he decided it was time to look for a good bar. Looking up recommendations for bars that were frequented by spacers, he settled for one called "*The Gamma Quadrant*". Therefore he wasn't surprised to find an assortment of ship's crews in there, from freighters to Star Fleet. What startled him was running into some familiar faces.

"Seems like we think alike," he told the people gathered about one of the tables.

Ceres grinned and said, "Might as well join us for a drink, Captain. They brew a pretty good beer here."

"Don't you believe it, Captain," Bethany said. "It seems Starwalkers have strange tastes."

"I wouldn't touch such weak stuff," Zelkie added.

"You chakats could drink straight ethanol and it would be scarcely strong enough for you," Risha retorted.

"I'll stick to what I know," Martin decided, and flagged down a waitress – a well-stacked (and apparently well-tipped) vixen. He placed his order before asking, "So where are the others?"

Ceres replied, "Did you know that they have a famous botanical garden in one of the caverns? It's part of the environmental system that helps keep the air smelling sweet, but it's awarded for its aesthetic design also."

"I suppose that explains where Danson is," Martin guessed.

Ceres nodded. "Yep. I had my fill after a couple of hours, but he's still exploring it. I told him I'd rendezvous with him later, and I went looking for a bar."

"And this is where I found hir when I arrived," Zelkie said. "My mates have taken the cubs to somewhere suitable for their age. Frankly their choice made me gag, so I begged off. I believe the Caitians have all gone to some family show. We have no idea where the others are." No one was going to use their comm to interrupt their R&R just to ask what they were up to.

"As long as they're back on time, it doesn't really matter," Martin conceded. The vixen turned up with his drink, and he tipped her a reasonable amount. With both Bethany and Risha there, he didn't want to show any excessive interest in the sexy fox.

Martin spent a bit of time with his shipmates before leaving to mingle with some of the other spacers. He was involved in a discussion with a couple of other independent shippers when the power suddenly glitched. The lights dimmed, and the artificial gravity oscillated, making his stomach lurch uncomfortably.

"What the hell?" the Voxxan he'd been chatting to exclaimed. "That's not supposed to be *able* to happen."

Martin hadn't known what to think. He started to ask a question when his wrist comm buzzed. "Yote here," he answered.

"*R'Murran here, Captain. There's been an incident that I thought you should know about.*"

"We noticed. Go ahead."

"*You are aware of a damaged freighter making its way to the repair facilities?*"

"Yes – *The Olympian* – attacked by pirates and barely functional."

"*Well, there was an explosion there that knocked us badly.*"

"Why in hell is the ship so close to Hesperia?" Martin demanded angrily. "And what damage has been done to the ship?"

"*Captain,* The Olympian *is nowhere near Hesperia yet – at least not for a conventional explosion. There was an E.M. pulse and a burst of radiation. I think they have an antimatter leak.*"

Madeline's voice cut in, "*Half our sensors were overloaded by a wave of radiation. I'm still seeing spots before my virtual eyes. The rest of the ship seems to have survived the pulse though.*"

Electro-Magnetic Pulse! That accounted for the effects on Hesperia. Although hardened for use in space, the electronics would have a harder time dealing with EMP. Martin said, "If it happened once, it could happen again. Put up what shields that you can and monitor the situation closely. What's *The Olympian's* current condition?"

"*Still there, but drifting,*" R'Murran replied. "*It must have been a fraction of a gram only, but that ship has to have been riddled with hard radiation. The crew is likely to be dead or dying. Tug ships have just been dispatched to deal with it."*

"*Captain!*" Madeline interrupted. "*I'm picking up a signal from* The Olympian. *Their First Officer is reporting massive systems failure and their engineering crew are not responding – presumed dead. They've tried to eject their power core, but it's not responding. Their captain has gone to try to trigger the manual ejection system.*"

"The radiation will surely kill him," Martin replied.

Martin's Voxxan acquaintance had been listening to the conversation with interest. He spoke up. "They're all as good as dead anyway – he might as well spend his last minutes doing something useful."

Martin had suspected as much, but had not wanted to articulate it. He got up from his chair. "Nice talking to you, but I've got to go."

The Voxxan nodded in understanding, and then set about contacting his own ship.

Martin left to find the others. It turns out that they were also trying to find him.

"Madeline let us know what's happening," Bethany said. "I think that we should head back to the *Phoenix*."

"I was thinking the same thing. I have this sinking feeling that the trouble has only just begun."

They started heading for the exit, but just then the vid screens switched to a live news feed. A concerned news reader started announcing what Martin had already learned, but then the picture switched to what seemed to be live video from a starship near *The Olympian*. The first thing that was obvious even from that distance was a gaping hole in the hull where the engineering section would be located.

"Hell! I don't know if they'll even be *able* to eject their power core in that condition," Ceres commented.

"I'm not waiting to find out," Martin replied. He continued out of the bar, followed closely by the others. Some of the other patrons had gotten similar ideas and weren't far behind. Outside, he called the *Phoenix* again. "Madeline – you there?"

"*Of course, Captain.*"

"Issue an immediate recall to all crew. No exceptions. No delays. I want the rest safely back on board as soon as possible."

"*Understood, Captain. Sending recalls now. We're still closely monitoring* The Olympian. *The tugs are nearly there. Wait... there appears to be some movement near Engineering. Debris seems to be being pushed out...*"

"*R'Murran here, Captain. According to the specs that I've pulled up, that's where the power core ejection port is located. It looks like somebody is managing to do something... yes... I see it. The core is definitely coming out. It's slow though – it must be catching on the wreckage. I hope that it doesn't get even more damaged. One tug is heading for the core... it looks like it's using its tractor beam to prise it out... yes, it's got it. The tug is starting to pull away from the ship. Still too close for comfort though. What is that pilot doing? He's taking a big risk if he doesn't..."*

There was loud short squeal on the comm, and the lights went out, followed by the artificial gravity. The background hum of electrical and mechanical equipment disappeared, only to be replaced by screams of fear and panic from the people who had never experienced weightlessness before, let alone in complete darkness. For the briefest moment, the blackness was absolute, and Martin felt a twinge of panic himself. Then the emergency lights came on. Pitifully few and not very bright, they nevertheless were able to relieve the stygian darkness sufficiently to enable people to be seen hanging helplessly in the air. It was immediately obvious who were spacers and who were tourists. While the latter futilely tried to get back to the floor, the experienced spacers either latched onto something secure, or waited calmly waited until they drifted within reach of something or somebody. Martin witnessed two Star Fleet officers brace against each other and push off in opposite directions to reach handholds on the walls. In zero gee, there was little point in sticking to the designated floor.

Martin had been caught mid-step when the artificial gravity failed, and his momentum carried him forward and slightly upward. He snagged a pole as he passed by it, and turned to check on his ship mates. Bethany was on a similar trajectory as he had been, but just out of reach of the pole, She calmly held a hand out to him, and he hauled her in. He spotted Zelkie walking along the floor as if the gravity plates were still on. Of course shi was using hir telekinetic ability to do it, but it looked odd when everybody else was weightless. For a moment he couldn't see Risha, then he found her drifting helplessly in a crowd of non-spacers who were more of a hindrance than a help.

"A little assistance, please!" she yelled to be heard over the racket when she caught Martin's eye.

Martin directed Zelkie to pull the cougar down to them, and then he looked for Ceres. He found the Starwalker already fetching the more helplessly stranded people. Ceres had of course reacted instantaneously when the gravity went off, and was in perfect control of hir movement at all times. Absolutely no one could match a Starwalker in hir element.

With everyone accounted for, Martin tried to get back in contact with the *Phoenix*. When no one answered, he started getting a horrible sense of dread. He tried again.

Bethany put a hand over his comm. "Captain – there's no point in trying to comm the ship. Your signal won't get through. We're inside an asteroid with many metres of rock and metal blocking low-powered comms like ours. Without power to the comm relays, they're useless."

Martin nodded in understanding, but remained frustrated. "I'm worried about R'Murran and Madeline, and has anything happened to the ship?"

"Hard to say. If that was another stronger EMP burst, the ship's shields should have coped. If it was something else, we won't know until we get back to the dock."

"Then we'd better get going. If the power doesn't come back on soon, we won't be able to use the transit tubes, and the dock is a couple of kilometres away."

"On the plus side, we don't have to walk it all. In freefall, we can push off and coast through the air," Bethany pointed out.

"As long as we don't bump into anyone along the way," Risha added.

"I can fend people off with TK nudges," Zelkie offered. "You will have to hang onto me though – action and reaction are still in effect."

"Let's do that. Zelkie, manoeuvre us against a wall so that we can push off..." Martin looked around to get his bearings, "...thataway." He looked for Ceres, and called out to hir, "Ceres! **Ceres!** We're headed for the ship now."

The foxtaur waved to show that shi had understood. Shi bounced off a statue, heading off in their intended direction.

Meanwhile Zelkie had got them all into position against a wall. Risha climbed onto hir back, locking her two lower arms around the chakat's waist. She held out her other two arms to either side, and Martin and Bethany took double arm grips on them.

Zelkie said, "Okay, brace yourselves against the wall, and push off when I say three. Ready? One, two, *three!*"

They shoved off as hard as they could. They sailed smoothly through the gloom at a fast pace, with only the occasional lurch as Zelkie pushed aside some hapless person, incidentally helping them to reach a secure point. They reached the end of the cavern that held the row of bars and restaurants, and another bounce aimed them for the connecting tunnel. There they were slowed down by the crowd in the confined space until they passed into the huge main cavern.

Risha gasped. "Omigod! There are people floating hundreds of metres up there! What will happen to them if the gravity comes back on now?"

"They'll have a heck of a harder landing than we would," Martin said grimly. "Hopefully the people in control will have the sense not to turn the grav-plates back on full as soon as the power is back on. Turning them on at a tenth of a gee for a couple of seconds could pull everyone downwards until everyone is safely anchored."

"Do you really trust them to do that?" Bethany asked.

Martin sighed. It was true – he couldn't. "Zelkie – can you reach that far with your telekinesis?"

"I'm... not really sure," shi replied doubtfully. "I've never tried from that distance. It's a clear line of sight... maybe."

"Park us somewhere safe and give it a try. Even a little pull should help them to drift down to safety."

Zelkie found a convenient sign to grab with four limbs to use as an anchor, then shi turned hir attention to one of the drifters. A frown furrowed hir face as shi concentrated hard on the distant figure. "It's like trying to hold a greasy eel with chopsticks, but I think I'm having an effect... yes, I can feel it... their delta vee is now towards the floor."

"Okay, don't take any more time than you have to. Move on to the next one. We'll just have to hope that they'll have the time to drift down to safety."

Zelkie chose hir next target, then the next, and the next. Shi must have done at least two dozen when Bethany spoke up.

"Look over there," she pointed. "There are people with zero gee manoeuvring packs. They've started picking up the drifters."

Martin nodded. "Looks like the authorities might finally be doing something. That's our cue to move on."

Zelkie said, "Okay – is everyone still hanging on firmly? We're off then." They shoved off in the direction of the docks. Crossing the main tunnel took some time, but they did it without incident, noting that people were calming down and getting more organised. Many were heading for the docks like they were.

"Some of those people might be in for a nasty surprise," Bethany commented.

"Why is that?" Risha asked.

"Let me guess," Martin answered. "If they didn't have their shields up, their ships might be as dead as Hesperia."

"Exactly. If EMP is the culprit, they're going to have to break out their emergency spares from the shielded stores just to get basic life-support operational again. At least here in Hesperia, there's a huge air reserve, although lack of circulation will be a major issue."

They reached the beginning of the docks and, as predicted, there were crowds trying to board their ships. It got too crowded for their formation, so they separated and manoeuvred through the tangle of people and objects.

"Try your comm now," Bethany suggested. "We may be close enough for a direct signal now."

"Good idea." Martin keyed his comm. "Yote to *Phoenix*."

"*Captain! Thank goodness – we've been trying to contact you,*" came Madeline's relieved voice.

"All of Hesperia has lost power, so the comm relays don't work. Fill me in as to what's happening. How's the *Phoenix*?"

"*We've burned out a number of sensors, and they're going to need replacing. Otherwise our shields held and protected us from the blast.*"

Martin sighed. There went the bonuses again. "Okay, what blast?"

"*As you've probably guessed, the damaged power core blew up. It was still far too close despite the efforts of the tug ship driver. That person is a hero for getting it as far away as they did. A pity that they were killed doing it.*"

"What about *The Olympian*?"

"It's dead. Nobody on board could still be alive after bearing the brunt of that radiation blast."

Martin was grateful for the sheer amount of rock that had shielded the inhabitants of Hesperia.

Madeline continued, "*The radiation hit a lot of ships here that didn't raise their shields in time. There could be a lot of sick or even dying people aboard.*"

"Damn!" Martin swore. "If Hesperia's problems go on too long, they're going to need to evacuate as many people as possible, but the ships might not be useable."

"*Captain!*" R'Murran's voice interrupted. "*Lack of power to the environmental systems may be the least of Hesperia's problems. I've been tracking* The Olympian, *and it's been knocked slightly off course by the blast. It's currently on an intersecting course with Hesperia!*"

"Hell! What about the second tug?"

"*It was too near the explosion, and their shields weren't good enough at that range to prevent them from being disabled.*"

"I don't suppose they have a third tug?"

"*I'm not sure, Captain, but I doubt it. The tugs are only for the maintenance site. Hesperia doesn't deal with those ships. The big space liners are assisted into the dock with the fixed tractor emplacements. They've also got a couple of super heavy-duty tractor beams that are used for warding off objects such as other asteroids in the region, and they could do the job, but of course they're out of action also.*"

Martin was worried. With over half the *Phoenix*'s complement still unaccounted for on Hesperia, he not only had to consider that they might be trapped, and even if they weren't, whether they could get to the ship before *The Olympian* crashed into Hesperia. "Keep a very close eye on the situation, and keep trying to contact the others. We'll be there soon."

"*Aye, Captain,*" came both R'Murran and Madeline's voices.

The Hesperia City Council had gone to a lot of effort to attract the tourist Fedcred. Amongst its more recent additions was a theme park intended to draw in families with children of all ages. Naturally this was the destination of choice for both the chakats and the Caitians, not to mention the playful mouse, Penny and the childlike Faleshkarti. Not that the chakats needed cubs as an excuse to enjoy the attraction; their general sense of playfulness made it almost irresistible. However, it was the opportunity to let the children let loose without the normal ship's restrictions that was the prime attraction, letting the kids be themselves out of the restrictions of shipboard life. They had even offered to take the Amur Tiger child, Katarina, along with them to give hir parents a bit of free time for themselves. Both children and adults were enjoying their day immensely.

The adult chakats wanted to do other things with their limited time though. Hotfoot wanted to shop for foods and items to prepare some special meals for Shintaro, not to mention adding to hir culinary repertoire. Burningbright wanted to shop for clothes and other knick-knacks. Zelkie had not wanted anything particular from the shops, but expressed a desire to visit some bars and gossip with other starship crews. So they divided up their available time and took turns indulging themselves, while the other two kept an eye on the cubs. Hotfoot went first, and after locating the market district, found much of what shi needed and dropped it off at the *Phoenix* before rejoining the others. Burningbright went next. By the time that shi returned, R'Murran had left to relieve Captain Yote. Zelkie then left, intending to meet up with everyone back at the ship. Everything was going perfectly.

There was a therefore a great deal of disappointment when the recall from *Phoenix* came in. However, all the children and some of the adults were already aboard a roller coaster ride, and they had to wait for that to complete first. While they knew that there had to be some sort of big problem, nobody expected total power failure. The one thing that the designers of the coaster system had not taken into account was the total lack of gravity. Without it, the precisely calculated and balanced forces on the ride were thrown out of kilter, and the carriage jammed at the top of a corkscrew loop, leaving its entire load of passengers stranded, locked into place by the safety bars.

M'Resk, who was heavily pregnant, had been refraining from the high-stress rides. She was kept company by M'Anissa'tk and Burningbright who had both had their fill of rides. Everyone else was aboard that coaster. Burningbright was nearly overwhelmed by the sudden flood of fear and panic, not the least of which was coming from the people trapped on that ride, especially hir children. For once, hir high empathic sensitivity was working to hir detriment.

M'Resk looked at the chakat in concern, unaware as yet of the predicament their cubs were in. "What's wrong, 'Bright?" She grabbed the chakat's foreleg as shi started drifting away, too preoccupied with the empathic onslaught to watch out for hirself.

"The cubs – they're so afraid. Everyone is afraid! It's too much! I'm… I'm trying to block it out… Must concentrate on calm… Focus down… Shut down the negative… Ooh… I…I think I have it under control now." Shi looked up and M'Resk could see the emergency lights reflected in the tears in hir eyes. "I feel fear everywhere, M'Resk. Whatever has happened has affected a lot of Hesperia, if not all. It must be something to do with that emergency recall that we just got."

M'Resk nodded. It had come in too late to get the children and the other adults off the ride, and they had been waiting for it to complete before they could head back to the *Phoenix*. She started to take out her comm to get back in contact with the *Phoenix*.

"Where's the coaster?" M'Anissa'tk asked, peering into the gloom.

Burningbright pointed up to where the coaster was stalled. "They're stuck up there. That's why they are so frightened."

"*Oh Goddess!*" M'Anissa'tk exclaimed in her native tongue.

M'Resk said, "I can't get through to anyone on the comm. What's going on?"

"It looks like a major power failure. If it's widespread, it may have knocked out the comm relays also," M'Anissa'tk replied.

"Then what are we going to do about the children?"

"See who is in charge first." M'Anissa'tk grabbed M'Resk's arm and pushed off in the direction of the coaster station, with Burningbright following behind. The morph at the controls was already besieged by other parents.

"Listen, lady," he repeated wearily, "I'm telling you what I told them – without power, I can't do anything. I can't call for help, and there's no walkway on the corkscrew to get them down that way either. You'll just have to wait until the power comes back on."

"Without gravity, you don't need a walkway," M'Anissa'tk pointed out.

"Are you nuts? If the gravity comes back on while anyone is up there unsecured, they'll fall to their deaths!"

The Caitian had to concede that he was right, and there was no choice but to wait and see what happened. The emergency recall had her worried though; they might not have the luxury of time. As the long minutes passed by and she watched people being plucked from mid air by some brave rescuers, she suddenly realised that if this was a Hesperia-wide problem, there would be no way that they would be turning the gravity back on soon. "I'm going up there," she announced. "How do you work the safety bars?" she asked the leopard morph.

"I can't let you do that, lady."

"You don't have a choice, mister. Hesperia has huge problems that aren't going to be fixed quickly."

"You don't know that," he replied.

"I'm a former Star Fleet maintenance technician with plenty of experience. I see nothing is working, not even the environmental systems. If anything is going to be restored fast, it's that. But *nothing* has. We have a major disaster developing, and we *need* to get those people down and evacuate."

"Don't you dare, lady!" He grabbed M'Anissa'tk's arm to restrain her. "Try anything, and I'll get Security to arrest you."

"Yeah, good luck with that," she told him. "Burningbright – this man is trying to stop me from rescuing our cubs and mates. Help me out, please."

The chakat had been hovering nearby, fretting over the delay. Shi came over to them, put a handpaw on the leopard's arm, and squeezed.

"Arrgh! Leggo!" yelled the leopard, releasing his grip on M'Anissa'tk.

The Caitian pushed back and floated out of reach, and only then did Burningbright release hir grip on the leopard.

"You're a fool, and you'll get all those people killed!" he shouted at her.

"I don't think so," M'Anissa'tk said as she positioned herself to shove off. "And I'm not going to wait around for ages for you to realise that I'm right." She sprang hard, and hurtled towards the stalled coaster.

Some of the captive passengers saw her coming. Her daughter, Keera, was one of them. "Mother's coming!" she shouted in excitement. "She'll get us out of this."

First M'Anissa'tk had to bring herself to a safe stop. Unfortunately, while her aim was very good, it was not perfect. She had to reach awkwardly for a handhold, and wrenched her shoulder bringing herself to a halt. Pushing the pain to the back of her mind, she started looking for the safety bar locking mechanism. It wasn't hard to find as it had to be easily accessible by the attendants. Keera, Ner'ritn, Kannekin and Katarina were in the first carriage.

"You know that you're not going to fall when I unlock the safety bars, don't you?" she asked them. "It's just like when you play Shaftball – push off towards the floor, but not too fast. You don't want to crash into it after all this."

They reassured her that they knew what to do – all except Kannekin who clung fanatically to the carriage.

"I'm scared, mamma, It's so far down!"

M'Anissa'tk put her uninjured arm around her son. "It's okay, cubling. It's not really down, after all." She lifted her arm above her head and pointed to where M'Resk was beckoning the others. "Here, it is *up*, and I know you're a great leaper. All it takes is one leap of faith from you. Can you do it for me?"

Kannekin looked again, and realised that it was indeed up, if he wanted it to be. "I'll do it, mamma."

"Good boy." She let him go, and he leapt.

M'Anissa'tk smiled proudly after her child for a moment before turning her attention to the people in the next carriage. This one was fitted out for taurs, and held Lemondrop and Candycane.

"Can I get a reassuring hug too?" Lemondrop asked with a grin.

"If it will help," M'Anissa'tk agreed.

She gave both chakats a hug and set them free.

"Whee!" cried Lemondrop as shi pushed off towards safety – a bit too fast, but that was normal for hir, and the Caitian didn't worry about the cub.

M'Anissa'tk worked her way along, freeing Pixiepaws and Hotfoot, then M'Lertiña, M'Rarrtikar, Penny, Loander and Presaith, and the rest of the passengers. One family of four absolutely refused to let her free them though.

"We're waiting for the proper authorities," a rather uptight Siamese cat morph informed her, despite the protestations of her children.

With a helpless shrug, M'Anissa'tk left them to wait for help that might be many hours coming. With everyone else free, she then followed the others back to the floor, although by now she was having a hard time regarding it as such. People being people though, everyone was aligning themselves perpendicular to that surface, so a floor it remained.

"Let's get back to the *Phoenix*," she declared, and the others readily agreed.

It was easier said than done though. Panicky people, many unsure of how to handle themselves in freefall, had caused a bottleneck at the theme park's exit, and it took them a long time to get out. Then there was the matter of figuring out which direction to take. They had arrived by transit tube, and without power, they had no access to navigation information. It took them a while to find a local inhabitant who could give them clear directions on how to get to the docks, and they were a long way distant. Riding herd on a number of cubs did not make the task any easier.

While they were traversing a connecting tunnel filled with people moving along at a slow pace from handhold to handhold, Burningbright sniffed deeply. "I don't like this. There's no air circulation, and the air is getting foul in here. Too many people in too small a volume."

"Nothing we can do about it except not waste time in here," M'Rarrtikar replied. "No dawdling, Kannekin!" she said with a glare in his direction.

"I'll keep him moving," Keera volunteered, exerting her authority as eldest child.

They forged ahead as best they could through the slowly moving mob.

Anastasiya and Valentina had invited Shintaro to tag along with them. While the kitsune had tasted the new and unfamiliar on the world of Pellucidar III, Hesperia made that place look dull by comparison. Shi was not a stranger to crowds and big events, but the loudness and brashness of the city within a rock was quite a revelation... and very exciting. One thing that Hesperia seemed to be big on was competition fights of various kinds. The tigers found an aikido championship was being held that day, and Shintaro was keenly interested.

Although Valentina did not practice martial arts like the other two, shi nevertheless enjoyed it as a spectator sport. The three spent several hours watching preliminary events, right through to the finals, with Shintaro critiquing the techniques of each competitor. After the final event, shi insisted on meeting up with the winner to offer hir congratulations. It was not easy, but shi did manage to do so, much to hir pleasure.

They were all very hungry by that time, and they set off for the restaurant sector in search of Japanese cuisine. Although Shintaro enjoyed the food that Hotfoot prepared, the chakat did not have much knowledge of Japanese style cuisine, nor all the necessities for making it, and so the kitsune was missing the foods with which shi was most familiar. The tigers liked variety though, so they happily went along with hir.

After a leisurely and very enjoyable meal, and not a little inebriated from generous quantities of saké, they set out in search of more fun. They found it in the form of a dance club. Shintaro had never been in anything like it before. Having been raised in a fairly traditional Japanese manner, nightclubs and such were very foreign to hir. However, after a lot of urging from Anastasiya and Valentina, the kitsune tried it out – perhaps encouraged by the inhibition-loosening quantity of alcohol that shi had drunk. Soon shi was enjoying hirself quite a lot, immersed in the music and energy of the experience. All three were so engrossed in it though that none of them heard the recall from the Phoenix, and so they had no forewarning when the lights and music died, and the gravity failed. Then Shintaro nearly lost hir lunch.

Feeling increasingly queasy as shi hung in mid air, shi called out loudly to be heard over the screams of fright. "Help, please, Anastasiya-san!"

The tiger had been caught by surprise also, but shi was within arm's reach of Valentina. Drawing hir wife close, shi said, "I need to push off you."

Valentina nodded in understanding, and looked around to see where shi would end up. There were panicky and frustrated people filling most of the volume of the dimly lit club, and with hir limited experience in freefall, colliding with some was inevitable. "OK – go!" shi confirmed.

Anastasiya shoved and floated quickly over to Shintaro, snagging hir as shi passed, then halting their drift by grabbing a fixture.

"What is happening, Anastasiya-san?" Shintaro asked while barely stopping hir self from throwing up at any moment.

"Major power failure. Grav plates are off. Maybe air too. If power does not come back soon, I think we must go back to *Phoenix*." Anastasiya looked closely at the kitsune. "Are you okay?"

"No – my stomach is falling and I am deathly sick."

Anastasiya grinned. "Don't worry, my friend – is not fatal. Freefall lessons for you when we leave Hesperia, and motion-sickness antidote too."

Meanwhile Valentina had drifted into a group of people. Shi fended off one easily enough, but ended up crashing into a wolf morph.

"Hey! What the hell do you think you're doing, bitch?"

"Apologies, comrade; I am not adept in freefall."

"I'm not your comrade, and I don't like your knee in my face!"

By now Valentina had realised that this was the kind of person who became belligerently angry when drunk. Shi tried to extricate hirself from the tangle of limbs, but lacked any hand or foothold except the wolf himself, and hir efforts only served to make him angrier.

"I said get out of my face, bitch!"

There was a glint of metal, and Valentina felt a jolt in hir abdomen. Shi looked down to see a spreading dark stain on hir clothes just below the left ribs. Shi then grunted in pain as the wolf kicked hir hard, sending hir spinning away helplessly. The last that shi saw of the wolf was him disappearing into a cloud of floating patrons. Shi grabbed for a handhold, and pain lanced through hir side as shi brought hir tumble to a halt. Shi looked about, trying to find Anastasiya and Shintaro, but shi could not see them. Shi was also completely disoriented, and could not see which way to go to get out of the club. Shi hung there, hand against hir wound, waiting to be found.

Eventually Anastasiya came floating up to Valentina, towing Shintaro behind hir. "Found you at last. These people are going crazy in here. Best to leave now while we can… what is wrong, Val?"

Valentina held up hir blood-covered hand.

"Chyort voz'mi! What happened? Let me see that!" Anastasiya started pulling up Valentina's shirt. "Damn! Is too dark in here to see properly. Keep your hand over it and we'll take you to a medic.

As soon as shi was able to, Anastasiya braced hirself against a rigid object and shoved off in the direction of the exit which shi had previously located, pulling Valentina along with hir and, with the space-sick kitsune still hanging onto hir tail, joined the growing throng attempting to leave the club. Anastasiya was not above using hir size and ferocity to intimidate other patrons into giving hir priority, and soon they were outside. They were dismayed though to find out that the entire cavern was in the same condition.

"How are we going to find medic?" Valentina wondered as shi grimaced in pain.

Anastasiya was wondering that too. Hir comm was apparently useless, and shi could not get access to information services. Shi did not have the slightest idea how to find a medic. Shi had another attempt at looking at Valentina's wound. Drifting close to one of the emergency lights, shi could at last see how bad it was.

"Is clean stab wound. Ship's autodoc should be able to fix. We need to get back to *Phoenix* as soon as possible if we can't find medic."

"Look up," Valentina instructed. "Transit tubes are dead too. We will have to travel there entirely by our own means."

"Yes, but I will do all work. You will not exert yourself. In zero gravity, I can handle you easily." Anastasiya looked at Shintaro. "But not two. You must pull yourself together and cope by yourself."

Shintaro nodded. "I understand, Anastasiya-san. Do not worry about me. I will keep up as best as I can." Privately the kitsune hoped that shi could do so without leaving a trail of vomit behind hir.

Anastasiya gathered hir wife into hir arms. Hoping that shi correctly remembered the direction back to the docks, shi pushed off, followed by the determined kitsune. The tigers had repeated encounters with other people as the various clubs emptied of patrons. Some were fellow spacers who were making their way to various destinations, but most were clumsy tourists. At one point, a hysterical rabbit morph latched onto Anastasiya and would not let go, slowing hir down considerably. When Shintaro caught up, shi managed to pry the morph off Anastasiya, and they continued until the next obstruction. That turned out to be an emergency bulkhead that was blocking the access tunnel between two of the caverns. A huge crowd was crammed into the tunnel, trying to get through.

"What is happening here?" Anastasiya asked a Caitian woman who was patiently waiting her turn.

She replied, "The power glitch that happened before the blackout caused the emergency bulkhead to trigger and lock down. They were in the process of lifting it when all power was lost. I'm told that there's only a gap big enough for one person to squeeze through."

"Damn! Do you know where is medic?"

"Sorry, no. If you need to get through in a hurry though, you can go before me."

"Thank you. I must get my wife to ship as soon as possible."

"Is that blood? Oh, goddess! Let me help." She started talking to the people in the queue ahead of them, and one by one, they allowed the tigers to cut in front of them. In that manner, they worked up to the front of the line relatively quickly. There Anastasiya pushed Valentina through a narrow gap that was barely big enough for the large tiger morphs, and then followed, with Shintaro bringing up the rear. The helpful Caitian was allowed to go next, and Anastasiya thanked her profusely before hastily continuing hir journey.

Emerging from the tunnel, they found themselves in one of the bigger caverns. Anastasiya was glad to see that the upper areas were relatively free of obstruction. Shi braced himself against the wall once again, and shoved off hard. They were making excellent progress and were about halfway across the cavern when shi realised that there was another figure approaching hir. With a sense of dread, shi realised that they were on a collision course. Shi curled protectively around Valentina and awaited impact. Fortunately the other person was an experienced spacer, and he fended them off as best as he could under the circumstances. There was a bruising blow, but they were otherwise fine… except that they were now knocked off course. Worse yet, they had lost a lot of momentum. Anastasiya was able to watch as Shintaro passed below them, unable to help the two. Very slowly, they were drifting towards the roof, losing precious time all the while.

Several minutes passed before a call alerted Anastasiya to someone's approach. Startled, shi realised that it was Shintaro. "Hold out your arm!" shi shouted again.

Anastasiya did so, and Shintaro grabbed it as shi passed, imparting a lot of momentum to them. The roof started approaching at a considerably faster speed.

"How did you do that?" Anastasiya asked in wonder.

"I may be space-sick right now, Anastasiya-san, but I am always a samurai, and I learn fast."

The tiger was hugely impressed, but shi had to give hir attention to the approaching rock ceiling. Looking back, shi could see the dimly illuminated portal to the docks. Shi carefully twisted in mid air to ensure that hir feet met the rock so that shi could push off toward it. Shi barely noticed that Shintaro did exactly the same, and they pushed off the roof in nearly perfect unison. They approached the portal, just above it where they could meet the wall feet-first to kill their momentum. They got lucky and had a couple of convenient poles nearby to use to make their way down to the portal and into the tunnel. Then they were in the corridor that passed by the docks. Unfortunately it was at the opposite end from where their ship was, so they had to run the gauntlet of the many crowds milling in front of the various docks.

Anastasiya called out to Shintaro, "Try contacting *Phoenix*!"

The kitsune grimaced. "I tried to do so as soon as we reached the docks, and have tried several times since. There is no response."

Anastasiya cursed under hir breath and continued to forge on as best shi could. Valentina was quiet – too quiet. Shi suspected that hir wife had lost consciousness. It was with relief that shi finally saw the sign indicating their dock number. They entered the dock and their hearts sank. The *Phoenix* was gone!

Heywood and Menalippe were excited – it had been too long since they'd had the opportunity to go on leave as a couple, and they intended to make full use of this opportunity. They first took a guided tour of Hesperia's highlights before choosing some attractions to patronise. Some shopping was done – most of it new clothes for the ferret woman. She tried on many outfits while he patiently indulged her whims. She chose just a couple of the outfits, trying to be frugal in her spending.

After they arranged to have her purchases forwarded to the *Phoenix's* dock, they indulged in a concert, followed by a formal meal at a swanky restaurant. The food was excellent, but it was the atmosphere of the place and the diligent attention to detail by the staff that made it special and romantic. It also cost a small fortune, but neither one cared. It was an extremely rare indulgence, but the occasion was special – their anniversary of becoming Companions.

They looked into a casino, but aside from a few trivial bets on a couple of games, they decided that it wasn't for them.

"Let's just do something fun," Menalippe suggested.

"Did you have anything in particular in mind?" Heywood asked curiously.

"The chakats mentioned that they were going to some kind of fun park. How about that?"

Heywood grinned. "Sure, why not? It's not something that we can do on the ship, so I'm all for it."

They continued on until they reached the elevators that took people up to the transit tube station. As they waited for it along with several other people, both Heywood and Menalippe's comm came alive with Madeline's voice.

"*Emergency recall. All* Phoenix *crewmembers are to report back to the ship as soon as possible. No exceptions. I repeat – everyone must return to the* Phoenix *immediately.*"

Menalippe sighed in disappointment. "Well, it was lovely while it lasted. I wonder if the emergency has anything to do with that power glitch we just had?"

"We'll find out soon enough. This transit tube goes to the docks in the opposite direction."

They piled into the elevator, and the doors closed. It was a round car, with the back third a clear window to the cavern beyond. As the car rose, they got an excellent view of the cavern landscape – until the lights died and the elevator came to an abrupt halt. The grav-plates failed too, so while the emergency brakes brought the car to a safe stop, its passengers' inertia made them keep going, and everyone was thrown into the roof. There were cries of pain and fear, and one person started screaming loud and long.

"For God's sake, shut up!" someone yelled.

The screaming continued however until a loud slap silenced the culprit. The passengers gradually sorted themselves out of the tangle they found themselves in. Someone had puked, and nobody escaped getting some of the floating vomit on them.

"Oh no, not this again," moaned Menalippe.

"Did you pack those anti-motion-sickness pills like I told you to?" Heywood asked, reaching for her purse.

She nodded. "Yes…urp!" She gulped back her rising gorge.

Heywood quickly found the AMS tablets and gave her one. She had a little difficulty swallowing it without water, but managed soon enough. The medicine was very efficacious, and within minutes, she was feeling reasonably good again. She still hated the weightlessness though.

Meanwhile, the elevator passengers speculated on what had happened.

"Must have blown a circuit-breaker," someone remarked.

"One circuit-breaker doesn't black out an entire cavern," another replied scornfully while indicating the gloomy scene beyond the glass.

"Try the emergency button again."

"There's no power, you fool. It's not working."

"My comm's not getting through to anyone or anything."

"Mine's not working either. The salesman said that it was their best model, and I'd never have any problems with it. I'm going to demand my money back!"

"People – listen to me! QUIET!" Heywood yelled.

Surprised, the other passengers shut up and looked at the human.

Heywood continued, "What nobody seems to have noticed is that the ventilation has died also."

"So what?" a rather fat feline morph asked. "So it'll get a little stuffy in here. I'm more concerned about missing my appointment if this thing goes on too long."

"You *should* care. In zero gravity, air doesn't circulate normally, and it has to be fan-forced or else oxygen starts depleting and carbon dioxide starts accumulating. Before too long, we're going to run out of air in this confined space."

"Omigod!" a vixen morph exclaimed. "We've got to get out of here!"

A couple of panicky people started clawing at the door, trying to prise them apart.

"Stop that! Heywood exclaimed. "You're just wasting your effort and our air. Even if you could get those doors open, there's nothing but the solid rock of the shaft on the other side."

"Have you got a better suggestion, smart-ass?" another human asked.

"The roof – maybe there's a service hatch," Heywood suggested.

They looked at the ceiling panels that had been knocked askew when they crashed into them. A couple of people started wrenching them out. One of them put his head into the gap.

"Damn! It's too dark to see anything. Wait a moment…." A light glowed from the man's comm, illuminating the recess. "Yes, I see a hinged lid… Shit! It's locked! Why the hell is it locked?"

"Probably to stop idiots from joyriding on top of the elevator," Heywood replied. "Can you break it open?"

"I'm sure going to try!"

There ensued a lot of pounding and cursing, but eventually the man came out of the recess with a scowl on his face.

"It's no use – it's too solid. I haven't been able to move it or break it."

"Let me try!" a burly wolf morph said.

"You'll be wasting your time."

Art © Heather Bruton

"Screw it! I'm not giving up!" But eventually he did. The elevator was simply too well built.

"What about the glass?" the vixen morph suggested.

"Shatterproof," Heywood answered. "Safety standards would require it."

"Then what can we do?"

"Nothing. Literally. Just hang about and stop wasting oxygen. We've already done too much. Let's just be calm, conserve the air we have left, and wait for the power to come back on, or for a rescue team. Watch the window for a chance to signal for help."

Amazingly, that's exactly what everyone did. By then, the panicky ones had calmed down to a state of mere worry, and they saw the logic of Heywood's advice.

Heywood gathered Menalippe close and quietly said to her, "I'm sorry that our day out was spoiled."

"It's not your fault, and it's been a wonderful day despite this. I'm happy just to be with you."

"Me too. I love you, Mena."

"I love you too, Heywood."

No more words needed to be said, so they kissed and cuddled in contented silence. Heywood's eyes continued to watch through the glass though, hoping to catch someone's attention and help them out of their predicament.

After several more minutes of struggling through the growing chaos, Martin and his compatriots had at last reached the *Phoenix's* dock. Naturally they could not access the ship through the main bay without power to open the doors, but the personnel airlock had a failsafe that enabled them to manually operate the door.

"Mind the gravity!" Martin warned as they approached the entry port to the starship. The steep gradient from zero gee to normal ship's gravity made their stomachs lurch, but otherwise they were glad to have weight again... except perhaps for Ceres.

Martin and Bethany hastened for the bridge, closely followed by the others. As they did so, Madeline's voice came from the speakers.

"*Welcome back! Have you heard from the others?*"

"No – I was hoping that you might have done so by now," Martin replied.

"*The last that I heard, most were in a section of the asteroid opposite to where you were. That would be more than enough to block person-to-person comm transmissions, and of course to the ship as well.*

Hopefully they're on their way, but we won't know until they get back in range, or Hesperia's power is restored."

"Any change to the situation with *The Olympian*?" Martin asked hopefully.

"No – it's still on collision course."

Martin brooded on this until they stepped onto the bridge. R'Murran got out of the command chair with relief. Madeline looked like she wanted to hug them, but her holo form couldn't do that, so she just stood there smiling happily.

"Glad to have you back, Captain," the Caitian said with relief.

Bethany said, "Do you know how many other ships were affected, and how many are still operational?"

R'Murran put a layout view of Hesperia on the main screen. "The ones in green also had their shields up before the second EMP hit. The ones in red did not. The ones in yellow are on the opposite side of the asteroid, and were presumably shielded from the EMP. Because normal comms are down, I can't verify that though. We can use sub-space radio if we really need to contact them though."

"How many of the remaining active ships have tractor beams powerful enough to deflect *The Olympian*?"

That class of ship was the interstellar equivalent of a super container ship. There were only a few in its class, and they were the heavyweights of the shipping industry. An ordinary docking tractor would be about as effective as a rowboat towing a tanker.

The Caitian studied the specs, then announced, "One."

"Which?" Martin queried.

"Us."

"*What?*"

"This former Star Corps ship was equipped to handle extraordinary situations out where there were no other facilities, so it has some high-powered tractors and the bracing needed to use them. All those other ships are normal commercial ships or passenger ships with standard equipment for docking purposes or cargo handling, which would not be up to the task."

"Are you sure *Phoenix* can do it?"

"I've studied the *Phoenix's* specs thoroughly, Captain. It would be marginal at best, but I believe we have a small chance. However, it's imperative that we leave immediately or else our efforts will definitely be too late."

"Madeline – any news from the rest of the crew?"

"No, sir."

"Then we can't wait. Prepare for immediate departure. R'Murran – how are the engines?"

"I've been warming them up since an immediate evacuation became a possibility."

"Good man! Zelkie, lay in our course. I'll take the con while we manoeuvre out of dock. Ceres – disengage the boarding tube and close the cargo access port. Disengage magnetic anchors." When all that was done, Martin took the ship smoothly out of dock, and then lined it up on the course that Zelkie provided.

"Watch out for traffic," Bethany advised. "Without Hesperia Control, things could be dangerous around here."

"All extra eyes on the screens! Madeline, watch our remaining sensors," Martin ordered before carefully engaging thrust.

Fortunately the ship was able to depart without any dangerous encounters. Once clear of the vicinity of Hesperia, *Phoenix* poured on the speed.

Martin considered the task that they had set themselves. "R'Murran – can you figure out the optimum points for us to attach our tractor beams?"

"Can do, Captain." Technical specs started flashing across his work-screen.

"Ceres, figure out the optimal direction in which we need to pull it."

The time spent closing the distance between the Phoenix and the derelict seemed tensely interminable, but they made good time, and soon Martin was manoeuvring their ship to take up the optimal position that R'Murran had calculated. The super-freighter dwarfed their ship, and Martin had to wonder if R'Murran's figures were right.

"Are we ready?" Martin demanded.

"Tractor beams ready, captain," Bethany replied.

"Full power available, sir," R'Murran confirmed.

"Engage!" Martin ordered.

The *Phoenix* had not one, but two heavy-duty tractor beams, and both flashed out to latch onto the chosen anchor points on *The Olympian*. Martin applied full power to the engines, and the superstructure of the ship audibly groaned under the strain.

Madeline looked nervous. "Captain – the strain gauges are red-lining."

"How far into the red?" Martin queried.

"Not far… yet."

"Keep an eye on them and let me know if they get worse. Zelkie – how are we doing?"

"Hard to say yet, Captain. We're an ant trying to move a melon. Wait… yes, it's deflecting. Calculating rate of change…."

There were several long, tense moments until the chakat spoke again.

"Oh hell. Captain – it's not enough. We're too close to Hesperia for our current rate of deflection to cause it to miss."

"Shit! R'Murran, can we get any more power out of the engines?"

"Not without probably blowing them up, sir. We need another ship to help us."

"What other ship? You said that the others aren't equipped with heavy-duty tractors."

"Maybe there a Star Fleet ship in the system. They might have the tractors," R'Murran suggested.

"Star Fleet? I saw Fleet personnel in Hesperia, so that means that at least one ship that we couldn't see on the opposite side has to be theirs." Martin activated the sub-space radio. "This is Captain Yote of the Merchant Vessel *Phoenix* calling any Star Fleet vessel docked at Hesperia. Please respond."

Martin was gratified to get a rapid response. The main screen lit up with the image of a canine morph in Fleet uniform, looking harassed. "This is Lieutenant Commander Alsace of the FSS Valiant. This had better be important – we're trying to cope with a bad situation."

"Whatever you're dealing with, you'd better drop it and help us. We need…" Martin began.

"Who the hell do you think you are, Yote? You can't just barge in and demand help from us. We have an asteroid full of people to worry about. Now stop bothering us…"

Bethany stepped into view and barked, "**Shut up and listen, Alsace!**"

Alsace jerked back in surprise. "Wha..? Who? Commander Oakwood! I didn't realise you were there."

"Still dithering and not listening to people, Alsace? You're never going to be promoted if you don't learn to find out the full situation before reacting. Where's Captain Lister?"

"He's out of contact on Hesperia, as well as the First Officer. I'm the most senior in charge at the moment."

"Then you're going to have to do. Are you aware of what has happened?"

"*The Olympian's* power core blew up and the EMP and radiation blast knocked out the power to Hesperia."

"What you cannot tell yet because you are on the wrong side of the asteroid, is that same explosion has also put *The Olympian* onto a collision course with Hesperia. If that isn't prevented, most of the people still in Hesperia will probably be killed."

Alsace looked stunned for a moment, then shook himself. "By the Makers! I didn't know. What did you have in mind?"

"We're trying to tow the ship. Captain Yote's ship is equipped with a strong tractor beam, but the ship isn't enough by itself. We need a second vessel to help tow *The Olympian* into a safe trajectory. I happen to know that the *Valiant* has a strong tractor also. In order to save the lives of tens of thousands of people, you are going to have to stop whatever you are doing and rendezvous with the *Phoenix* and help deflect that freighter."

"Right. Give me one minute to drop off all our rescue personnel and shuttles so that they can keep working while the *Valiant* joins you."

"Now *that's* good thinking. Rendezvous with us at the coordinates we will transmit to you. Mr Sandblossom, please calculate the optimum rendezvous point and transmit them to *Valiant*."

Zelkie was already doing that, and shi very quickly had the coordinates for Alsace.

"Coordinates received. We'll meet you there soon. *Valiant* out."

The screen blanked, and Bethany turned to Martin and said, "My apologies for interrupting you, Captain."

Martin waved it off. "You were obviously in a better position to deal with them than I. An old acquaintance of yours?"

"I served on the *Valiant* with Alsace before I was transferred to my last ship. He's always been too easily flustered, and he needs to be handled firmly. I don't think he even realises that I'm not in Fleet any more."

"That's to everyone's advantage right now. The last thing that we want is a jurisdictional dispute when every minute counts."

A few minutes later, Madeline reported, "There's a ship coming from the direction of Hesperia on an intercept course. Transponder says it's the *Valiant*."

Martin keyed the comm. "*Phoenix* to *Valiant* – come in please."

The screen lit up to show Alsace once again. "Yes, Captain Yote?" he asked far more politely.

"My engineer has figured out the optimum attachment point for your tractors, as well as the delta vee you need to apply."

"Send us the details and we'll be ready, Captain."

"Thanks, Commander. *Phoenix* out."

The Valiant quickly approached the stricken super freighter. Even *two* ships seemed inadequate to move that behemoth. Nevertheless the *Valiant* got into position, attached its tractor beams, and began adding its considerable might to the task of deflecting the gigantic ship. Even so, much time had been lost waiting for the *Valiant*, and they still could not be sure that it was enough.

'*Good grief!*' thought Martin. '*How big* was *that explosion to have knocked this gigantic mass off course?*'

Several long minutes passed as they kept up their effort. R'Murran started to look concerned about the power output and strain that they were putting on the ship.

"Zelkie, how much longer?" Martin asked.

"We still won't clear if we quit now, sir."

Fifty seconds later though, R'Murran said, "Captain, I advise shutting down very soon."

"Zelkie?" Martin pleaded.

"Not yet," shi advised.

Madeline was the next to speak, her tone very concerned. "Captain, strain gauges are peaking. We risk major structural damage if we don't quit."

"And everyone on Hesperia, including our crew mates risk death if we quit too soon," Martin replied grimly.

The seconds ticked by until Zelkie announced, "We have to disconnect and move *Phoenix*, or else *we're* going to crash into Hesperia too."

"Shut down tractor beam!" Martin commanded, and then immediately set a course to avoid the asteroid. Keying the comm, he said, "*Phoenix* to *Valiant* – we've had to shut off our tractor. What is your situation?"

"We were just about to ask you the same, *Phoenix*. Tractor beams aren't supposed to be run at full power non-stop for so long. We're just about to shut off ours also and manoeuvre away from Hesperia. My navigator says that we've might not have done enough though."

Martin looked at Zelkie, who said, "He's right. It's going to scrape the asteroid, but there's some big structure there that's going to take a direct hit."

"Put it on the screen."

Zelkie switched the view to show the approaching structure. "It looks like one of the control towers. There are also other structures close enough to be affected. I hope that they know that they've got a ship about to hit them, and have evacuated."

"Without power, there's no way to warn them if they haven't."

Martin brought the ship to a relatively stationary position a few hundred metres away from the point of impact. "Shields on full," he ordered. "I don't know what's going to happen, but I want to be ready for anything."

It was like watching a train wreck in slow motion. With imponderable force, *The Olympian* struck the asteroid, gouging out chunks of rock, and continued on unchecked into the structures. There were explosions, with gouts of flame jetting out of various places until the oxygen that fed them was exhausted. Those watching on the bridge imagined the sound of tortured metal on rock and steel as the two giants of space struggled for supremacy. It seemed to take forever before the derelict passed the asteroid with a gigantic gash scarring its side.

Martin heaved a sigh of relief. While Hesperia might have suffered some shaking, it had not broken. Their crew mates and family would have their chance of getting back to the ship alive. He called the Star Fleet vessel again. "Thanks for your help, *Valiant*. We could not have done it without you."

"Thanks for being on the ball, Captain Yote. Now you'll have to pardon us – *The Olympian* is a radiation hazard, and we also have to ensure nobody gets into a collision course with this hulk, then get back to Hesperia to help with the rescue operations."

"We have crew to pick up also. *Phoenix* out." Martin leaned back in his chair and allowed himself a moment to let out the tension. He then took a deep breath and ordered, "Let's get back to our dock as quickly as possible. All eyes on the screens again."

This time they encountered a couple of ships leaving the stricken city. That slowed them down, but they were able to pull into their dock without incident, although this time they had to do it much more slowly and carefully without the benefit of the automated docking system. They encountered one problem though – without power, the docking tube could not be extended and reattached.

"I can go out and manually haul it into place," volunteered Ceres.

"OK. How long will it take you to suit up?" Martin asked.

"For that little job, and with time being at a premium, I won't bother suiting up."

"Say what?" Martin said with his jaw agape.

Ceres grinned. "Just a little ability we don't talk about, Captain. There's a reason why we're called Starwalkers."

Shi left the bridge, and the stunned coyote looked at Bethany. "Can shi really…?"

Bethany nodded. "Yes, shi can. Their bodies are impervious to vacuum, and they can store about an hour's worth of oxygen. They don't usually operate without suits though because they normally work for long hours in space, and hard work also reduces the time that they can survive without replenishing their oxygen supply. And one last thing – they don't want some idiot seeing them working without suits believing that they can do it too."

"I've known hir all this time, and I never knew shi could do that. I've got to watch this! Turn on the camera in the personnel airlock."

They watched as Ceres arrived and closed the airlock door behind hir. Then shi grinned at the camera, realising that shi was being watched. Shi slowly blinked, and when hir eyes opened again, they showed solid gold orbs.

"Third eyelid," murmured Bethany. "Seals the eyes and protects from radiation."

Ceres cycled the airlock, and while the air was being pumped out, shi withdrew a safety harness from a cupboard. Fastening it around hir waist, shi then opened the bulkhead door and pushed out confidently. They watched hir float over to the tube where it coiled lifelessly. Shi grabbed the frame with hir two dextrous forepaws, and started hauling hirself back to the port hand over hand using the safety line. Somehow shi imparted a bit of rotation to the frame and it turned to line up with the port. Shi released it a moment before the magnets in the frame clanged onto the hull. Then the ship's docking system took over, clamping the frame and completing the seal. Ceres then overrode the safety control in order to start filling the airlock with air without closing the bulkhead door first, thus pressurising the access tube. When the pressure equalised, Ceres blinked hir eyes back to normal and pressed the comm button. "Boarding tube is ready, Captain."

"Well done, Ceres, and thanks for the show."

Ceres grinned. "You're welcome, sir."

Martin turned to Madeline. Before he could ask, she shook her head. "No – no contact with the others yet."

R'Murran spoke up. "Permission to go look for them, Captain?"

Martin nodded. "Your entire family is out there, as well as Zelkie's. You two do that. Ceres can go with you as shi's best equipped to function in there in these conditions, and shi has hir mate to look for also."

"Aye, Captain," R'Murran said, and left the bridge with Zelkie following immediately behind.

Hundreds of frightened and frustrated starship crewmembers were gathered at the ports of their disabled ships at a loss for what to do. The air was noticeably fouler by now, and they found it hard to push through the chaotic crowds.

"If those people had a gram of sense, they'd be moving back out to the big main cavern. They're using up all the air here," Ceres commented.

"That's why I had us bring these oxygen tanks," R'Murran replied. "We could encounter even worse conditions in some of the smaller tunnels and caverns."

"When do you think that they'll be able to restore power? *If* they can, that is," Zelkie queried.

"Hard to say. It depends on what back-up equipment they have in their stores. If I was in charge, I'd have back-ups for *all* the vital equipment in shielded stores, but I don't know what Hesperia's situation is. It wouldn't be the first time that the relevant authority has skimped on certain items because they cost too much, or they thought that the likelihood of disaster was virtually nil." R'Murran gave his head a doleful shake.

"Why was the power knocked out anyway?" Zelkie asked. "Everything else inside Hesperia was shielded by all this rock and metal, so why did that fail?"

"Because of Hesperia's power source. Like a normal space station, they have an antimatter power core. Actually they have four, with one kept in reserve for downtime on any of the others. Because antimatter reactions produce a lot of radiation, the safest and simplest option is to locate the power cores on the outside of the asteroid."

"So the EMP was able to knock out the power cores because they weren't protected by many metres of rock and metal?"

"Well, yes and no. If the actual power cores had been affected, we'd all be dead because the antimatter containment would have failed, and there would have been an explosion even bigger than *The Olympian's* power core. However, the power cores are well-shielded and still producing power. Unfortunately, all the controls, monitoring, and distribution grid are also located outside, next to the power cores, and while they are adequately shielded against normal radiation peaks such as solar flares, they weren't up to blocking EMP and radiation of that magnitude. The good news is that the repairs needed should be confined to just that one facility. The bad news is that most of that facility is probably junk now."

"Then does that mean that Hesperia is doomed?"

"Not if they had any sense when they designed the system. All they need to do is get one thing going – the power supply to the environmental system. The rest can wait until later."

"So they won't turn the gravity back on immediately?"

"That's likely to be one of the last things restored. Grav-plates are rather energy hungry."

"So the time that I spent hauling people down from the big cavern was wasted?"

"What do you mean?"

Zelkie explained what shi had done in the big cavern.

"I see," R'Murran said with a nod. "No, your efforts weren't wasted. It would be pretty terrifying for anyone, even hardened spacers, thinking that the gravity might come back on at any moment and they'd plummet to their doom. The less time that they spent up there, the better."

"You're right," Zelkie said with gratitude.

The group emerged into one of the larger caverns. They travelled quickly to the other side, with R'Murran hanging onto Zelkie as shi provided the same service as previously. By now though, the only people not on the floor were those who were deliberately travelling in freefall like they were. At the far end, they found two access tunnels to other parts of Hesperia.

"Okay – the map that I downloaded onto my comm shows that the right one should take us to theme park."

Ceres said, "Can we take the left one? That leads to the botanic gardens, and that's where I left Danson."

"How can you be sure he's still there? He could have moved since you left him, especially if he heard our recall message," Zelkie pointed out.

"He'll be there. There's nowhere else that he could be because he wasn't comfortable anywhere else. He had been getting pretty freaked out by all the noise and crowds. When we found the gardens, it was like a lifeboat to him. He didn't want to leave."

"You told us that he was having too much fun exploring it."

Ceres' ears drooped. "That's what he was doing, but only because he refused to go back out with me unless we returned to the ship. I didn't want to go back to the ship, and I was getting bored with the gardens, so I left him there. Oh Makers! I've been so selfish! It's always been what *I* wanted, and now he's in danger again because of me."

"It's not your fault that this has happened," Zelkie reassured hir.

"But it is! Without me, he would never have left that farm that he grew up on. I wanted to follow my dream of working in space. That's what I was made for – that's where I belong. But I'd fallen in love with the silly tod and insisted that he come along with me. That's why you seldom see him outside of hydroponics. He just isn't at home within steel walls, with machinery to keep him alive every moment. I knew that when I dragged him into space with him, but I did it anyway because I was only thinking of what *I* wanted. Since then his life has been threatened by pirates, a herm symbiont, and now a derelict freighter. He never wanted any of this. It's all *my* fault."

Zelkie hugged the distraught Starwalker. "Ceres, you may have been selfish, but you can't put the blame squarely on you alone. Danson would never have followed you into space if he didn't truly love you – and he does. I may not have an E-rating as strong as Burningbright's, but even my average empathic sense can tell how happy he is in your company. He loves you as much or more than you love him. He sacrificed a lot just to be with you, so don't overlook that."

Ceres sniffled. "I hope you're right."

"I know I am. Now go find him and bring him back to the ship. R'Murran and I will go the other way. We have families to find too."

"Thank you! Good luck!" With that, Ceres was off like a shot down the left tunnel, leaving Zelkie and R'Murran to head off down the right tunnel.

Danson had not liked the compulsory freefall training that he'd had to do aboard *Phoenix*, but he had to admit to being glad that he had not been totally useless when the gravity was lost. In fact, after a bit of initial queasiness, his stomach had settled down, and he was kind of enjoying the lack of weight. It was rather surreal in the gardens right now. With just the emergency lights adding a bit of illumination, it was like a moonlit night in the forest back home. He drifted amongst the branches of the trees like he was in a flying dream. Pausing to smell some of the blossoms occasionally, he was curiously content. In blissful ignorance of the degree of peril that he was currently in, he waited patiently for his lifemate to turn up to guide him back to the ship. Shi had told him that shi would be back, and he had utter faith in hir.

He must have drifted off to sleep because it seemed like no time at all before he heard hir voice. It was coming from his wrist comm. Shi had to be near because all attempts to contact anyone before had been futile. He pushed out of the tree that had stopped him from drifting, and he floated 'skywards', trying to catch sight of Ceres while he returned hir call.

"I'm up here, my love," he sent.

Ceres had been searching the ground where shi had expected to find Danson, but now shi looked upwards. Shi spotted a foxtaur shape silhouetted against one of the emergency lights, and shi gasped in surprise. He looked like a Starwalker at complete ease. Shi bounced off a rock and closed in on him. He spotted hir coming, and opened his arms to hir. They came together in a joyous reunion, hir momentum imparting a spin, and they orbited each other as they kissed.

When they eventually broke off the kiss, Ceres said, "I'm sorry for leaving you here alone, my love. It must have been terrifying for you when the power failed."

"I must confess that it freaked me out at first. It was the not knowing what was happening that bothered me the most. Eventually though, I found myself beginning to enjoy the experience, and I think I'm starting to see what attracts you to working out here. Maybe you can teach me to move about in no gravity the way you do."

"I would love to give you lessons, dear. I would have offered sooner, but I thought you wouldn't be interested."

Danson chuckled. "I love my plants, but I'm not entirely a basket-case away from them, although I admit that Hesperia was a bit too much at once. I followed you out into space because I wanted to be with you, to do things *with* you. I think we can share *some* of those things, don't you?"

"You're right. From now on, I'll be taking better notice of what *you* want, I promise. Right now though, I've got to get you back to the *Phoenix*. I'm glad that you stayed here – it made you much easier to find." Ceres took a firm grip around Danson's waist and started orienting them to push off from an approaching feature wall.

"I knew that you'd be back for me, no matter how long it took, or what obstacles were in the way. So the best place to be was right here. So what *has* happened?"

"I'll explain along the way. Be prepared to push off in a moment when I say 'go'. Ready? Three…two…one… Go!"

With precise timing, their hind legs shoved off the wall in synchronisation, and they shot off in the direction of the access tunnel, skimming over the tops of trees in perfect unison.

As Martin watched Zelkie, Ceres and R'Murran departing on the monitor, Madeline announced, "Incoming call from the *Nebula Queen*, Captain."

"Which is that?" Martin queried.

"That's the huge cruise ship berthed nearby."

"I wonder why a cruise ship is calling us? Put them on, please."

The main screen lit up with the visage of a fox morph… no, a Voxxan, judging by the unusual fur pattern. He was smartly dressed in formal whites.

"Ahoy, *Phoenix*! Would I be addressing Captain Yote?"

"That would be me. What can I do for you, sir?"

"My name is T'eelix, and I'm the captain of the *Nebula Queen*. First of all, I'd like to offer my thanks for that magnificent effort in diverting *The Olympian*. I would have lost many of my passengers and some of my crew if that disaster hadn't been averted."

"You're welcome, Captain. I gather that you also survived the EMP pulse that has put so many of the other ships out of action."

"Yes, and again it's thanks to you in part. When I saw you put up your shields after the first pulse, I thought that it might be wise to follow suit. A few other ships took notice also, but far too many were complacent. We're taking on many refugees from them and Hesperia also. My bosses back home aren't going to be happy, but you don't turn your back on disaster victims."

"I understand. I'm still trying to locate many of my crew."

"Well, that brings me to another reason for me calling." He gestured to someone off-screen.

Anastasiya stepped into view. "Hello, Captain. I'm happy that you did not leave without us after all," shi said with a grin.

"Ana! Is Valentina there with you? Why are you on the *Nebula Queen*?"

Anastasiya's grin faded. "Valentina was attacked with knife. I needed to find medic. *Nebula Queen* was first ship that I found that was still operational and could give help."

"Makers! How is shi?"

"Good medic here. Valentina is fine. Just needs a few days rest to recuperate."

"That's a relief. Can you come back over now, or will you be waiting for Val? And is Shintaro with you?"

"Yes shi is. I was just checking to see what situation was like first, Captain."

"I'd like you back here as soon as possible. I've sent out a search party to try to find the others, and we're undermanned here."

"I will return immediately with Valentina then."

"Good." Martin turned his attention back to T'eelix. "Thank you for aiding my crew, Captain."

T'eelix waved it off. "It was the very least that I could do in return for what you did, Captain Yote. I hope you find your crew soon, and I wish you well for the future. *Nebula Queen* out."

"Whew! Three down. Let's hope we find the others soon."

It was some time though before they got more news. By that time, Valentina was resting comfortably in hir quarters and Anastasiya and Shintaro had joined the others on the bridge.

The comm chimed. "*Ceres to bridge. I've just come aboard with Danson.*"

"Good to hear, Ceres. Send Danson to his post and get ready to go out again. I'm going to send you out with Anastasiya to look for Heywood and Menalippe."

"*Understood, Captain. Ceres out.*"

"Where to start looking for them, Captain?" Anastasiya asked. "Ceres knew where Danson likely to be. Zelkie and R'Murran knew where their families were planning to go. But Heywood and Menalippe had no specific plans. They could be anywhere in huge city."

"I know, Ana, and that's what worries me. I feel almost completely helpless."

Despite the seriousness of their task, Zelkie couldn't help blowing the minds of a few people as they passed through the tunnel. Shi used hir telekinetic ability again to give hirself sure footing, but used the ceiling as a floor instead. Shi left some very confused people in hir wake.

"Behave yourself, Zelkie," R'Murran chided.

"What?" Zelkie asked innocently. "It's roomier on the ceiling."

It was true enough. Despite there being no true up or down in zero gravity, most people still oriented themselves to the usual floor despite the extra chance of bumping into others.

They passed into the next cavern.

"According to the map, the route to the theme park is to our right – that way," R'Murran said, pointing in the right direction.

"We can use the transit tubes as guides," Zelkie pointed out.

"You're right. Let's pour on the speed now that we're in the open again."

The duo got enough elevation that they could clear all the edifices in the cavern, and pushed off hard in the direction of the next tunnel. Most of the traffic was in the opposite direction as people evacuated the theme park, but not many had the confidence to freefall so far above the floor, so Zelkie rarely had to nudge anybody aside from a potential collision. As they got close enough to see clearly despite the poor illumination, they could see a constant stream of people coming out of the tunnel.

Zelkie frowned. "That's a small tunnel. So many people in such a small space can't be good. The only thing circulating the air at the moment is all those people moving in the same direction."

"Worse yet, the map shows one of the longest tunnels in Hesperia. The air is probably pretty bad in there right now. I'm really glad that I brought this oxygen," R'Murran replied.

They reached the end of the cavern and Zelkie started pulling them down to street level. "*Phwaugh*! That air is really foul in there." The chakat's nose wrinkled in distaste.

"Yeah, let's not waste any time in there."

"It's going to be hard going against the flow."

"I know. Can't be helped," R'Murran echoed.

The Caitian let Zelkie lead the way, hir Talent gently clearing a way through the slowly-moving throng. After only a short time though, Zelkie said, "I can sense Hotfoot and Burningbright! Something has

Art © Kat (Foxenawolf)

them very worried." Shi looked about, trying to see past the crowd of floating people. "There they are!"

The chakat took them in that direction. Burningbright had already sensed Zelkie's approach, and was overjoyed to spot them. Shi pointed them out to the others in the group.

R'Murran immediately noticed that something was wrong.

M'Rarrtikar said, "Thank the goddess that you're here! M'Resk is very unwell. I think it's the air. None of us are feeling too good right now."

"We brought oxygen tanks. Let me get a breathing mask on her." As R'Murran proceeded to do that, he continued saying, "You're not too far from the end of the tunnel. Don't slow down for me, Get everyone out into the next cavern as soon as possible."

"I'll boost you along," Zelkie informed them, and started telekinetically hauling the group. There were too many for hir to control well all at once, but at least shi could impart more speed. Shi was starting to feel thick-headed too, and knew that they needed to get out as soon as possible. Shi decided that it was time to start using hir own oxygen tank that shi had been saving until it was really needed.

R'Murran followed as best as he could while assisting M'Resk. His wife started responding to the oxygen though, and soon was looking much better. R'Murran took an occasional breath from the oxygen mask also to ensure he did not succumb to the lack of breathable air. He wondered how the rest of the people in the tunnel were faring. They exited the tunnel and found themselves being hauled telekinetically upwards into the clear open air where the others were waiting and breathing deeply to clear their heads.

M'Anissa'tk asked, "Are you okay, M'Resk?"

M'Resk nodded. "I... I'm still a bit woozy, but I think I'll be fine." She put her hands on her swollen abdomen. "I'm just worried about the effect this may have had on the child."

R'Murran said, "Just take it easy on the way back to the ship. Let us do all the work. We'll check you over in sick bay when we get back."

Zelkie said to R'Murran, "I'm worried about the people that are still in the tunnel."

"I know, but what can we do about it? Our oxygen tanks aren't going to be much help."

"Actually, one tank might be enough for what I have in mind. You continue to the ship with the rest of the group."

R'Murran asked, "What did you have in mind?"

"Turning on the ventilation," shi replied, then took off without wasting more time explaining hirself.

R'Murran wanted answers, but he realised that it was more

important to get everyone else back to the ship. "Okay – everyone link up. We're going to all jump in that direction. As long as we keep together, we're all going to be okay. Are you ready? Jump!"

It was an awkward effort, but they managed to stay together and headed in the right direction.

Meanwhile, Zelkie had put hir mask back on and was heading back up the tunnel as fast as shi could. Without having to worry about anyone else, shi made much better speed despite going against the traffic. Time was of the essence now. The tunnel seemed ridiculously long, but shi had to remind hirself that they had made use of existing mining shafts rather than planning it this way, and it wasn't the main access to the park. Shi was very glad to have the oxygen mask to keep hir clear-headed. Eventually shi came out into the open again and saw that that there were still many people trying to enter the tunnel. Shi positioned hirself in the middle of the entrance and started blocking people from entering.

"**STOP!**" shi yelled as loudly as possible, which for a chakat was very loud with the full force of hir taur lungs behind it. "**Nobody enter the tunnel! The air has gotten too bad!**"

The people nearest to hir stopped and started paying attention, although some people still foolishly tried to ignore hir.

Zelkie continued, "There are lot of people getting very sick from lack of oxygen and too much carbon dioxide because there's nothing to ventilate the tunnel at the moment. Adding more people will just make it worse."

"Are you saying we're trapped here then?" someone called from the crowd.

"I hope not. I'm going to try something. I have a strong telekinetic Talent. I am going to try pushing air into the tunnel. If I can get some sort of flow going, not only will it help the people in the tunnel already, it will enable the rest of you to follow soon after."

"Are you sure you can do that?" another concerned person asked.

Zelkie shrugged. "I've never tried it before, but it seems possible, and it's not as if we have much choice. Now please move back from the tunnel and give me a bit of room to work."

It was difficult to make the crowd move back from the entrance, but when the people had moved away sufficiently, the chakat braced hirself against a post that was almost opposite the tunnel entrance. Shi spread hir hands wide and closed hir eyes. The people thought that shi must be guiding hir telekinesis through hir hands, but Zelkie was doing it partly for putting on a show for the people so that they would not think shi was just standing there doing nothing. The other reason was that shi was trying to envisage pushing a large volume of air into the tunnel mouth. It worked. A large volume of air moved into the tunnel, and of

Art © Shawntae Howard

course was immediately replaced by air flowing in from the cavern which was in turn pushed into the tunnel. As shi got a better handle on what shi was trying to do, the process got more efficient, and the air speed picked up. The people closest to the tunnel could feel a draft heading in the direction of the tunnel. After a lengthy period of this going on though, some people started to get restless.

"When can we go into the tunnel?" a canine morph asked with a trace of annoyance.

The constant effort was taking its toll on the chakat, and shi gasped, "Soon! This... isn't exactly... easy, y'know!" Shi gritted hir teeth and kept up the pressure as long as shi could. Then with a moan, shi stopped and nearly passed out. Shi panted heavily for several seconds before saying, "OK. That's as much as I can do. I hope it's enough. Please don't crowd too much."

The crowd surged forward, pretty much ignoring hir advice.

A strange chakat stopped next to Zelkie. "That was impressive. Thanks for doing that. I had not realised that it was so bad in there. My name is Chakat Spinner, and my cubs and I will always be grateful."

Zelkie smiled. "I'm Zelkie Sandblossom, and my family was in the same situation; how could I not do anything about it?"

"Of course. Do you require assistance? You look pretty wiped out."

"I think I'll take you up on that. I think I've pretty much burned up my energy reserves with that stunt. My body is drawing on my milkwater right now, but it will take a bit to get back up to speed."

"Okay, then let me do the work," Spinner said, putting hir arm around Zelkie's waist to pull hir along. "Cubs – hang onto my tail and don't let go." Spinner joined the crowd still pouring into the refreshed tunnel.

"Here, use the oxygen mask," Zelkie instructed.

"Isn't the air okay though?"

"Don't want to waste the oxygen in the air, and you're the one doing the most exertion."

"Makes sense," Spinner agreed, and continued taking them down the tunnel while drawing fresh oxygen.

As soon as R'Murran had reached the other side of the cavern, he tried sending the others ahead to the *Phoenix* while he waited for Zelkie.

M'Rarrtikar interrupted, "No you won't. You are going to take our children, your wives, and the chakats back to the Phoenix. *I* will stay here and wait for Zelkie."

"As you say, dear." The Firstwife had spoken, and there was no debating her decision. It was her responsibility after all.

M'Rarrtikar was thinking about the good of the ship also though. *Phoenix* needed her engineer more than her purser. She settled into a suitable position to wait.

It was a long time coming, and shi almost overlooked her crewmate in the poor light as she wasn't expecting to see hir grouped with other chakats.

In fact, Zelkie had seen M'Rarrtikar waiting, and as soon as they reached the cavern wall, had asked Spinner to let hir go. Only when shi had separated from the group did the Caitian notice the familiar pattern. When they came together, Zelkie said, "M'Rarrtikar, this is Spinner. Shi helped me after I exhausted myself trying to ventilate the tunnel."

"My thanks for helping my crewmate, Spinner."

"No problem; glad to help. Will you be okay now, Zelkie?"

"I think so. I'm feeling better now, and I have M'Rarrtikar to help me if necessary."

"Good. I'll be on my way now." Shi looked at the connecting tunnel. "Um... is that tunnel safe?"

"It's much bigger and shorter, so I think so," Zelkie reassured hir.

"Great! Tail high!" Hir cubs echoed hir words.

"Tail high to all of you too!" Zelkie replied. As they left, shi said to M'Rarrtikar, "No need to rush back – this oxygen should last until we get back to the ship if we need it, and I'm not up to full speed yet."

"Fine with me. We can head back at whatever speed you're most comfortable with, and you can tell how you managed to ventilate that tunnel."

Long before any of the Caitians or chakats had gotten back to the *Phoenix*, Martin had sent out Ceres and Anastasiya to look for Heywood and Menalippe, plus any of their missing passengers. Four of them had turned up so far, but that still left a few unaccounted for.

"I know that this is pretty futile because it's like looking for a needle in a haystack, but I can't just do nothing," Martin had told the Starwalker and tiger. "But I cannot risk sending out anyone else at this stage either. Ceres is by far the best equipped to deal with the current situation, but I'm not sending hir out alone, especially when we can't even stay in contact. Both of you are to take breathing apparatus with you just in case, if not for yourself, but for others. Every minute that the power is off, it's getting worse in there, so there's likely to be problems. Help if you must, but try to keep on mission. Good luck to you both."

Because one direction was as good as another, they chose to start off from the same cavern, but headed for the tunnels at the other side from the ones taken earlier. They avoided the open areas because they were the safest and easiest to traverse. They headed for the most crowded areas, looking for any places likely to cause hold-ups or preventing people from getting through. They found plenty of those, but nothing insurmountable. They did start encountering people dressed in high-vis clothing with the letters H.E.R. on them - the Hesperia Emergency Response team. Although seriously overstretched, they were helping to coordinate evacuations in the worst affected places. The duo decided that they would be wasting their time wherever the H.E.R. personnel could be found on the job. They had a lot of ground to try to cover, and all the while they kept hoping that their crewmates had returned to the ship in their absence.

"Is it my imagination, or is it getting darker in here?" Anastasiya asked.

"At a guess, I would say that some battery-powered emergency lights are running out of power," Ceres replied. "Hopefully they have some running on power-packs which won't run out of power, but given that they are way more expensive, I don't think they're going to be very common."

"I don't think that even you can work in complete darkness, my friend."

"No, I can't, and this is just making our job harder."

They continued on their quest with a renewed sense of urgency.

Martin welcomed back the chakats, Penny, and the Caitians with much relief. He was much concerned about M'Resk though as she still looked unwell, and after hearing what had happened, he ordered hir to the sick bay, and instructed M'Lertiña to give her a thorough check with the autodoc. Then he had nothing more to do than nervously wait. Unfortunately, the first news came from the sickbay, and it wasn't good.

"*Captain,*" came M'Lertiña's voice from the comm. "*M'Resk has gone into premature labour. We need a real medic here!*"

Martin cursed, then replied, "I'll try asking the *Nebula Queen* if we can borrow theirs."

"*Thanks, Captain.*"

Martin immediately contacted *Nebula Queen* and explained the situation to T'eelix. The Voxxan looked concerned when he replied, "My medic has been kept busy due to this incident, but I will see if he can be freed up. I'll get back to you soon."

The Voxxan was true to his word. It was not long before their medic was at the *Phoenix's* airlock, and he was led to the sick bay to lend his expert help. Martin was left to fret over yet another thing over which he had no control.

Hours after Zelkie and M'Rarrtikar had rejoined the ship, he was still waiting for good news when Madeline materialised on the bridge in front of him.

"Captain! They've restored power to the environmental systems! Fresh air is being circulated into the docks."

"What about comms?" he dared hope.

"No, not yet, but surely it can't be far... Whoa! They just came online, and there's an insane amount of traffic from queued communications. We're going to have to wait a bit for that to clear before we can contact anyone."

"Do your best to get through to them the second that there's bandwidth."

"Aye, captain."

It seemed like an eternity, but it really wasn't too long before they got in contact with Ceres and Anastasiya.

"Captain, do you have good news for us?"

Martin's heart sank a little. "No. Neither Heywood nor Menalippe have checked in. Madeline – is there any response at all from their comms?"

"Sorry, Captain, but the system says that the signal should be getting through, but there's no response."

"Right. Ceres – what's your situation out there?"

"Some more lights have come on, and we're noticing draughts from the ventilation system, so we are assuming that they've gotten the environmental systems back online. Other than that, the situation is much the same. No power to most things, and of course the gravity is still off."

"Can you continue searching?"

"Can do, Captain. We'll report back at least every fifteen minutes."

"Acknowledged. *Phoenix* out."

Martin settled in to wait for more news. He refused to let anyone relieve him on the bridge, and Hotfoot had to bring some food and drink to him there to get him to eat. Not knowing what was happening was gnawing at him constantly though, and he hardly managed half the food.

At last, Madeline excitedly announced, "Incoming signal from Heywood's comm, Captain!"

Martin pounded the acknowledgement button and said, "Heywood, is that you? Where are you and Menalippe?"

Instead of Heywood though, a strange man's voice replied, *"This is*

Garth Blake from the Hesperia Emergency Response unit. Who am I addressing, please?"

Puzzled, Martin responded, "This is Captain Yote of the commercial starship *Phoenix*. Why are you using that comm?"

"Would this Heywood person be a male human about thirty years old?"

"Yes! Is there a female ferret morph with him, about the same age?"

"Yes, there is. We have just found them together while trapped in an elevator with a number of other people. It's my sad duty to inform you that all on board were asphyxiated from lack of oxygen."

Madeline gasped, and Martin felt like he was hit in the gut. "Are... are you sure?"

"Sorry, but yes. I have been contacting relatives and acquaintances of all these people using their comms, and it isn't getting any easier to pass on this news."

"I see. Thank you, Mr Blake. Where can I collect their... remains?"

The H.E.R. man gave them the details and then excused himself as he was very busy.

Martin slumped in his chair, and all of the bridge crew were stunned silent by the horrible news. Eventually Martin punched the comm again to contact Ceres and Anastasiya. He passed on the news and instructed them to bring their bodies back home.

Everyone was gathered in the hydroponics bay, even Madeline whose holo-projector had been temporarily relocated from the recreation room. Martin and Danson stood next to an odd anomaly in the high-tech plant farm – a two metre square plot of real earth. It was one of the few things that Danson had insisted on bringing with him when they joined the *Phoenix* – some of his home soil from the farm where he grew up. He reserved it for some special plants, but today it was going to serve another purpose.

Martin held up his hand to indicate he wanted everyone's attention, and the quiet conversations stopped.

"I have asked you all to come here now to pay tribute to our lost comrades. Not all of you know this, but Heywood and Menalippe both originally came from Celeste, a planet belonging to the League of Non-Aligned Worlds. And yes, that means that Menalippe was a former slave. I almost did not even consider Heywood for his position on the *Phoenix* due to that fact, but I was persuaded to at least hear his case first. I am glad that I did. Heywood and Menalippe defied his family, their world's customs, and the planet's laws to be together as true lifemates, not master and slave. His devotion to her was undeniable and complete."

Martin paused because emotion was threatening to overcome his speech. After a moment, he continued, "Heywood was sometimes an abrasive person, with strong opinions about unpopular subjects, but two things that were never in doubt were his competence and loyalty to the ship which became their home. Menalippe who had never been trained for a life in space, nevertheless made herself a valuable member of this crew, up to the point of having a major role in regaining control of the ship when it was hijacked. Both of them deserved better than to die in such a meaningless way, but their contributions to the *Phoenix* will be remembered for as long as the ship survives."

Martin paused to wipe a tear from his eye before continuing. "Even more tragic is the loss of someone who never even got the chance to live. M'Resk's miscarriage caused the loss of her first child, and deprived us of our first ship's baby. We all mourn for her loss."

He turned to a nearby bench on which were three small urns. "These are the ashes of our dear comrades and M'Resk's child. Because *Phoenix* is their home now, I have asked Danson to prepare part of his special garden where we will scatter their ashes. This is similar to the foxtaur tradition of returning their relatives to the soil in the cycle of life." He handed one of the urns to Danson, another to M'Resk, and the last for himself. They each carefully scattered the ashes onto the prepared area. Then the foxtaur raked the ashes into the soil.

"Danson has selected a plant that he has been cultivating since he picked them up on Voxxa. They are known simply as the Lovers' Embrace. This species has distinctive male and female plants, and are always found growing in pairs. Despite their love for each other, Heywood and Menalippe could never have children in life, but in death they will nourish these plants and they will produce fine fruit year after year. I ask Penny and Burningbright to please plant these in the garden."

The mouse and the chakat each took one of the pots that Danson offered to them, and carefully planted them close to each other.

Martin continued, "Unfortunately we do not have any plants from Cait, but Danson has a dwarf rose that I am told resembles the Caitian *thornflower*. This we plant in memory of the lost child."

Danson handed the pot with the rose in it to M'Resk . She was still weak from her ordeal, but she managed to plant it with the support of R'Murran. Then the foxtaur watered them all thoroughly.

Martin continued, "My crew… my friends… my *family*… We have lost too many of our own today, but they will always be with us in spirit, and I hope that they watch over the *Phoenix* for as long as she sails the stars. Thank you everyone."

The crew exchanged hugs, many of them with tears in their eyes, before they started departing for duty stations. Before they left though, Martin asked Bethany and Zelkie to join him in his office.

He settled in his chair with a sigh, rubbed his eyes for a moment, then straightened up and said, "With Heywood gone, we are short a master pilot. Until we find a replacement, Zelkie, I am going to have to ask you to step up and take the back-up role."

"But I'm only rated for shuttles, Captain," Zelkie protested. "I haven't gotten a master pilot's licence."

"I know, but I'm the only one with that rating, and I can't be on duty 24 hours a day. You will only be expected to relieve me when there is nothing of that nature expected, but I suggest that you study up on those skills anyway. If nothing else, you will be able to increase your skill set, not to mention be eligible for a higher rate of pay. But for now, I need you to fill that gap. Can I count on you?"

"Of course, Captain."

"Thank you, Zelkie."

"What about Menalippe's position?" shi asked.

"What about it? I don't expect you to do her odd jobs too."

"No, I meant did you have anyone in mind to replace her?"

"Not yet. It's not as if she had a vital role. For now, everyone is going to have to pitch in a little more to do those odd jobs."

"Can I make a suggestion, sir?"

"Go ahead."

"I'd like to recommend my brother."

"Your... *brother*? Oh yes, your sire is a skunktaur, and you must have a skunktaur sibling."

"Correct. Hys name is Darkwave Quanda."

"Hy has a chakat-style name while you have a skunktaur type?"

Zelkie shrugged. "So my parents are a bit weird sometimes."

"Okay. So why are you suggesting hym?"

"Hy's a bit like Menalippe – smart but untrained. Hy is not lazy but hy has always been too restless to settle into one job. I reckon that this job might be well suited to him."

"Hy sounds promising. I'll check hym out when we get back to Earth and see if hy's interested."

"Thank you, Captain." Zelkie then left.

"What happens now?" Bethany asked.

Martin took a deep breath and let it out with a deep sigh. "We're badly behind schedule, we've expended much fuel, and now we're being asked to take some refugees to our next destination. We're badly in need of some good news right now."

As if on cue, the comm buzzed. "Captain – I have the Hesperia City Administrator on the line."

Surprised, Martin said, "Put them through please."

The desk's screen lit up with the image of a female lion morph. "*Would I be addressing Captain Yote?*" she asked.

"I am Captain Yote. And you are…?"

"*My name is Sarabi Keller, and I am the Hesperia City Administrator. I have a report on how you were instrumental in saving Hesperia from a fatal crash with* The Olympian."

"I had a lot of help from the *Valiant*."

"*Which would not have been in time to prevent the disaster if you hadn't acted when you did. We owe you a huge debt, Captain. Due to the magnitude of the disaster that we have to deal with, there's little more than our thanks that we can offer right now. However, as a token of our gratitude, we are waiving your docking fees now, and in perpetuity.*"

"That's much appreciated, Madam Administrator, but right now, we could do with a lot of fuel to replace that which we expended."

The Administrator looked off-screen at someone. After a moment, she nodded and turned her attention back to Martin. "*I am authorising a refill for you, Captain. I am happy that I could do this much for you before you left. Now I hope that you will pardon me, but I have a lot more to get done right now. Bon voyage, Captain Yote.*"

"Thank you, Ma'am."

The screen blanked out and Martin looked at Bethany. She said, "Do you suppose that she knows just how much fuel a ship of this class can hold?"

"I don't know, but I'm going to take her at her word and fill up. I'm going to burning a lot to make up for lost time."

Three and a half hours later, with refugees crammed into every spare cabin, and their antimatter stores filled to capacity, *Phoenix* departed for her next destination.

The ship had never seemed so crowded. It was never intended to carry so many people, and interstellar trips took days with everyone forced to rub shoulders in relative discomfort. Ilya had not had much luck in finding time with Madeline lately. However, he found out that the holo-suite was scheduled to be set up with a tranquil forest program, intended for both crew and passengers to get a break from the sterility of the starship, and the aggravation of the crowding. He hoped that he could 'bump into' Madeline there. As usual, when entering the sophisticated holo-suite, it was hard to believe that the room was not hugely vaster than it actually was, and he knew that he'd have his work cut out for him if he was going to find her here. He ran into several chakats, two Caitians, some Voxxans, many morphs, and one foxtaur before he finally heard the sound of a familiar female voice. No – *two* female voices.

Approaching cautiously so as not to simply barge into them, he caught sight of the owners of those voices. He froze, watched for a moment, then quietly backed away, the sight of Penny and Madeline ardently kissing, burned into his mind.

Chapter 7: Changes

The six-day journey to New Hong Kong colony was not pleasant. *Phoenix* was uncomfortably full of refugees who kept interfering with normal ship's business, and keeping them out of mischief was a fulltime job for several of the crew. M'Resk and Penny did their best, but Anastasiya and Shintaro were still constantly having to chase bored people out of areas where they did not belong. Keeping them all fed was a task beyond Hotfoot alone, and shi had to beg help from whichever of the crew were free to lend a helping hand. Even Martin helped out a few times, and once had the indignity of being called a waiter by some clueless tourist.

The crowding and Spartan conditions inevitably led to a couple of fights breaking out, and *Phoenix's* brig was put to use more than once to let those involved cool off for a while. It was with great relief that they reached the Chinese colony world, and were able to unload most of their unplanned passengers. A few of them whose destination was Cait – *Phoenix's* next port of call – paid to stay aboard, but that brought their number down to within the maximum number that Martin had planned for. The New Hong Kong authorities were less than happy to have the refugees dumped upon them, but Federation law required them to accept them.

Under the circumstances, stopping for shore leave was not thought to be a good idea, and as soon as they had collected their loads, *Phoenix* departed for Cait. Soon after, M'Rarrtikar met Martin in his office.

"So, how do we stand after this little episode?" Martin asked her.

"That depends on whether you look at it in the long term or the short term," she replied.

"The difference being?"

"We can expect compensation and reward for our actions at Hesperia. However, bureaucracy being what it is, we cannot count on seeing any of that for many months, if not years, so that is not going to help us in the short term when we most need it. The cost of carrying those refugees was considerable, partly because of the increased strain on our systems which weren't intended to cope with so many, but mostly having to feed them. Without food stocks, most of their meals came from the food replicators, the energy requirements for which were a constant drain on our anti-matter supply. This is balanced against the refill that we got before we left Hesperia, but considering that we were only on the first leg of our voyage, our gains were not greatly significant compared to the losses we incurred. There is also the as yet unknown amount that will be needed to effect heavy maintenance on the ship due to the heavy stresses that we put upon it...."

"Please," interrupted Martin, "just give me the short version. You can give me the details later."

"The short version?" she asked with an exasperated sigh. "We lost a significant amount of money. We should recoup all of that when we get recompensed, but that won't pay the bills now."

"I was afraid of that," Martin said glumly. "I'm going to have to have a word with our creditors."

"Before you do, you might want to take one other thing into account."

"Why didn't you include that into your figures?"

"Because it's the money that Heywood and Menalippe saved. It's a considerable amount. What are we going to do with it?"

"How much are we talking about?"

M'Rarrtikar named a very large sum, and Martin blinked in astonishment. "Didn't they spend any of their wages?"

M'Rarrtikar shook her head. "They were very frugal. Their outing at Hesperia was their biggest indulgence they've had since they joined the crew, and that was because they were celebrating their anniversary. The rest they asked me to put into a long-term investment account."

"I wonder why? Did they tell you?" Martin's curiosity was piqued.

"They did. They wanted to have children, but of course they were genetically incompatible. They researched the cost of gene surgery to enable him to fertilize her, and it is very expensive. They've been saving their wages ever since."

"He would have sired ferret morphs? And to think that I almost didn't interview him for the job because I thought he would see morphs as slaves."

"It's because of his past that I bring this up. Normally the money would default to his relatives, but he left all that behind him when he eloped with Menalippe, and she has no relatives anyway. As I see it, the crew of the Phoenix was their family, and I think that they would be happy to see their savings go towards helping that family in its time of need."

Martin nodded thoughtfully. "I wouldn't be surprised if you were right. Obviously though, they didn't leave a will, or you wouldn't be running this by me."

"No, but one thing that might bend this in our favour is that the money never went into their personal accounts. I immediately deducted the amount from their wages and put it into the investment account for them."

Martin pondered for a moment, then said, "We could really use that money, so go check out the legalities and get back to me."

"Aye, Captain."

In the end, the Federation taxation department wanted a bite out of the pie, but the remainder went into the Phoenix Inc. business account, and it made a huge difference to their financial situation. After a thankfully uneventful remainder of the voyage and they got back to Earth, they were able to make their creditors happy for a while longer. Martin prayed that this would be their last hurdle though on his way to his goal. The way things were going, he would be cutting things mighty fine.

As it was, *Phoenix* was laid up for an extra week while tests and repairs were made to the structure. Although it was an added unbudgeted expense, it was one that he hoped to be able to pay in full when the anticipated compensation and/or reward came through... eventually. He was more concerned about lost time. As when they had been quarantined, the business was losing money every hour that they had to put back their departure date. Martin tried to make good use of the downtime though by chasing down more possible clients. As news of their feat had spread to Earth by this time, it did lend them a bit of welcome publicity, and that was advertising worth its weight in gold, offsetting the harm that the Windsor incident continued to cause.

One other thing that needed to be done as a matter of priority was hiring a new pilot, and of course a replacement for Menalippe. The former was not so easy. It was not a coincidence that Baxter had been the only one to answer Martin's original call for pilots. Qualified pilots were always in high demand, and one's willing to work for what he could afford to pay were few and far between. Six nerve-wracking days passed before he finally got an enquiry.

The person who turned up for the interview turned out to be a kangaroo morph, a couple of years younger than Martin. His first impression was of a fashionably dressed and cocksure character.

"Mr Bruce Hopper, is it? Please take a seat."

The kangaroo sat on the indicated seat, his large tail barely fitting through the tail slot. "I prefer to be called Bruce Roo, actually. I've

Art © Sara "Caribou" Palmer

always thought Hopper's a pretty silly name for a kangaroo," he replied with a grin.

Martin found himself smiling back. "You could be right. Anyway, I see from your résumé that you've just graduated as a master pilot. Why are you interested in joining my ship when you might be able to get employment with some major company with your qualifications?"

"Pretty simple really. I became a starship pilot fer just one reason – I want to travel and see lots of places. Any job that I could get with a big mob would have me stuck in a rut, and I wouldn't see much of anythin'. I don't care much if I'm on a fancy ship, or earn the big bucks, just so long as I get to see new worlds on a regular basis. Guarantee that, and I'm yer man!"

"And you think *Phoenix* will take you to those worlds?"

"I know she will. I did me homework. Yer ship is famous, and I found out that you've been to many worlds and colonies. I want in on that."

"I'm impressed, Mr Hop… er, Roo, but you do realise that as a commercial trader, we don't stop long at most worlds?"

"Yeah, I'm not silly. I know that I'd be doin' a job first, and playin' tourist only when there's shore leave."

"Good. The flip side to going to so many places is that you don't get to come back home here much. Is that going to be a problem?"

"No worries! Me folks are alright, but in small doses, you know what I mean? Droppin' in on the rellies every few months is fine by me. Nothin' much to hold me back."

Martin glanced to the side of the room where Burningbright was sitting in on the interview. The chakat had a big grin on hir face, so he didn't really need to ask hir opinion. Bruce seemed a bit brash, but was otherwise of good character.

"Well then, Mr Roo, I would like to offer you the job of assistant pilot of the *Phoenix*." He pushed his PADD over the desk, the contract and pay rate displayed upon it. "If you're happy with the pay and conditions, just sign where indicated."

"Suits me, Captain, And call me Bruce," he added as he signed.

"When can you be ready to start work, Bruce?" Martin asked as he took back his PADD.

"Right now if you want. Me bags are packed, and I'm eager to go."

"Well, we won't be doing any cargo loading until tomorrow when we get the ship back from being serviced, so come to this address at midday and I'll introduce you to some of the team and put you to work." Martin transmitted the details to Bruce's PADD along with a copy of the signed contract.

"Great! I'll see you then." Bruce got up and shook Martin's hand, turned and winked at Burningbright. "Catch ya later, luv!"

When the kangaroo had left, Martin looked at the chakat and asked, "So why are you grinning your fool head off?"

Burningbright shrugged. "I can't help it. Bruce just radiates irrepressible joy of life. He'd be a good match for Penny if she wasn't gay."

"Judging from the way he dresses, he could be gay too."

"Ha! You obviously didn't see him checking out my boobs. Of course he might be bi, but I think he's just a snappy dresser. Either way, I like him."

"As long as he's a good pilot and gets along with the rest of the crew, he can be whatever he wants to be," Martin concluded as they left the office.

Replacing Menalippe was not as vital, but she had made herself useful in such a variety of ways that Martin could see the value of replacing her. As Zelkie had requested, he gave hir brother, Darkwave, the first opportunity to take the job if hy was interested. Hy came to meet hir before shi went on leave while *Phoenix* was being repaired, and Martin took the opportunity to interview hym then. Zelkie brought hym back up with hir after the last load had been taken down to the spaceport, and hy got a brief look around the ship before being shown into Martin's office.

As chakat-kin skunktaurs usually preferred, Darkwave was in male mode, and he was dressed solely in a smart vest with a hip pouch belted around hys waist. He was patterned like a normal skunktaur, but where they would normally have white stripes, hys were a creamy colour instead, as was the short ruff of fur on hys head, probably resulting from having a chakat as hys sire. Hys most distinctive feature though were hys bright violet eyes. Other than that though, hy looked like any other twenty-one year old skunktaur.

Martin shook hands with Darkwave. "Welcome aboard. Is this your first time in a spaceship?"

"Yes it is. You'd think that with a sister working on a star cruiser for years, shi'd get you a freebie or something," Darkwave replied with a teasing look at Zelkie, who rolled hir eyes but said nothing.

"Well, shi's recommended you for a job on this one, so I'd say that shi's finally come through for you. The question is – are you interested?"

"Zelkie's told you that I'm just a jack of all trades?"

"Yes. Shi says you never settled into one career path."

Darkwave nodded. "It's true. I just get bored when focusing on just one type of job. I like to be doing all sorts of different things, especially stuff that I've never done before. As I've never worked on a starship before, of course I've never encountered the jobs that are unique

Art © Kacey Miyagami

to them. I find the idea challenging."

"There certainly are going to be some challenges, but there are also going to be plenty of relatively boring tasks. If you take the job, am I going to be able to rely on you?" Martin asked pointedly.

"Captain, I've always left my jobs voluntarily, not because I was fired or found lacking. I know that no job is going to be interesting all the time – I'm not that naïve. If I take the job, I will always give you 100%, and I'll be committed to the complete round-trip voyage. If I still find it sufficiently interesting, then I'll sign up for another voyage."

"Sounds good enough for me. The job is yours if you want it."

"What are the pay and benefits?"

Martin outlined the details for him.

Darkwave nodded. "That looks fine, and I've been curious about this job since my sister told me about it, so... where do I sign?"

Martin completed the formalities and then said, "Welcome to the crew of the *Phoenix*. You start the same day that Zelkie comes back to work when repairs are completed on the ship, and we start loading her up for our next voyage. Enjoy these last few days on Earth. I recommend getting your sister's advice on what and how to pack for the voyage."

"Thanks, Captain. I'm really looking forward to this."

After the last load was taken down and the *Phoenix* left in the hands of the shipyard, the entire crew went on leave, mostly taking the opportunity to visit family for a while. Anastasiya insisted that Shintaro visit with them, and they both could show off their pregnancies. Because Penny could not feel safe down on Earth though, she elected to stay on the gateway station where Star Fleet's heavy presence could ensure her security. Captain Karnak had given Martin his personal assurance that Penny would be discreetly guarded. Madeline's life-support unit was transferred there also, and she was installed in one of the holosuites for the week, the expense being willingly covered by her father. The two enjoyed a carefree vacation together, exploring all the possibilities of the holosuite.

Martin had decided that it would be good to visit his parents, but was not looking forward to hearing what his father would say about his latest financial setback. Still, he would not have to face him without some moral support. He had invited Bethany to join him there after the vixen had confessed that her sister was unavailable, and she had no other particular place to go.

"You might as well come stay with my family if you have nothing else that you'd prefer to do. You've seen the family mansion before, so you know that there are plenty of guest rooms."

"What about Risha? Is she coming too? It would look improper if you brought two females with you."

Martin gave her an odd look before replying, "Risha intends to spend the time with *her* family. She's been missing them a bit."

"Well… if it's alright with your parents…"

"Standing practice that my siblings and I can invite anyone, so long as we let our parents know in advance. Our folks may be rich, but they've never let that go to their heads, and they welcome guests."

"Yes, I got that impression when we visited last time."

Bethany was delighted with the warm welcome back that she received, and greatly impressed with the bedroom she was given. It was huge, although she supposed that it might be a pretty normal size for a mansion. It was tastefully decorated, and had its own en suite bathroom. It also had doors opening out into the garden, and she was enchanted by its beauty. It certainly made her cabin look dull in comparison.

It did not take her long to unpack and change out of her ship uniform. The butler, Alain, showed her to where Martin was sitting out on the sun deck with his mother, enjoying some afternoon tea. They chatted pleasantly for a while, and she found herself relaxing more than she could remember doing so in a long time. There was one moment though that startled the vixen. Martin had excused himself for a few minutes, while his mother continued talking with Bethany.

"So how long have you and Martin been in a relationship, my dear?"

Bethany nearly choked on her café latte. "I'm afraid that you're mistaken, Mrs Yote. Martin and I are just crew-mates, friends at most. Besides, I'm fourteen years older than him."

"Ah – my mistake. My other children have only ever invited to stay at our home people with whom they are in a relationship. I assumed the same thing for Martin. Forgive me."

"Of course. It's not important."

Mrs Yote smiled. "Such things are never unimportant, dear. However, I will not mention it again."

But although the subject was never brought up again, Bethany went to bed that evening wondering how Martin's mother could make that silly assumption.

Martin had been correct in his guess that his father would not be so harshly critical in front of a guest, and he had a very pleasant evening. He went to sleep in his old familiar bedroom reasonably contented with the world.

Although she had planned to do some shopping, Bethany found herself relaxing in the mansion's gardens instead. The beauty and tranquillity of the grounds had a very calming effect, and she found that the accumulated stresses of her work simply melted away while she lay on a deck chair in the warmth of the April sun. Spring leant a growth spurt to all the plants, many of which were flowering and spreading their delightful scent her way. And when she tired of that, she took advantage of the heated swimming pool for a while. She was very glad that she had taken Martin's invitation.

On her second afternoon, she had encountered Martin's mother in the garden with an easel and oils, painting a landscape. She was very impressed with what she saw.

"Am I disturbing you, Mrs Yote?"

"Not at all, dear, and please call me Lydia."

"I don't know much about art, but that seems very good to my eyes. How long have you been painting?"

"Since the birth of my first child. I used to work for a living, and when I married Arthur, I worked with him to help his business get going. But when we could afford it, we decided to have children, and I would stay at home to raise them. However, I felt the need to do something with the time not spent with the children, so I decided to take up a hobby. That's when I started painting, and I haven't stopped since."

"Well the years of practice really show. You seem to have captured the essence of the landscape without going into every detail."

"I paint what I see, Bethany. I look for that essence, as you call it. Once you get that essential part, the rest comes readily enough."

"You make it sound easy, Lydia."

The coyote woman laughed. "I suppose that it would seem so after something like three decades of practice, but I'm still finding new things to learn."

Bethany and Lydia spent another two hours together discussing painting. The vixen was encouraged to try her hand, but while she was unimpressed with the result, Lydia was supportive in her criticism.

"I was no better at first. You have gotten off to a reasonable start, and if you choose to pursue painting as a hobby, you will soon find yourself getting much better. Don't believe anyone who tells you that it's just a matter of having talent; it's mostly hard work that yields the results. Put the time and effort into it that it needs, and you will reap the rewards."

"Running a starship keeps me fairly busy, but I'll think about it. Unfortunately I won't have this magnificent garden for inspiration, but perhaps a scene from a holosuite program will do."

"Not quite as good as the real thing, but if you look, you will find the beauty in it as well."

*** 28 April 2334 ***

The week went by faster than Bethany thought possible, and she and Martin reluctantly made their farewells and went to the spaceport to rendezvous with the rest of the crew. Half of them were there already, including the two Amur Tigers.

"Hi, Anastasiya," Martin greeted hir as he entered their warehouse base. "That baby of yours looks like shi's put on two weeks worth of weight in just one week."

Anastasiya rubbed hir swelling belly a bit self-consciously. Hir masculine bias had made hir a little embarrassed to be pregnant, but Valentina was very happy, and that made it worthwhile. "Mother thinks Hotfoot does not feed us enough. I think both of us have put on weight."

"I'm sure you're both doing fine," Martin reassured hir, and then went to chat with the others before starting work.

Bruce was put to the test immediately, and was found to be every bit as good as his résumé had suggested despite his lack of experience. He also set about ingratiating himself with the rest of the crew, but he especially had his eyes set on one person in particular.

"Hey, luv, can I get you a coffee," he asked Risha with a roguish grin.

"Why? Don't you think I'm capable of getting my own?" she retorted.

"No, I just want you to try my special blend."

"You have your own blend?" Risha asked, her curiosity piqued.

"Me dad is a barista. Taught me what good coffee tastes like. Packed me own mini coffee maker so that I'm not forced to drink this mediocre swill."

"I *like* this swill," Risha said defiantly.

"You won't be so keen after you try mine," Bruce replied confidently.

Risha stared at him for a moment, then laughed. "Okay, that's one of the better pick-up lines that I've heard. I'll give your coffee a try."

"Great! Yer gonna love it!"

Bruce was a good as his word, and Risha was impressed. So were the rest of the coffee-drinking crew who tried his brew. Hotfoot offered to program it into the food replicator, but Bruce was scandalised.

"Good coffee isn't replicated – it is created by an artist!" he proclaimed.

So the crew humoured Bruce, and his special blend was never replicated. It did get him that foot in the doorway with Risha however. Being of similar age and unmated, not to mention exotic, she was easily the most attractive to his mind, and he set about learning more about her.

Risha found herself liking the cocky kangaroo more and more. He was always upbeat, never lost for words, and shared a lot of her interests. It was not long before she realised why she liked him so much – he was so much like Carson!

Six days into their voyage, Risha stopped coming to Martin's room at night. It was not for another four days before he realised that this was not going to be one of those lulls in her visits. That was when Bethany let him know the reason why.

"Looks like you've lost your lover, Captain," she remarked with some satisfaction when she saw him as she walked down the corridor past his room.

"And why do you say that, Commander?"

"I just saw her go into Bruce's room."

"Hmm. Can't say I'm surprised." He opened the door to his quarters.

"You don't seem terribly cut-up about it," Bethany remarked suspiciously.

"Oh, I'll miss having her in bed with me, and it was good while it lasted, but I didn't expect it to go on forever."

"Why not? You were pretty adamant about having a relationship with her."

"And as I told you then, she was mostly looking for company to allay her feelings of insecurity and loneliness. I was the only person available really."

"So are you going to try to tell me that you didn't have sex with her night after night," Bethany said scornfully.

"Actually only two or three nights a week at most," Martin admitted. "Risha has a strong libido, and as the only unmated male on board this ship, of course she came to me for sex. And as an unmated heterosexual male, of course I took what she offered. But that's all it was – a mutually pleasurable bed sex partnership. There was never any real chance of anything more."

"Why not? It lasted this long."

"Because we have very little in common. We both knew long ago that one day, one of us would find someone that they really liked, and then we would be finished. It seems that Risha may have found that someone, and I'm happy for her. That's all." Martin entered his room and was about to close the door when Bethany asked a final question.

"If Risha didn't really interest you, what kind of person would?"

Martin paused thoughtfully, then replied, "Someone like you, Bethany."

She was too stunned to correct his informality, and by the time that she had recovered her poise, he had closed the door. She wanted to ask what the hell he meant by that, but she was not going to beat down the door and demand an answer. Her smug sense of satisfaction had been turned into intense frustration though, and with a growl of anger, she turned from Martin's door and marched off to her own room.

"Damn idiot males!" she cursed as she stripped off her uniform. "Always screwing around and making my life a complete mess!" She practically hurled herself into the shower and turned it on full blast. She let the water pummel her face, washing away the tears that she would deny crying.

Bruce's relationship with Risha hadn't been the only impact that he had made on the crew. Burningbright had been correct when shi had reckoned that he and Penny would get along well. In fact they became instant best friends, and frequently tried to top each other with jokes. However, friends was all they were, with Bruce's romantic interests lying firmly with Risha, while Penny retained her relationship with Madeline. Not that Madeline had not given the handsome kangaroo a look or two. By now, the rest of the crew knew what Penny had learned long ago – the rabbit swung both ways. If that bothered any of them, they kept it to themselves. However, in the interests of crew harmony, Martin felt that he could not ignore it.

"Madeline," he addressed the empty air in his office, "I'd like a word with you if you're not doing anything important."

"Nothing that I can't have the computer do by itself," she replied, her face appearing on his desk comm unit. While she could not project her holo-body there, she could reproduce her image on the comm with but a fraction of the computing power required for the hologram. "What's up, Captain?"

"I'd like to ask you a question that is of a personal nature. I'll understand if you don't want to discuss it, but I need to ask."

"Ask away, Captain. I promise to not get upset."

"What is your relationship with Penny really like? Are you just steady girlfriends, or is it more serious?"

"We're pretty serious. Why do you ask?"

"Yeah, I thought you two had a very nice relationship going, but how does she feel about you looking at Bruce or the male passengers the same way? I don't want her hurt in any way."

Madeline's face grew serious. "You're very protective of her, aren't you?"

Martin nodded. "She didn't have the good fortune of having a father like yours."

"Yeah, I know. She's told me all about her controlling father and her attempts to get out from under his thumb before she managed to stow-away on *Phoenix*. It's a wonder that she came out as well-adjusted as she did. Her indomitable will is one of the things that I find attractive about her. However I was upfront with her about my own nature. I made sure that she understood that I like boys as much as I like girls, and whatever I feel for her would not change that."

"That may be so, but unlike chakats or Caitians, most people commit to a relationship with just one person. If *I* can see you being interested in a guy while still being in a relationship with Penny, how will *she* react? I'm not pretending that I know what will happen, Madeline, but I am concerned."

"Captain – I don't think that you understand me well enough to be critical of what I do, but I promise you that I will do my best to not hurt Penny in any way."

Martin could sense the subtle rebuke in that answer, and knew that it was time to end that conversation. "Thank you, Madeline. That will be all."

Madeline's image blinked out, and Martin was left wondering if he'd overstepped the boundaries of his authority. Nevertheless he could not regret asking. Penny was family, and he would protect her any way that it took.

On the morning of day twelve of their voyage, Martin was surprised to discover Zelkie waiting outside of his quarters as he emerged. Not ever having done this before it set him wondering why.

"Good morning, Captain," Zelkie said. Shi seemed on the verge of saying more, then nothing happened.

"Good morning, Zelkie. Anything wrong?"

"Um… no. Not exactly." Zelkie's expression was awkward and undecided.

'*Well, that was unconvincing,*' Martin thought. "Tell me what's bothering you on the way to the mess hall."

The chakat sighed. "It's a bit of touchy subject, but I thought I'd better tell you something about my brother before you confronted it for yourself."

"Oh? And what is that? Not something that will affect the ship, I hope?"

"Oh no! Nothing like that! Umm… how familiar are you with the nature of chakat-kin skunktaurs?"

"Like your brother? Well I know that they're cyclic herms, and can change from male to female and back again pretty much at will, although when they go into heat, they change to female whether they want to or not. Most of them seem to prefer the male form for some reason, so it's more common to see them that way in public."

"It's probably because they are all born in the male form," Zelkie explained. "In fact they don't change sex until they reach puberty and go into heat for the first time. The male form feels more normal to them, so when heat is over, they frequently change back. Not all though. Just as the chakats have their gender bias, some skunktaurs actually like the female form and stay that way until a rut phase forces the opposite change."

"I didn't know that they were male until puberty. That explains a lot. So what has this got to do with you wanting to talk to me? Has Darkwave changed?"

"Yes, hy has," shi confirmed as they stepped out of the trans-lift and headed for the mess hall.

"Thanks for the warning, but I wouldn't have been shocked by that."

"I know, but you haven't seen my brother. Hy isn't exactly normal by skunktaur standards, and it embarrasses him a lot."

"How so?"

"You'll see. I'm just asking you to be tactful," Zelkie said as they entered the mess hall.

Martin noticed the skunktaur immediately, but hy had hys back to them while seated at a table. All he could see was that hys ruff of tan fur on hys head had lengthened several centimetres. Then he noticed that the other occupants of the room that had a better view of hym kept glancing at hym. They obviously could see something he couldn't. It couldn't be something like hys genitals as hy was sitting on those. Then suddenly it became clear as Darkwave got up with hys empty plate and took it to add to the pile of plates and cutlery to be washed.

Martin's eyes nearly bugged out. He knew that skunktaurs grew fairly large breasts in their female phase, but Darkwave's put those utterly to shame. Martin had seen breasts that large before, but that wasn't all there was to it. Usually gravity dragged at breasts, stretching them, and creating a perfectly normal amount of sag. However, Darkwave's had grown overnight, and gravity had not had a chance to affect them, so they stood up and stuck out proudly, almost preposterously so. Hy was a living cliché of bad porn artists.

Darkwave headed out of the mess hall, avoiding talking to most people, but in passing Martin who was still riveted next to the doorway, hy said, "Good morning, Captain. Zelkie," before hurrying on hys way. Hys voice had also changed to a more sultry feminine timbre, compounding the visual effect.

When the skunktaur was out of earshot, Martin turned to Zelkie and just looked at hir with an incredulous look on his face.

"Told you so," shi said.

"Was one of hys parents that much endowed?"

"Nope. Nor hys grandparents. None of hys siblings either. Hy's just a freak of nature, and I don't mean that unkindly." Shi moved off to the breakfast buffet and Martin followed. "Hy's even inherited the chakat internal breast support from hys sire, compounding the problem."

"I can see why hy would be embarrassed by all the stares hy would get."

"Hy might have gotten used to them except for the unfortunate timing of hys first change."

"Can you tell me?" Martin asked as he served himself some scrambled eggs and bacon.

"As I said, skunktaurs change for the first time during puberty. Hys first heat didn't hit until hy was fourteen, much later than average. There's some debate that the lateness might have caused the problem, but that's pure speculation. It was during the school week when hy switched sex for the first time. Unfortunately it was also on the day of a big soccer match, and hy was one of the star players. Hy not only had to deal with the reactions from hys classmates, but the whole of both football teams. Hy had to borrow some big guy's uniform top just to cover them, but it ended up looking even more ridiculous because of the bad fit. Worse still, those huge boobs of hys threw off hys centre of balance and kept getting in hys way. Hy was playing so badly that the coach pulled hym out of the game halfway through the first half of the game. Hy never lived down that humiliation, and for a while hy started skipping classes whenever hy went to female phase, until our parents found out and cracked down on hym. Hy still won't stay female for one minute longer than hy is forced to even now."

"So what do you think I should do, if anything?"

Zelkie shrugged. "While hy does have quite an effect on everyone who looks at hym, they'll get used to it. I wouldn't let hym avoid public contact any more than our parents would. Hy needs to learn to live with them also, and hy won't ever do that hiding in hys room. Other than that, it's up to you."

Martin decided that he would just watch to see what would happen and deal with it if necessary. For now, if it was not affecting the ship, it wasn't his business.

However, Darkwave did cause a greater reaction when hy was eating dinner later. While everyone was avoiding mentioning hys endowments, they kept stealing peeks. Then Ceres and Danson arrived.

Neither had been present earlier at breakfast when Darkwave was there, so it was a surprise to them.

"Great Makers!" exclaimed Ceres. "How'd you get that gorgeous rack?"

After everyone tiptoeing around the subject, hir blunt question came as a bit of a shock to everyone, especially Darkwave. "Huh?"

Danson weighed in also. "Shi's right, you look hot!"

Martin had to remind himself that foxtaurs had a very down-to-earth attitude about everything, and were pretty blunt about such things.

"Umm... I changed sex last night," Darkwave replied uncertainly. "This is how big they always get."

"Well, you're sure looking sexy, hon," Ceres said with a wink as shi sat down next to hym. Danson sat down on hys other side with a grin on his face.

Darkwave was flustered. Hy simply was not used to getting such open admiration. Sure, hy got a lot of leering looks from strangers, and hy was used to the teasing that hy got from hys siblings and friends, but hy just did not usually get these honest frank flattering opinions on hys looks. "Thanks... I think."

"Hey Danson," Ceres said. "Do you reckon Dark's boobs are as big as Kaleesha's?"

"Nobody's boobs are bigger than Kaleesha's," he replied. "But Dark's are a lot more shapely."

"Mmm. You got that right, hon!"

By now, Darkwave's ears were burning with embarrassment. However, unlike the humiliation he normally felt, their candid admiration made him ask, "You... really like them? You don't think they look ridiculous?"

That genuinely surprised the foxtaurs. Ceres replied, "Why on Earth would you think they're ridiculous? Hon, I know a couple of vixens who'd kill for a rack like yours. Hell, I'd like a bigger rack, although I'm not quite so ambitious as that. Do you know what some vixens go through to try to attract a tod? You'd have half the vixens in our home village jealous of you!"

"I'm more than a set of tits, y'know."

"Good thing too. A good rack is just advertising. Nobody keeps a tod with just tits to offer. At least, not the ones worth going after anyway."

"I wouldn't know," Darkwave said self-pityingly.

Ceres suddenly understood that Darkwave's endowments were not necessarily the advantage they would be in the typical foxtaur village. "Aw hon, I'm sorry to hear that. Dan – how about we show Dark a little of what it would be like back home?"

"How far should we go?" he replied.

"As far as you like, or until hy says otherwise."

"What are you two up to?" Darkwave asked suspiciously.

"We're going to show you what it's like when someone like you gets the interest of people like us," Danson answered with a grin on his muzzle.

"Should I be worried now?"

"Only if you have no ability to enjoy yourself," Ceres replied, and gave the skunktaur a kiss on the cheek.

"Eep! Help?" hy asked Zelkie who had been watching in fascination.

Hys sister just shook hir head with a smile. "You're on your own, brother. My advice is go with the flow."

The foxtaurs stood up, and they each took an elbow of the nervous skunktaur and insistently pulled hym away from the table. Not knowing what else to do, Darkwave complied, but protested, "But you haven't had your meal yet!"

"We're hungry for your company right now," Ceres replied, and they led hym out of the mess hall.

Martin turned to Zelkie and asked, "What do you think those two are going to do?"

Shi looked thoughtful. "Probably treat hym like they would a vixen in their foxtaur village. If hy is lucky, they might end up screwing hys brains out. As far as I know, hy's still a virgin... or at least hy is in female mode."

"Ceres must be in male phase," Martin opined.

"Yeah, but that wouldn't necessarily change things. You're not a herm, Captain. You don't truly understand that some things are irrelevant to whatever phase we're in. I know Ceres already found Darkwave attractive when hy was in male mode. Shi just gets a bit more in-your-face about such things when shi's in male phase."

"I suppose so. I wonder how Danson feels when shi gets like that though."

"Ever been to a foxtaur village? They're even more open about sex than chakats, and that's saying a lot! Tods are used to getting attention from several vixens, Vixens are used to having to share. They had a couple of dozen herm Starwalkers thrown into the mix, and adapted to that too. My guess is that it doesn't bother Danson at all. When you eliminate sex as something to be jealous about, then only the things that really matter are left. Danson and Ceres really love each other, truly and deeply, so nothing is going to affect their relationship. It doesn't mean though that they can't feel something for someone else also. Frankly, only two foxtaurs in a relationship after a few years is very rare. Three or four is the norm. Hmm... and maybe that's exactly what my brother needs the most."

"As it happens, I do know a lot about foxtaurs, but our friends are hardly typical ones. Yet you reckon you can tell all that from just this one incident?" Martin asked sceptically.

"I know my brother, and I'm pretty familiar with foxtaurs. I'm betting I'm right."

Martin couldn't argue with that, but he sure was going to be watching with interest to see what happened.

Later that evening, Martin was ready to go to bed, but was not feeling sleepy, so he decided to head off to the rec room and get a mug of hot chocolate. To his surprise, he found Darkwave there already, sitting by hymself by the observation port, watching the light streaks of hyperspace, a steaming mug of some brew in hys hand. The skunktaur was apparently lost in thought and did not notice the coyote until Martin sat in a chair beside hym. Martin sipped his very hot chocolate carefully while watching the light show for a while before finally commenting, "So, what happened, if I may ask?"

Darkwave shrugged. "Not much. They took me to their quarters, and kept complimenting me on my looks. They asked me to take off my top so they could have a better look at my breasts. That didn't bother me – after all I come from a family of chakats who are nudists in private, even if my sibs like to tease me about them. More compliments on how they looked, then they started asking about more personal stuff – whether I had lots of boyfriends, or other gender friends, what I liked to do... lots of little details. And they told me about themselves and their own likes and such. They would occasionally stroke my back fur or tail-caress... but nothing else! Then eventually they said it was about time we all had dinner, and we came back to the mess hall to eat. Then after the meal, Ceres gave me a kiss on the cheek and they went back to their quarters. I came here to try to think about what had happened, and all I feel is that there was something left uncompleted." Darkwave looked at Martin earnestly. "Can you please tell what I'm missing?"

Martin sympathised with the skunktaur. Hy had been thrust into an unfamiliar situation, and hys responses were so naïve. "How much do you know about foxtaurs?" he asked.

"Not much," Darkwave admitted. "Before I came on board *Phoenix*, I'd met two or three, but I can't say that I talked to them much."

"Okay, then let me tell you about Joocinda, a foxtaur vixen whom I met at pilot training school. She had a lot of aptitude, and I actually approached her to ask whether she would be interested in my plans for *Phoenix*. She was tempted, but she was already committed to following in her sire's footsteps as flight crew for a cruise-line. However, we struck up a friendship, and I learned much about foxtaur customs from Joocinda. The thing that you most need to realise is that many of them are based around the fact that females outnumber males three or four to one, so there's always a great deal of competition amongst the vixens for the available tods. They also developed gender roles that are pretty consistent across all the sub-species of foxtaur, such as *Vixen's Choice*. Basically it means that the females have the dominant roles in foxtaur society, and it's the vixens who are the sexual aggressors. However, if a male is interested in a female who has *not* approached him, he can show his interest in her by compliments, conversation, gifts, and so forth – everything except asking about sex. That's *her* role."

A light dawned in Darkwave's eyes. "You're saying that *I'm* the vixen in this case. They were waiting for *me* to ask *them* for sexual relations."

"Pretty much. That's the thing about foxtaurs – if they are interested in you, they are very bluntly obvious about it, but they still do it within their defined gender roles."

"But Ceres is a herm. Shi surely could have said something!"

"Ceres was raised in a normal foxtaur village, and shi seems to have developed hir own way of relating to the gender roles depending on who shi's relating to, and perhaps what phase shi's in. You are in female phase, and shi's in male phase. You are still the one in control."

"So you're saying that I should have asked them for sex?"

"Good grief, no. I'm saying that if you wanted sex, it was *your* place to ask for it. The choice is still completely up to you, no matter how much they're interested in you." Martin finished the remainder of his hot chocolate and stood up. He looked at the skunktaur and said, "But if you want my *opinion*, then I'd say you'd be an idiot not to. They're good people, and I think you could do worse than to take their offer. Goodnight, Dark."

Martin left Darkwave to think about his parting words, hoping the repressed skunktaur would make the best choice for hymself.

Darkwave sat for a while longer, staring at hys half-finished drink, trying to sort out hys feelings. Eventually hy got up and put the mug on the returns tray, then headed off to the crew quarters. Hy tapped the call button on door of Ceres and Danson's quarters.

Half a minute passed before a nude and slightly dishevelled Ceres answered the door. Hir eyes widened in surprise. "Dark! I thought you'd gone to bed?"

Hy shook hys head. "No, I needed to do some thinking. Thankfully the Captain was able to clear some things up for me, and I realised that I left something undone. May I join you for the night?"

Ceres smiled happily. "Certainly! Come in!" shi said as shi

ushered the skunktaur inside. "Danson! We have company!"

Martin was slightly disappointed that both Darkwave and the foxtaurs were close-lipped about the previous evening. While foxtaurs might not be shy about their relationships, it did not mean that they went around blabbing about the details. However he did notice that Darkwave seemed to be a lot more upbeat than hy had been yesterday, so he guessed that hy may have taken his advice.

Darkwave spent the next evening with the foxtaurs, but was back in hys usual male mode after two days as female. However, Ceres and Danson apparently had not lost interest in hym. More and more they were found socialising with the skunktaur, and Darkwave certainly didn't seem to be embarrassed about it anymore. Zelkie finally realised that shi and hir family may have made a mistake in not discussing the matter, trying not to cause hym further embarrassment. What hy apparently had needed was a reason to *like* how hy looked.

Weeks later when hy reverted to female form at hys next heat, hy stayed that way for an extra day. Zelkie was amazed as shi had never seen hym stay female one moment longer than hy had to. However, shi was happy that hir brother seemed to have finally started to like hys whole self.

And so were the foxtaurs!

Chapter 8: Side Trip

While the relationships between several of the crew members had changed significantly in the days that it took to get to Relay Station R23, the voyage and job of resupplying the station was perfectly normal. R'Murran pronounced great satisfaction with the repair work done on the ship's structure, and the replacement equipment for those that had been destroyed back at Hesperia were working flawlessly. The only fly in the ointment was their continuing financial problems. When Martin finally got a call from Star Fleet while on the way to Kantorg, he eagerly hastened to take the call in his office. After the call, he asked M'Rarrtikar to join him.

An hour later, as the shift was about to end, he put out a call on the ship's public address system for all crew to attend a special meeting. Only Bethany was left on the bridge, watching and listening via comm, while Madeline monitored systems even as she was present in the room as a hologram.

Martin called for attention when the last of the crew arrived. "We finally have gotten word back from Star Fleet with regards to the Hesperia incident."

There was a smattering of cheers, and Anastasiya said, "It's about time!"

Martin waited for them to quiet down before continuing, "The *Phoenix* and its entire crew have been officially commended for their actions which saved the lives of tens of thousands of people. Those of us who were aboard the ship while undertaking the task of deflecting *The Olympian* are due to get medals too."

"And well deserved too," declared the tiger. "Now how much compensation are we getting?"

Martin looked sour. "Well, we might get a few credits for the medals if we sell them."

"*What?*" There were multiple cries of shock and outrage until Martin managed to get them to quiet down again.

"It seems we are the victims of a technicality. Hesperia City is not a world, nor a colony. The whole asteroid is a business. While the Federation will recognise our efforts in saving lives, it is their position that it is up to that business to allocate any compensation and/or reward. In other words, we *won't* be getting Federation money. If we want to get anything, we will have to persuade Hesperia Incorporated to reward us, or alternatively sue for damages. Either way we're not going to see any money soon because Hesperia is spending every credit they have to repair the city, and they're losing money every day that they are shut for business. Court action will take years. We may get something eventually, but not now when we need it the most. I am sorry, but that means that we're going to have to be very austere for a while. We can only hope that the bad times are behind us now, and we can build back up again."

"What about saving the whole Federation from the herm plague?" Burningbright demanded. "*That's* not a business. Why haven't we heard about that?"

"I asked about that also. It seems that the Federation fears a reprisal against the Asahikawans, or a panic due to how close it came to happening, and so they are keeping the incident hush-hush. So trying to arrange a reward for us while not telling anyone is slowing down the process mightily. Even then it probably won't be huge."

"So they'd let *Phoenix* die through their bureaucracy? I say let's tell the Federation what we did, and cut through this red tape!" Burningbright replied.

You're forgetting two things – firstly, have you considered the possibility that some nutcases might think *Phoenix* is a plague ship, and try to destroy us? Secondly, and more importantly, are you going to risk the lives of all those people on Asahikawa if the Federation Council is right? I certainly won't risk anyone's life, and if that's not good enough for any of you, then I regret that I will have to ask you to leave the crew."

There was a moment of shocked silence before Martin continued.

"Most of you have been with me for a year and a half now. You're more like a family to me than just my crew. It would kill me to lose any of you, but I will fight to keep *Phoenix* sailing the stars by doing this by the book, and not by drastic action that may cause more harm than good. I will understand if you feel you cannot afford to go on this way, but I hope that you will all stay."

Burningbright contritely stepped up to Martin and hugged him. "I'm sorry, Captain. I spoke in haste and anger. But don't you dare speak of breaking us apart again!"

Martin smiled and hugged hir back. "I promise that I won't. Now it's time for everyone to get back to their normal schedule, don't you think? We've got a great business to run!"

This was *Phoenix's* first trip to Kantorg, the home world of the Merraki. The reptiloids were well known for their superior scientific test and measurement equipment, and that was their principle export. Martin had scored a contract to pick up a consignment, and he had been lucky enough to find a load of goods to take there as well, thus making better use of the time spent travelling in that direction which was near the outer edge of the Federation. Kantorg was not exactly known for its tourism though, so there was not much to attract the crew of the *Phoenix*, but any chance to get away from the ship for a little R&R was nevertheless seized upon readily by most.

Martin elected to settle for hanging out at the spaceport bar with some other starship crewmembers. He had been warned to avoid the Merraki cuisine, but apparently they made some fine alcoholic beverages, and he was judiciously sampling them when a comm call came in.

"Would I be talking to Captain Yote of the commercial starship, Phoenix?" came a voice that Martin recognised as being synthesised by a Merraki translation device.

"Yes, this is Captain Yote."

"I am Falthiss, procurement officer for the Kantorg branch of the Star Corps, and I would like to know if you would be available for an urgent consignment to be taken to a planet currently under exploration?"

Martin was intrigued but cautious. "It may be possible. Would you like to meet up and discuss the details?"

"That would be best. Can you do so immediately?"

"I can."

"Then please come to my office, third level, Star Corps Complex, Block Two. I am transmitting travel coordinates."

Martin noted the coordinates arriving and said, "Received, and on my way."

Having not left the spaceport, Martin was delayed slightly by having to have his passport processed, but was soon on his way in a taxi. Totally automated, the vehicle nevertheless had no trouble accepting directions from an alien, and the trip was swift and brief, if not totally comfortable. Merraki were significantly smaller than the average Terran, and their taxis were built accordingly. He wondered if the chakats had squeezed themselves into one.

Martin was intrigued by the Merraki concept of a city. They tended to build down rather than up, and few structures extended beyond ground level. Below ground however, the structures could be very extensive. In their hot climate, it made sense to burrow to get away from the heat. The address that Martin had been given referred to the third level *down*, and there was no such thing as a room with a view. Also, like the taxi, the rooms were built to accommodate Merraki, and Martin found himself having to watch out for low doorways. Despite this though, it seemed that the Merraki working there were used to seeing aliens, and he was directed to Falthiss' office without a qualm.

"Thank you for coming so promptly, Captain," came Falthiss' translated speech from a device sitting on his desk. Almost no Merraki bothered to learn another language, relying instead on their superior technology and near-infallible translation devices.

"Not a problem, sir," Martin replied. Now that he was in the reptiloid's presence, he could tell that the raptor-like Falthiss was a male, with their more conservative crest and scale colours. "However, I'm curious as to why you would need an independent trader when you normally do your own shipping."

"It is a matter of urgency and availability. An exploration team requires a replacement machine, and we do not currently have a ship in port. Their own ship would have to interrupt its assignment and return here to pick it up, losing several days. You are here now though, and if you are willing to make a long detour, you would save us much valuable time, and be amply compensated for doing so."

"That sounds promising, but I would need to know how much of a delay that would mean to my own schedule. Too much, and I won't be able to afford the lost time. What are the details?"

Falthiss activated a holo-projector and displayed a 3D star map with Kantorg's star centred on it, and other major stars highlighted on it. One other point was highlighted in red. "Here is the location of the planet Sylvania. It is approximately thirteen standard cruising days from Kantorg."

Martin compared its location with their next intended port of call. "I see that it's angled towards Aintak Tharl, so I won't lose too many days. If I put on more speed, I can cut that down by a couple more days, but that will cost me more in fuel. How much are you offering for this job?"

"We are prepared to accept any reasonable price due to the urgency of this matter. What is your quote?" he countered.

"Give me a moment to calculate time and costs, please."

"Of course," Falthiss agreed.

Martin took out his PADD and calculated fuel expenditure for the extra distance and speed balanced against delivery requirements to Aintak Tharl and making up for lost time on the next leg. He threw in incidental costs, and then included a premium for express delivery service. He quoted a bit higher than normal, gambling that the Star Corps needed his services badly enough to pay what he asked.

"**That will be satisfactory**," Falthis agreed promptly.

Martin wondered if he could have gone higher still, but decided that it might have been pushing his luck. "Okay, let's sign the contract and we'll get onto this right away."

After all the niceties were observed, Martin was soon on his way. He activated his comm and called back to the ship. "Yote to *Phoenix*."

"*Madeline here, Captain,*" came the prompt response. "*What's up?*"

"Put in a recall to all personnel. We've got ourselves a priority job, and I'm moving up our departure time."

"*Aye Captain. Anything else?*"

"Ask Zelkie or Risha – whoever gets back soonest – to prepare a container bay for me. I'll be bringing up our load as soon as I can. That's all."

"*Will do, Captain.* Phoenix *out.*"

Martin directed his taxi to the Star Corps warehouse where their load was waiting. A Merraki female with a gaudy crest confirmed his pick-up order and told him to get into the passenger side of the container loader. Then she drove them to the spaceport apron where Martin's shuttle was parked. They loaded the container onto the shuttle, and Martin signed for the delivery. The Merraki wished him safe voyage, and then departed.

Martin was just about to close up when Risha and Bruce arrived in a small automated ground car.

"Ho, Captain! Give us a lift?" Bruce called out.

"Of course. Any others coming?"

"Nah. The rest beat us to Zelkie's shuttle and all the seats are full. Shi told us that if we hurried, we could ride up with you, or else shi'd have to make a return trip."

"Good. Get in and buckle up. We're lifting as soon as possible. Call the tower and get us clearance while I finish closing up."

The kangaroo headed off to the cockpit, while Risha took it upon herself to ensure that their load was secure before getting into a passenger seat. Martin meanwhile closed the hatch, secured it and double-checked the seal, then joined Bruce in the cockpit.

As he slid into the chief pilot's seat, Bruce said, "Tower control has given us clearance to lift in four minutes. I'm halfway through the pre-flight checks. We should be ready with a minute spare."

"Cutting it a bit close, weren't you?" Martin commented.

The roo shrugged. "It was either now or in 27 minutes for the next available slot."

"Good call." Martin then concentrated on completing the pre-flight checks. As Bruce had said, they were completed almost a minute before the designated time.

"Did you drink any alcohol?" Martin asked.

"No, Captain. I stayed dry as you requested. Pity though – this hot weather was giving me quite a thirst."

Martin could empathise with that. The Merraki liked their hot, dry climate, but it was a bit harder on the Terran morphs. The Caitians might have found it a bit more comfortable though. "Good. You have the con. It's been too soon since I had my last drink, and I don't want to bend any safety regulations if I don't have to."

"Aye Captain. So what are the local brews like?"

"Not bad, actually. I did bring along a few samples for you to compensate for having to lay off the booze."

"You're a prince, Captain!" Bruce replied with a broad grin. "Time to go," he added as he switched on the comm. "Phoenix Shuttle Baker to tower control. Request final clearance for scheduled departure."

"*You are clear to depart, Phoenix shuttle Baker,*" came the prompt reply.

They boosted off into orbit and rendezvoused with *Phoenix*. While Zelkie and Risha saw to their important load, Martin headed off to the bridge and updated Bethany and the others on their change of plans. After confirming that their load was secured and all the crew had reported in and taken their posts, *Phoenix* departed for virtually unknown territory.

*** 3 June 2334 ***

They made it to Sylvania in just over ten days, the best speed they could make without wasting too much expensive anti-matter fuel. The bridge crew watched the planet as they moved into orbit.

"Doesn't it look a lot like Earth?" Ceres remarked.

Martin replied, "According to the data that I was given, it's closer to being Earth-like than any planet found so far. It looks like being very promising for another colony."

"Do we really need another colony world though?" Madeline's holo-form asked. "The computer library tells me that we already have enough resources at the moment which will fill our needs for a century."

Bethany answered. "You aren't taking some things into account. First – finding worlds suitable for colonisation is rare. For every useful one we find, we reject hundreds of others. It's possible that we may not find another one like this in our lifetimes. Secondly – it takes a long time to survey a world and make preparations to colonise and/or exploit its resources."

"Thirdly," interjected Martin, "you've forgotten about Loander's people." He nodded to their comptech seated at hir station. "While chatting with our Star Fleet friends about our Faleshkarti representatives, they told me that they would be looking for somewhere for them to colonise when they have licked the problems with their sexual maturity. Their other colonies virtually ruined those worlds, so they want to give the new generation of 'corrected' adults a fresh start. It's also a kind of incentive to join the Federation as contributing members. It seems that they're very impressed with what the Faleshkarti envoys have been doing."

Loander nodded agreement with Martin. "It's true. The Hona Council is keen to show what the Faleshkarti can contribute in order to gain the benefits of what the Federation has to offer."

"The Federation is just going to hand over a whole planet to the Faleshkarti?" Ceres asked incredulously.

"Not exactly," Bethany answered. "It will be developed as a Federation colony world, but with the Faleshkarti as the principle population, just like the chakats developed Chakona, or the Terran-Caitian Alliance developed T'Karr Paradisio. The idea is to foster greater integration between our races."

"And give us one more place for us to trade in the future," Martin added with a smile. "Even if it's a bit out of our way for the moment…"

He was interrupted by Madeline. "Pardon me, Captain. Incoming communication."

Madeline switched the call to the main screen. It lit up to reveal a silver fox in Star Corps uniform and captain's insignia.

"Would I be addressing Captain Yote of the commercial vessel, Phoenix?"

"Yes," Martin answered. "And you are…?"

"I'm Captain Blackwood of the Star Corps exploration ship, Endeavour. We've been eagerly awaiting your arrival."

"We got here as fast as we could, Captain. Just let us know where you want the shipment delivered."

"No need to deliver it. Just put your ship into parking orbit one kilometre from the Endeavour, and a shuttle will rendezvous with you and take it off your hands."

"Easily done. We won't be long. Yote out."

Ceres was already laying in the course, and *Phoenix* was soon parked exactly one kilometre from the Star Corps ship. It was not so different from *Phoenix*, although a little newer and more modern, but considering that *Phoenix* used to serve the same function as *Endeavour*, it was hardly surprising.

"That's odd," Madeline said, turning her holo-body towards Martin. "I 'see' a shuttle coming up from the planet on an intercept course with our ship, but it's only a small personnel type. They couldn't possibly fit the shipment into that."

Martin pondered that anomaly for a moment. "Maybe it's just an advance team sent to check it out before shipping it down?"

"Still seems odd to me."

"I agree." Martin shrugged. "We'll just have to wait and see. On the other hand, I don't like unexplained things, so I think I'll have Anastasiya come watch over whoever this is. Hmmm... maybe Burningbright also to get an empathic impression."

"Getting a little paranoid, Captain?" Bethany asked.

"No, just a little more cautious after all we've been through."

The approaching shuttle contacted *Phoenix* and was directed to the shuttle bay where their consignment was being held. Martin and Zelkie were there to meet them, with Anastasiya and Burningbright standing back a bit, alert but not too concerned.

The shuttle's door opened, and three chakats exited. The first was golden-furred, cougar-patterned, with long blond hair tied back in a ponytail. The second was black-furred, with creamy-white stripes like a skunk, with long hair of the same creamy colour. The third was also cougar-patterned, although with darker fur than the first, and was a brunette instead.

The first stepped up to Martin and said, "I'm guessing that you're Captain Yote?"

At a nod from him, shi continued, "I'm Chakat Goldfur, and these are Chakats Swiftwalk," shi indicated the skunk-patterned one, "and Oceanrider. I'm here to check the consignment before delivery, and then hand it over to Swiftwalk to take it onsite. Oceanrider is our taxi driver."

"Welcome to the *Phoenix*, Shir Goldfur," Martin replied. "This is Zelkie, my Loadmaster, and behind me are Anastasiya, our Security Chief, and Burningbright, our Environmental Engineer who helps me out with other odd jobs."

Goldfur smiled and offered a greeting hug, and the others followed suit. When shi got to Anastasiya, shi said, "Good grief! You're almost big enough to be mistaken for a Rakshani."

Anastasiya grinned. "Except Rakshani are not herm like me."

"Wanna bet?" Goldfur asked with a mischievous grin.

That startled the tiger, but before shi could query the chakat, shi was called away to check the cargo.

The crate was opened, and the machine was given a thorough inspection by Goldfur's experienced eyes. Finally shi closed the crate

Art © Foxene

and said, "It looks like everything is there and in good condition. I'll be able to install it right away."

"Great," Martin said, holding out a PADD. "Please sign here and you can take it as soon as your cargo shuttle arrives."

Goldfur signed, saying, "We already have the transport here, Captain, and seeing as we've been waiting for this impatiently, we'd better get going right away.. Shi held out a hand to Swiftwalk who took it and then placed hir other hand on the crate. "It was nice meeting you, Captain Yote."

And then shi, Swiftwalk, and the machine vanished, leaving only a flurry of air in their wake.

"What the hell?" exclaimed Martin. "I've seen a Transporter in action, and that wasn't it!"

Oceanrider grinned. "It's a bit startling when you see it for the first time. Swiftwalk is a teleporter. They're already at the site where the machine is to be installed."

"Wow! I've heard of teleporters, but they're so rare that I thought I'd never see one, let alone meet one. How come shi didn't just teleport up here though?"

"For the same reason that shi didn't teleport to Kantorg and fetch the machine back – shi has to have been to that place before, or get a lock on it some other way. Shi's never been to your ship before, so I had to shuttle hir up."

"Wait – you said something about teleporting to Kantorg. You're not telling me that shi can teleport that far, surely?"

"Further," Oceanrider answered him. "Shi teleports back and forth to Earth all the time. In fact they can't tell if shi has any distance limit at all."

"That's amazing," Martin said as he shook his head in disbelief. "A few people like that could put people like me out of business."

Oceanrider laughed. "No fear of that. Not enough of them for a start, and there are other limitations. Shi still needs people like you and me to get hir places shi hasn't been, and the more shi teleports, the harder it is on hir. Anyway, I've got other work to do, so I'll say goodbye for now. Good to meet you folks!"

Oceanrider was soon on hir way, while the *Phoenix* crew left for their respective stations.

When Martin got back to the bridge, he had to explain to them how they had managed to deliver a large machine in such a small shuttle. There were quite a few who were disappointed at not having met a genuine teleporter.

"Any chance we could go meet hir?" asked Bruce. "After all, while we're all the way out here, we might as well take a bit of time to have a look around."

"You know we have to hurry to our next destination to get back on schedule," Martin replied.

"But if we teleport down, we could have a look around, and still leave fairly quickly," the kangaroo said slyly.

"Brilliant idea, except that I have no say in what Swiftwalk does."

"Could it hurt to ask?"

Martin was about to tell Bruce to forget about it when he realised that the roo had a point, and he was getting too much like a stuffy businessman. He had decided on this career in order to see and do things that most people did not get to do, and here he was at a brand new world and he was going to leave without taking a look? No way!

Martin tapped his comm unit. "*Phoenix* to *Endeavour* – could I talk to Captain Blackwood, please?"

Half a minute later, the main screen lit up with Blackwood's face. "Captain Yote – is there a problem?"

"No, Captain Blackwood. Instead, I would like to ask a big favour on behalf of my crew, as well as myself."

"What would that be?"

"We've come out all this way, so we'd like to have a look around while we're here, if possible."

"The planet isn't interdicted, so I have no legal authority to stop you, but I would prefer it if you did not land anywhere and possibly interfere with some of our work, or get into trouble somehow."

"Well, I have a solution for that, and that's where the favour really comes in. If your teleporter – Swiftwalk – were to take a couple of parties down for a quick look around, we could stay safely in designated areas, *and* do it all quickly. We really need to leave again soon, you see."

"Ah yes, that makes sense. However, I cannot drag Swiftwalk away from hir work willy-nilly, nor is shi obliged to provide such a service. In fact this urgent delivery was a special exception that shi made from hir normal duties. However, as you provided us such excellent service, I will do you that favour and ask if shi can spare the time."

"Thank you, Captain."

"I'll call you back with the result soon. *Endeavour* out."

They only had to wait about five minutes before they got a call back.

"Good news, Captain – Swiftwalk has consented to giving you a brief visit. Shi will be available in about half an hour from now, so please be ready for hir. Shi will teleport to your ship at the point that you met hir."

"Thank you! That's good news. We'll be ready when shi arrives. Is there anything that we should prepare for the visit?"

"No, shi will only be showing the secure or safe sites. Now I must attend to other matters. Good day to you and your crew."

Martin organised the crew into two parties, and was ready with the first group in the shuttle bay when Swiftwalk reappeared at the exact same spot from which shi had departed. However, whereas shi had been wearing a full uniform top on hir first visit, this time shi was wearing only a halter with a single strap over hir left shoulder. It revealed a black patch of fur shaped like a paw-mark on the creamy fur over hir right breast.

"Pardon my informal dress," Swiftwalk said. "It's very warm where I work, and we tend to dress as lightly as possible so as to not overheat."

"So I'd better take off my jacket?" Martin asked.

"I'd recommend it. So are these everyone?"

All the chakats including children were there, as well as the Faleshkarti, Bruce, Penny, Ceres, Danson and Risha.

Martin replied, "Half the crew. I did say to Captain Blackwood that we'd be sending a couple of parties."

"I suppose that you can't all simply abandon your ship," Swiftwalk said with a grin. "Okay, here's the drill. Everyone lay a hand on me somewhere – no groping please," shi added with a wink. "Everyone ready? Okay, we're… here!"

And just like that, the group was standing in a small clearing in a forest. Several people were either putting up tents, attending to scientific instruments, or preparing meals. Glowing force-field poles encircled the encampment.

"Welcome to Sylvania! In case you're wondering, I'm normally a planetary scout, and this is the team that I lead with my mate. We've just finished travelling for the day, hence why I'm reasonably free to play tour guide for a short while. And this is the forest that we've been trekking through for the past sixteen days for the biologists in the team."

"You weren't kidding about the heat," Risha said with feeling.

"I'll take you somewhere a bit cooler in a moment, but this is the tropics, so these temperatures are pretty normal around here."

A familiar golden-furred cougar chakat stepped up to the group, and said, "Not exactly the most comfortable climate for those of us with fur, but it makes for some spectacular vegetation and the wildlife that inhabits it. So you're all from *Phoenix*, eh?"

Martin blinked in surprise. "Didn't you have long hair in a ponytail before?"

The chakat laughed. "You're talking about my identical twin sister,

Goldfur. I'm Goldendale, Swiftwalk's lifemate, and I prefer my hair shoulder-length. It's a lot more practical out here, despite Swiftwalk preferring to keeping hirs long."

"Ah! That explains it. I've never met twin chakats before. Yes, we're all from the *Phoenix*, and taking a chance to look around while we can."

"I don't blame you. That's why I love my work."

Swiftwalk said, "I had better move on, Love. I've got to show this lot around a bit, and then go back and get a second group. The sun will go down in less than two hours, so I can't muck around. I'll give our cub a feed after that."

Goldendale nodded. "Have fun, folks!"

Swiftwalk held out hir arms. "You know the drill, everyone."

The skunk-patterned chakat teleported the group around to various sites, including the base of operations. Shi took them to some of hir favourite scenic spots that shi had found while on hir treks, including one that was high on a cliff and gave a panoramic view of the fantastic landscape below. The whirlwind tour took a bit over half an hour, and then shi returned them to the ship where the second group was waiting.

Valentina was carrying a holo-camera, and Martin remarked to hir, "I don't think that you'll have much time to do much holography."

"Maybe," shi replied, "but Madeline wants to get look at Sylvania too, so I promised to be getting shots for her."

"Why doesn't this Madeline come along also?" Swiftwalk asked curiously.

"Because I can't leave the ship," Madeline's voice came over the public address.

Martin explained the situation to the chakat.

"I see," shi said. "In that case, I'll try to give your tiger friend a fair chance to take some good shots for you, Ms Madeline."

"Thank you, Swiftwalk!"

"You're welcome, but we'd better hurry, or else we'll lose the light."

"One more question, please," Anastasiya said. Shi indicated hir and Shintaro's gravid bellies. "Does teleportation affect pregnant people like us?"

Swiftwalk shook hir head. "As far as I know, it should not. The way teleportation works is totally different from how a Transporter does. Now, if that satisfies everyone, let's get going."

The second group was organised like the first, and in a moment they were gone. Their return took a quarter hour longer than Martin's group, and Valentina was able to report that shi had been able to get some very nice shots.

They thanked Swiftwalk profusely, exchanging lots of hugs before they had to part company. The chakat had hir dinner and hir lifemate waiting, and the *Phoenix* had to begin its journey back to more familiar territory.

Martin stopped by the holosuite after dinner, and found the familiar sight of the cliff-side vista reproduced virtually perfectly. The only exception was because it was from a recording rather than a program, the scene kept looping. If you watched carefully for long enough, the same pair of avians swooped past on exactly the same path, and the same colourful insects landed on the same flower, and the handful of clouds went back to where they were a few minutes ago.

Madeline was standing close to the cliff's edge watching the view, a holosuite generated wind blowing her hair around. She noticed Martin approaching and said, "Beautiful, isn't it?"

"Yes it is. I'm sorry that you couldn't get to see it in person."

Madeline smiled gently. "Captain, you've got to stop that. I've come to terms with how my life will be lived. Besides, how long did you get to stay on the planet? Mere minutes! While I have this…" she waved her hand to indicate the whole landscape, "…whenever I want, for as long as I want. How many people back on Earth would ever get even a glimpse of what I get to see while travelling with you? I'm really the lucky one."

Martin nodded. "You're right, and I'm happy that we're able to give you this opportunity."

"Watch the scenery with me for a little while," said Madeline as she put her arm around Martin's waist.

"Gladly," Martin replied, putting his own arm around her shoulders.

The coyote later realised how much more he really got to see of Sylvania in that time spent with Madeline.

Chapter 9: To Snare A Firebird

(**Note:** The bulk of this chapter was written by Allen "Redbear" Fesler as a separate story by the same name. I have added and/or updated some parts in view of episodes written since this story was first published.)

Phoenix arrived at Aintak Tharl two and a half days later than originally scheduled on their itinerary. The extra speed that they had poured on for their side trip had cut the delay considerably, but could not economically eliminate it. Although he definitely did not regret taking on the consignment to Sylvania, Martin knew that it entailed the risk of losing their consignments at Aintak Tharl. Two days could make or break an independent shipping company's reputation in the interstellar shipping business.

Martin had been greatly relieved therefore that their tardy arrival had not caused problems, either in deliveries or pick-ups. In fact he was surprised to pick up a bit more unexpected business. Windsor's attempts at harassment had been unremitting, but perhaps his influence far out here was considerably less. Martin decided to count his blessings.

Because they were running behind schedule, and also because they had gotten a small break at Sylvania, Martin did not allow any shore leave at Aintak Tharl. There would be other opportunities to check out that particular world. Instead, they departed as soon as possible for their next port of call. As journeys went, this one was totally uneventful until they reached the Carswell star system.

*** 19 June 2334 ***

Phoenix currently coasted along at a small fraction of light speed on her way sunward towards the planet Carswell. Carswell's sun was large but dim, placing the sun's 'habitable zone' planets well within the sun's gravity well and thus it kept ships from getting too close to Carswell while still in warp. This forced several extra hours of travel time for those trying to enter or leave the system.

As had become standard, downtime meant cross-training time for most of the on-shift crew as they waited to be needed at their primary tasks again. At this time, R'Murran was at the bridge controls as he and his engineering second, Presaith, were simulating a docking maneuver on a slowly tumbling ship. Bethany was controlling the simulation from another console as Loander and Ceres were going over the computer-enhanced sensor logs.

"See, there it is again, Loander," Ceres told the Faleshkarti. "The sensor system just started picking up these ghosts soon after we dropped out of warp."

"Well it's not the software, I've been over it twice now, and both primary and backup computers are giving us the same answers. Is it possible the sensors themselves have become damaged?" Loander asked the Stellar Foxtaur.

"I'd say *maybe*, except then there should be other problems showing up," Ceres admitted.

"I would have to agree," Madeline said from a nearby speaker. "Everything else looks good, but something *external* is causing those distortions."

"Problems?" Bethany asked when she noticed that Loander had started a diagnostic test on their backup systems.

"Sensor 'ghosts', Commander," Loander told her. "We weren't seeing them until we reached this system."

"Humph," R'Murran half grunted. "Madeline? Send your raw data to my console, if you would please. Sometimes ghosts *aren't*," he said giving the commander a look.

"True," Bethany agreed, "though we're close enough to Carswell to call for help if this was an attack of some kind."

"Should I move us away from them?" Presaith asked as shi cleared the simulation from hir board and brought up the navigation controls.

"No!" Ceres and Bethany both half shouted almost simultaneously. They grinned at each other as Ceres explained, "Any departure from what we'd normally do at this point could tell them they've been spotted."

"So we pretend we don't see anything out there?" Presaith asked in surprise.

"We don't know who might be out there watching or why, so we don't give them reason to think we're on to them," Bethany told hir.

"I think I found *something*," Madeline reported, "One of my inspection cameras seems to have caught whatever it is."

"Hmmm, I *think* I might know the *who*," R'Murran said as he sent the image to the commander's console. "Ever seen one of *these* before?" he asked her.

"Damn," she quietly muttered at the picture Madeline's inspection camera had taken before tapping in a command. "Captain to the bridge – at your convenience, sir."

R'Murran nodded. "Thought so. 'Fleet had us working from images and sensor readings, trying to figure out how he made them and what their full potential might be."

"Who?" Loander asked for the others.

"Someone we really don't want to run afoul of," Bethany sourly said as the hatch opened and Martin stepped in.

"Run afoul of who?" the coyote morph asked as he leaned over Bethany to look at her display; he could tell whatever it was it concerned her when she didn't make a fuss over him being so close. Their camera had caught what looked like a small warp engine nacelle, but minus the ship it should have been attached to. There were other differences, such as what looked like a series of sensor arrays down its length.

"What have you heard of a ship named *Folly* or her Captain Foster?" Bethany asked, cocking her head at him as she brought up the ghost readings that had led to them finding the probe running along side *Phoenix*.

Martin snorted. "My dad warned me about him. 'Piss him off and you might as well drop your ship into the sun', he told me."

"Colourful," Bethany agreed. "Even 'Fleet has to watch themselves around him. We know he's helped a few times; if he's hurt anyone he hasn't left any witnesses."

"And *that*?" her captain asked.

"Is what R'Murran and I think is one of his probes."

"Why would it be following us?"

"If I was still in Star Fleet, I'd guess that probe was testing our sensors."

"While this was a Star Corps ship at one point, there's no way they'd mistake us for 'Fleet," Martin pointed out.

R'Murran huffed lightly before saying, "'Fleet thinks he carries on anti-pirate patrols – though his ship and the probes *appear* to be unarmed."

Bethany snorted. "That probe doesn't *need* a weapon, it *is* a weapon."

"Drag its warp bubble across another ship; or simply ram it," R'Murran agreed.

"Are we at risk?" Martin asked as R'Murran sent more tactical information to their screen.

"As the commander pointed out before you came in, we're too close to Carswell for the probe to do something without it being noticed. Hardly the 'out of sight' the *Folly* and her captain are reported to prefer," his engineer informed him.

"So, what do you suggest we do about that probe?"

"Well," R'Murran said with a grin, "in 'Fleet we'd just bounce a scan pulse or comm laser off it. A little 'Yeah, we see you, now go away'."

Martin looked thoughtful for a moment before he grinned and said, "Do it. Bounce a comm laser off it."

"Any message?"

"As you said, 'Yeah, we see you, now buzz off'."

"Sent," R'Murran said, only to let out a laugh a minute later. "I sent them a text message, but the probe is now sending us an audio one in return!" he told them as he directed the reply to the speakers.

"Sorry! We was just playin'!" protested the voice, that of a very young feline. In the background they heard another young voice saying 'Hey! You're not suppose to be *talking* to them!' before the audio suddenly cut off.

"That was *not* what we'd normally hear from the *Folly*," R'Murran remarked as Martin and Bethany exchanged bemused looks.

Madeline's image nodded as she said, "I picked up a third person, young and giggling in the background. Somehow I'm finding it hard to think of this as an attack."

"Open an audio channel, please," Martin said. At Bethany's nod he said, "This is Captain Yote of the *Phoenix*. Let me speak to your captain, please."

There was silence for almost a minute before the reply came back. "It'll be just a minute," said the young voice from before, "Really, we didn't mean nothin'," it pleaded a little quieter while yet another voice was calling out 'Mom!' in the background.

Presaith and Loander both giggled as the older members of the crew smiled or smirked. Whoever was controlling the probe, it sounded like a family-run ship, and not one where the cubs were taught to be wary of everyone they met.

Since the other ship hadn't muted or dropped their audio connection, they heard 'mom' before she knew they were listening in. 'Ok, what did you brats get into this time?' a much older voice growled.

"We was just testin' them like *you* do," said one of the younger voices while another was saying, "We didn't mean to …" while a slightly older voice responded with, "I didn't do nothing," before they were all cut off by 'mom'.

"*You* were in charge – which means you *allowed* them to do whatever it is we're talking about. Which is?"

Silence reigned on both ships as 'mom' must have been looking over something. A little softer she said, "There was no reason to take either of your unshielded probes in that close; the other two had already proven their sensors aren't up to our standards, and that they're probably running some of that hacked software."

The looks Martin and Bethany were now exchanging were not happy ones as R'Murran bent over his console muttering.

"*And* you little idiots went and left the comm on!" they suddenly heard *mom* chuckle when she finally noticed the still active communications panel. A moment later and much closer to a pick up, they heard, "*Maverick* to *Phoenix*, you guys still there?" the bandwidth increased as a video channel was added to what the probe was already sending them.

As soon as Madeline keyed the video to the main screen they found a Rakshani female grinning down at them; her fur was almost silver with white and light gray stripes. Sitting down in his captain's chair, Martin took a moment to compose himself before nodding at Bethany to send his image in reply.

"This is Captain Yote of the *Phoenix* – whom do I have the pleasure of addressing?" he politely asked.

"You mean the *pleasure* of finding that things are able to get closer than you thought?" she replied with a smirk. "I am Captain Frosty ap Rawhen na Pridefang of the *Maverick*. Normally we'd wait until both ships are in dock to chat, but my unruly cubs have forced the issue upon us."

"We heard something that hinted that you had probes closer than the one we spotted?"

"Close enough that one of them was able to catch your inspection camera turning to look at the one you *did* spot," Frosty agreed. "Suggest you look 'up'," she added with another grin.

R'Murran switched feeds and instantly found another probe sitting directly 'above' them, a mere twenty meters beyond where their warp bubble would form had *Phoenix* been able to properly form one that deep in a gravity well.

"Permission to go active?" he asked. At Martin's nod he sent an active sensor pulse at the probe, only to get no return from it at all. "What the hell?" he muttered, "Hologram?"

"No," Frosty assured him with another toothy grin, "it's real; it's your sensors that are the issue." Appearing to look back at Martin, she added, "Rumour control tells me you have a pair of Faleshkarti youths onboard, and that one of them is a software witch?"

Loander stepped into range of the camera. "I am Loander."

"I have heard good things about you Faleshkarti. I'll bet I'll hear even better after they find a cure for you," the Rakshani softly told hir. "In the meantime, I'm sending you a series of code strings to check against your sensor suite software. A couple of manufacturers got hacked and some code was added to their updates. The corrupted code lets anyone broadcasting the right signal hide in plain sight – as our probe is doing to you right now."

The Faleshkarti youth sat down at hir station and began inspecting the message that had just come in. Not finding any hidden tricks in it, shi started running a scan against the backup systems. The others watched hir work quietly for a minute before hir head came up. "We have strings U2 and SR71," shi stated.

"Nasty, the both of them," Frosty agreed. "Sending you both a bug-free upgraded version as well as the steps to kill it in your own system."

"Why would you be doing us such a *favour*?" Martin asked.

"Ha, I was wondering when you'd start worrying about getting something that sounded too good to be true."

"Well, you are the competition …"

"Oh, little pup, if only you knew," Frosty openly teased him. "I and some of my friends have been keeping our eyes on you and your little ship and crew for a while now."

"Oh?"

"Indeed," Frosty growled. "For example, when your father pulled some strings to get you a cargo after a certain mouse heist, our sister ship *Good Deal* had to go without for a while."

"I didn't know …"

Grinning again, she said, "No reason you would have, Captain; it was neither your choice nor decision to make. Sharptongue isn't one known for being played the fool, and she quickly discovered the *why* of the shipment changes. Since cause and effect revolved around one little mouse and her father, we were happy to show our displeasure at the kidnapping and attempt to run your little *Phoenix* into the ground."

"Meaning?" Bethany half demanded.

"Meaning, Commander Oakwood, that the senior Windsor is finding it much harder to get things shipped, so hard in fact that he might soon be begging *you guys* to take his cargo."

"There's no way," Martin choked out as if it left a bad taste in his mouth.

"Probably not," she agreed, "but he's having to settle for much less reputable shippers than he's used to dealing with. Like stepping across a picket line, some will do anything for money, while others won't for principle."

"And what *principle* would that be?" Bethany asked with a frown.

Frosty gave her a wink before saying, "The same type of principle that is giving a certain tod officer in 'Fleet a *slight* problem in finding his next command. It seems he bragged where the wrong ears could hear him, and a little message was sent to 'Fleet. It was something along the lines that if people like that tod were allowed to run over other people with 'Fleet's blessing, then certain resources that 'Fleet has become accustomed to could be withheld."

Bethany shook her head. "Not even that Captain Foster could *force* Star Fleet to do what he wants."

Frosty shrugged. "Depends on the type of force applied. There was more than enough evidence showing that dirty tricks were used to smear your reputation, Commander. And over a quarter of the antimatter 'Fleet now uses comes from a *certain* private sector that can cut them off with a word. With shippers it's closer to a third, so running counter to this supplier can mean paying a lot more for your fuel."

"So you're saying you could crush me," Martin slowly said.

"Maybe, but only if I could get the others to agree that you needed to be stepped on. But I see no need; you're too little to bother with!" she laughed at him.

"So why are you?" Presaith demanded into the new silence on the bridge. The Faleshkarti youth moved to stand next to Martin as shi said, "You test and spy on us, you offer help and threats, so why *are* you bothering with us?"

"*YES!*" Frosty laughed, "Finally, why *would* I bother with you? Well, your captain has built up a good team and a very promising ship. We've even given him a few chances at dealing dirty to make credits at someone else's expense, and he refused to take the bait. Then on your last stop at Gateway station, he agreed to take a shipment for *Night Hawk* and not only didn't he gouge them – your Captain Yote even offered up some tips on cargo heading the way they needed to go!"

"You want *Phoenix* in your *group*," Presaith accused.

"It would be nice," Frosty admitted. "We could use a ship like yours. But all those in this group are free agents. Other than a few basic rules, no one tells you what to do."

"Rules?" Bethany growled.

"Yeah, very basic rules, so basic that even old man Foster could follow them."

"He didn't *make* them?" Bethany asked surprise.

Frosty grinned at her. "Not the type of rules you may be thinking, methinks. We have a of couple *lists*. One is of people, groups or ships that we *don't* deal with. The other is a warning list of who has dealt dirt in the past and what to watch out for."

"I'll have to think about it," Martin said.

"Take all the time you need," Frosty agreed. "In the meantime, I'm sending you those lists. Follow them or not, at your own risk, of course," she said with a toothy grin as her image disappeared from the screen.

"At your own risk? I don't like the sound of that," Presaith stated.

"Not following it means we could be working with people even Foster's group wouldn't risk dealing with," Bethany pointed out. "And I was on a couple of cruises where we were refueled by remote automated stations, I wonder if those belonged to Foster ..."

"Wouldn't 'Fleet just go in a take what they want?" Martin wondered.

"I think someone might have tried it, *once*," R'Murran muttered as he looked at the list Frosty had sent them. "Rumors say a 'Fleet captain pissed Foster off and Foster refused to refuel them. They then reportedly followed him out to one of his stations and then tried to steal from it."

"I don't remember hearing of that one," Bethany commented.

"Rumours say a destroyer came in with much of its armor plate 'sand blasted' away. The official story was they went unshielded through a dusty system far too fast, but scuttlebutt says the damage looked more like it had tried to fly through a cloud of *antimatter*."

"So much for 'unarmed' stations."

"Can't really blame him, you don't want him giving pirates free fuel either. Huh, Windsor's company is on their list for dirty tricks ... Ha! Yote is too!"

"What?" Martin said in surprise.

"Just a minor note. Says here your father plays favours; also says he will then try to make up for it if he can."

"Frosty did say we got some of the cargo that was bound for *Good Deal*," Bethany pointed out, "though she didn't sound *too* upset about it ..."

"What now?" Loander asked. "Do I patch our software or just load theirs?"

"Can you confirm it doesn't do more than she said it did?" Bethany asked in return.

"The patches appear to do just what she said they do, but the software has more in it than I can figure out without more time."

"Just the patch then for now," Martin agreed. "While they seem friendly enough, there's no reason to take unnecessary risks with our systems."

"We have a little time, deceleration in thirty, station docking twenty after that," Ceres reminded them.

Madeline's image nodded. "Plenty of time then for me to use my extra systems to simulate our sensor systems and see if there are any tricks in their software."

"Is that safe for you to do?" Martin asked.

"Completely safe, Captain. I can isolate the subsystems and watch it run through another layer of interfaces. Think of it this way, I'll be doing the equivalent of you looking at the sun through one of our cameras – and the screen has been preset to not get bright enough to hurt your eyes."

"So long as you're taking precautions," he acknowledged.

Loander soon had their backup systems cleared of the 'hacks', and they could now see the other probes clearly, as well as the *Maverick*, which had been trailing a ways behind them.

Once docked, there were more chores to be done as *Phoenix* was placed in the queue for unloading. While some were tasked with moving the cargo, others were in charge of the kids.

A surprise awaited *Phoenix's* youths when they left the shipping docks for the station's main concourse. A teenage Rakshani female smiled when she saw them coming, while the younger Rakshani male and a pair of chakat youths didn't seem quite as pleased.

"You guys from the *Phoenix*?" the teen asked.

Penny had been leading the group and cautiously nodded as a very pregnant Shintaro moved to stand beside her.

"Excellent! I am Greeneyes, and these are Graytail, Starburst and Renniky. As they managed to bother your captain and crew, our captain has decided that they would make up for it by treating you guys to the ice-cream parlor in the shopping section."

"And how do we know this isn't a prank or some type of trap you're setting for us?" Penny asked, having heard a bit of what had happened on the bridge.

Greeneyes shrugged. "I picked the parlor because it would be out in the open and neutral, neither group having an advantage."

Penny cocked her head a little and asked, "Do you always see everything as challenge and challenger?"

Greeneyes laughed. "When you deal with many different species and the many different customs, you learn to not look too overbearing – but not appear to be a rollover either."

"I think you mean a pushover, but I get your drift," Penny admitted. "And if our captains don't see eye to eye?"

"Doesn't matter," Greeneyes assured her, "This is just a 'getting to know you' thing." She grinned even bigger before adding, "Though if this were an *attack*, you really *should* expect it to be a multi-prong one."

Penny frowned as she pulled out her comm. "Lane to *Phoenix*, I've got the kids; who's unaccounted for?"

"Hotfoot's gone shopping, everyone else is either unloading or still onboard," Madeline told her. "Is there a problem?"

"Check on hir, *now*."

"Shi's with Sergio, *Maverick's* chef," Greeneyes cheerfully told her. "Ask them to swing by when they're done shopping."

"Hey, Penny! What's up?" Hotfoot's voice asked a moment later.

"Watch out for Sergio, he's from *Maverick*," Penny replied.

"So he admitted when we first met. He also told me *Maverick's* cubs and their keeper would be treating you guys to ice-cream. We'll see *you* there later," Hotfoot laughed before disconnecting.

Penny was still frowning up at the much larger – and still grinning – Greeneyes when her comm chirped. "Yote to Penny Lane," it said.

"Yes, Captain?" Penny replied.

"Madeline told me you'd felt the need to call in to check on things. *Maverick's* captain is with me in my dayroom, and she has *advised* me that her crew would be looking up ours. An offer of being treated to ice-cream sounds safe enough, and we *will* be joining you there in a little while."

"Yes, Captain," Penny said again, this time with a lot less stress.

The combined group of youths and keepers didn't quite make it to the ice-cream parlor though, the spicy aromas from a restaurant two doors down detoured them. Greeneyes informed someone named Spencer while Penny updated Madeline.

Sergio and Hotfoot must have been told of the change in venue, as they were there just a little later. Sergio turned out to be a rather large wolf morph; the rusty coloring in his fur suggested some possible fox in his ancestry. Wolf and chakat placed their orders and then sat at a table a little away from the others, their conversation hardly impacted by outside influences.

"Hey, Boss! I'm defecting!" Sergio called out a little later as Frosty and Martin came in with most of the rest of their two crews behind them.

"Like *hell*," Frosty growled back, "I'm not going back to eating my own cooking!"

"Ha," he scoffed, "I'll wait until I'm sure you guys won't poison yourselves, but I do want to spend some leave time in this kitten's kitchen."

"Yote here will think I sent you to spy on him," Frosty pointed out.

"Na, his chakats would see through that. The only things I want to spy on are Hotfoot's cooking skills. Hell, I'll pay full passenger rates for a cabin if I have to."

"Between you and them then," Frosty grudgingly agreed. "*After* you train your replacement!"

"Ha, I'll make sure the replicators have plenty of healthy choices," he countered.

Frosty just shook her head. "Do you have this type of trouble with *your* crew?" she asked Martin.

The coyote morph just chuckled before replying. "We aren't such an old ship that my crew has had time to become jaded," he pointed out.

"Hmmm, we sometimes trade crews to better train them," she admitted. "But only with ships that can handle the surprises that can come with new deckhands."

Martin nodded. "You caught us doing some cross training when your probes started ghosting our sensors."

Frosty grinned. "It's always interesting to see how a ship will react when they realize the Zulus are there," she admitted. "My favorites are the random pirates that thinks they've been caught out. I've had three of them roll out their 'concealed' guns and fire – while in clear view of a Star Fleet base no less!"

Martin shook his head. "So you guys also flush out game for 'Fleet to hunt?"

"It's something of a hobby," the large Rakshani said with a grin. "With Neal and his *Folly* out visiting his colonies, we have to show the pirates it's still not safe to come out and play."

"I've heard rumors that *Folly* now has *armed* probes," Bethany commented with a side look at Frosty.

Looking down at the smaller gray fox morph, Frosty placed a finger along side her muzzle before flicking it away. "His one ship is carrying over half a million colonists, it damn well better be ready to protect them," she stated. "Though that doesn't mean he took *all* the good stuff with him," she added with a sly grin.

"Are you saying *you're* armed?" Martin said mildly. He figured they were already in deep water, time to sink or swim.

"A *few* things we don't bring into port," Frosty admitted. "'Fleet is spread too thin to cover or patrol what is needed." She snorted lightly before adding, "They've been grateful the couple times they've found us there to back them up."

"May I ask what type of weapons?" Bethany asked.

"You saw one of our older probes," Frosty told them. "The new baby Zulus are three quarters the size and have a pair of fighter-based phasers – though that's just the start. Neal also has a manned Zulu with transporter capability. Rather than arm it too, it has twelve hard points that can either mount the baby Zulus or fuel and cargo containers."

"And the little ones can be used as remote guns or missiles?" Bethany suggested.

"Just so," the Rakshani agreed. "Their sensors are still just as sensitive as the originals, so they're great for the hunt or a search and rescue."

"To give you a wider envelope, I thought that's what I saw once we could properly see them," R'Murran commented.

Frosty nodded. "We do wide scans where we can, and we hide the Zulus if they might scare or offend the locals."

"And Star Fleet?" Bethany asked with a smirk.

"*Some* members of 'Fleet get pissy about us patrolling their space," Frosty agreed, "but there are a lot of others that are glad we do it. Even Nightwatch has been asking us to look into a few things – don't try giving me that look, Commander! *You* of all people should know that groups hunting shadows will eventually run into each other," Frosty exclaimed at the astonished look Bethany was giving her.

"Okay you two … just what is *Nightwatch*?" Martin asked.

"A group that among other things watches for strange comings and goings, so of course *Folly* and her friends have attracted their attention on numerous occasions," Frosty told him, ignoring Bethany. "'Fleet likes to think Nightwatch is a big secret, but we've picked up their activity often enough that they had to 'fess up'." Looking Bethany in the eye, she added, "*Folly* came up on what looked like two pirates fighting over a kill. Imagine the Nightwatch ship's surprise when Neal not only went after the real pirates, he then offered them aid."

"He already *knew*," Bethany stated for her.

"Just so. Knowing the players helps keep you from hurting the wrong team."

"And what do you know about *us*?" she demanded.

"Quite a bit actually," Frosty admitted. "Otherwise we wouldn't be *bothering* with you," she added with a grin. "*Phoenix* is a solid little ship and pretty well run from what we can tell. Others of our group liked what they saw and suggested that you joining our team would be beneficial to all parties. As one of the oldest ships in the group, *Maverick* was appointed to make the offer."

"That, and we were the *closest*," they could all hear Sergio telling Hotfoot from the neighboring table. "They also thought the practice would be good for our still wet behind the ears captain."

"Sergio!" Frosty snarled as her ears folded back in rage and embarrassment.

"You're not such an old hand to be putting on such airs, *Captain*. Your uncle requested we keep you from getting too swollen a head with your new position," he reminded her with a cheeky grin.

"How long *have* you been a captain?" Martin asked.

"Six Earth months," Frosty admitted.

Martin chuckled. "And most of your crew has more time and experience than you do? I can relate; my ex-Fleet people have had to point things out to me on several occasions," he said.

"She's a good kid, just needs a little more *seasoning*," Sergio said with a grin at the sour look his captain was giving him.

"Do you always dress down your superiors in public?" Bethany asked, frowning slightly.

Sergio shrugged. "It was that, and let her make more of a fool of herself when you did find out, or say 'excuse me' – grab her by the ear and drag her around the corner to have a couple words. If it had been your captain, would you have let it ride?" he countered.

Martin frowned as he said, "There's a couple looks and words they like to use to 'warn' me that I'm about to make a major blunder – I find I ignore them at my own peril."

Presaith nodded from where shi had joined Penny and the kids from both ships. "I saw the wolf try to get his captain's attention before he butted in. I think this might be another 'showing of faith' in that they're willing to correct her in front of us."

R'Murran chuckled, "Like me teasing you in front of the others when you've missed something?"

"Just like that," shi agreed, "it's in house or in the family. They think they know us well enough to trust us with their family business."

"So ..." Penny said, looking slyly at Greeneyes, "What's the *family* rate for things?"

Greeneyes grinned back. "Such *as*?" she countered.

"Listening to the kids, it sounds like yours have a few more *toys* ... is there a *sharing* program?"

"It's not that so much as a 'hand me down' program," Greeneyes laughed. "It seems that we've managed to stagger the generations on most of the ships so that while the cubs on one ship are outgrowing something, another ship has cubs just getting old enough to be interested in it."

"So we'd be depriving some other ship's cubs?" Penny asked.

"Not really, as the cubs aren't always interested in the same things. Depending on who wants what, we may be glad you're taking it off our hands," she assured the mouse.

"Hmmm, something to think about," Penny said with a grin towards her charges.

"That can also include tech and hardware," Sergio said as he looked over at Presaith and R'Murran. "Old man Foster hates losing friends, so he's a strong believer in everyone running the best they can afford."

"Well, as a fairly new ship, affording new toys takes a little time," Martin admitted.

"Some just cost you a little time and practice," Frosty assured him. "Like that software update I sent you. It can run crosschecks between your primary and backup sensor computers – or it can tie them together for a much more sensitive system."

"And you just *gave* it to us?" Bethany said.

"Yup."

"It's too good a deal," she stated, "Why are you doing this?"

Frosty let out a small sigh, "Honestly?" At Bethany's nod she gave them a sheepish grin as she said, "Neal's latest colony push pulled far more ships and personnel than even *he* had anticipated. You've already helped us move things a couple times without you knowing it, and it also didn't hurt when we discovered how you've dealt with the *strays* you've come across," she said, looking over at Penny and Shintaro. "In case you hadn't heard, Old Man Foster picked up a few strays of his own his last trip through the Federation. Let's just say we all thought it might be time to offer you some of the benefits that come with being a part of us.

"Such as?" Martin wondered.

"Such as what cargoes we've seen going where at what rates, where you can refuel on the cheap," Frosty told him.

"What extra toys or gear the others in the group might be willing to part with, a list of what they might be interested in return," Sergio added.

"So you *do* pay for fuel?" R'Murran asked.

"Oh, yes – but far less than the going rates," Frosty assured them. "Neal uses the extra credits from the group to pay for things he can't trade for – like that software we sent you."

"Another *minor* advantage is ready access to *The Tinker*," a new voice said as a tall arctic wolf walked towards their table with a loaded plate. As he sat down he added, "Schedule your major refits when and where they are to get our engineering experts Arcs and Sparks working with you."

Frosty smirked. "This is Spencer, my first officer, second pilot and comm specialist."

"I thought *The Tinker* was one of Foster's ships," Bethany said.

"He may have laid out a little capital to get them started, but Arcs and Sparks own it outright," Frosty assured her with a grin. "Though he does send a lot of work their way."

"He didn't on that *little* upgrade he did to *Good Deal*, word has it he has a couple new tech witches he's training in the '*Foster* school of engineering'," Spencer told her. "Give them another decade or two and I'll bet his newest pair will be setting up their own shop."

"You've been holding out on the rest of us?" Frosty demanded, grinning, "Give!"

Taking a drink to wash down his food, Spencer said, "Neal's got a pair of nine-year-olds in training as both engineering and pilots. I have it on very good Intel that *Pegasus's* engineers coined the handle 'Terror Twins' for them. They, and one of Sharptongue's daughters did most of

Good Deal's upgrade. In the two weeks they were at Chakona, Starbase 2 fined *Folly* for those two racing through their shipping lanes, they performed a ship rescue using one of Neal's heavy shuttles, and they were in control of *Gwen* when Starbase 2 later got a sample of just how low into a gravity well she can use her warp systems for high sub-light maneuvers."

"Ha! Bet 'Fleet didn't like that!" Frosty laughed.

Spencer shrugged. "Neal probably did it to wake them up a bit before he left, if he can do it, so might others …"

"Just how *low* can he go?" R'Murran half demanded.

"With what I heard about *Gwen*? Warp in maybe half again closer than you did, sub-light maneuvers all the way down to this station," Spencer told him with a grin. "*Folly*, we don't really know for sure, Neal holds his cards close to his chest on that info."

"Wow," was all Bethany had to say, while Martin looked interested.

"What can *Maverick* do?" he asked.

Frosty smiled before saying, "A bit better than your *Phoenix*, but we're quite a bit larger too. And like Neal, we don't show *all* of our tricks to 'Fleet."

"The better to surprise a problem that thinks you're in too deep to escape," R'Murran agreed. "Rumours also said they're getting better speed and economy out of older ships?" he hinted with a grin.

"In their spare time Arcs and Sparks also refurbish the stuff they pull from those refits," Spencer told him. "Which means we paid the cost of refurbishing for a trio of class three warp cores – whose numbers can best the ones you'd get from a set of fresh-out-of-the-box class fives that 'Fleet pays way too much for," he said with a grin.

"Someone close Presaith's muzzle and wipe R'Murran's chin – he's actually drooling over there!" Penny laughed.

Martin was a little surprised to find that his mouth had been hanging open as well. He closed it gently and carefully ignored the snap of a set of jaws beside him – safer he not look over at his second in command until she'd had more time to compose herself. Taking a sip of his drink to give himself a minute to think, he glanced around. Other than Frosty's toothy grin, which he was now pretty sure held more humour than malice; the rest of her crew was cool and collected, just another day to them. *His* crew though was another story.

He caught a feeling and looked over at Chakat Burningbright. Shi smiled and nodded when he finally realized that shi had been gently trying to get his attention for a while now. Knowing he was now watching, shi looked at each of *Maverick's* crew before looking back at him and nodding. He nodded in return for shi had just told him shi felt no deceit from the others, they believed in what they were saying.

R'Murran was saying, "I've got Presaith fairly well trained, perhaps when your cook is visiting *Phoenix* I could … or not!" he hastily added when he saw the looks his captain and first officer were now giving him.

Frosty appeared to be ignoring the interplay as she said, "Depending on what type of upgrades your captain goes for, there's on and offsite training. If needed, this includes help setting up an advanced holosuite to give you some 'hands on training' even before you get the gear."

Martin thought he heard a snort beside him, but it might have been his imagination, that and the suddenly louder talking from the kids' table at the word that there might be holosuite programs to trade.

Frosty's grin widened, they were *hooked*, as Neal would say. Had this been real fishing she'd just give a little yank to set the hook, but that wouldn't work here. While well baited, her hook had no barb, it wasn't even really a hook as it couldn't get caught in the 'fish's' mouth, the moment her catch opened their mouth to protest they were free. The trick here was making her catch actually *want* to follow her line and leap into her boat on their own accord – trying to force them could cause her to lose them entirely. She said nothing, letting the others ask and answer questions. Turning, she found one of the *Phoenix's* chakats looking hard at her, a raised eyebrow at hir and had hir return a rueful grin and headshake. Giving hir a wink in return, she turned back to Martin. The poor coyote morph looked like he really just wanted to go someplace quiet and sort things out.

"For those that haven't *stuffed* themselves too much, there's still ice cream," Frosty reminded them all as she got up. Looking down at Martin she added, "You can take all the time you need to decide. Yea or nay, it was nice meeting you and your crew, Captain."

Martin stood as well before saying, "And you and yours, Captain."

Giving him a wink, Frosty left, quickly followed by the youngsters from both ships.

Penny got up to follow, but Martin waved her down. "Finish your meal, I think they'll be safe enough. Loander and Presaith went with them," he told her. He also tried to wave down Shintaro, but the twin-tailed fox just gave him a smile as shi followed the kids out with a rub of hir swollen belly.

"I've got an ear on them," Spencer assured them. "Never mind that the captain takes her crew's safety very seriously."

"That looked like a rather heavy duty stunner," Bethany commented.

"Yeah, that's what it looks like," Spencer agreed with a grin.

"It's *more*?" she demanded.

Spencer smiled at her as he said, "When you're 'in' we can then discuss the different methods we use to protect our crews and ships."

Bethany looked like she had a hot retort ready, but Martin held up his hand as he said, "No more than we would give away our secrets."

"Precisely," Spencer agreed as he also got up, as did the rest of *Maverick's* crew. "We'll leave you to get your crew's assessment of us," he said as they filed out.

"Do you think they left behind a bug?" Penny asked once they were 'alone'.

"No," Burningbright told her. "To do so and then get caught would destroy what trust we *do* have in them."

"So *do* we trust them?" Penny asked.

"I think we do," Martin admitted. "I think we would have heard of any strong-arming to force others to join."

R'Murran chuckled, "'Fleet's been trying for years to get *trusted* enough to get someone in Foster's little group."

"It'll never happen," M'Anissa'tk, R'Murran's Secondwife told them. "While they might be able to put their trust in someone *in* Star Fleet, they can never trust that someone higher up the chain of command won't order them to then abuse that trust."

"And yet they're just handing it to us," Martin pointed out.

"Only after testing us," Bethany reminded him. "I guess it's just lucky you didn't bite on some of those things that were offered."

"Some of the things I saw offered weren't things I could then be proud of doing," Martin told her. "That type of person might also like to abuse their relationships with their crew …"

"Then I for one am glad we have you for a skipper and not some ass like the one Bethany has mentioned," Penny stated.

"Who is on their list too it seems," R'Murran commented. "I'm surprised the tod hasn't tried to make the commander here 'get them off his back' as it were."

"He may have tried," Bethany admitted. "I'd asked Madeline to simply delete anything he sent me."

Madeline 'cleared her throat' through Martin's comm badge before saying, "I detect no bugs, and I have moved the almost weekly demands from that tod to a secure folder on the off chance he threatens the Commander or those she cares for."

"From sound of tod, he would try other ways to force you – or himself come," Anastasiya said. The Amur Tiger rubbed hir belly as hir cub kicked before shi frowned and added, "Could this be more Foster group playing in background?"

"Why would they have?" Bethany countered.

"What if you're not the only one that the tod did a number on – and they were already watching him when he pulled that number on you?" Penny asked.

"But this sounds like they hit tod *and* tod's power base, so helping someone on shit list put you in same bucket," Anastasiya pointed out. "He may not be able to bother commander because they fear wrong side of Foster's group."

"So, will we end up on their bad side if we don't join?" Hotfoot asked.

"No," Burningbright told hir lifemate. "Their offer is freely given, the only strings involved will be those we ask to be tied with."

M'Rarrtikar, R'Murran's Firstwife and ship's Purser, grinned as she said, "If the benefits are even half of what they claim, we can easily handle the upgrades, maintenance, *and* the bonuses you keep hoping to hand out …"

"You're telling me I should take it," Martin said.

"I'm saying it looks very *appealing*, but the decision falls on *you*, Captain," she replied.

"To think on," Martin agreed. "Well, shall we see if they left any ice cream for the rest of us?"

It was late into the ship's night, but Martin was still at his desk. As a going away present Frosty had handed him a number of memory chits. While some were for his engineers, he had several that only he could decide on. He was just finishing one when the next command brought up a link that said, 'Had enough yet?' Curious, he clicked it.

Greetings Captain Yote. We hope Frosty wasn't *too* overpowering. In case she didn't admit it, this was a group decision to ask if *Phoenix* would be willing to join us. As she was also supposed to tell you, joining us is totally optional on your part, and you get some of benefits whether you join up or not. I've included a few things that you might find useful, including my *Night Hawk's* comm codes and a set of FTL relays you now have access to. Drop us a line if you have any questions – or just want to talk.

Colin Steppes, Captain of the *Night Hawk*

Martin looked thoughtful a moment before grinning like a kid at Christmas and punched in the release code. Looking over the new data it revealed; he tapped a key on the intercom.

"Bridge," a youthful voice replied.

"I take it I'm not the only one burning the midnight oil," Martin said with a smile. "Your people are going to think we never let you guys rest."

Loander's smile could be heard in hir voice as shi said, "Better that than us telling them you're finding fascinating new toys and then sending us to bed without even letting us look them over!"

"Well, *my* toy chest included some access codes to things that are hard to believe. Including what it claims are comm codes that can even reach the Faleshkarti home-world," Martin told hir.

"That's impossible! The Federation has been talking about a FTL link, but the cost isn't in the budget," Loander informed him.

"And yet they gave us a comm code and instructions on how to use it," Martin told hir. "I'm game if you are."

"The worst that can happen is we waste a little time, and they laugh at us for falling for their joke," Loander agreed.

It took them only a few minutes to run the commands and then a voice came on speaking a language Martin had never heard before. Loander replied in kind and then they started talking even faster.

After five minutes – and no signs that they were going to slow down, Martin cleared his throat before saying, "I take it it worked as advertised?"

Speaking in a quick burst, Loander then stopped for a moment before saying, "Sorry, Captain. Yes I got through and thoroughly confused them. They didn't even know the relay was there until my call came from it as regular local traffic."

"Were you able to get high enough to get someone that will hear things out before they act on what they've learned?" he asked, a little concerned now that he had just exposed a previously hidden FTL array.

Loander actually snickered before answering, "Trust me, anyone we speak to at this point will be *very* interested in anything we may wish to say."

"Let them know that we don't have the rights to give them access to it," he warned hir.

"I already did, along with what little we know about the group – or human – that most likely did it."

"I'll ask the group next chance I get what plans they have for that relay, among other things."

Loander went back into high-speed mode and two or three other voices were soon mixed in with hirs.

Shaking his head in amusement, Martin dropped the connection to the bridge. "I wonder what that little call is costing us," he murmured.

"Almost nothing, Captain," Madeline informed him.

"Martin please, as we're well off our shifts by now. And how do *you* know what the charges will be?"

"You're forgetting I'm your systems controller. Other than staying out of your personal screens and rooms as a courtesy, I see all and know all; and that comm link included additional information …"

Martin grinned in spite of himself. "Quit smirking in there and tell me already."

"Yes, Captain. Unlike the regular network, this one has more options to choose from, including feedback on how busy the path is and what priority you wish to place on your message. The lower the priority, the cheaper the link, no matter how much data you're sending down it. As Loander is the first person to ever open that link, I chose the lowest level with an option to upgrade if it became busy." A corner of his display changed to the link in use and the growing charge.

"You're sure that's correct?" Martin asked, for the amount wasn't up to that needed to send an email to Earth.

"Positive, Martin. In fact, with your permission, I'd like to call home too."

"Let me know what it comes to," Martin asked.

"Of course," Madeline agreed as a second line showed up on his display. She was quiet for a moment before saying, "Whoa, this thing looks like it has enough bandwidth to …"

"To what?" Martin asked into the silence, the cost on the second line was climbing faster now, but still slower than a voice only call to Earth on the regular FTL service.

"Oops, sorry, Martin. I didn't mean to leave you hanging. I'm running a full holosuite simulation at home right now, just gave Adele a long distance hug."

"I'll let you enjoy your 'shore leave' then," Martin said.

Opening a third channel, he keyed in a number he knew by heart.

"Do you know what time it is?" his father's voice growled a minute later.

"At least this way I know your aide can't tell me you're in a meeting," he quipped back.

"Ha!" the older Yote laughed. "But how *did* you get through without them telling me you were calling?" he half wondered out loud.

"Dad? Have your team run a trace on this call. I'll be surprised though if they get very far."

"Really? Interesting – give me a minute."

The younger Yote was quiet as his father placed the query, pondering just how extensive this secondary network might be.

"Ok," his father said a few minutes later, "My experts are now very confused. They are insisting that this is a local call – though they do seem to be having problems locating the endpoint …"

"Do you remember telling me I might as well drop *Phoenix* into the sun if I annoyed a *particular* freighter captain?"

"*Yes ...*"

"It seems I've been granted access to *his* network and an option of joining the group."

"I ... see," the elder Yote said after almost a minute of silence. "The word was he was clear out of the Federation."

"He may well be, but it seems his friends can invite others they deem worthy."

"You've actually managed to impress me, my boy."

"Don't read too much into it, it seems they're more strapped for ships after their colony group went out."

"Ha! Don't you read too *little* into it. There's a lot of ships and crews out there that would do *anything* in their power to get picked to join."

"That might be part of what got us in," he confessed. "They admitted to having thrown a couple things my way that I rejected on principal."

His father nodded. "I had wondered about a few of the things that had filtered down to me."

Smiling slightly, the son said, "They have a couple 'lists' I now have access to. Your name is on one of them for nepotism ..."

"I was only putting the boot up Windsor. Any benefit you received was just *luck* on your part," he retorted. "Still, I'd do it again under the circumstances."

Martin hid a smile – his father would never openly admit to helping him. "They know, and they added that you'd make up for it if you could."

"This wouldn't have anything to do with a Caitian run ship named *Good Deal*, would it?"

"I could double check, but I think that was the one they mentioned."

"That one was easy to remember, their Firstwife has a tongue on her you don't want lashing out in your direction. You know how our network works here, well despite that, she was able to yell at me directly a mere hour after I diverted their loads."

Leaning back in his seat, the younger looked surprised. "I didn't think that was possible for anyone not already on your cleared list."

"It isn't, but she did it. It seems she had already gotten 'where' her load had gone and did a little browbeating on me about it."

"And you *let* her?"

"Let's just say that by that point I was more interested in how she came by her information than whether she was calm or yelling. At a pause in her rant I cut in and told her why I'd changed carriers and suggested she could probably go get the loads that you'd been denied. She actually laughed at me! One moment you'd swear she'd tear my ears off if she could only reach them, the next she was leaning back in her chair laughing like I'd told the best joke ever. Then she agreed to the alternate loads one of my managers had tried to offer her, saying the forced delay would give them an excuse to do a little sightseeing."

"Windsor's name is also on their list. Unlike your little warning, his carries the full report of the kidnapping and his trying to use Star Fleet to do it. None of them will ship anything relating to him."

"So I'm on their watch list while Windsor's on their shit list."

"More or less," the younger agreed. "One other thing that might interest you, they have some kind of 'buddy system' with cargo loads. While we can take what loads we like, we are to let the others know of the ones we didn't."

"In case one of the others wants them, that makes sense."

"There's more. It looks like I have their shipping manifests and timetables for the last year or so, so I did a little snooping. One of the group members, *Time Bandit*, needed to get somewhere well off their normal route. They sent out the request, and in a *day* there was a new route for them to follow with good cargo loads all the way. Among other things, I also found where they were deliberately leaving some non time-critical cargoes loads where we would find them – including the one that caused us to come out here to Carswell."

"Sounds like they were already working you into their system, son. I wonder how *he* manages all of that?"

"I don't know that *he* does, but from what was said, he has to follow the rules just like everybody else."

"What stories I've heard make him sound like a hell of a taskmaster."

"Hmm, what if they're doing the same thing *your* managers do? 'Well friend, I'd really like to help you with that, but my *boss* can be a real hard-ass about this/that or the other'."

The elder Yote chuckled at the tone his son had used; it had sounded exactly like one of his senior managers. "And you think they might be doing the same?"

"Come on, Dad. I know you employ several of your chakats for the sole reason of sniffing out lies, and I lucked into having a couple of my own. Other than some teasing and their young captain trying to act a little pompous, the crew we met was a happy one. There's no way they're being forced to be a part of something they don't want to be."

"Easy son, you trust what you saw and I trust you ... so, you said 'an option to join', you taking the plunge?"

"I'm thinking about it," he answered honestly. "They said there wasn't a time limit so I'm making use of it."

"Wise. You didn't call for *my* input I suppose?"

"Not really, you have even less data on them than I do now."

"Hmmm, I'd ask for a copy of what you have, but I have this funny feeling you'd then have to tell me no ..." at his son's lopsided grin he smiled. "I think they picked well in choosing you. Might actually make something of that foolish business of yours."

"Gee, thanks, Dad. Tell mom I send my love."

"I will," his father said before the display went dark.

Staring at the blank screen, Martin thought for a moment before going back into the list of names and numbers. The name was there, as it should be, but should he try it? Deciding that it could be the best way to separate fact from fiction, he keyed in the number.

'Establishing connection' flashed on his screen for several minutes, along with tracking data and link information across the bottom.

The message finally changed to 'Connection complete – Ringing' just before it cleared to reveal a sandy-colored chakat with dark red hair and piercing blue eyes.

"Hello?" shi asked, cocking hir head slightly at him.

"Ah, I'm sorry, the code I entered –," he started, only to have the chakat grin at him.

"You were looking for a particularly troublesome human? I'm afraid he's indisposed at the moment; you're stuck dealing with *me*," shi told him with a warmer smile. "And you might be who?"

"Martin Yote, Captain of the F.S.S. *Phoenix*."

"Ah, *Phoenix*, I was wondering when we'd be hearing from you. So you girded your loins and decided to check to see if there really is a dragon hiding in yonder cave," shi chuckled.

"Who *are* you?" he asked, more than a little confused.

"Ah, call me Red, everyone else does. As to who I am? I'm just the final say in a *group* dispute, the tiebreaker vote if you will. Sadly, or perhaps not so sadly, the group runs so smoothly that they seldom have need of me for that purpose. So, how can I help you, Captain Yote?"

"The correct comm number so I don't have to bother you again?" he suggested with a smile.

"Sorry, Captain, but you dialed the right number and reached just who you should have," shi replied. Shi then just sat there grinning as if shi could see the penny making that long drop.

"Captain Foster," he finally said.

"Captain Yote," shi said back, "don't let the muzzle and fur fool you, I'm still that bastard others have warned you about."

"I've read a very old book, *The Wizard of Oz*, I think it was. Why am I suspecting that *you* are that little man hiding behind the curtain?"

Red chuckled. "Hmmm, I can vaguely remember that title. So, you think I'm all smoke and mirrors?" shi asked with a toothy grin.

"Not all of it," Martin admitted. "This conversation proves you have some very real tricks behind that smoke you use to hide things. By the way, we made use of your link to the Faleshkarti home world, I'm hoping that isn't going to cause you any problems."

"No, I was looking for a good excuse to bring it to their attention, you just beat me to it," shi said with a smile. "If you dig deeper into your pack you'll find the stuff that we'd prefer you not use outside the group – or only in dire emergency."

"Does it include your definitions of 'dire'?"

The chakat shrugged. "I'd say you almost getting locked up and losing Ms Lane would have fallen under dire ... While I frown on throwing away perfectly good hardware, I have yet to find a way to replace a living being. I don't know how much you heard, but *Folly* was attacked and heavily damaged a while back. I traded the aft end and a good bit of my cargo for six chakats, a Rakshani, and a fox youth. I still think *I* got the better deal ..."

Martin slowly nodded. R'Murran still had connections in Star Fleet, and they had painted a much grimmer picture of the H1 attack, including proof that *Folly* could have escaped with little or no damage – *if* her captain had just blown them away immediately – rather than trying to look for and recover any furs being held.

"I can work with that," he finally said.

"I thought you might," shi agreed with a smile. "Not everyone wants to fully join the group. Find your comfort level and let it ride – you can always go deeper at a later date if you have the desire."

"Or bail?" he asked with a grin.

"You're no good to us if you're unwilling," shi pointed out in agreement. Shi looked ready to say more but shi suddenly had a minor distraction at hir end.

"Ddaaaadddddddeeee," a very youthful voice was heard calling out.

"Wwhhaaaatt--eee?" the chakat called back, turning to the side with a smile.

Martin couldn't help but notice that as Red turned to face the unseen cub, shi had reached back to rub hir swollen lower torso. He didn't have to be a doctor or midwife to know that the chakat before him was getting close to hir time.

"Eedtim," the younger voice was complaining.

"Yes, it will soon be *your* bedtime," shi agreed, wincing slightly at a sharp kick from within.

"Stoorree? Youu rommissed." the cub half pleaded.

Looking back at Martin with a smile, Red said, "If there's nothing else, duty calls."

Martin shook his head as he completely failed to contain his grin.

"I think you've given me enough information for now, and it sounds like *you* have a story to tell."

Red grinned. "Perhaps tonight's tale will be about how a no longer elderly firebird likes to take bubble baths to wash off the ashes of her rebirth!" shi suggested as the connection dropped.

Martin sat staring at the screen for a full minute before giving himself a shake. "I really should have recorded that," he muttered as he locked his console, "no one's going to believe me …"

With the console off, Martin missed Madeline's giggle as she quietly saved a copy of his call where he could find it in the morning.

Chapter 10: Children, Children!

Martin paused in his exercises to watch Anastasiya and Shintaro sparring. Both were conspicuously pregnant, the kitsune even more so than the tiger, but aside from some moderation in their attacks, it did not seem to be slowing either of them significantly. Nevertheless, Martin was concerned. Both were going to be first-time mothers, and had no way of knowing how well their birthings would proceed, and all he had to offer was a paramedic for medical supervision. He had dodged this problem once when M'Resk had miscarried, but that was something he hoped would not be repeated this time. He sighed. "Time to bite the bullet," he murmured to himself, then went back to his exercises.

When he had completed his routine, he went back to his cabin, showered, then got dressed in his uniform. He tapped his wrist comm and said, "Commander Oakwood, please meet me in my office." He then repeated his request to M'Lertiña.

Bethany was waiting for him when he got to his office, while M'Lertiña followed mere seconds later. He invited them to be seated, then said, "Have either of you considered what to do when Shintaro and Anastasiya come due?"

M'Lertiña replied, "As a paramedic, I've been trained to deal with births on an emergency basis, but I am not qualified to deal with problems arising from them. I would prefer it if you did not place total responsibility for them in my hands."

Bethany added, "In Fleet, we did have qualified doctors on staff, but most people nevertheless chose to spend the last few weeks of their pregnancies on their home worlds with their families, and of course proper maternity hospitals."

Martin nodded. "I didn't seriously consider leaving their births in your hands, M'Lertiña. Your paramedic skills are always going to be a last resort. As for having them stay on a planet for a few weeks, well... Shintaro has no home nor family outside of *Phoenix*, and I'm pretty sure Anastasiya will threaten mayhem if I try to put hir off the ship for such a 'trivial' reason."

"You're talking yourself into the only alternative," Bethany observed.

Martin gave her a lopsided smile. "Yeah, you're right. I was hoping against hope that you might have some alternative that I'd overlooked, but it looks like I'm going to have to try to hire a doctor's services for a while."

"That's not going to be cheap," M'Lertiña remarked.

"Do you happen to know the going rate for a ship's doctor?"

"As a matter of fact, I do have a good idea. As a paramedic, I was frequently called on to help the ship's doctor on the ship, and we were good friends. He gave me a good idea of how much they can earn." She quoted a pay range and Martin winced.

"Ouch. Even just for a few weeks, that's going to hurt the purse. Maybe tussling with Anastasiya wouldn't be such a bad idea after all."

Bethany frowned at him. "You can't be serious?"

Martin shook his head. "No, not really, but I don't know if I can afford that."

"Did you think you could afford several Star Fleet trained personnel when you were putting together the crew?" Bethany asked pointedly.

"No, I didn't; so you're saying that I should put out the offer and see what comes?"

"What have you got to lose?"

Martin could not think of anything. "Okay, I'll do that. For the sake of us all, I hope that we get lucky."

As usual, *Phoenix* had taken on some passengers looking for cheap fares to their next destination. It was not often that those passengers were Rakshani however. A female and her teenage son in this case. Their species was not exactly renowned for their sociability with other races, so it was no surprise that the mother did not leave the privacy of her cabin. The son, however, was another case. Quickly bored with confinement, it did not take him long to find the holosuite. As it happened, it was currently running a program for the children – a basketball court was set up, and three chakat children, two Caitians, two Faleshkarti and a tiger cub, were playing a game. A young rabbit woman was acting as referee, dressed in the traditional black and white striped shirt. The Rakshani boy was not familiar with the game, but he decided that it looked simple enough.

"Hey! Can I join in?"

The children looked at each and shrugged. Madeline said, "Sure. You can join with Katarina's side. That will help balance against the chakats on the other team."

"What's your name?" Candycane asked.

"I'm Zarej na Parshak ap Lorensar."

"I'm Candycane, Zarej." Shi introduced the others, but when shi got to Katarina, the boy snorted in contempt.

"You're the scrawniest Rakshani that I've ever seen," he said, looming over hir.

Katarina was a timid soul, and did not take this well. "I'm an Amur tiger, not a Rakshani," shi mumbled.

"And shi's a lot younger than you too!" Lemondrop said with a frown.

"Okay, okay – let's get on with this game already," Zarej said impatiently.

The game restarted, and it soon turned out that the Rakshani teen was a pretty quick learner. Unfortunately, he was also proving to be a rather selfish player, taking risky shots rather than passing the ball to a teammate with a better chance. He was also a very rough player.

Madeline blew her whistle yet again to pull him up for yet another foul. "Zarej, if you can't play this game properly, I'm going to have to ask you to leave."

Zarej scowled. "Fine then! Play your stupid game without me! Let's see this *glisp* do anything without me." He threw the ball straight in Katarina's face, and the child was knocked to the ground, yowling in pain.

"Go back to your cabin!" ordered Madeline. "The captain will be hearing about this."

Zarej snorted in contempt, but left anyway.

Madeline turned back to Katarina. The others were gathered around hir, one of them calling on her comm for M'Lertiña to come to attend to the tiger whose nose was bleeding profusely. "Damn, what's going to happen when Anastasiya finds out about this?" she murmured to herself before putting in a call to Martin.

The coyote was even more alarmed. If the boy's mother decided to defend her son, the hellcat might pose a real threat to Anastasiya, especially in hir gravid condition. In the end though, Martin realised that a confrontation was inevitable, so it would be best to do it under the most controlled conditions. He called both Anastasiya and Shintaro to his office, and explained the incident to the tiger. To his surprise, hir reaction was a lot more restrained than he expected.

"In part of Arkhangelsk where I grew up, bloody noses were badge of honour. Katarina could stand some toughening up. However..." Shi put hir hand on hir phaser significantly. "...does not mean that assault should be ignored." The tone of hir voice brooked no argument.

Martin nodded in agreement. "That's why I asked Shintaro to come along also. I'd like you both here when I confront the boy's mother."

"A wise idea," Shintaro agreed. "I hear that Rakshani can be very aggressive when defending their family."

"Yes, and ocean is a bit wet," Anastasiya added dryly.

Martin got on the comm and requested M'Resk to ask the Rakshani mother to come to his office.. "Just tell her that the captain requests her presence. I don't want her getting aggravated with you. If she does anyway, don't hesitate to leave."

"*Understood, Captain.*"

As it turned out, the Rakshani woman was calm when she arrived, although she became wary when she saw both of the security staff there, standing on either side of Martin's desk.

"You asked to see me, Captain?"

"Thank you for coming, Ms Palayeth. Would you like to take a seat?"

"No, thanks. Your Terran chairs tend to be uncomfortable for me."

"Very well, I'll come to the point. Are you aware that your son assaulted one of our children?"

Palayeth stiffened, then scowled. "No, I was not aware of any such thing," she declared.

"Zarej had joined the children in playing a game of basketball in the holosuite. He was unduly rough, and when reprimanded, deliberately threw the ball into the child's face, injuring hir. This is totally unacceptable, and I want to know what you intend to do about it?"

The Rakshani looked as if she was going to explode into rage, and both kitsune and tiger firmed their grip on their weapons. However, Palayeth abruptly sighed and deflated.

"My apologies for my son's actions, Captain, to the child and hir parents. Life has been difficult for me trying to raise my son on my own, but without a father to help keep him disciplined, I fear that events such as these have been becoming more frequent."

"May I ask what happened to the father?" Martin asked gently.

"He was killed in a stupid incident, and Zarej blames him for being careless and leaving us behind. Now I'm trying to stop my son from following the same self-destructive course."

"I see. However, I am now presented with a problem. I either have to confine the boy to his cabin for the remainder of the journey, or run the risk of another incident."

"With all due respect, Captain, you can't keep Zarej confined to the cabin for that many days. The journey is dull enough as it is without being restricted access to many diversions."

"I still must put the interests of my crew and their children first..." Martin began.

"Pardon me, Captain," Madeline's voice interrupted.

"Yes, Madeline?"

"I have a suggestion, if I may. Confine him to his cabin for the rest of the day as punishment, but let him go out again tomorrow. In fact, encourage him to play again. If he relapses, I have a special program in mind for him."

"Nothing too extreme, I hope?" Martin asked.

"That depends on his mother."

Palayeth hooked her thumb in the general direction of Madeline's voice. "Who?"

"Madeline Cottonfield, our ship's systems controller, and also my special assistant. She can't be present right now, but she was the one refereeing the game that Zarej was playing in."

"I see. Well then, Ms Cottonfield, would it help to know that we Rakshani usually consider you Terrans too soft on discipline? I doubt that you would do more than a stern Rakshani father would."

"My methods might differ, but I think I know how to handle him."

"What are you? A big tiger like this one here?"

"No, just a defenceless little bunny girl."

Palayeth wondered at the tone of that statement, and was even more puzzled at the grins on the faces of the *Phoenix* crew.

They all had to wait to find out what Madeline intended though. After the tongue-lashing that his mother gave him after the incident, he mostly avoided the other children for the two days that it took to get to Chakona. Although the Rakshani were continuing on to the *Phoenix's* next destination – a Rakshan colony world – they took the opportunity to visit the chakat home-world at the same time as the crew took shore leave.

It was pretty much a normal visit to that world. The timing was ideal in that it was early Autumn, and the weather was perfect. Because *Phoenix* was running nicely on schedule, they had the luxury of time to relax and recharge in a pleasant atmosphere. The chakats headed for the beach, volunteering to take all the crew's children, while the rest of the adults entertained themselves in various ways. Martin was the only one of the crew who had yet to go off-duty because, beyond all expectations, he had gotten a response to his request for a ship's doctor, and he headed to the Amistad Spaceport recruitment centre.

Martin had arranged an appointment with the applicant for shortly after they finished the unloading and loading of shipments. At the reception desk, he was informed that the applicant had already arrived, and was waiting in interview room seven. He was pointed in the right direction and found the room occupied by a female serval morph. She had short hair, looked about middle-aged, and was quite attractive despite fairly conservative clothing.

"Hello, you must be Doctor Andrea Leptailurus. I'm Captain Martin Yote," he said as he extended his hand.

She got up and shook his hand. "Yes, and I presume that you're from the *Phoenix*?"

"That's correct. Please be seated and we can get this interview under way."

Martin took his place behind the interview desk and looked at his PADD. "I took the time to look over your qualifications, and I see that you have the necessary licences for practicing as a ship's doctor, although you have never taken such a job before. Why now?"

"I have only just got those licences so that I could take a break from my life here."

"Looking for a glamorous life aboard a starship? I'm afraid that you won't find such on a commercial starship such as mine."

"No, nothing like that. In fact it's the opposite to what I want. I'm leaving all that behind me."

"You *want* a relatively dull life for a couple of months?" Martin asked in surprise.

"Exactly. Longer than that even. I have belatedly realised that my work has become my life, to the detriment of everything else. I am trying to make a break from all of that."

"Hmm... well, I might have moved to a small country town to try to achieve that, but if that's the way that you feel, I'm not going to look a gift horse in the mouth." Martin scrolled through her résumé. I note that you're experienced in maternity. Both our prospective mothers are herms, by the way."

"So are the majority on this world," Andrea pointed out.

Martin grinned. "Yes, but they're not chakats in this case."

"I've had my share of those also. It's rarely a problem."

"Good. You seem to have had experience in a broad range of areas, which makes you very suited towards being a starship doctor. However, as you have never done this before, are you sure that you will be suited to such a life?"

"To be honest, Captain, I've no experience to go by, either my own or someone else's, so I can't be sure that I'd be suited to it on a long-term basis. However, I am certain that I can do the job effectively for the minimum period that you have indicated that you will need me."

"I can accept that. Now about compensation – my advertisement for the position indicated that you would be payed at the low end of the scale, subject to negotiation. To put it bluntly, Doctor, *Phoenix* is a privately owned business with very tight margins. We simply cannot afford to pay you too much. If you request a higher scale, I will have to shorten the length of your employment, but I would rather have you stay on longer to watch over the babies and their mothers for several weeks."

"The agency informed me of all that. As I told them, money is the least of my concerns. I would be happy to stay on for as long as you are prepared to have me for the minimum rate."

Martin's eyebrows raised in surprise. "You'd make a terrible negotiator, Doctor. May I ask why you're so set on getting this job that you're willing to do it so long for so little?"

"You're suspicious of my motives?" Her mouth quirked in a lopsided smile. "I suppose it does sound very odd, and you wouldn't want some nutcase on the crew. Firstly – frankly I'm far from poor and I don't need the money. Oh, I won't work for free, but as long as I get the basics, it doesn't really matter. You see, as I said, my life was dominated by my work. I spent very long hours at it, and I was well-compensated for it money-wise. However, I let *everything* else lapse while I spent practically my whole time at the hospital. Then one day I came home very late as usual, and the house was empty. My mate had left me, taking our son with him. Only then did it get through to me that he had been trying for a while to tell me that we were growing apart. It's too late to fix that now, but it's not too late to get a life. The trouble is, even if I find some little backwater town to settle down, I'd soon be taking on more and more work until it took over my life once more. I recognise that obsessiveness in me, and it's inevitable because I love my job. I've always wanted to be a doctor, and I've always put my career before everything else. It's a wonder that I even found time to get mated in the first place, let alone have a child. I need to find some way to limit that tendency to obsess, and I believe that a job on a starship will achieve that. There is only so much that I can do with such a small crew, and that means that I will be forced to socialise the rest of the time."

"I understand," Martin replied. "I must admit that I did not expect that as a motivation, but several of our crew have had some odd experiences of their own that led to them joining *Phoenix*. I think that it has helped to make us a very close-knit and sociable group, so we can offer that much for you. So if you're happy with the basic pay and conditions, I am happy to offer you the position."

"I'm satisfied. Where do I sign?"

Martin passed over his PADD with the contract displayed. Andrea signed the screen, and it took her biometric reading for positive identification. Martin then transmitted the document up to *Phoenix*.

"Welcome to the crew, Doctor."

"Thank you, Captain. When and where do I board?"

"We are all on shore leave today. Come back to the spaceport tomorrow and be at Pad 37 by 1300 local time. Anything else that you need to know?"

"Have the two patients had proper tests by a gynaecologist yet?"

"I believe that they made an appointment with one at the maternity hospital today."

"Could you contact them and ask them to get their doctor to transmit their full details to me for their records? Give them my licence number for authorisation."

"I'll do that."

"That should be all. I'll be bringing along all my personal equipment which, in addition to yours, should cover all our needs."

"Very good. I'll see you tomorrow then."

As realistic as the holosuite scenes were, in some ways they were too perfect. The beach scene, for example, did not reproduce the sudden gusts of hot wind that sent fine sand in your face, the holographic sun never burned, and you did not tread on dead sea creatures or plants. That's why the children so loved the real thing – it was more exciting than the sterile sameness of the reproduction. They thoroughly enjoyed themselves amongst the crowds of the popular beach, and the hours flew by before the adults finally declared that it was time for dinner. Only then did the youngster realise how much of an appetite that they had worked up. By then, several of the other adults had rendezvoused with the beachgoers, and they all wandered off to find a suitable venue. An adjacent park had a family restaurant set in the middle, which seemed to be very popular, judging by the crowds taking advantage of the excellent weather to enjoy some open air dining. Too popular in fact, because they were told that their large group would have a considerable wait before they could be seated. After a short discussion, they decided that they would wait a while for the space to open up, but the younger children soon started fidgeting impatiently. Eventually Kannekin asked if they could go off exploring.

"Alright," M'Rarrtikar conceded, "but stay together, and don't go too far. Come back immediately when we call you on your comms. As the eldest, Keera is in charge."

The cubs willingly agreed, and they left as a group and headed towards the shops that faced onto the park on the other side of the road. The waited for the lights to stop the vehicles that rolled past nearly silently. Chakona's traffic was always a contrast to most places that they visited due to its reliance on almost totally electric vehicles which were quiet and pollution-free. Occasionally a totally empty vehicle would pass by – an A.I.-controlled Public PTV, a kind of automated taxi, on its way to collect a fare. They crossed the road and headed down the sidewalk, looking for something to interest them. Two blocks down and they struck paydirt with an amusement arcade.

The modern arcade featured interactive games that relied on multiple players, often featuring holographic displays and sense feedback that were far more sophisticated than any home system. They also had dance competition games that were very popular. The children spread out seeking their favourite diversions.

For a while nothing unusual happened. There were the normal waits while people took their turns while others watched. Then a pair of older teen wolf morphs decided that they were not finished playing with one of the games and refused to yield it to the next people in line. Those people were Candycane and Pixiepaws.

"Hey! You've had your turn," Pixiepaws objected.

The tall wolf boy moved up close to the chakat to glare down at hir, trying to dominate hir. "What's it to you, greenie?"

"We've been waiting, and your turn is finished," Pixiepaws said firmly, not at all intimidated by the teen after doing self-defence sessions with Anastasiya.

The boy's companion stepped up next to the other, crossed his arms and snarled. "Well you can wait a bit longer. We're having a re-match, so beat it."

Candycane came to hir sister's assistance. "No, you can get back in line with everyone else."

The first wolf said, "What is this? Freak-show day? Did your parents mate with clowns?"

Pixiepaws could sense that the boy was trying to needle them, but shi rose to the bait anyway. "You leave our parents out of this! They at least know how to raise cubs that know how to take their fair turns!"

The boy just laughed and they both turned to go back to the game. Pixiepaws reached out to grab the arm of the first boy, who whirled around and knocked the arm aside. He then put both hands on hir chest and shoved hir aside hard. The chakat's four-footed stance prevented hir from being knocked off hir feet, but that did not stop hir from getting angry. Without thinking, shi reached out with hir mind and gave the teen a huge telekinetic shove. The wolf flew off his feet and knocked over his companion, and they landed in a tangle of limbs.

The dispute had attracted some attention, and the onlookers gasped in surprise. Some of them turned to glare accusingly at the chakat who suddenly realised what shi had done. The wolves were already getting to

Art © Seth Triggs

their feet, and they were looking very pissed off. Candycane knew that the situation was getting worse, and moved up close to hir sister to help defend hir. However, before anything more could happen, a voice roared over the excited babble.

"What the smegging hell is going on here?!"

A very irate renzar – an ursine alien species – came striding up to the group. He wore a badge that indicated that he was the manager, and he was not in any mood to put up with people disrupting his business. He stopped next to the game and took in the scene. "Oh, it's you two again. What have I told you about hogging the games?"

The renzar was no taller than the wolves, but easily out-massed them, and it was mostly muscle. It was clear that the wolves knew they were outclassed and remained sulkily silent.

"Right – you two are out of here now, and I don't want to see you back!" He hooked his thumb in the direction of the exit, and the wolves slinked off.

Pixiepaws and Candycane were about to move off when the renzar turned his attention back their way. "And who was part of that ruckus? Was it you two?"

Pixiepaws meekly replied, "Yes, sir."

"I run a family business here, and I won't tolerate any troublemakers. I haven't seen you two here before, so you get one warning. Any more trouble from you two, and you'll be banned like those wolves. Now get out of here. You're done for today."

The chakats slunk out, embarrassed at letting things get out of hand. They saw Keera glaring at them on their way, and knew that they were going to cop it from their parents later. They stopped outside the arcade, wondering what they should do next. Minutes later, the others came out and joined them.

"We were told to stay together," Keera sternly told them, "so you've forced the rest of us to leave. I hope you're happy."

"Hey! That wolf started it!" Pixiepaws objected. "And he insulted our parents."

"Yeah, and what do you think they'll say when they hear about this?"

"Do you really have to tell them?"

"I've been left in charge of you, so what do you think?"

The chakat had nothing to say, and the Caitian sighed.

"Okay, I won't say anything this time, but only because I don't want everyone else to get into trouble along with you. But I won't do it again."

Pixiepaws and Candycane heaved a sigh of relief. The group started to move off in search of alternative distraction, but only a minute later, Keera's comm went off, and they were told that it was time to rejoin the adults at the restaurant.

Martin picked up a last-moment consignment before Andrea arrived with a van full of medical equipment. He helped her stow it securely aboard the shuttle.

"Aren't there any others people coming with us?" Andrea asked.

"Everyone else is already aboard *Phoenix*. They went up in our other shuttle. That means you can sit in the co-pilot's seat and enjoy the view if you'd like?"

Andrea accepted with a little trepidation.

"Been in space at all before?" Martin asked.

She shook her head.

"It's not much more than a normal aircraft ride, but the view is more spectacular. Don't worry about the controls in front of you – they've been deactivated. Just enjoy the ride."

Andrea was not sure that she had not made a mistake anyway. Sure, the view was amazing, but it was also a little bit terrifying. When they went into freefall, her claws punctured the material of the armrests, and they did not retract until they docked in *Phoenix's* shuttle bay.

Because his attention had been on the piloting, Martin had not realised Andrea's state until he had shut down the shuttle. He grinned as he said, "I'm going to have to dock your pay to fix those."

Andrea's ears grew hot as she blushed in embarrassment. It was not the way that she had hoped to start off her employment.

Martin took pity on her. "I'm just teasing, Doctor. If that's the worst that happens on your tour of duty, then you'll be doing very well. Now let's get you unloaded."

Martin enlisted Risha's help to get the equipment up to the sick bay while he headed for the bridge. As soon as all departments had acknowledged their readiness, he ordered departure for the Rakshan colony that was next on their itinerary. As soon as they had escaped Chakona's gravitic influence and gone into warp, he left the bridge in Bethany's care and headed to the sick bay to see how Andrea was settling in. He found it crowded with opened crates and equipment in various states of assembly, and her personal luggage set on the floor to one side.

"Doctor, you could have unpacked your own stuff before getting down to work. Didn't Risha point out the medic's quarters that are adjacent?"

"Um... yes, she did. I just thought it best to set up as much as I could before we departed."

"We've been on our way for the past half hour," Martin pointed out.

Andrea blinked in surprise. "But I didn't hear or feel anything."

"In a properly functioning starship, you would have to be paying attention to notice anything. Inertial compensators cancel out acceleration, and warp drive is reactionless. However, that's beside the point. It's obvious that you're letting your work obsession affect you, so I'm ordering you to stop this for now, unpack your personal stuff, and settle in properly. Once you've done that, come to the rec room and meet with the off-duty crew, and get to know them over a cup of coffee, or whatever your favourite beverage happens to be. If you have any questions, just ask Madeline."

"Who's Madeline?"

"That would be me," Madeline's voice appeared to come from the air between them.

"Oh!" Andrea was slightly startled. "Are you always listening in on people's conversations?"

"Part of my job, Doctor. If you want privacy, just tell me. When you want things back to normal, just use your comm to let me know."

"Speaking of which," Martin said as he dug into one of his pockets, "I have your personal wrist comm. Please make sure that you're wearing it at all times when you're on duty, which while on this ship pretty much means all the time that you're not in bed or in the shower."

"I understand the need to be on call, Captain."

"Good. Now get settled in, Doctor."

"Yes, Captain, but please just call me Andrea when we're not talking on a professional basis. I... it's just one of the things that I want to do to help disassociate myself from my job."

"You want people to talk to the person, and not to the profession, so to speak?"

"That's a good way of putting it."

"Fair enough. Outside of sick bay, I won't call you 'Doctor' unless you're specifically doing your job. I'll see you in the rec room soon."

***

Andrea did not take very long to settle into her quarters. While she had brought along plenty of equipment, her personal effects were considerably less. She found a ship's uniform neatly folded on her bed and took the time to change and freshen up before heading for the rec room. As she stepped into the corridor though, she realised that the captain had not given her directions to it.

"Madeline?" she said hesitantly.

"Here, doc," came the prompt reply.

"How do I get to the rec room?"

"Easy! Head to the translift at your right...." Madeline continued to give Andrea directions as she walked, concluding with, "See you there."

Andrea resolved that one of the first things that she would do would be to get hold of a map to the ship and memorise its layout. She could hardly stop to ask directions in an emergency, nor could she expect Madeline to be available 24 hours a day.

Andrea found the rec room readily enough, and found Martin there as well as Risha, a black foxtaur, a rabbit, a chakat, a pregnant tiger, and an even more gravid fox with two tails.

"Ah, Andrea – come in!" Martin said. "Everybody, this is Doctor Andrea Leptailurus."

There was a chorus of welcomes.

"Let me guess – you would have to be Anastasiya," Andrea said to the tiger.

"Pleasure to meet you, Comrade Doctor."

"I will want you to see me soon after I finish setting up all my equipment in sick bay."

"No rush, Doctor. Little one is not due for several weeks yet," Anastasiya said as shi patted hir belly.

Andrea turned to the kitsune. "And you must be Shintaro. I believe that you're due much sooner."

"I am honoured to meet you, Doctor-san," Shintaro said as shi bowed as much as hir pregnant condition allowed.

Martin then introduced Ceres and Zelkie, but before he could introduce Madeline, she beat him to it.

"And I'm the resident ghost," Madeline said, extending her hand to the serval.

"I recognise your voice. Why do you – *eek!*" Andrea squealed as her hand passed through the rabbit's.

"Told you I was a ghost," Madeline said with a grin. "I haunt this ship."

Andrea hesitantly put her hand out again and passed it through Madeline's arm. "You're a hologram. Why?"

"Aw! She caught on too fast," Madeline said with a wry grin.

Martin said, "You're getting more like Penny every day. Stop teasing Andrea and tell her about yourself."

Madeline did so, and Andrea was quite intrigued. "Could I have a look at your life-support unit?"

"Sure, but there's not much to see. I'm totally sealed inside to keep

Art © P_Moss

the interior sterile."

"What? Not even a visual inspection window?"

"Well, yeah, but you don't see much anyway. The suspension gel that my body is in tends to make me look a bit weird."

"What if you have a medical problem?"

"The life-support unit is state of the art, and can cope with just about anything."

"What about the things that it can't cope with?"

"Just like everybody else, there's always the possibility that I could have an emergency when I am a long way from help. Life is a risk, Andrea."

"I realise that, but I hope that I can be considered an alternative while I'm aboard."

Martin interjected, "I'll be getting the entire crew to have full check-ups with you, Doctor. I can't see why that would not include Madeline."

"Excellent!" Andrea declared. "Now, didn't somebody promise me a coffee?"

Andrea was gradually introduced to the rest of the crew, and everybody soon had received the most thorough health check of their lives. The doctor was most intrigued by the Faleshkarti physiology which had significant differences from Terran biology, and even Caitian biology which was almost as familiar to her. However, most of her attention was focused on the two who were the reason that she was aboard. Shintaro's biology was so similar to a normal fox morph's that she decided that it made no difference, and she confidently predicted the baby's arrival to within a day's leeway. She observed hir exercise routine and got hir to modify it a bit, as well as Anastasiya's. After that, it was mostly a matter of waiting.

The day came on the sooner side of Andrea's prediction, presumably triggered by the kitsune's exercises that day, mild though they were. In the middle of hir session, Shintaro was hit by hir first contraction. Anastasiya anxiously hustled hir friend to the sick bay, getting Madeline to alert Andrea along the way. The doctor made Shintaro comfortable on a bed that had been specifically prepared for that moment, and they settled in for the period of labour.

Not long after, Hotfoot and Zelkie turned up and asked to come in, and Andrea asked why.

"We'd like to witness the birth," Zelkie explained as if it should be quite obvious.

"I thought as much," Andrea replied. "For starters, the birth could be many hours away. Second of all, your chakat traditions notwithstanding, you don't belong here unless Shintaro invites you, and so far the only person that shi seems to want at hir side is Anastasiya. So shoo!"

The two chakats slinked off in disappointment.

"Chakats!" Andrea muttered with a roll of her eyes before she turned her attention back to Shintaro.

As it happened, the labour only lasted about an hour and a half from the time of hir first contraction. Doctor Hiro's genetic engineering that defined how the herms were built meant that they were made for relatively easy births. With Anastasiya there for support, Shintaro delivered a healthy kitsune kit.

"Your child is beautiful, my friend," Anastasiya said with a grin. "What are you going to name hir?"

"Shi will be Kiku-chan in honour of hir sire. Shi will receive all the love and devotion that I can no longer give my lifemate."

"That is good choice, I think. Rest now. If you need me, call me any time."

"Thank you, Anastasiya-san," Shintaro replied as shi gazed proudly at the baby in hir arms. "Please tell everyone that we are both doing well."

Zarej had basically kept to himself and found what amusement that he could, but he was now bored enough to reluctantly approach the other youths in the hopes of joining in. By coincidence, it was during another basketball game, although he would have been happy to play any other sport with them.

Madeline of course spotted him approaching even before he got to the holosuite, and she warned Keera. "Looks like we might be able to put my plan into action. Zarej is heading here."

"Okay, I'll take over refereeing the game. You get ready."

Madeline's form morphed from a young adult female to that of a mid-teen male. "How do I look?" she asked, her voice altered to sound like a boy of that age.

"Like an awkward, gangly teenage buck rabbit," Keera reassured her.

"Perfect! 'Madden' is ready to play. Now we'll see if Zarej has learned his lesson and is prepared to play nicely, or not."

Madeline had discussed her plan with the youths so that they could act accordingly, so as soon as they saw 'Madden', they knew the ploy was about to be initiated. Not everyone was thrilled about it though.

"I don't want to play with that jerk!" Pixiepaws declared.

"Everyone deserves a second chance, Pix," Madeline said. "Besides, I won't let anything happen to anyone this time."

"He can have his second chance without me," Pixiepaws stubbornly replied.

Keera frowned at hir. "We need you to fill out the team. And if that's not a good enough reason, then I call in a favour. You owe me big time for not telling how you got us kicked out of the arcade."

Pixiepaws' ears lay flat in humiliation. "Oh, alright."

That was resolved just in time as Zarej had entered the room, and was approaching the group.

Keera turned to look at him coolly. "What do *you* want?" she asked with just a trace of hostility. She did not actually want to put him off.

"I'm bored and I want to play. I'm not banned, so I'm allowed to join in."

"Are you going to play like a team member, not play rough, and not hog the ball?"

"Yeah, sure."

Keera looked towards the others. "Will we let him play?" she asked them.

They made a show of reluctance, then begrudgingly said, "Okay."

Zarej was put against 'Madden's' team, and the game recommenced. For the moment, everyone played it straight. If Zarej behaved himself, nothing exceptional would happen, and they could be satisfied that he had learned his lesson. Madeline made sure that she was competing with him wherever possible, and leaving openings for his teammates for him to take advantage of, encouraging him to work with the team. At first he was calm and cooperative, passing the ball at most opportunities, but gradually he started to get more and more aggressive, and hogging the ball. After Keera pulled him up for yet another foul, Madeline caught Keera's eye and several of the others. It was time to start the lesson.

Up until then, Madeline had restricted herself to the skills of the average teen, but she happened to be a good basketball player, and with some enhancement from the holosuite systems, she stepped up the pressure on Zarej. She constantly blocked him, stealing the ball occasionally. Without breaking any rules, she made it nearly impossible for him to achieve anything. She made a point of passing the ball to her teammates, while his loudly griped that he would not pass even when he had a clear opening. In general, they made it the most high-pressure scenario that they could, expecting him to reach the breaking point.

And he eventually snapped. Upon having the ball stolen yet again by Madeline, with a loud growl, he grabbed her and hurled her several metres. She crashed to the floor in a manner that may have broken a bone or two, if she did not happen to be an energy construct rather than having a real body. Of course she was totally unhurt, but she lay there dramatically for a long moment. The others had stopped to watch, knowing that the real fun was about to start.

Zarej just stood there, panting and growling at 'Madden', his ears folded back and his muzzle wrinkled in a snarl, oblivious to the others. Then he was startled as the rabbit started to laugh. Madeline got to her feet, her laughter growing louder, mocking him. She walked up to the Rakshani youth, craning her neck up to gaze at him in contempt, despite the fact that he was 35 centimetres taller than her, and nearly twice her apparent mass.

"What's the matter? Can't play properly, so you have to take your frustrations out on little guys like me? It will never make you a better player."

"I won't be mocked by a plant-eater!" he yelled, making a grab for her.

She dodged him easily, and grinned infuriatingly. "Can't even catch helpless prey either, I see."

That stung him, and he leaped at her. She dodged again, giving him a hard kick on the backside as he passed, and he stumbled to the floor.

"Better get someone to hold me so that you can actually hit me. Oh wait – you don't need anybody else to help you. You're too big and strong to need anybody else."

He howled in rage and leaped at her, but she moved impossibly fast. Each time she was almost within his grasp, she slid away, laughing.

"Hold still, you pathetic flea! I'll show you what it means to be strong!"

"Okay," Madeline said obligingly. She stood there with her arms folded, a mere three metres away.

With a cry of triumph, he charged the rabbit, intending to tackle 'him' to the floor and pummelling 'him' into submission. Instead he crashed into an immovable object; the rabbit may as well have been carved from stone. He dropped to the floor, heavily stunned, his head pounding and his vision swimming.

"Smeg!" Madeline swore. "I didn't expect him to lead with his face."

Zarej's mother stepped out of the concealment that Madeline had set up for her. "Do not worry too much. We Rakshani are tough enough to cope with something like that."

"I've called the doctor to come look at him anyway," Madeline replied. She had not intended to cause major injury, only to teach him a lesson. She had taken the precaution of discussing her plan with his mother to ensure that there were no unwanted repercussions against the crew. His mother had actually been impressed by the idea.

"You would make a good Rakshani parent," was her comment. "There is no honour in strength alone, and he needs to learn that."

Madeline reflected that she did not want to raise rabbit children that way, but it did seem that tough love was the preferred Rakshan way.

Andrea arrived quickly, and scanned the boy. "He has a broken collar bone, and mild concussion. Nothing that we can't fix immediately. Let's get him to sick bay."

Zarej was carried out by his mother, and the players drifted out of the holosuite, leaving Madeline with just Keera. The rabbit resumed her normal form and looked glumly at the Caitian. "This seemed like a much better idea before."

"We all thought so, Maddy. Don't be too hard on yourself."

"I suppose so. If Palayeth isn't mad, I suppose it will work out."

"Let's wait and see if Zarej's attitude has changed before we get too bent out of shape about it."

"Yeah, you're right. I'd hate to get all cut-up about this only to find out that he hadn't learned anything from the experience."

Keera grinned. "At least he will probably have learned not to crash-tackle rabbits in future!"

Zarej recovered quickly enough, or at least physically anyway. His humiliation at the hands of the little 'plant-eater' however stung for days after, exacerbated by his mother's lecture on honour and self-control. It remained to be seen whether the Rakshani boy had at last learned his lesson, but for the remainder of the trip to the Rakshan colony, Zarej gave nobody any trouble.

With little to do until Anastasiya gave birth, Andrea offered to give M'Lertiña more medical training to make her more useful both as an assistant to her, and as a better paramedic when she was gone. Martin approved, but with a caution to keep it to keep it to a normal shift. Andrea reassured him that she would not be sacrificing any personal time.

The chakats were again disappointed when Anastasiya went into labour weeks later. Valentina supported hir wife during the event, and Katarina asked to be present at the birth of hir sister, but aside from Andrea and M'Lertiña, they kept the birthing within the family.

After a five and a half hour period of labour, the child was born and declared to be strong and healthy. Shintaro was the first and only one to see Anastasiya before the tiger got some rest, but shi was able to tell the others that the proud parents had named their child Petrushka. The rest of the crew got to celebrate the event with Anastasiya the next day.

Several weeks later, a couple of days out from Chakona, Martin came into the rec room at an odd hour, looking for some refreshment. As he had suspected, Bruce was not there to be a barista for him. That happened frequently enough that Martin had one day surreptitiously had his perfect espresso patterned, and he could get it from the replicator whenever he wanted – as long as nobody was there to witness his sneakiness. Tonight there was just one person, but she was sitting by the observation window with her attention on the view outside, so he was able to get his favourite brew. Then he wandered over to the window and quietly sat beside Andrea.

The doctor glanced his way and said, "Good evening, Martin."

"Feeling a bit introspective tonight, Andrea?"

"Yes, a bit. How did you know?"

"This seems to be a favourite choice of many people when they're in that mood. Is it about the upcoming end of your contract aboard the *Phoenix*?"

"Right again. I have mixed emotions about it. On the one hand, I've achieved what I wanted to do by going out into space – finding time to be myself and socialise. I've made many dear friends on this job. However, on the other hand, I feel under-utilised. This is such a well-run ship with a relatively young and healthy crew that you don't really need a doctor most of the time. M'Lertiña is certainly competent enough to meet your needs."

"So you should be happy that we'll be back at Chakona in two days," Martin commented.

"You would think so, but I'm not really looking forward to returning to what I left behind. I've enjoyed my stay on *Phoenix*, and I'm reluctant to leave as yet."

"Heh! You're not the first to feel that way. I wouldn't mind you staying on for a while longer, but frankly I can't afford to be paying for a full-time doctor who has so little to do."

"I certainly understand that, and I'm not asking you to keep me on, but it does make me wonder what exactly I want to do with my life when I get home. If I go back to my old job, my compulsiveness will inevitably lead me back into my bad habits, and I don't really want that to happen. Then there's the small town option, but would I be willing to settle for that? That has been the beauty of my stay here – I could not stray from my goal even if I wanted to. But as I have already said, it's the opposite extreme, and I'm finding myself getting bored occasionally."

"Perhaps you might want to take up some hobby?"

"Ha! Maybe I should." She grinned at him before turning to look at the streaks of light that were the fascinating sights of hyperspace. "I'm going to miss this."

"And we'll miss you," Martin said sincerely.

After a day off for shore leave, the last of the crew were gathering to ride back with Martin in his shuttle. As usual, one of his last tasks was to check with spaceport's booking office to see if there were any more people looking for a cheap fare to their next destinations. Two had already been shuttled up on previous loading trips, but it paid to keep checking up until the last moment. He was pleased to hear that there was one looking to go their way.

"She's in the waiting room. I told her that you would be showing up soon," the desk clerk informed him.

"Thanks!" Martin said, heading for the lounge. He opened the door and immediately spotted the sole occupant. "Andrea! What are you doing here?"

"I thought that this was where you got to hitch a ride on commercial starships," she replied with a smile. "Going my way?"

"You know as well as I do where we're headed. What's going on?"

"Well I went back to the hospital where I was working before, and they were quite willing to have me back on staff. But I was not there long before I realised something – I did not *know* most of those people. I'd been working alongside them for years, and yet hardly knew much more than the names of some of them, whereas I had become very familiar with everyone aboard *Phoenix*. I knew then that I could not go back to that life. Or should I say lack of life? So I decided that I would quit and do something more with my life, so here I am."

"I still can't afford you, Andrea."

"Who said you had to? I'm here as a paying passenger. One thing about being a workaholic is that you don't have much time to actually spend your wages. However, I was thinking that perhaps I could work my passage?" she replied with a mischievous grin.

Martin caught on, and returned the smile. "And what services can you offer, Ms Leptailurus?"

"Oh, I was thinking medical services, but I hear that you have children aboard also who might benefit from some biology lessons."

"And in the boring parts in between?" Martin prompted.

"Someone suggested that I take up a hobby. I was thinking

gardening. You do have a hydroponics section, I believe? I brought some flower seeds that I'd like to see if I could grow."

"Excellent! And how far do you intend to go?"

"I'll let you know when I get there."

"Then welcome to the *Phoenix*. I hope you enjoy your journey with us!"

Chapter 11: Encounters

Hesperia City certainly was a shadow of its former self. The gaudy and brazen displays that made it a beacon to tourists in the blackness of space were still absent after many months, the energy needed to power them more urgently needed elsewhere. The number of ships docked at its ports were far fewer also, and *Phoenix* had no difficulty with traffic as it manoeuvred to its designated dock.

Out of both curiosity and business, Martin had kept an eye on the progress of Hesperia since the disaster. While power had been restored for lighting and basic emergency needs at the time they had left, that had only been achieved through the usage of emergency spares that they'd had in storage. However, no one had anticipated the need to replace *everything*, and it took time to acquire and install a whole electrical station's worth of transformers, switching equipment, and other vital machinery. Meanwhile, no businesses could be run, no tourists catered for, and of course no money coming in. The management was rebuilding as fast as they could before they were bled white, and shipping companies were doing good business because of it.

That was why *Phoenix* had returned. They had been at the right place at the right time to pick up another replacement piece of equipment, and with the added incentive of waived docking fees, Martin had not been able to pass it up, although returning stirred up bitter memories.

The crew were unusually subdued as the automatic docking system brought them to a smooth stop and the mooring mechanism engaged. They too were remembering their loss. However, they had a job to do.

Martin hit the comm button. "Valentina – prepare the shuttle bay for transferring the shipment. The repair crew is eagerly awaiting it."

"*Understood, Captain,*" came the reply.

They had some other supplies to offload via the dock, but the priority shipment would be shuttled directly to the power station still perched on the outside of the asteroid, although hopefully better shielded now.

"Commander," he said to Bethany, "I've been assured that Hesperia can cater for the crews of the ships here, so if anyone wants to take a few hours shore leave after we've finished unloading, they may do so. We depart at 2300 ship's time though."

"Aye, Captain," she replied.

"I'll be in my office checking for any more business. I don't think it's likely under the circumstances, but you never know. You have the bridge."

"Aye, Captain," she repeated.

When he got to his office, Martin said, "Madeline – see if you can get a hold of the city administrator for me."

"*Yes, Captain,*" came her voice from mid air.

Martin busied himself on the hypernet until an incoming call beeped on the comm. It lit up with Madeline image. She was 'dressed' in ship uniform as she played Martin's assistant for the comm call.

"I have her on the line now, Captain."

"Thanks, Madeline."

The image shifted to that of a familiar lion morph. "Captain Yote – good to see you again. I hear that you've brought us some more equipment for the repairs."

"That's correct, Ms Keller. How are they coming along?"

"Quite well, thanks. We expect to re-open for business within a few weeks, although not everything will be back online immediately. However, I expect that you didn't call me just to find that out."

"I'm afraid not. After submitting a request for compensation and not hearing anything back for a while, I feel that I deserve some kind of update. Considering how grateful everyone was for us saving them back then, I would have thought we'd deserve some priority on our case."

Keller grimaced. "I may be the City Administrator, but I am still beholden to the higher-ups in the company, and they're the ones dragging their feet. Believe me, I did put in a good word on your behalf. Several good words actually. However that's as much as is within my power. I suggest that your lawyers have a word with them."

"I'm already doing that. Are you sure that you can't do more for me?"

Keller looked uncomfortable. "Captain Yote... my hands are tied."

"I see. Then we don't have anything more to discuss. Have a good day, Administrator."

Martin cut the comm before she could respond.

"*For someone with so much authority, she seemed to me unusually helpless*," Madeline commented.

Martin nodded. "There's something that she's not telling us, although I have the impression that she wishes she could. Ah well, if a personal appeal doesn't work, it's back to legal recourse. I just hate having to pay the lawyers so much without getting any results."

"*May I suggest that you stop stressing over this, and go take a break with the others?*"

Martin grinned. "You don't have to mother me, Maddy."

"*Just being a good executive assistant is all,*" she replied.

Martin nevertheless thought her suggestion was a good one, so when the unloading was complete, he joined the group of people who wanted to take a bit of shore leave.

Much as Martin loved his ship, it was good to be able to get out and see something else besides the same corridors again. Emerging from the personnel lock, he looked around the docking area. While there were a few other ships in port, dock activity was a far cry from the frenzy that had greeted him the first time that he had set foot here, or even the chaos after the loss of power. The artificial gravity was on though because the unloading mechanisms were not designed to work in freefall. However, he had been advised that many sections of Hesperia still had no gravity in order to conserve the available power, and he should watch and listen for the warnings.

"The air smells pretty good," Ceres remarked. Shi and Danson had heard that the botanic gardens were fully operational, and had elected to spend some time there. They particularly wanted to show them to Darkwave. The skunktaur happened to have hit hys female peak just before arrival, and hy was dressed in a flattering bodice, so much less self-conscious than when hy first changed aboard *Phoenix*. Hy was arm in arm with Danson who had been persistent in his attentions, resulting in Darkwave's shift in attitude.

Martin nodded. "The gardens are an essential part of their air freshening system, so that would have been one of the first places that would have restored to normal."

"Well, me an' Risha ain't interested in gardens," Bruce commented. "Seems to us there oughta be a pub or two open with all these workers though."

"I think I might join you," Martin said. "How about you, Commander? I'll buy the first round."

"I suppose," Bethany said a bit uncertainly. "Not much else to do with the majority of the attractions closed."

"What's the bet that at least one casino is open still to relieve these workers of their earnings?" Risha commented.

Anastasiya snorted in amusement. "Is sucker bet. Flashy lights and amusements are for tourists. All casino needs is dice and cards for workers."

"Try not to blow all your money," Martin said dryly.

The big tiger grinned back at him. "Well I can't drink alcohol while breastfeeding, so I must find something to do here." Then shi noticed the glare shi was getting from hir wife. "Of course we have to think about baby's needs too," shi added hastily. "Must get back to Petrushka soon, and not leave her with Shintaro all day."

The group had to go through one large cavern to reach the section open for business. They were able to use the transit system however. They rode up to the station in an elevator not dissimilar to the one that had trapped Heywood and Menalippe. Martin did not consider himself paranoid for carrying a multi-tool that would enable him to escape one of those in the unlikely event of a repeat occurrence.

Ceres, Darkwave and Danson parted ways with them there. Penny, the chakats and the Caitians herded the youngsters off in another direction to go exploring under their watchful eyes, accompanied by the two Faleshkarti. Moments after Martin and his companions boarded, the transit carriage moved off, and the public address came alive.

"Warning – zero gravity section ahead. Prepare for freefall."

Everyone took a secure grip before their stomachs lurched as they left behind the active artificial gravity field. The *Phoenix* crew were acclimated to freefall, and Martin noticed that the other occupants of the carriage did not even pause in whatever they were doing – blasé from familiarity, he presumed.

They had a good view from the transparent transit tube. While power was not being wasted on the artificial gravity in this mostly unused section, it did have a decent amount of illumination. It was a far cry from when they had floated through the near-darkness relieved only by the occasional emergency lamp. It was impressive in its size, but a little sad in its emptiness. Martin could see rows of shops and cafés which were all closed and dark within. He wondered what the proprietors were doing in the interim, and how long it would be before this section came back to life.

They pulled up to a station as the P.A. announced, *"Shopping district three. Freefall conditions still apply."*

Two workers exited from their carriage with a crate, and Martin wondered if they still used the elevators, only to see the answer immediately. A section of the station wall had been opened, and the duo simply manoeuvred themselves and their load through it, pushing themselves off to their destination at a casual pace.

The carriage took off again. As they approached the far side of the cavern, the P.A. announced, *"Gravity resumes in ten seconds. Please brace yourselves."*

They passed through the solid rock wall that separated the shopping district from the next, and abruptly they were pulled firmly back into their seats as they emerged into the casino district. Soon they were pulling into another station.

"Jade Palace Casino and Entertainment district."
They all emerged from the carriage. Rather than having to go down an elevator, the station exited straight into the casino. Anastasiya was proved right when they passed by a number of games in operation.

While the gaudy and power-hungry machines were all turned off, there were still roulette tables, craps and poker games all doing reasonable business under the circumstances.

Anastasiya and Valentina parted company with them there, while the rest of them went in search of somewhere to find a drink and socialise. Inevitably the casino had its own bar and grill that was being well patronised by visiting starship crew members, and since there was unlikely to be much alternative, the group elected to try it out.

A large number of Caitians were there – crew from another freighter. M'Rarrtikar led the charge amongst the *Phoenix's* Caitian members to chat with their own kind, and get some news from their home world. Unfortunately for R'Murran, he had drawn the short straw amongst the senior crew, and he had been left behind on the ship with just Madeline and Shintaro to keep him company. Of course the kitsune's attention was primarily focused on hir cub to whom shi had given birth only a few eeks ago, as well as babysitting for Anastasiya's cub.

Burningbright and Zelkie were surprised and delighted to spot some former colleagues in the crowd, and they were greeted enthusiastically and invited to join them.

That left just Bruce, Risha, Bethany and Martin. They found themselves a free table, and Martin took orders for drinks, keeping his promise to buy the first round. "Only one drink for me though," he said. "One of us has to be sober when we leave tonight."

"Good of you, Captain," Bruce replied. "I've worked meself up quite a thirst."

After a short while, a few people started dropping by the table and introducing themselves. Some joined them for a conversation and they exchanged stories. Risha and Bruce eventually left to see if they could find something more exciting to do together. Martin was happy to see that Bethany seemed to be enjoying the convivial atmosphere.

Martin ordered meals – steaks for both of them. While they could get replicated steaks (when Hotfoot let them), there was a sameness about them that palled. Martin liked to try out how different restaurants prepared their steaks, and he was rarely disappointed. He also indulged in a bottle of fine wine to go with the meal.

They were just finishing dessert when Bethany got up from the table, excusing herself to visit the restroom. Martin continued finishing his deep-dish apple pie, but after only a short time, he noticed someone sit in the vacant chair in his peripheral vision. Knowing that it was too soon for Bethany to have returned, he looked up, and was stunned.

"Hi, handsome. Why haven't I seen you here before?"

A drop-dead gorgeous female coyote morph gazed sultrily back at him. Unlike himself, she had human-type hair to shoulder length, framing a mischievous face. She was lean like a typical coyote, but padded and curved in all the right places. A low-cut dress emphasised decent-sized breasts for her kind, and she oozed sex appeal.

Martin was momentarily lost for words. When he regained his tongue, he replied, "We just got in a few hours ago. I'm Captain Martin Yote of the starship *Phoenix*."

"A starship captain? Even better! Call me Hecate."

"Isn't that a name that they normally give to black cats?"

She grinned. "Perhaps, but it suits me too."

"So what are you doing here, Ms Hecate?" Martin asked, his conversation with the others forgotten.

"Oh please, drop the Ms. I work at the casino – customer relations. It's been a bit quiet for the last few months though." She put a familiar hand over Martin's and gave it a gentle squeeze.

Martin thought that he knew what kind of customer relations she was talking about, but he did not press the point. He tried to pull back his hand gently, but she resisted. "I suppose that you're lucky that the casino is still open to cater for us and the people doing the repairs," he said, trying to keep the conversation innocuous.

"Yes, and I really hit the jackpot today," she replied, leaning in closer and letting Martin get an eyeful of her cleavage, and a noseful of her scent. Whatever she was using exaggerated her femaleness, stimulating him almost as much as if she was on heat, and it was arousing him quite thoroughly.

"You're in my chair," a deadly cold voice behind them said.

Martin looked up to see Bethany glaring at both of them, and he realised that she must have caught him unintentionally drooling over Hecate. He cringed inside, knowing how it must look.

"Bethany... umm... this is Hecate. She's casino customer relations," he said lamely.

"So I can see. Well, I'll let her do her job and leave you two alone." Bethany turned away stiffly.

"Wait, Bethany!" Martin called out, too late realising his mistake.

The vixen ignored him, however, and quickly disappeared from view.

"Ooh, burn!" one of the spacers said with a grin.

Martin sighed. Things had been going so well up until then.

Hecate put her arm around Martin and said, "Don't worry about her. She's a big girl and can take care of herself. Besides, wouldn't you rather spend some time with me? We're not only the same species, but we're a lot closer in age, if I am judging correctly."

By now, Martin's arousal was completely gone. He shrugged off her arm and said seriously, "Her age and species is irrelevant, as is yours. I don't require your companionship, Hecate."

"No? I think you're fooling yourself, handsome. Someone like you needs someone like me."

"Wants? Maybe. Needs? No, I don't think so. I suggest that you find someone else who needs 'customer service'."

Hecate sensed that it was a lost cause for now. She stood up, making even that simple thing a production. "Okay, cutie, but you know who to look for if you need... help."

Martin steadfastly averted his eyes and tried not to breathe her scent. She was very good, and under other circumstances, a delight to be with, but she wasn't what he needed right now.

"You're an idiot for passing her up," the wolf morph opposite commented.

Martin looked at him. "Am I? Maybe I'm after something more than what she has to offer."

"You're too picky. Life doesn't usually throw the ideal woman at you. You've got to take what you can get while it's available."

"Normally I might agree with you, but maybe fate has been kinder to me. I just need to be patient."

The guy shrugged. "Your funeral," he opined.

Martin hoped that he was wrong.

Keera was chafing at having to tag along with her siblings and the chakat cubs, but even though she was seventeen, she was still not allowed to go off by herself. It didn't help that her parents had a good excuse to keep their children close by – the current condition of Hesperia being unsuitable for unsupervised exploration. She considered herself almost an adult, soon to take her Coming-of-Age ceremony. She was now officially apprenticed with Commander Oakwood as her teacher. She was a responsible person, so why did she have to be watched like a cub?

She had almost decided not to go with the others at all, but like everyone else on board, she wanted to get away from the ship for a while, and she was curious as to how the asteroid city looked after all those months. It did not mean that she had to be happy about tagging along with the others, and she moped along with the group, responding sulkily whenever anyone talked to her.

They were herded into a transit carriage going the opposite direction to Captain Yote's group, and they all watched through the windows as they passed through cavern after cavern on a sightseeing tour which was a bit like a rollercoaster ride because of the occasional shifts from gravity to freefall and back again. Keera observed that the shutdown portions of the city far outnumbered the active parts. However, one area that seemed relatively normal was evidently a residential area. Not too surprising considering that many of the inhabitants of Hesperia were permanent residents, and life went on in spite of the problems.

They eventually alighted on the return trip at the entrance to the botanical gardens. Here at least, everything was completely normal. There was plenty of light for the plant life, and the air circulation and watering systems were fully functional. Plenty of gardeners were at work planting, trimming, fertilising, and every other horticultural activity. The trees, shrubs and flowers were all the picture of health, and the air was suffused with a mixture of pleasant scents, bees, butterflies, and even some birds that flitted about from tree to tree. In spite of herself, Keera's mood lightened. It was not like Cait, but it did resemble other worlds she was familiar with, and it was beautiful and peaceful anyway.

It was impossible keeping the children together. They all wanted to explore in different directions. Some wanted to stop and look at something more closely, while others wanted to hasten ahead to something that had caught their eye. A plethora of side paths soon meant that the group was split into many smaller ones – an adult tagging along with one or two cubs each. Abruptly Keera found herself alone. She was surprised at this turn of events, but relieved that apparently no one thought that she needed a minder. She took the opportunity to explore in another direction.

Ten minutes later, she turned the corner of one of the meandering paths and almost ran into someone coming the other way.

"Oops! Sorry! I... um... hello." Her apology trailed off into a surprised greeting when she realised with whom she had nearly collided. A youthful male Caitian grinned back at her – he could not have been more than a year older than her.

"Hello yourself," the male replied. "I didn't know that there was another Caitian ship in port here."

"I'm from *Phoenix*, a mixed ship based on Earth."

"*Phoenix*? I think I know that name from somewhere."

"Our ship saved Hesperia from *The Olympian* crashing into it."

"That's right – I remember now. Wow! I never thought that I'd get to meet someone from that ship. You're famous!"

Keera's ears warmed with a blush. "Well, it's not as if I did anything. I'm just an apprentice," she replied modestly.

"Yeah, but it's not likely that I'll meet anyone else, and you were a part of the rescue."

Keera decided not to tell him that she had not actually been on the ship while that had happened. It would not sound quite so exciting if she told him that she had been trapped on a rollercoaster at the time. To change the subject, she said, "My name is Keera."

He smiled back, his tail twitching excitedly. "I'm R'Kassaran. Still haven't had your Coming-of-Age?"

She shook her head. "No, but I'll be having it in a couple of weeks," she replied earnestly.

"Hey, it's okay. I just had mine eighteen days ago."

"So you're unmated?"

His smile grew wider. "Nope. First chance that I've had to meet girls since the ceremony, and not much opportunity to date before that."

"I thought that you came from a Caitian-run ship? Or at least that seems to me what you implied."

"I am, but there aren't any available females on board. They're either mated or too young. What about you?"

"Only my brother."

"You said you're from a mixed species ship, and I hear that some Caitians take mates from other species – any prospect there?"

"What? No! I mean – I like them, but I'm not interested in them as mates."

"Didn't think so, but I wanted to be sure. Want to join me in exploring these gardens?"

Keera replied a little shyly, "I think I'd like that."

A couple of hours later, Keera was startled by someone yelling at the top of their lungs, "**FOUND HER!**" She turned to see Candycane and Pixiepaws standing there, grinning.

"Goddess! You nearly made me jump out of my fur!"

"Your mum wanted us to find you, so we did," Candycane explained.

"That doesn't mean you had to yell. You have comms, y'know?"

"So do you. Except that it doesn't seem to be responding. Any reason why that might be?" shi asked ingenuously.

Keera had muted it in order to be undisturbed for a while, and had forgotten to turn it back on. She hastened to do so, while the cubs merely grinned knowingly.

"Didn't want to let the grown-ups know that you had wandered off with a boy," Pixiepaws explained with a knowing grin.

"Who are these?" R'Kassaran asked.

"Two of the cubs from my ship – Candycane and Pixiepaws," Keera explained.

"Colourful, aren't they?" Then he noticed some adults approaching. "And those would be your parents and theirs?" He indicated with his eyes.

Keera sighed. "Yeah. I guess this means that we have to go now."

M'Rarrtikar padded up to them and looked over R'Kassaran. "I was going to ask where you've been, youngling, but I think I see the answer."

Keera was so relieved to hear no rebuke in her mother's voice that she didn't object to being called a youngling. "This is R'Kassaran. We met on one of the paths. He and I have been exploring the gardens together."

"Just the gardens?" M'Rarrtikar asked with an arch of an eye.

"Yes, mother, just the gardens," Keera replied with a touch of exasperation.

"Then I hope that you two enjoyed them as much as we did. However, it's time for us to head back to the ship."

"Oh, already? It seems like we've only been here for a short time."

"Yes – time does seem fleeting when you're enjoying yourself."

Keera turned to R'Kassaran and said, "I'll contact you on your ship. I hope to talk with you again soon."

"I'll look forward to that, Keera."

With some regret, Keera left with the group. As they walked, Keera asked her mother, "We're due to go to Cait soon, aren't we?"

"Yes, via one colony first though."

"We're due for a few days shore leave to visit family then?"

"Again yes, although I suspect that it's not family that you're keen to see."

Keera's ears lowered with a touch of embarrassment at being so obvious. "R'Kassaran's ship is headed for Cait also. I said that I'd try to meet up with him there."

M'Rarrtikar nodded. "You will soon have your Coming-of-Age ceremony, and will want to start looking for a potential husband. R'Kassaran looks like a fine young mel – is he mated as yet?"

"No."

"Better yet. To be a Firstwife will give you much more status."

"I'm not so worried about status as finding a boyfriend at all!"

"I understand, daughter. We asked for a few days shore leave not merely to visit family, but to also give you your first chance to look for potential mates. It's fortuitous that you may have already found one.

However, since he is your first, please remember the First Virtue – Intelligence. Choose with your head, and not just with your heart."

"He comes from a trader ship much like ours, so we have much in common."

"That is good to hear. Tell me more about this young man."

Keera happily espoused R'Kassaran's virtues as they walked to the transit tube. She did not even mind her siblings giggling and making comments. Her mood was too good to be spoiled so easily.

Martin's mood had improved considerably after he had lost interest in the bar and headed back to his ship. Upon his arrival, Madeline had informed him that he had gotten a call from Hesperia's procurement office, and could he contact them when he returned? He had done so, and had come away with a contract to pick up another load of equipment that was ready to be shipped from Cait. The loads had been a bit light of late, so this was very good news. The only bad point was that he was going to have to shorten their stay at Cait. M'Rarrtikar was going to give him hell over that, but he would have to make it up to the Caitians another time. Besides, as *Phoenix's* accountant, she should be mollified a bit by the extra income.

He was braced for M'Rarrtikar's reaction, but he was not expecting the drama that would come from her daughter. There were some drawbacks to running a family ship rather than a pure business, he reflected. He was pondering what to do still as he took his place in the Captain's Chair on the bridge in preparation for departure.

"Priority call coming in for you, Captain," Madeline announced.

"Put it on screen, please," Martin ordered without bothering to ask from whom the call was coming. A moment later, he wished he had not skipped that step.

"Hi, handsome," Hecate said, batting her eyes at him. She had changed into an even more breathtaking top than before. She leaned into the video pick-up. "I was afraid that I would miss you before you left. I want you to know I'll miss you, and I hope you'll come back and see me again soon."

Martin could swear that he felt the temperature drop several degrees to his left where Bethany stood. He massaged his forehead with his left hand, trying to forestall a headache. "Hecate, I told you that I'm not interested in seeing you again."

"Oh, come on, Captain," she cooed, "you know that we're good together."

"In your dreams!"

"Why, of course, and yours too, I bet. I'll be waiting!"

The woman was a nutcase! He hit the button to disconnect the call, and the screen switched to a status display. He spent the next few days wishing that he could thaw out his First Officer's frosty attitude as easily.

M'Rarrtikar and R'Murran invited everyone to their daughter's Coming-of-Age ceremony. Although it was generally held with just family members, they felt that the crewmates were as good as family to them all anyway. They gathered in the recreation room which was the only place besides the holosuite that was large enough and suitable for the ceremony. Ceres had volunteered to man the bridge for the short time that the ceremony would take, and with Madeline monitoring the ship's systems, everyone else was able to attend. Keera was dressed in a new green day-robe for the event – a gift from her parents. She stood within a large circle formed by her family and friends, along with her parents.

R'Murran held up his hands to call for attention. "Quiet please!" When conversation had stopped, he continued. "Keera, daughter of M'Rarrtikar, step forth."

Keera stepped up to within two paces of her parents. "I am Keera, M'Rarrtikar's daughter," she stated.

"Why are you here today, daughter?" R'Murran asked formally.

"I have trod the path of childhood for eighteen years, father, and it has come to an end. I now demand the right to travel the path of adulthood."

"The path of adulthood is not an easy one to walk, my child. Are you prepared for the journey?"

"I am. I face the path with confidence and anticipation of its challenges."

"Then take the final step from childhood to the responsibilities of adulthood. Cross the stream of life and begin your journey."

M'Rarrtikar was holding a pitcher of water. She poured some of it carefully on the floor in front of Keera, a symbolic stream of life. Keera stepped forward through it and stopped in front of her father, who placed his hands on her shoulders.

"Farewell child. I welcome M'Keera, daughter of Cait and the Goddess. So everyone witness!"

That was the cue for the people witnessing the ceremony who cheered their approval.

M'Keera turned around, smiling, acknowledging their acceptance of her into adulthood.

When the cheers died down, Hotfoot said, "If that's the end of the ceremony, I have an old-fashioned Terran birthday cake made for the occasion. It's Black Forest cake."

R'Murran stepped up quickly. "All ceremonies must end with Black Forest cake!" he declared with a grin. "It's an ancient Caitian tradition, don't you know?"

There were lots of laughs, but R'Murran got his slice only second to M'Keera. There was no getting between the mel and his favourite dessert.

"He's here!" M'Keera announced excitedly.

No one had any doubt that he would not turn up. R'Kassaran and M'Keera had exchanged messages whenever they were not under warp. Martin was glad to have the benefit of the Foster network, considering the charges that they would have run up otherwise. And that was only for the trip from Hesperia to Cait via Huxton Mining Station!

R'Kassaran's ship had arrived long before *Phoenix*, and the pair had arranged for him to meet her as soon as she came down in the shuttle. Wisely, no one got between M'Keera and the hatch as it opened. She rushed out to greet him, and he enfolded her in a hug before leading her away. She never even thought to wave goodbye to her family.

Martin said to M'Rarrtikar, "I'm glad that she's *your* daughter. I'm not so sure I'd let mine go with someone whom she's known for so little time."

"Yes, but is it really so different from Terran dating customs? A male and a female need to get to know each other."

"Of course, but we don't usually let them stay overnight with their boyfriend on the first date."

"She will be staying with his family, not just him. It's rushing things a bit, but still acceptable."

Martin shrugged. This had been the best compromise that they had been able to work out. M'Keera would get to spend her entire stay on Cait with R'Kassaran's family. It had been surprisingly easy to arrange it with his parents until M'Rarrtikar pointed out that they too were interested in their son's prospects for a Firstwife.

That stay would only be until tomorrow though when *Phoenix* departed for her return trip to Hesperia. The rest of the Caitians were off to visit family as originally planned. Aside from them though, no others from the crew were getting shore leave. There was too much to do, with some of them filling the Caitians' places for a day, so they had to settle for a brief visit to the spaceport's facilities, or nothing at all.

The next day, Martin was ready at the appointed time with his shuttle.. Most of the Caitian crew were there, but they were still waiting for M'Keera. They were beginning to worry that they were going to miss their assigned departure window, when a small ground vehicle raced out to the landing pad. M'Keera and R'Kassaran climbed out, and they embraced and kissed before she very reluctantly parted.

"M'Keera – move it!" shouted R'Murran from the hatch.

The young lady snapped out of her daydream and hastened into the shuttle. R'Murran secured the hatch and let Martin know that everything was ready.

"Prepare for take-off," Martin announced over the P.A.

R'Murran dived into his seat and fastened the safety harness. Moments later, the hum of the contra-grav units rose to a peak, and the thrusters lifted them into the air. From there it was a regulation flight to meet *Phoenix* in orbit. It was not a quiet one though.

"What was the idea of arriving so late?" M'Rarrtikar started scolding her daughter. "You of all our children should know the importance of keeping to a schedule. You're an adult now, and you're expected to be more responsible."

"I'm sorry, *Satri*. (*Mother, formal address) R'Kassaran and I were trying to make some future arrangements, but his captain and first officer were away, and we had to clear things with them first.

"I don't think that there are any arrangements that can excuse holding up our ship."

"*Nearly* holding it up," M'Keera corrected. "I was on time."

"Don't get smart with me. You used up every minute of leeway that we had to make it on time. That is unacceptable for my daughter, and even worse for a junior member of the crew. What kind of example do you think you are setting for your sibs, or the other children?"

"Look, Mother, I'm really sorry, but it really couldn't be helped. Can we talk about this later when we're back on the ship?"

"Why not now?"

"Because I need to discuss this with the captain also."

That surprised M'Rarrtikar. "Alright, we will talk once we're under way to Hesperia." That decision made, she shifted topic. "So how was your stay with R'Kassaran's family?"

M'Keera's expression shifted to fond reminiscence. "It was wonderful. They were very welcoming, and I had a wonderful time."

"I'm very happy to hear that. I regret that we could not stay longer. I realise that our lifestyle makes it hard for you now that you've grown up."

"Yes, but at least I got lucky and found R'Kassaran."

"*Tara* (*Daughter, formal address), it's good that you and he get along so well, but he is your first boyfriend. Don't read too much into this yet."

"Are you saying that I can't find a potential husband first try?"

"No. In fact by necessity, many females often do, but that doesn't mean that you should. He has had as little experience as you, so he might just be infatuated. Have you considered whether it's in *his* best interests? Or you might simply have had insufficient time together to realise the ways that you are *not* compatible."

"We *have* thought about those things, "M'Keera insisted. "But that's part of what we have to discuss later."

"It seems that our conversation keeps coming around to that. Very well, I can be patient. So, what *can* you tell us now?"

M'Keera was happy to expound on how R'Kassaran had proudly given her a tour around his ship, shown her what he did, and introduced her to the entire crew who were in effect one big family. Then they spent what time was available on shore leave activities of the kind that young adults enjoyed the most. They'd had very little sleep, which was hardly surprising – none of the others had much either due to trying to cram as much as they could into the little time they had available.

While it was hardly a quick trip to go into orbit and rendezvous with *Phoenix*, M'Keera and her family still did not have enough time to recount everything that they had done. However, M'Rarrtikar was impressed with how well things were working out for her daughter. There only remained the postponed discussion, and that had to wait until *Phoenix* left orbit and was under warp back to Hesperia. With everything down to mere monitoring, the Caitians were at last able to gather in Martin's office.

"So, M'Keera, what is it that you wanted to discuss?" Martin asked.

"As you can probably guess, it involves R'Kassaran and me finding more opportunity to be together. As my mother pointed out, it's too soon for us to be sure that we are right for each other. However, I think we will be, but we need to arrange ways to learn more about each other, and under circumstances that we are likely to experience for years. In other words – daily ship life rather than shore leave occasions. We discussed this with his family, and now I'm doing the same with you. We propose that R'Kassaran join *Phoenix* as a junior crew member for a while so that we will have the time and opportunity to be together and get to know each other better." M'Keera paused there, waiting for some reaction from the others.

Martin looked to M'Rarrtikar and asked, "What are your thoughts on this?"

M'Rarrtikar replied, "Mixed. I'm a bit surprised that R'Kassaran's family is so willing to let him come over to our ship. On the other hand,

M'Keera is right in that this would give them time and opportunity to interact more and find out if they are really suited to each other. It would seem like a good idea."

"Persuading R'Kassaran's family wasn't that easy," M'Keera admitted. "It's what delayed us more than we had intended, but in the end they did agree."

M'Rarrtikar looked back to Martin. "I suppose it comes down to whether you are willing to take him on."

Martin leaned back in his chair and pondered for a moment, then said, "I agree that it sounds like a good idea, and to be fair to M'Keera, she definitely needs more social opportunities. However, taking on even a junior member of the crew will put more strain on our finances. It's not something I'd do lightly." Martin noticed M'Keera's distressed expression, and before she could argue, he continued. "On the other hand, it's not as if I hadn't anticipated this possibility, although I had hoped that it would be later than this. What are R'Kassaran's skills?"

M'Keera could sense the real possibility of persuading the captain. "He's training in structural engineering, both theoretical and applied. He'd fit in between Father's and Mama M'Anissa'tk's disciplines."

"That could come in handy," Martin admitted. "Okay, I'm willing to give it a shot – as long as your parents approve."

R'Murran nodded to M'Rarrtikar who turned to Martin and said, "We approve a trial of this idea."

Martin nodded. "Okay, it's decided. So when and where shall we be acquiring our new member?"

M'Keera replied, "Are we still scheduled to be going to New Hong Kong?"

Martin nodded. "Second stop after Hesperia."

"R'Kassaran's ship is going there after their next port of call. We only need to let them know, and they will leave him there for us to pick him up a few days later."

"You seem to have this all worked out," Martin remarked with a grin.

"We put a lot of thought into the possibilities, including me going to his ship instead."

"Then it's settled. Next time that we drop out of warp, you can send a message to his ship and let them know when to expect us to arrive at New Hong Kong." Martin tapped a few keys on his desk PADD and confirmed *Phoenix's* E.T.A. there.

The Caitians started leaving his office, but not before M'Keera gave M'Rarrtikar a hug. "Thank you, *Satri*. This means a lot to me."

"I still remember what it was like when I met your father, dear, so I do hope that this works out well for you," she replied fondly.

Martin would never have anticipated their reception at Hesperia. While they were happy enough to accept the priority shipment from Cait, they seemed to be very evasive when he tried to sound out the possibility of more work. After a series of frustrations, he resorted to calling the general manager, knowing full well that she did not normally deal with such things directly, but hoping to play on her sense of indebtedness. He was shocked at the response.

"I'm truly sorry, Captain Yote, but we do not, and will not have any work for you in the future." Someone of her seniority would normally impart such news with equanimity, but she looked distinctly unhappy telling Martin this.

"What do you mean by not having anything in the future?" Martin asked suspiciously.

"I mean that my hands are tied by orders from above."

"What! Why? You can't do that! It's restriction of fair trade."

"Nevertheless, you will not win any more contracts here. I regret that I cannot help you."

Martin would have been inclined to argue more, but he could not only recognise the futility of doing so, but he also sensed that she was truly upset at the decision. And if she could not defy the orders, then no one here could. "Very well, Ms Keller, I won't bother you any more. Adieu."

Martin disconnected the call and slumped back in his chair.

Bethany was seated on the other side of the desk, and had been listening in. "Do you want me to take a wild guess as to why we have been black banned?"

"If it involves a certain mouse whose surname begins with W, then I'm with you."

"I wonder how though? It does not seem to be his usual line of business."

"I suppose we'll find out sooner or later. Meanwhile we've lost a lucrative destination. Hesperia will be back in business soon, but we're not going to get any benefit...."

Martin was interrupted by the comm beeping.

"Pardon me, Captain," came Loander's voice from the bridge. "There's a lady on the comm who insists on talking to you. She won't say her name – just that you'll know her."

"Hmm... maybe it's a customer after all. Okay, put her through, please."

Martin's desk comm lit up with a familiar face. "Hi, handsome.

Heard that you'd returned, and I wanted to see if you'd join me for dinner."

"Hecate! How did you know that I was in port?" Martin noticed Bethany stiffen, then get up from her seat. "Wait, Commander..."

"I'll leave you two in private, Captain," Bethany said tersely, then marched out of Martin's office.

"Don't leave..." Martin started trying to say.

"You haven't answered my question, Captain," Hecate interrupted.

Martin frowned at her. "I thought that I had made it clear that I am not interested, Hecate. And you didn't answer *my* question."

"I hear a lot in my line of work, and people owe me favours, so I knew pretty quickly that you had returned. I knew you couldn't stay away, and you would want to see me," she said coyly.

"I'm *not* here to see you. Can't you get that through your head?"

"Your words say no, but I bet something else is saying yes," she said smugly.

"Argh! Good! Bye!" Martin cut the connection, annoyed that he seemed to have picked up a stalker, but infuriated that she was at least partially right. She oozed such sex appeal that his body betrayed him.

"Madeline!"

"Yes, Captain?" came her voice from mid air.

"Filter all communications from that woman. I don't want to see or hear from Hecate ever again."

"Aye, Captain!" the bunny replied, wishing that she had been on comm duty when that call had come in, so that she could have warned Martin.

Soon after, *Phoenix* departed without taking on any cargo. Martin decided that there would be no shore leave there this time, but instead would add a day onto their next scheduled stopover. There were too many bad memories associated with Hesperia to want to stick around any longer.

To say M'Keera was excited was somewhat of an understatement. No sooner had they gotten into orbit around New Hong Kong than she was on the comm, contacting R'Kassaran. As arranged, he was waiting at the spaceport after enjoying a few days shore leave by himself. Martin allowed M'Keera to come down in the first shuttle so that she could spend some time with him on the planet, but he warned her to return promptly as this was only a brief stop to load and unload.

The pair did return well before the last scheduled lift up to their ship. They looked very happy together, and Martin was pleased for her.

A life aboard a ship was never going to be easy on the youth of *Phoenix*, so if this worked out for her, it was one hurdle successfully passed.

Hotfoot made a special meal to welcome R'Kassaran aboard. He got a chance to meet almost everyone then, and it was clear that he was a little nervous.

"I've lived my entire life aboard *Añarra'tssik Kaasrr*, and that ship is crewed entirely by Caitians," explained R'Kassaran in strongly accented Terranglo. "While I've met most of the sentient species over the years, I've never lived and worked with them before, so I hope you'll be understanding if I make any mistakes because of that."

Martin replied, "Don't worry too much, R'Kassaran. We've all lived together for a few years now, so I think we'll know what's happening if you put a foot wrong. As long as you put in the effort, we'll all get along fine."

As it turned out, they had more problems with M'Keera than with him. She kept getting distracted from her training whenever R'Kassaran was off-shift when she was supposed to be on-shift. R'Murran had to reschedule all of his training sessions with R'Kassaran so that they coincided with M'Keera's, and M'Rarrtikar gave her daughter a stern lecture about appropriate times for socialising.

Once the settling-in period was over, R'Kassaran found himself enjoying the change from his home ship. He had not anticipated the difference that interacting with several other species would make, but he was young enough to adapt readily. It would be several months before *Phoenix* and *Añarra'tssik Kaasrr* crossed paths again, so it was a relief to everyone that this was working out. In fact the time flew by too quickly for both him and M'Keera.

Phoenix arrived at Cait on the eve of the Spring Goddess Festival, bringing a load of exotic foodstuffs to be consumed during the celebrations. *Añarra'tssik Kaasrr* arrived barely an hour after *Phoenix*, and the two crews arranged to meet at a local restaurant that evening. In fact they booked out the entire premises in order to cope with the entire number. *Añarra'tssik Kaasrr's* crew was considerably larger than the *Phoenix's*, but they had been in the shipping business for a few generations.

Although Martin had communicated regularly with M'Kennisin'tr, the captain of *Añarra'tssik Kaasrr*, it had been little more than keeping her updated about the status of her cousin, R'Kassaran. This was the first real opportunity for the two crews to socialise.

The *Phoenix* Caitians relished the opportunity to talk with a Caitian starship crew, although some of those were unenthusiastic about the intermingling with non-Caitians. The majority were more than happy to learn more about the people with whom one of their own had spent so much time. R'Kassaran of course was kept quite busy telling everyone about his experiences, while M'Keera was occupied by the curiosity of his family and friends.

Only the serving of the food slowed down conversation. Despite the best efforts of the cooks from both ships, the crews did look forward to eating something different that had not been prepared in their galleys. This particular restaurant had a reputation for serving exotic fare, so it was a good change of pace for both Caitians and Terrans alike.

As the meal drew to a close, as expected, R'Kassaran and M'Keera stood up and asked for everyone's attention. When everybody had quieted, R'Kassaran spoke for the both of them.

"My time aboard *Phoenix* was both instructive and pleasant. I have very much enjoyed spending time with such a varied crew, and they have made me feel very welcome." He cast a look at some of the females from *Añarra'tssik Kaasrr*. "I've also enjoyed being away from my sisters for a change," he added with a grin.

"Hey!" one of them said. "You're going to pay for that crack!"

R'Kassaran just grinned wider. "However, that's not what you've been waiting to hear." He turned to M'Keera and took her hand. "M'Keera and I have agreed that we would be suitable mates, and I am now formally asking her to be my Firstwife."

M'Keera gazed adoringly back at him. "I accept your proposal."

There were cheers all around, some more enthusiastic than others. M'Rarrtikar in particular felt that they should have taken more time to get engaged, but she had nothing against R'Kassaran.

When the congratulations had died down, M'Keera said, "We intend to have the traditional pre-mating night together to confirm our compatibility on board *Añarra'tssik Kaasrr* this evening. If all goes well as we feel it will, we will want to have the mating ceremony immediately while both our families are together here on Cait." She sat down, smiling happily.

"I suppose we had better check the local temples to see if a Mentarkan priestess is available to perform the ceremony," M'Kennisin'tr said to M'Rarrtikar.

"With the festival tomorrow, that might be difficult," M'Rarrtikar replied.

"I agree, but we are not scheduled to leave until the evening of the day after, so we have time to spare if we are not successful."

"Good. Are you Orthodox or Progressive sect?"

"We're Progressives, but we'll accept either."

"That works for us also."

"Very well, it's settled. I will start making arrangements for your daughter to join our crew. She will be your first, won't she?"

M'Rarrtikar nodded. "It had to happen sooner or later, but I admit that it's a little earlier than I thought. However, I can't deny that it was good fortune for her to meet your cousin. I believe that she has chosen well."

"I will make sure that she fits in well with us, and is happy. Perhaps in time, one of ours will seek your son for a mate."

M'Rarrtikar rolled her eyes. "If we can ever get him to focus on his studies and make himself a worthwhile catch."

M'Kennisin'tr grinned. "You're supposed to talk up his prospects, you know?"

"Hmmph! Speak to me again in a year, and I might be more enthusiastic."

The two continued to chat about the merits of their children or grandchildren, and M'Kennisin'tr passed on some of the wisdom gained on a multi-generation starship.

Unlike humans, morphs, or other alien species, Caitians are not sexually receptive all the time. While they may have some physical attraction to a male, the actual desire for sex rarely came outside of oestrus for the females, and the males usually had to be stimulated by the pheromones of the female on heat. Otherwise neither was sexually oriented in physical manner. However, it is possible for a couple to stimulate each other to bring about a sexual response, and that was the basis of the pre-mating night test. It was believed that if a couple could successfully bring themselves to sexual orgasm outside of her oestrus, then they were indeed compatible, and the ceremony of union could go ahead.

This tradition dated back thousands of years to when the Caitian people consisted of nomadic tribes that followed the herds of prey species. Occasionally tribes would meet and the opportunity for the youth of each to find mates would happen. However, two tribes could not stay together too long, hunting the same resources, so the youths had to decide very quickly if they were a good match. The final test was the pre-mating night, and if they were successful, the priestess who witnessed the event would marry them the next day, and then the tribes would go their separate ways.

That practice continued even after their species started building a civilisation with permanent villages and farms, then industries and cities. Nowadays though, females tended to leave their home town to seek a mate in another. It was always the females who hunted a male because they so outnumbered them, and competition for one grew more intense.

The concept of status grew with that competition. A Firstwife always had the greatest status as it was shown that she had the ability, appeal, and talent to be the male's first choice. For the male, the more females that he could attract, the greater his status became, and with it, his family's.

M'Keera and R'Kassaran were determined that their pre-mating night would be a success. Although pre-marital sex was originally banned in the old days, today the Orthodox sect turned a blind eye to it, and the Progressive sect outright condoned it because it gave the couples a better chance to get to know each other before the pre-mating night. On the last two occasions that M'Keera had been on heat, she and R'Kassaran had made love, although with the appropriate contraceptives of course. Both sects still frowned upon pregnancy before marriage. Consequently they had a much better idea of what each other liked, and they were able to use that knowledge to bring success to their efforts while she was not on heat. Unlike the old days, a priestess did not have to be there to bear witness. Instead, it was usually the male's mother who filled that role for a potential Firstwife, although others might. In their case, M'Kennisin'tr took that role and witnessed their success. Later on in life, if R'Kassaran took on more wives, it would be M'Keera's task to fill that role to ensure that a potential co-wife was worthy.

The young couple were pleased to succeed quite easily. In fact they had a far harder time trying to find a priestess available to formally unite them because the Spring Goddess Festival was a popular time for such ceremonies. However, they were eventually able to find one who could do it early that evening. Both crews attended that ceremony, and the parents of each extolled the virtues of their children, witnessed by the priestess. She gave the couple a speech on the duties and responsibilities of each in their marriage, then the two exchanged vows. The priestess then pronounced M'Keera to be Firstwife to R'Kassaran, and formally assigning her the Virtue of Intelligence as all Firstwives were due.

After the ceremony, all the *Phoenix* crew were invited back to *Añarra'tssik Kaasrr* where a big celebration was held. Everything went perfectly, a good omen for their future. It was not until the next day that M'Keera dropped the bomb.

I don't want to want to move to *Añarra'tssik Kaasrr*. I want to stay on *Phoenix*," she told her parents.

"What?" M'Rarrtikar exclaimed. "Don't be ridiculous. The wife *always* joins the husband's family, or his ship in this case."

"Why? Don't I have any say in this? Don't *we* have any say in it? R'Kassaran is quite happy to join me here, otherwise I would not have asked."

M'Rarrtikar frowned at her contrary daughter. "You are not only going up against centuries of tradition, but you're also trying to set up an impractical precedent. Males can't change homes every time they get a new mate, so it's the females who must join him. That's the way it is. That's the way it always will be."

"But I'm his first mate – he doesn't have any other wives to drag along, so that means he's free to make a choice. I've told him why I want to stay here, and he agrees with me. He also has motivation to leave *Añarra'tssik Kaasrr*. We're both adults capable of making our own decisions, and we've decided to do it this way." M'Keera folded her arms and glared at her mother defiantly.

"You would be taking a male away from *Añarra'tssik Kaasrr* – you know that you cannot do that lightly. Every family – every ship – needs its males."

"They have enough even so. Besides, there's nothing stopping them from doing what we want to do – have first-time mated males move to their ship. They could do with some males from outside the family. We, on the other hand, have no males available – only my brother and father. We *need* males more than their ship."

"What? As competition for Kannekin when he grows up?"

"No, to start building a Caitian community. We can't do it alone."

"And what of others affected by your decision? Captain M'Kennisin'tr has made arrangements to fit you into her ship...."

"*Squeeze* me in to her ship, you mean! It's a multi-generational family ship, and there are really too many of them aboard for comfort already. They need *fewer* people, not *more*. One of the first things that R'Kassaran mentioned to me after he came to stay with us was how much more room everyone had here. It's one of the reasons that he wants to stay here. Then there's the fact that there's only so many jobs to go around. On *Phoenix*, he has the potential to be so much more than he's ever likely to be back on *Añarra'tssik Kaasrr*. Surely you can see that as his Firstwife, I'm looking after *his* interests as much as mine."

That point hit home to M'Rarrtikar, but she was nowhere near ready to concede as yet. "But you would be going up against centuries of family tradition that has stood the test of time and served us well. The family is what has made our kind strong. Cait would not be the world it is today if we had ignored such things at our whim."

"Whim?" M'Keera responded angrily. "Why is a carefully reasoned course of action that benefits all of us considered a whim? On *Phoenix*, I'm an apprentice with a future as bridge crew. On *Añarra'tssik Kaasrr*,

Art © Jameless

I'd be one of many competing for the rare opening. What has tradition got to do with that?"

"If you have the talent, you will get that bridge position on R'Kassaran's ship. By staying on *Phoenix*, you ignore our culture and heritage..."

M'Keera interrupted her mother. "Culture and heritage? Mother - I've spent my entire life on starships! Cait is an exotic holiday destination for me. I'm not a Caitian - I'm a child of the stars! What is the relevance of any culture that does not directly affect me? I know Terranglo better than Ratarsk. A ship's cabin is more home to me than a Caitian house. My family consists of many species. I will *not* leave them behind to pander to your outdated concepts of tradition. I *will* live my life as I see fit, and I will do it with or without your blessing."

For once, M'Rarrtikar was lost for words. In desperation, she turned to R'Murran who had made no comment so far. "Husband, tell her why she is wrong."

For a long moment, R'Murran continued his silence, then he closed his eyes and shook his head. "Wife, I cannot back you on this. Our daughter argues well, and I will support her in this." Of course, he did not have the ultimate say in the family – that was the Firstwife's prerogative, but as the guiding and uniting voice for all his wives, his opinion carried much weight. He knew that he was going to cop hell from her later though, but he could do no less. M'Rarrtikar glared balefully at R'Murran. Without even looking, he could feel her eyes boring into him, but he remained steadfast.

Eventually she turned back to M'Keera. She had one more card to play. "What about Captain Yote? Have you considered how this will affect his business – our livelihood? He was prepared to take on R'Kassaran for a few months, but you're asking him to commit to having him on board indefinitely, not to mention any children you may choose to have. You know quite well that our finances are tight, and this is asking no small thing of him."

"I know, mother, and I always knew that that would be the one *real* problem. R'Kassaran and I have agreed that we don't want any children for a few years, so that is not a major factor. I approached the Captain this morning about the possibility of staying on. He told me that he could cope, but he said that he would prefer it if I got your approval."

For a moment, M'Rarrtikar could see herself winning the argument on that technicality, but M'Keera continued. "He also said that I was an adult capable of making my own choices, and he would not force us off the ship if we decided to stay in spite of what you say."

M'Rarrtikar fumed. "So you're saying that the decision is made, and all you want me to do is rubber stamp the approval?"

M'Keera stepped up to M'Rarrtikar, took her hands, and looked deeply into her eyes. "No, *Satri*, I want you to see that this is the right course for us, and to be happy for us. How could I continue to live on *Phoenix* knowing that every day that you would be bitter about this? You are my mother. You are family. I want your approval. I *need* it to be totally happy. But I will not change my mind about this."

For a long while, M'Keera did not know if her final appeal would work. Then tears welled in M'Rarrtikar's eyes and she leaned in to hug her daughter.

"When did you get so strong, *Tara*? You are right – it *is* your life to lead. You have my blessing."

"Thank you. Thank you from both of us, mother," M'Keera replied, hugging her back.

For a while, the two just stood there, embracing each other. Eventually though, M'Rarrtikar pulled back and asked, "What is R'Kassaran doing?"

"He's waiting to hear from me. As soon as I confirm that we have come to an agreement, he's going to see Captain M'Kennisin'tr and let her know that he intends to leave and join *Phoenix*."

"She will be very reluctant to let him go, of course."

M'Keera nodded in agreement. "However, she will have no choice really. As an adult, he can't be forced to stay on their ship. He has the right to do what he wants with his life, so she can either be graceful about it or nasty, but it won't change anything. She would be best off wishing him well and keeping close ties with us, and we think that's what she'll think too."

"You're thinking about Kannekin, aren't you?"

"Yes. It's like the ancient tribes of our past – we would occasionally meet and exchange members. Captain M'Kenissin'tr will want to keep her options open."

"Wise thinking. Anyway, I had better get back to work. I will need to refigure our finances with both of you to take into account now. People may come and go, but the bills just keep coming."

M'Kennisin'tr gave her blessing as predicted. R'Kassaran was formally added to the crew roster by Martin, and Hotfoot laid on one of her famous feasts to celebrate the occasion. *Phoenix* departed Cait with full holds and full hearts.

Madeline dumped yet another message from Hecate to Martin into a special trash archive, then turned to the mouse seated next to her in the holosuite environment. "I just trashed message number twenty three."

"Told you she wouldn't give up," Penny said smugly.

"No one can go without getting any response whatsoever indefinitely," the rabbit replied.

"Oh? Stalkers don't give up that easily. I bet you fifty creds that he gets at least fifty messages."

"You're on!"

"Who's on?" came a voice from behind them. Martin approached the pair down the track through the holographic environment.

"Oh, just a private bet I have with Penny." Madeline naturally had been aware of his approach since he had entered the holosuite. She patted the mouldering log that they were sitting on, indicating that he should sit down next to her on the opposite side to Penny. Since their trip to Sylvania, the bunny had enjoyed the company of both of them in the one environment where she could touch and be touched.

Martin took the proffered spot and gave Madeline a hug.

Madeline gave him a kiss on the cheek in return. "Still couldn't persuade the commander to take a walk with you?"

Martin sighed. "No. She just doesn't seem to want to let go of that Hecate bitch's unwanted attention."

Penny said, "Don't worry too much, Captain. It might take time, but eventually she will put it aside. Meanwhile, keep doing what you're doing."

"I agree," Madeline added. "You're too good a man to be ignored for long. I know that you make me feel happy when you're with me."

"Thanks, Maddy. I like being with you too."

The three of them sat in companionable silence to watch the scenery from the mountain lookout. Martin reflected that not everyone's relationships came together as quickly and easily as M'Keera and R'Kassaran's had. The girls were right – he just had to be patient and persistent. The goal might be distant, but it was worth it.

Chapter 12: Faleshkarti Catch-22

Two and a half years passed after the marriage of M'Keera and R'Kassaran with the Caitian mel fitting in with the *Phoenix* family as if he had always belonged. Two and a half years of kitsune and tiger cubs growing up together like siblings. Shintaro had never sought another companion since hir beloved's death, but shi had drifted into a de facto relationship with Anastasiya. It filled the gap in hir heart that the loss of hir lifemate had opened, and Anastasiya acted as a surrogate father to Kiku-chan. Valentina never begrudged the relationship between the two – shi had recognised kindred spirits from the first time they had met.

The fortunes of *Phoenix* had steadily improved, and their lives had settled down to a comfortable normality that had been frequently missing during their first two years. In retrospect, they were overdue for some drama.

Over the years, Martin had chatted with all the crew members many times as they relaxed in the recreation room. Sitting around on one of the comfy chairs, mats, or sofas, watching the streaking trails of hyperspace with a mug of one's favourite brew in hand was conducive to conversation, and that was true as much for the alien Faleshkarti as it was for the Terran species. Therefore the coyote had learned much of the fennec-like race in the four years they had been part of the crew. Nevertheless it still came as a surprise to him one day when he accidentally bumped into Loander as he was leaving his office, and he realised that something had drastically changed.

"When did you get so tall?" Martin asked.

Not counting their exceptionally long ears, the *Phoenix's* Faleshkarti crew members were only about 120 centimetres tall (about 4 feet), except now, Loander was not. Shi had put on about fifteen centimetres in a remarkably short time.

"It's the growth spurt that precedes the Change," Loander explained.

"Oh. That would explain why you've been so ravenous at meal times lately."

"Exactly. And that's what I was coming to talk to you about. Do you have a moment to spare, Captain?"

"More than a moment, actually. Come on in."

They made themselves comfortable, and Martin said, "So, you've kept me informed on the state of research into your species. Has that drug the Federation produced proven effective in stopping your loss of intelligence?"

Loander nodded. "Since they started the program, the drug has proven to be 100% effective and reliable. No Hona has lost hir intelligence since reaching sexual maturity, and their sex drive has been brought under control. I'm told that they desire sex only twice a day now, instead of six to eight times. Of course the most important benefit is that we can exercise contraception for the first time in our history, and start reining in the runaway population growth."

"*Only* twice a day," Martin repeated with a grin. "How will you cope?"

Loander smiled. "I'm sure Presaith and I will be able to bear that burden."

Martin laughed, then said, "Has Presaith shown signs of the Change yet?"

"Yes, it has just started for hir, so you won't notice anything obvious yet, but hir appetite will soon match mine, and hir growth will be rapid also."

"I suppose you have to arrange to get a shipment of that drug sent to you when we arrive at Earth?"

"Actually, we want to return to Namath," Loander said a little reluctantly.

Martin was shocked. "But I thought you wanted to stay on *Phoenix*?"

"We do, but it's something that we learned here that makes us want to return to our home world."

"That sounds… contradictory," Martin said in puzzlement.

"We've told you about how we are raised in nurseries from birth, and nobody ever knows their parents. The concept of family was literally alien to us. When we joined *Phoenix*, it was with the intention of learning about the Federation and its cultures. One thing that we found was universal amongst the sentients is family. Parents raise their children. Mates support each other. Children grow up and support the family, and become parents in turn. On Namath, we have a saying – "Only the Hona can know love", but this is not true for any other intelligent species we've encountered. And amazingly, it doesn't even have to be within the species. *Phoenix* has many species, but we are all family. *That* is the most amazing thing that Presaith and I have learned while we have been with you. The sense of belonging, the real *love* we have for one another, is what drives us. Presaith and I have agreed to be mates when we have made the Change, and we intend to have our own children to raise within a family, and that is why we must return to Namath."

"I understand your motivations, but not why you have to go to Namath to achieve it."

"Because like you, we want our children to have the best future that they can, and that means not having to go through what we will have to put up with. The drug that is our salvation, is only a stop-gap. We will need to use it for the rest of our lives, or else we will revert and become dull-witted Zora. The only permanent solution is a change to our genes. The Federation has begun a gene-surgery program that will alter our reproductive system so that our children will be permanently free from this curse. However, it has to be done before the Change happens, or else it will be too late."

"Then have them do that for you on Earth. Even if you have to pay for it, you should be able to afford it."

"It's not a matter of being able to afford it. It's a matter of having the expertise to do it, and every person that they can find who can do it, and is available, has been taken to Namath to undertake the biggest gene-surgery program in the history of the Federation. There are 70 billion Faleshkarti on the home-world alone, and many more in our colonies. About a third of them have not made the Change as yet, and that is a huge number to try to deal with. An impossible number, actually. Many will make the Change before they get the chance of gene surgery. The Federation simply cannot spare someone to deal with us here, so we must go back to Namath."

"But won't you run the risk of missing out on the gene-surgery too?"

"For our services to Namath, all envoys have been guaranteed a place in the queue, and we will be on time. But first we must get to Namath. We have a standing reservation with Star Fleet to be taken back whenever our missions were complete, but while they were complete for us a long while back although we chose to stay on *Phoenix*, the offer still stands."

"I see. Then we will have to get along without you for several weeks until you can return. Well, it won't be easy, but we did it before you joined, and I'm sure that the rest of the crew will be understanding of the need."

Loander looked sad. "Captain... Star Fleet guaranteed to take us back to Namath. They did not say anything about bringing us back home here. I honestly don't know if we *can* return."

Martin was stunned. He had not even given a moment's thought to the possibility that the Faleshkarti would leave, let alone not come back.

It had become clear years ago that Loander and Presaith were more than happy to make *Phoenix* their permanent home.

"Is there... might there be some way that you can persuade Star Fleet to send you out again?" Martin knew that this was a slim hope – the duo's official mission had ended a long time ago. They were still on *Phoenix* because they wanted to be, not because it was their assignment.

Loander shrugged. "I don't know, but we will certainly be trying to find a way back. It is our dream to raise our children here on *Phoenix*."

"Maybe we can pick you up ourselves?" Martin suggested.

"Captain, do you know where Namath is? We've never needed to go out that way, so you've probably never looked it up, but the Federation only came to our world after one of your exploration ships encountered one of ours coming from the opposite direction. It's at least half again as far as Sylvania is from Earth. How are you going to cover the cost of going out all that way just to pick us up?"

Martin had to admit that Loander had a point. It was not one that he liked, but neither could he afford to ignore it. The budget was still tight despite years of good business. Nevertheless he had no intention of giving up. "You keep looking at your options, and I'll look at mine. We'll find a way – just you wait and see."

Loander smiled. "I know you will. I have great confidence in you." Shi got up, and Martin followed suit, but instead of leaving, shi walked up to him and gave him a warm hug. "Thank you, Martin."

The Faleshkarti never used his name normally. To do so now indicated that shi was very emotional – touched by his desire to get them back again.

"You're welcome, Loander," Martin replied softly.

By the time that they reached Earth, Loander had grown another ten centimetres, and Presaith had grown twelve. After a farewell party with the crew, the two Faleshkarti were officially put on indefinite leave. They disembarked at Earth's Gateway station, and met up with the Star Fleet officer who would see to their transport back to Namath.

Just hours later, they departed for Namath, along with four other Faleshkarti who had also remained in their Federation posts after their missions had been completed. Loander and Presaith were the last of the envoys to arrive, so there was no need to delay departure.

All six Faleshkarti got acquainted, and found out that they had similar stories – they had all liked their postings so much that they had not wanted to leave until biology had forced it upon them. None of the other four had had quite the family experience that the *Phoenix* crew had though, so they spent much time talking about that, comparing it to the experiences of the others. All expressed the same intentions however – to return and continue their lives in the Federation. Sadly, none of them knew how to accomplish that as yet.

The return to Namath came as a bit of a shock to Loander and Presaith. After nearly five years away from their home world, they were surprised to discover that they had gotten used to the lack of crowds, and the degree of privacy that this world could not afford. For the first time in their lives, they felt cramped – their sense of personal space had grown. Thankfully as Hona, they could still get a room to themselves, tiny though they were.

As promised, both were immediately placed in line to be treated by the gene techs. That happened the day after they arrived, and Loander took the opportunity to ask the Federation tech a question that had been puzzling hir.

"Why can't you treat the Hona who have made the Change? I'm sure that there are many who have been taking the drug who would want to bear children who would be without the curse of the Change hanging over their heads."

The med tech was a male hare – they had long ago run out of qualified herm personnel to send – and he had heard this question several times from the returning envoys. Patiently he explained, "It's not so much that we couldn't, it's that it's more complicated. The Change introduces factors that makes it more difficult to treat you reliably. There are changes to your ovaries and testes, and there are more hormones to make things more difficult. Still, I'm sure that we could crack those problems too. However, we already lack the time and manpower to treat all the Hona who have yet to make the Change, so we certainly can't spare the people to work on something we simply can't find the opportunity to use anyway. We are training Faleshkarti techs just as fast as we can to speed up the process, but there are still billions of you, so it's going to be a project measured in many years."

"I see. I'm grateful to get this opportunity," Loander said fervently.

The hare grinned. "You're hardly the first to say that. Now hold still for this next bit...."

With all the cross-training that the crew had done over the years, it was easier to take up the slack left by the two absent Faleshkarti. However, the extra workload was still harder on everyone. Martin was not yet prepared to write off Loander and Presaith though, so he was reluctant to consider hiring replacements. He decided to put it to the rest of the crew, and the response was unanimous – they wanted to see if the Faleshkarti could find a way to return, so they were happy to put up with the extra work for a while.

Martin was glad that everyone was in agreement, but he was not going to just wait and see if things worked out. He began researching what worlds and colonies lay out that way. After all, if the Foster network could find the opportunity to set up FTL communication relays to Namath, surely there had to be freight opportunities out that way also?

Loander was bored. Shi had been assigned a computer job as befitted hir skills, but it was incredibly simplistic compared to the work on *Phoenix*. There were just too many other Faleshkarti to ever get enough work to occupy hir mind. Shi wondered how shi had ever been satisfied before the opportunity to be an envoy had come along. Shi shared hir troubles with Presaith a few days after returning to Namath.

"I understand completely." Presaith said sympathetically, "although I'm not in the same position as you. We're still building colony ships as fast as we can to alleviate the population problem, so my skills are needed more than yours. However, with so many others under me doing the grunt work, I'm not being as utilised as much as I was on *Phoenix*. Still, I'm not bored like you. Have you found out anything from the council about returning to our Federation jobs?"

"Not really. All I've learned so far is that there are no plans to send out envoys again. There will be ambassadors, but we aren't considered to be qualified for that."

"What about trading opportunities? If ships come here, maybe we can leave with them?"

"Under negotiation still," Loander reported glumly. "Official word is that they are 'excited at the future possibilities', which seems to mean that sometime in the distant future, they might do something about it."

Presaith gave Loander a hug. "Don't be so pessimistic, Lo'. I'm sure that something will come up. Tell you what – let's go to the play that the Federation support staff are putting on. It ought to be fun, and it might cheer you up a bit."

Loander smiled at hir mate-to-be. "Yeah, I think I'd like that."

Loander had reached hir full height of 148cm, and hir breasts had filled out after two weeks back at Namath. Other than that, shi still felt little different from normal. Shi knew from talking to hir friends on

Phoenix that this was not how they experienced puberty, with a steady growth of sexual interest. For hir species though, it was more like turning on a switch. One day the brain would decide that shi was old enough and turn on hitherto dormant organs, and hir body would be flooded with sexual hormones. Then shi would know sexual desire for the first time. Shi hoped that it would be as pleasant as hir friends said it would be. All shi was familiar with were the Zora, and their sexual compulsiveness. They seemed to enjoy it, but there was no love in it at all. They were little more than rutting animals. Shi was so very glad that shi got to escape that fate.

Loander wished that shi could share hir first sexual encounter with Presaith, but shi was two to three weeks behind hir in physical maturity. Loander would have to seek out another Hona who had made the Change at the same time because shi would not be able to wait for Presaith. Shi *literally* could not. Shi had been told that the compulsion to have sex for the first time was as strong in the treated Hona as it was for the untreated. It saddened hir that shi could not make it a moment of bonding with hir intended mate, but shi consoled hirself with the thought that shi would be able to do so when Presaith made the Change, and neither of them would become dull-minded Zora as trillions of others had done throughout the history of their race.

On the fifteenth day, the final sign of imminent Change happened – spontaneous lactation. Loander was working at hir desk in a half-hearted way when hir chest suddenly felt odd. Looking down, shi saw two damp spots spreading on hir shirt where milk was leaking from the nipples. Shi closed off the work that shi was doing on the computer, checked with the department head who dismissed hir from duty, and then shi made hir way to a new facility that had been created specifically for the Hona who had been treated, and were making the Change.

Half the facility was little more than a giant waiting room. Row upon row of chairs filled a huge hall. There was a steady flow of Faleshkarti coming into the room, with a roughly equal number leaving by another door that led to a multitude of tiny private rooms. While the Zora did not care where they had sex, and frequently had it in public, the Hona did not want their first sexual experience to be a public spectacle, and the treated Hona retained their desire for privacy. Several Faleshkarti were seated at desks at the entrance, ensuring that each new arrival got their first dose of the protective drug before they were allowed to proceed further.

Loander found a vacant seat and sat down. There was a terminal that offered various forms of diversion while shi waited, but like the majority of those present, shi was too keyed up to take advantage of it. Instead shi spent hir time watching the others. Shi saw some who seemed nervous, others excited at the oncoming Change, and others were just bored. However, every one of them had the same reaction when the Change hit. Their eyes widened, their jaws dropped, and their bodies trembled as the sex hormones coursed through their bodies, and their pants started to bulge as their first erection filled them. They stood up and looked around for another who had made the Change. It did not matter who it was – the first one that they laid eyes on was good enough. They came together in an awkward embrace, then hastened off to find an empty private room.

Loander waited for about three farnigs (around 2.5 hours) before shi got to find out for herself what that was like. It happened so fast that it startled hir. No wonder everyone's reaction was the same. Then shi felt the sexual urges grow, hir penis react, and burning need that could not be resisted. Shi stood up and looked around. Two rows over, shi locked eyes with another, and they both moved to meet in the aisle.

"I am Loander," shi said as they embraced. Oh! The feelings that touch stirred in hir!

"My name is Kartaiss," the other replied.

Without further preamble, they headed for the exit to the private rooms. An indicator board showed which were available in green. They selected the nearest one, and it changed to yellow. They walked down the indicated corridor past many doors with red lights on them until they reached their room with a yellow light illuminating the number. They entered and closed the door, and the light (and indicator board) changed from yellow to red.

Inside the room was a simple bed with a pad and replaceable cover. They had passed a Zora who had a cart full of the covers whose task apparently was to replace the covers after each use of the room. Loander was barely able to appreciate that fact with the desire to have sex growing constantly. However, a huge sign still managed to gain hir attention. It said in bold red letters: 'REMEMBER TO TAKE THE CONTRACEPTIVE FIRST!'

The only other objects in the room were a shower stall, and the contraceptive dispenser unit. The latter was unique in the history of Namath as no generation had ever used, nor been *able* to use, contraceptives. It was a simple oral medication designed by the Federation med techs, and each Faleshkarti swallowed one before frantically stripping off their clothes and getting on the bed. There was some amateurish fondling and groping before they settled on Kartaiss mounting Loander first. The experience was intense, and as physically pleasurable as promised, but relief from the incessant urges only came when Kartaiss ejaculated into hir, passing along the special hormone that not only signalled sexual success to hir body, but also would have doomed hir higher intelligence but for the special drug that counteracted it. Despite all the reassurances and the unfailing efficacy of the drug so far, Loander had been nervous about this moment. It was necessary to let the semen-borne hormone be taken in by hir body or else shi would never be relieved of the need for sex, but its side-effects would have been disastrous for hir if the drug had failed. However, as the glow of orgasm spread through hir body, shi realised that hir mind was not fading, and shi finally relaxed.

But not for long, for Kartaiss' needs had yet to be fulfilled. Only then did Loander get to experience the male orgasm also. Once both had their immediate urges quelled, they started to more carefully explore each other's body and learn more about having sex. That was the sole thing that bothered Loander now – it felt *really* good, but it was fairly empty emotionally.

When their sexual needs were completely satisfied at last, the two stepped into the shower stall to clean up. As they washed and dried their fur, they took the opportunity to talk for the first time since they introduced themselves.

"Have you got someone you want to have a relationship with after the Change?" Loander asked.

"Maybe," Kartaiss replied. "We weren't sure what it would be like for us after the Change, so we haven't committed ourselves as yet. What about you?"

"Oh, yes. Presaith and I were envoys to the Federation, and what we learned there made us very much want to be what they call *mates* – a long-term committed relationship. Shi is still a couple of *tansa* (Namath week) or so from the Change though, but when shi does, I'll be there for hir."

"I've heard how many of the envoys came back with that same desire. It makes me a bit envious of your experience."

"It was the best part of my life so far, and Presaith and I want to go back very much. The Council has no plans to send us out again, but I am hoping that I can persuade Star Fleet to take us back with them when their next ship comes to relieve the staff stationed on Namath."

"Will that get you back to where you were assigned?"

"Not quite. We were assigned to a commercial starship, but its home base is on Earth. If we can get to that world and to the right spaceport, eventually the ship will come back."

"You sound very determined. I wish you luck with that."

"Thank you. I hope that you find a true mate and a good future also. Umm… I don't really want to have sex with lots of different people while I wait for Presaith to make the Change, so would you like to spend that time with me until then?" Loander asked hopefully.

"I understand. I'm not keen on asking strangers to meet my needs either. I can meet you in your room each evening if you wish."

"That sounds like a good plan. I'm told that we will be needing sex twice a day, so if we do it before we go to sleep, and again when we wake, that should be the minimum inconvenience for both of us."

"I agree. Let's do that."

When they had finished drying off and redressed, they exited the room. Loander noted that the light on the door had turned blue. As they walked away, a Zora with a cart hastened up to the vacated room to get it ready for the next couple.

The work shift was almost over when Loander left the facility, so shi decided to go meet Presaith. Shi took the train reserved for the Hona because although shi had made the Change, shi was not a Zora, but a new designation called a Kana-Ra. In fact shi got a couple of challenges from Hona, but hir obvious intelligence soon confirmed hir right to use their designated transport.

While shi rode the train, shi took time to take stock of hirself. Despite the extended sexual activity, shi still felt a background urge that shi realised would be with hir for the rest of hir life. That urge would build up into that twice-a-day need, and still leave hir capable of more if shi desired. Shi noticed that the scent of the Hona seemed different to hir now, and when a Hona who was at the cusp of making the Change also boarded the train, hir body reacted to the sight and the smell of the almost fully sexually mature Faleshkarti. Shi wondered if shi would ever get used to the feelings that they stirred in hir.

Presaith was surprised but pleased to find Loander waiting for hir as shi exited the factory to which shi had been assigned. Shi gave Loander a hug, not realising the strong reaction that engendered. "I'm happy to see you, but why are you here?" shi asked.

"I was dismissed from work for the rest of the day because I made the Change today, so I thought that I'd meet you and we could go to the food hall together.

"You've Changed?" Presaith asked, looking intently at Loander. I didn't notice anything different... oh..." Shi had stepped back to look over Loander, and only then noticed the bulge in hir crotch that hir hug had caused.

"Believe me," Loander said, "you'll notice a lot more things after you've Changed that you've never noticed before."

"What was it like?"

"The physical pleasure was not exaggerated. The urge to have sex was utterly irresistible, and I had no hesitation whatsoever in taking Kartaiss as my partner when it happened."

"Kartaiss was another to make the Change?"

"Yes. Shi has agreed that we'll meet each other's needs until you make the Change also. I'm sorry, Presaith, but my evenings must be spent with hir until then."

"We knew that something like this would have to happen. I'll miss having you around, and I'll be counting the days until I can take hir place."

"As will I, dear one."

As promised, Kartaiss turned up each evening at Loander's room, and they took care of each other's urges. Although the Hona beds were not designed for two, they slept together each night, and then made love again in the morning. After freshening up, they then went to the food hall together where they met up with Presaith. In this manner, they got more acquainted with the Faleshkarti, and became good friends. It made Loander's time spent with hir more pleasant now that shi had some emotional involvement. Nevertheless, when Presaith called Loander one day to tell hir that shi had just spontaneously lactated, and would be heading for the Change facility, Loander was nearly overcome with relief and happiness that at last they would be together. Shi asked to be relieved from hir task, and headed to the facility to rendezvous with Presaith. Along the way, shi called Kartaiss to let hir know that the time had come to end their arrangement.

"I admit that I will regret the end of our nights together," Kartaiss said, "but I am pleased that you will be able to bond with your... *mate*. Don't be a stranger, Loander."

"I won't. Goodbye for now, Kartaiss."

Presaith beat hir to the facility, and was waiting outside for hir. Loander embraced hir, and they proceeded inside. Loander had to explain to the desk attendants that shi did not need another dose of the drug because shi had one already that day because shi had already gone through the Change. This bemused them, but they could not see any reason to not to let hir in. They managed to find two empty seats together, and sat down to wait. Unlike any of the others, they held hands while waiting for the Change to hit Presaith. Loander knew immediately when it had because the hand that held hirs suddenly tightened its hold. Shi looked around to see the same wide-eyed, slack-jawed look that hit every person making the Change. Their eyes met and Loander smiled.

"Come with me, love," shi told hir.

As shi had before, Loander found an empty room, and they both took contraceptives. This time though, Loander was more familiar with what to do, and shi soon had hir lover writhing in pleasure as shi

Art © Foxene

mounted hir. Because Presaith had the urgent need to be fulfilled, Loander quickly brought them both to coitus together, and they both cried out in the ecstasy of their first time together. Then, with much more time to be intimate, Loander made love to Presaith with much more imagination and less haste. A lot later, when Presaith was satiated at last, Loander took Presaith's hands and looked into hir eyes.

"Presaith, my companion, my lover, my beautiful Kana-Ra, will you consent to be my lifemate?" shi asked formally.

"I will, Loander, my beloved. May our lives together be long and filled with happiness."

Their fervent kiss to seal the commitment was in many ways so much more pleasurable than the sex had been.

Loander and Presaith were hardly the first Kana-Ra to make a permanent relationship, and because Hona quarters were not designed for couples, they had to be relocated to another facility. A newly constructed building that had been intended to house Zora was repurposed to deal with the Kana-Ra, and the mates moved into it just as quickly as they could move their meagre possessions from their old quarters. The bed was much larger than they needed, but not all Kana-Ra were settling for a monogamous relationship, so the standardised beds were all made to cope. Aside from a bit more cupboard space and an extra desk, the room was not much greater than their old one, but to the average Faleshkarti it was palatial in comparison. Their species simply did not have the luxury of wasted space, but a couple made more efficient use of the slightly larger room than two single person rooms.

For a while, their lives slipped into a bit of a routine. They would make love each morning before going to the food hall for breakfast, then going their separate ways to their assigned jobs. Then they would meet up after work to indulge in some form of entertainment before having the evening meal and going back to their room to make love once more. It may have become a bit boring after some time, except that they both continued to entertain hopes of leaving Namath again, and they spent their free time trying to find ways of achieving it.

It was Loander who had the less taxing job and the greater amount of time to devote to the task, who found their way out. Using hir skills with computers, shi was able to access some information that the Federation did not tell just anyone, such as their staff rotation schedules. Shi got in contact with one of the staff who was due to leave on the next staff turnover, and befriended her. Thus shi was able to be on hand when it was announced that the starship had arrived at Namath. Loander contacted Presaith and told hir mate to rendezvous at the landing site of the shuttles. They were going to get on one of those shuttles whatever it took, whether it took begging, bribes, or working their way back to Earth. They still had access to the fedcreds that they had earned as starship crew, and they were willing to give it all away in exchange for passage.

Each Faleshkarti had pre-packed a bag with all the things that they wanted to take with them off-world. Amongst them were supplies of the drug they needed. The med techs had assured them that standard replicators could reproduce the drug as needed, but they wanted to have a back-up supply anyway. There wasn't much else in the packs. Most of it were mementoes that they had brought with them from *Phoenix*. There really was not much on Namath that they needed, or wanted to remember.

When the doors opened to access the shuttle landing pad, Loander and Presaith shuffled along with the rest of the group in the hopes of stealing aboard without being noticed as not belonging. Although they got a few curious looks from the other passengers, they wore their *Phoenix* uniforms to make them look more like they belonged in the Federation rather than Namath. Their small stature made them less conspicuous amidst the group, and they actually made it onto the shuttle before someone spotted them.

"Hey, you two! What are you doing here?" The voice was incredibly familiar.

The two Faleshkarti's heads whipped around to behold the familiar coyote grin of Martin Yote. "Captain!" they both cried in unison, and nearly knocked over some people in their rush to hug him. There were a few amused chuckles from the passengers as they took in the obvious delight in their reunion.

Loander belatedly realised that they were in Phoenix shuttle Alpha. In trying to be inconspicuous and hiding in the crowd, they had not gotten a good look at the vehicle before now. What it was doing here though was still a mystery. "Captain, how did you get here?"

Martin's grin never faltered. "Remember when we picked up the people from Asahikawa? Star Fleet does not do taxi service – they contract that out to others. Guess who won that contract?"

The two laughed and hugged him again. "We *knew* you'd find a way here," Presaith said.

"Says the Faleshkarti trying to sneak on board my shuttle." Martin winked. "I knew you two would not let yourselves get stuck on Namath too long. Looks like I was just in time."

They looked a bit sheepish but unrepentant.

"Anyway, find yourselves a seat – we've got lots of pick-ups to do, and time is money!"

"Yes, sir!" they chorused, and headed for available seats.

Apparently Martin had called ahead to inform the crew that he was bringing their two lost sheep home, because every one of them except Madeline were crowded into the shuttle bay to welcome them home, and she voiced her welcome over the ship's PA. M'Resk was allowed to be one of the first as she had to take care of the passengers immediately, but the rest took their time. Martin had to shoo them out of the shuttle bay so that he could do another run down to the surface.

"Go on! It's about time you both got back to your posts. You're long overdue back from your leaves of absence."

You could not have wiped the grins of happiness from the faces of the Faleshkarti if you tried.

Chapter 13: The Final Challenge

Martin checked the calendar again – four years, eleven months, and twenty-seven days since he received his bequeathal. Three days short of five years since he had bought this starship, renamed it *Phoenix*, and made it his home as well as his business. Half a decade spent with a crew that were more like his family now. In two days they would arrive at Earth. In three days, he might lose it all.

M'Rarrtikar and he had pored over the books, checked every financial detail, chased up every debt, but in the end it still was not going to be enough to pay off the bequeathal. Although their recent years had been reasonably profitable, and indeed in some cases had been a bit more than Martin had estimated back when he started, it had fallen just short of making up for the financial disasters that they had incurred in the first couple of years when it would hurt the most. The ultra-low bid that he had put in to guarantee winning the Faleshkarti contract had also eaten into time that could have been spent more profitably. Martin's last ray of hope had been to finally get some reward from the Hesperia Corporation, and in fact they had managed at last to get a promise for a significant amount for compensation after unbelievable delays. Unfortunately they would get it too late to be of help right now, and it was only after they had started legal action to get that compensation had they found out why the delay had been so great.

Like other big companies, Hesperia had many shareholders, and one of the biggest shareholders turned out to be Windsor. Behind the scenes, he had been throwing every barrier and delay that he could manage within his power. He had even been behind trying to get Hesperia to renege on the promise of docking fees waived in perpetuity, but the ever efficient Madeline had recorded and archived that conversation with Hesperia's manager, so that had been quickly dealt with. Not that that was currently of any use to them. However, the legal wheels ground around slowly, and getting that compensation was not so quickly achieved. Martin wondered if the man had somehow become aware of his financial deadline, or was just plain obsessive. Maybe he was feeling the hurt from the embargos that had been put on his business, and was lashing out even more? He also wondered if Windsor was acting alone, because it seemed a bit much even for a man of his resources. However, if there were others, Martin had not been able to confirm his suspicions.

A knock at Martin's office door interrupted his introspection, and when he looked, he saw Burningbright, M'Resk, Penny, and Valentina standing in the doorway.

"Can we talk with you for a moment?" Burningbright asked.

"Sure! Come in! What can I do for you?" Martin asked as cheerfully as he could manage.

"It's what we can do for you," the chakat replied. "We've heard from M'Rarrtikar about our problem."

Martin noticed how shi had said '*our*' problem rather than '*your*'.

Burningbright continued, "We've all discussed this, and we'd like to offer to loan you our savings to help pay off your debt. Whatever it takes to meet the deadline."

Martin was touched, but also a little saddened. "I appreciate the offer immensely. Thank you, everybody, but I cannot accept it."

"Why not?" Penny asked with a touch of annoyance. "We all want to keep this crew together. We're all prepared to do whatever it takes to make it so."

Martin sighed. "It's not because I don't want to, but because it would make no difference. Paying off the bequeathal isn't just a matter of giving my father the money. It's a matter of paying off the entire debt. Getting the money from you merely transfers the debt, not pay it off. It's the principle of the bequeathal – to prove that I can be successful and debt-free within a specified period. Even if you couched it as a gift, for the purposes of the bequeathal, it would still be regarded as part of the debt."

The looks of disappointment were heartbreaking. Martin added, "Look – we're not dead yet. There are one or two things that I can try when we reach Earth. Just keep your fingers crossed."

They left with more hope than Martin felt. Realistically there was virtually nothing more that he could do to get the money, but he did not want them fretting more than necessary.

Bethany arrived not long after that. She closed the office door and sat down in one of the chairs without bothering to ask. Looking up into the air, she said, "Madeline – privacy please!"

Madeline's voice replied, "I'm outta here!"

Bethany then fixed Martin with her gaze and said, "You're not fooling me – you've got nothing left, have you?"

There was still a touch of mischievousness left in the coyote. "Are you so sure of that?"

"I think I've gotten to know you better than most, Martin."

First name terms, was it? That was unusual. "I think I may yet surprise you, Bethany."

"Prove it! Tell me what you have in mind."

"No, I'm going to leave it until the last day. It really is my final option."

Bethany looked intensely frustrated. "Damn it, Martin, stop being so coy! Can't you tell that I'm trying to help?"

"*Everyone* is trying to help, Beth. We're all in the same boat. Literally, as it happens. Why should I make a special exception for you?"

"Because I have so much more to lose!"

Martin was shocked by that admission. "How so?"

"Because I might lose *you*, you damn idiot!" she yelled at him, her eyes bright with incipient tears.

Martin's heart felt like it almost stopped for a moment, then he got up out of his chair and placed his hands on her shoulders reassuringly. "You don't know how long I've been waiting to hear something like that. If that's how you truly feel, then I promise that you won't lose me, Beth."

"How... how can I be sure of that if you won't tell me your plans?"

"What I have planned is very risky, and I don't want to involve someone that I care deeply about. But if that person is willing to share my life, no matter the outcome – good or bad, then I would be willing to take the risk. I would share everything without reserve."

"That almost sounded like a proposal," Bethany said hesitantly.

"Remember a few years back when you asked what kind of person interested me? It wasn't someone just *like* you. It was you specifically, but first you had to come to terms with the past. I've waited years for that, Bethany. I don't want to lose you either."

"What about the other girls you've had in your life? First Risha, then Madeline, and that coyote tart at Hesperia. All of them close to your age. Why would you want a vixen fourteen years older than you?"

"I would never have realised our age difference was so great if I didn't know your background, and frankly it never mattered to me. You already know what my relationships to Risha and Madeline were really, and that so-called tart was sexy, but she was chasing me, not I her. No, I've only been really interested in one person for years, and that person is *you*." But you had built a wall around yourself that I had to chip away slowly until you were ready to trust again, and to forgive yourself."

"What? Why should I need to forgive myself?" she asked, jerking away from Martin's arms in annoyance.

"Beth, that creep, Russ, was the worst kind of slimeball, I know, and what he did to you was truly terrible. However, you went out with him solely on the basis of the fact that he was a handsome tod, and then you accepted an invitation to his place. Both actions were very naïve for a vixen of your maturity, and you have never forgiven yourself for those mistakes, have you?"

She reluctantly shook her head.

Martin continued, "Well, we all make mistakes, Beth. You learned the hard way, but it's time that you lay that to rest and get on with your life. Forgive yourself and learn to live again. And please, live it with me."

Bethany looked woebegone, and the tears welled in her eyes, brimming over. She stepped back into Martin's arms, burying her face in his chest. He could feel her body shudder as she sobbed for several minutes. Martin knew that he had said more than enough, and he let go on like that for several minutes until the catharsis brought her back under control.

"Are you feeling better now?" he asked gently.

She nodded, and then murmured, "Say it."

"Say what?" he asked in puzzlement.

"You know what I mean. Say it."

Martin realised what she was wanting to hear, and pushed her chin up so that he could look into her eyes. "I love you, Bethany. Will you be my wife?"

"Wife? Not mate?" she asked in surprise.

"My parents are married. Seemed to work for them."

Bethany smiled. "Yes, I could see that, and I think that I like that idea. I love you too, Martin. I've loved you for far longer than I've been willing to admit to myself. I accept your proposal."

They kissed for the first time, long and hungrily. When they broke at last, Bethany said, "*Now* will you tell me what you have planned for *us*?"

"Of course. I promised, didn't I?" Martin explained what he intended to do, and her face grew grave.

"You're right – it *is* risky. We could end up with all sorts of problems."

"You don't want to try it?"

"Of course I want to try it. We have our family at stake."

"Then it's agreed." Martin heaved a huge sigh. "Phew! Honestly, sharing this with you has made this a whole lot less daunting."

"That's the beauty of sharing our lives – it halves the load. Speaking of sharing though, there's one more thing that I'm wanting you to share with me."

"Oh? What's that?"

"I'll need to show you back at your quarters."

"Oh! Are you sure?"

"Yes, my love; and this time it's no mistake."

The news of their engagement cheered up the crew for a while. Hotfoot insisted on whipping up something special to celebrate, and Martin and Bethany encouraged it for the purposes of morale. They had already celebrated in the most intimate of fashions.

They had all sobered up somewhat by the time they reached Earth. Before they started the unloading process though, Martin called them all to a special meeting in the rec room. Everyone soon arrived with the exception of Bethany who was on watch on the bridge. However, she already knew what he was going to tell the crew, so he began without preamble.

"You all know that I am due to pay off my debt by tomorrow, and you also know that I cannot do it by then. By the terms of the bequeathal, I will then be required to close down my business and take up a job with my father. That would mean that the entire crew would be out of a job, and a lot of my clients will be very angry. Well, I am not going to go down without a fight. I want everyone to treat this as a normal stopover. We will unload all the cargo, and we will pick up our scheduled consignments and bring them back to the ship as originally planned. Then tomorrow, this is what I intend to do...."

Martin explained his intentions, and then said, "If anyone of you feels that they cannot participate in this, please let me know, and I will settle up your pay and entitlements and give you a glowing letter of recommendation. You will be able to leave *Phoenix* tomorrow with my blessing." He paused for a moment, and then asked, "Anyone?"

Penny spoke up, "Captain – stop wasting our time. We're all behind you 100%."

There was a chorus of agreements to that, and Martin had to smile.

"Okay! Thanks everyone for your support. Now let's get to work. We've got a lot to do before the real fun begins!"

Earth being *Phoenix's* home base, it was normal for there to be at least a 3-day R&R break after the cargo had been dealt with. This time though, everybody was still aboard the next day. Martin decided that he might as well not put off his confrontation with his father any longer than he had to, and so he gathered all the crew together again, but this time they all crowded onto the bridge. It was the only other place that Madeline could produce her holo-body, and nobody had to be absent on watch.

Martin took his seat in the Captain's chair. "Okay, Maddy, connect us to my father, please."

It was business hours there, so he was not surprised that he had to get to him at his office. The main view screen lit up with the image of the elder Yote.

"Well, well, I must admit I'm a little surprised. Considering what my people have been telling me, I would have thought that you would have let this go until the last minute. So tell me, son – are my people wrong? Have you got the funds to repay your debt?"

"No, I haven't, although if your people are that good, you know just how close I am to that goal."

"Irrelevant, and you know it. You have disappointed me greatly, son. I will be sending one of my administrators to begin the process of winding up your foolish business. I expect you to report to me tomorrow, and I will inform you what job I have chosen for you."

"No," Martin said.

Yote senior scowled at Martin. "What was that?"

"I said no, father. I will not let you do this."

The elder coyote's visage grew thunderous. "You have no choice! You know the terms of the bequeathal, and they are absolute. You took the risk and failed, and now you must accept the consequences."

Martin's looked sorrowful but resolute. "I regret that I must fight you over this, but there is no way in hell that I am going to let you destroy what I have built over these five years. I have a beautiful starship which embodies my dreams. I have a successful business with an excellent reputation, and with great profit projections. But most of all, I have this crew…" He waved his arms to indicate everyone gathered about him. "…that are family to me now, and they mean far more to me than your bloody bequeathal bullshit!"

Arthur Yote leaned into the video pick-up and growled, "How dare you defy me! You *will* honour your commitment, or else I will be forced to shut you down the hard way. I will get you black-banned for breaking contracts and non-payment of debts, and your crew won't get another job on a starship. This is your very last chance, so think very carefully before you speak."

Martin sighed. "Very well, father. I am sorry that it has come to this but… go to hell."

His father looked as if he was going to burst from apoplexy, and Martin braced for the inevitable tirade. Instead he was shocked when instead he burst into uproarious laughter.

"Hahahahahahahaaaa! Go to hell indeed. Well said, son. Right now I am so proud of you, I could burst. I knew you had it in you, and you didn't disappoint me one little bit."

Martin wondered if his father had suddenly lost his marbles. "What are you talking about, dad? One moment you're threatening me, and the next you're praising me?"

Arthur Yote leaned back in his chair, quite at ease and with a grin on his face. "It's taken over ten years for me to find out whether I had judged you correctly. Five years since I was certain that you had the potential in you to be great. A man only shows his true colours under adversity, and I have seen yours shine through despite all the obstacles in your path. You rightfully told me off for trying to destroy what you have built, and that's why I am telling you right now that you can consider the terms of the bequeathal to be fulfilled."

There were cries of delight from various crew members, but Martin was not ready yet to celebrate. "What game are you playing at, dad? Is this some sort of ruse to get me to let down my guard?"

His father's grin grew wider. "Instead of making a quick getaway in your ship to parts unknown? Oh yes, I know that you've been busily loading *Phoenix* up with cargo, and filed a flight plan for not long after this conversation. Admittedly I would not have known if I hadn't been looking specifically for things like that. It really got my expectations up when I did. So let's make this formal and binding. Turn on your recorder."

"It's already recording," Madeline spoke up.

"Very efficient, young lady. Haydn is right to be proud of you. Anyway, here's the official bit: I, Arthur Yote, confirm that my son, Martin Yote, has fulfilled the terms of the bequeathal to my complete satisfaction, and he is now free and clear to pursue his career as he sees fit."

The whole bridge was unrestrained this time as they whooped and cheered in joy.

Yote senior waited for them to calm down a bit before continuing, "I further decree that I am officially naming Martin Yote as my successor. The family business will be his when I pass on."

"***What?***" Martin exclaimed. "Father, you have me hopelessly confused. This is all coming out of the blue. Why are you doing this?"

"I suppose I've had my bit of fun now, so I will explain. This started back on Hank's twenty-first birthday. Do you recall what happened then?"

"Isn't that when I first told you that I wanted to be a starship captain?"

"Yes, and start your own interstellar shipping business."

"Which you promptly told me was foolish and risky, and I should look at some other career."

"And it was all true. It was also bold and independent of you. Unlike your siblings, you had chosen a more difficult path, but one with potentially great rewards. I hoped that you had the strength of will to follow that dream."

"But you never said anything like that. In fact, right up until I turned twenty one, you kept telling me all the ways this business could fail."

"Yep. Made you more determined to prove me wrong, didn't it? Also made you research all those problems, so that when you did begin business, you had a head-start on avoiding the pitfalls. Why else do you think that I continued to pay for your education, no matter what classes you took to fulfil your dream? Starship pilot training doesn't come cheap y'know, and I was under no obligation to pay for that, but I didn't want you distracting yourself with a part-time job. I wanted you to succeed, son, but you had to be doing it for yourself, not for me."

"But you still said you disapproved even after I put together the business. And what's this about naming me your successor? Shouldn't that go to your eldest child? Surely Brandon will be pissed off about that?"

Arthur shook his head. "I explained the second purpose of the bequeathal to all your siblings long ago, and they all know that my decision on who would be my successor would only be made when the last of you had completed it. You see, it wasn't just a test to see if you had the talent to run a successful business. Every one of them did well with their choices. Some were more ambitious than others, some more cautious, but in the end they are all very competent business people. However, I was looking for that something extra, the something that built the family business from nothing into the major company that it is today. Merely keeping it running at the level it is would be good safe business practice, but I want it to continue to grow and adapt to meet future needs, and for that I needed someone with both the vision and the talent and determination to make it happen. You defied me when I told you to forget your dream. You went ahead and made it a reality regardless of everything I did. You made it a success despite some of the worst disasters that were beyond your control. And you had the great big hairy balls to ask for help against Windsor's machinations despite that being against the rules. You have everything it takes to do the job, and take Yote Industries into the future."

Martin still felt a sense of unreality. "But... I don't *want* to be head of Yote Industries. Didn't I also say that I just wanted to have a relatively small business where I could devote time to my family, instead of always being in the office like you?"

His father waved a hand dismissively. "For starters, son, I don't expect to be shuffling off this mortal coil anytime soon. My doctor says he's going to have to force me to retire at gunpoint because I'm so healthy. Strange man. Anyway, circumstances can change a lot in that time. Besides, you can appoint a general manager to take care of the day-to-day operations, while leaving the big decisions to you. I'm sure that you can fit that into those boring intervals while travelling between ports, and with access to that fantastic network that you're in, you can certainly telecommute at will. I don't foresee any real problems."

Martin tried to take that all in. "I... thank you, Father. This really is a shock to me... but I must admit that I am proud of my achievements. Best of all though..." He looked about him at the grinning faces of the crew, before turning back to his father with a huge grin on his face. "*Phoenix* lives!"

There was a roar of approval from everyone.

Arthur Yote waited for the cries of celebration to die down before saying, "So are you going to take off on that scheduled flight, or are you going to come home and celebrate with your mother and I?"

Martin replied, "We can certainly put back our departure to the original date, but I won't be coming home, because I *am* home. When would you like us to come down to visit?"

"Right away. In anticipation of this outcome, your mother has been preparing a special party for days now. We expect to see all of you there, Madeline included. We've installed several holo-projectors in various rooms, one of them with energy-construct capability so that she can have a solid presence too."

"Wow! You're really going all out on this. We can make it even more of a celebration though." Martin took Bethany's hand and said, "Bethany and I are engaged to be married."

His father smiled. "Whaddya know? Your mother was right again – she said that you two would get hitched."

Bethany was startled. "Lydia knew? How long?"

"Hmm, maybe three years or so ago after one of your visits. It's a wonder it took you this long."

"That was incredibly perceptive of her. I certainly never thought I would then."

"Your future mother-in-law is a very perceptive woman. She helped me build Yote Industries from the beginning, and only semi-retired from the business to raise our children."

"Oh? Well maybe she could arrange a celebrant so that we can kill two birds with one stone."

"Knowing my wife, she might well have that contingency planned already. I'll let her know. Anyhow, I suggest you all get ready for the party, and I will see you at the house when you arrive. I have to wind up

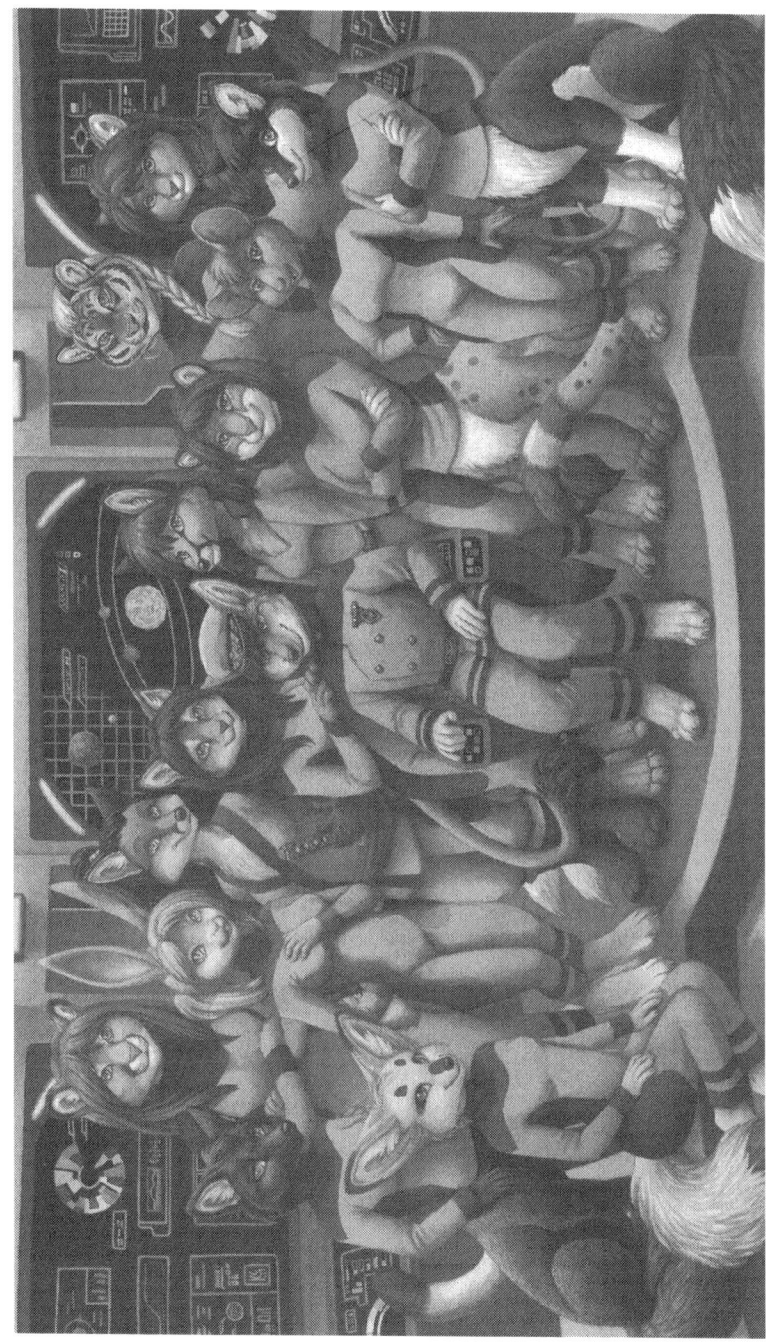

a couple of things and head off home too. After all, family is more important than business, isn't it, son?"

"Right, dad. See you soon."

The crew burst into excited discussion, and Martin pulled Bethany gently towards him. He kissed her, and she returned it in full.

"You've really taken to this idea of marriage, haven't you?" Martin murmured.

"Seems like I've been waiting years for it," she smugly replied.

Martin laughed. He then called everybody's attention. "Okay everybody – put all your stations into standby or station-keeping mode, then get ready to party! We shuttle down in one hour…"

"Make it an hour and a half," Bethany interrupted.

"Like I said, we shuttle down in ninety minutes. Anyone later than that gets to do janitor duty while the rest of us are having fun."

The bridge quickly empty of everyone except those who needed to do their work there. Martin headed off to his office, taking along Bethany whose hand he did not want to relinquish. There he contacted the maintenance shipyard and managed to snag a technician who could do some light maintenance while managing to babysit *Phoenix* in their absence. Then they headed to the Captain's quarters, now both of theirs. Bethany had not had any opportunity to move anything in as yet besides a few toiletries and some clothes.

"Did you need the extra time to get ready?" Martin asked.

"Of course, and so do the other ladies and chakats. This will be a formal party, not a little social call! Besides, it gives us a bit of time to celebrate together." She towed him into the bathroom and started undressing.

Martin took the hint and followed suit. Soon they were in the shower together, but getting clean was hardly the thing they had uppermost in mind.

As it turned out, all of Martin's siblings attended the party as well. Despite what his father had said, Martin was still unsure about how they would take the news that the youngest child had scored the mantle of successor. He need not have worried. His siblings all sincerely congratulated him, and Burningbright later confirmed that they meant what they said. He was so proud of them that day. After hearing all the horror stories about envious siblings fighting over the family business, it was good to see that that particular cliché wasn't going to happen here.

Haydn and Adele Cottonfield were at the party also. Many of the other crew's parents who could get there on short notice were also in attendance. Conspicuously absent of course were Penny's parents, and she sincerely hoped that they did not even know she was there. Arthur had reassured her that extra security precautions had been taken, but he doubted that there was anything that bitter old man could do anymore.

Lydia had indeed foreseen the possibility of a celebration of union between her son and Bethany, and she had a celebrant on call. With the cooperation of the weather, the ceremony was held in the formal gardens in the gentle warmth of a Spring afternoon. Martin had found a nice suit in the wardrobe of his room, but Bethany looked radiant in a dress that Lydia had arranged for her. Before their entire extended family, they exchanged vows and were pronounced husband and wife.

The party lasted late into the night, and it was a long time before the newlyweds had the opportunity to consummate their marriage. In the afterglow of their lovemaking, Martin reflected on his good fortune in meeting Bethany. Her misfortune seemed more like fate pushing her his way, for he could not think of a more perfect mate, not even if she was a coyote too. After all, they were both canines, and that meant that they were physically compatible too.

"Darling," Bethany interrupted his reverie.

"Yes, Love?"

"I remember you saying something a while back about wanting children too."

"Yes, but I was not going to rush you into that."

"Thank you, but I'm forty years old, and biology waits for no woman. It would be best that I have them sooner rather than later."

"So you want to try on your next heat?"

"Yes I do. Would you want a boy or a girl?"

"Hon, you know I would be happy with either. Look at the joy that Madeline brings Haydn. But I am a typical male in that I have teeny-weenie preference for a son."

Bethany laughed. "Fair enough. However, whichever we have first, I hope that they have an equal chance of taking over from you as captain."

"I promise to be as fair with our children as my father was with me and my sibs. Whoever would make the best captain will get the job. However, like my father, I intend to be around for a lot longer, and spending every moment with you, my love."

"Sounds perfect to me, dear."

*** 18 September 2337 ***

Fond farewells had been made, and the crew of the *Phoenix* gathered once more in the rec room. Martin nodded to Bethany who tapped her PADD, and the sound of the bos'n's whistle came through the P.A., bringing conversation to a halt.

Martin said, "I asked you all to gather here first before taking your stations in order to make an important announcement. I've said a lot about how this crew is more like a family, and now that we're clear of debt, there are some things that I can do that I could not afford before. One of them is this – I am giving every one of you a share in the ownership of *Phoenix*."

There was an excited babble of comment at that news, but Martin held up his hands for quiet.

"While Bethany and I will retain a majority ownership, I want you all to know that while you are a part of this crew, your input is valuable to us, and your reward will be reflected in the value of your share of the business. Once we're under way, I will issue you with the official documents. If you have any questions, I'll answer them then. Right now though, it's time for all hands to go to your stations. We have a schedule to keep!

A little while later, Martin was receiving reports of readiness from the departments. Finally Bethany said, "All stations ready for departure, Captain."

"Thank you, Commander." He contacted Earth Orbit Control and received clearance to depart on schedule. Right on the mark, he said, "Take us out of here, Mr Roo."

"Aye, Captain," came Bruce's reply.

The starship *Phoenix* eased out of orbit and soon was beyond Earth's gravitational influence, on its way to the interstellar depths where it could once again truly fly.

Character Art Gallery

Art © Kashmere

Art © SharpK

Art © Heather Bruton

M'Nissa'tk

Art © David Bliss

Art © Dan "Flinters" Canaan

Art © Silent Ravyn

Art © Ishaway

Art © Dark Natasha

Made in the USA
Charleston, SC
03 December 2013